THE SHIPPI

E. Annie Proulx is the author of a
Songs and Other Stories (1988), and two novels: *Postcards* (1991) and *The Shipping News* (1993). For *Postcards*, E. Annie Proulx became the first woman ever to win the coveted Pen/Faulkner prize. *The Shipping News* won the 1993 *Irish Times* International Prize and, in America, both the 1994 Pulitzer Prize for fiction and the 1993 National Book Award. The author lives in Vermont.

THE SHIPPING NEWS

E. ANNIE PROULX

TED SMART

This is a work of fiction. No resemblance is intended to living or dead persons, extant or failed newspapers, real government departments, specific towns or villages, actual roads or highways. The skiffs, trawlers and yachts, the upholstery needle, the logans, thumbies, and plates of cod cheeks, the bakeapples and those who pick them, the fish traps, the cats and dogs, the houses and seabirds described here are all fancies. The Newfoundland in this book, though salted with grains of truth, is an island of invention.

This edition produced for The Book People Ltd,
Hall Wood Avenue, Haydock, St Helens WA11 9UL

First published in Great Britain in 1993 by
Fourth Estate
A Division of HarperCollinsPublishers
77–85 Fulham Palace Road
London W6 8JB
www.4thestate.co.uk

This paperback edition first published 1994

31 33 35 37 39 40 38 36 34 32

ISBN 0 00766 658 6

A catalogue record for this book is available from the British Library.

Books design by Cora Lee Drew

Printed in Great Britain by Clays Ltd, St Ives plc

For Jon, Gillis and Morgan

"In a knot of eight crossings, which is about the average-size knot, there are 256 different 'over-and-under' arrangements possible. . . . Make only one change in this 'over and under' sequence and either an entirely different knot is made or no knot at all may result."

THE ASHLEY BOOK OF KNOTS

Acknowledgments

Help came from many directions in the writing of *The Shipping News*. I am grateful to the National Endowment for the Arts for financial support, and to the Ucross Foundation of Wyoming for a quiet place to work. In Newfoundland, advice, commentary and information from many people helped me understand old ways and contemporary changes on The Rock. The Newfoundland wit and taste for conversation made the most casual encounters a pleasure. I am particularly grateful for the kindness and good company of Bella Hodge of Gunner's Cove and Goose Bay who suffered dog bite on my account and showed me the delights of Newfoundland home cooking. Carolyn Lavers opened my eyes to the complexities and strengths of Newfoundland women, as did novelist Bill Gough in his 1984 *Maud's House*. Canadian Coast Guard Search and Rescue personnel, the staff of the *Northern Pen* in St. Anthony, fishermen and loggers, the Atmospheric Environment Service of Environment Canada all told me how things worked. John Glusman's fine-tuned antennae caught the names of Newfoundland books I would otherwise have missed. Walter Punch of the Massachusetts Horticultural Society Library confirmed some obscure horticultural references. Thanks also to travel companions on trips to Atlantic Canada: Tom Watkin, who battled wind, bears and mosquitoes; my son Morgan Lang who shared an April storm, icebergs and caribou. I am grateful for the advice and friendship of Abi Thomas. Barbara Grossman is the editor of my dreams—clear blue sky in the heaviest fog. And without the inspiration of Clifford W. Ashley's wonderful 1944 work, *The Ashley Book of Knots*, which I had the good fortune to find at a yard sale for a quarter, this book would have remained just the thread of an idea.

THE SHIPPING NEWS

1

Quoyle

Quoyle: A coil of rope.

"A Flemish flake is a spiral coil of one layer only. It is made on deck, so that it may be walked on if necessary."

THE ASHLEY BOOK OF KNOTS

HERE is an account of a few years in the life of Quoyle, born in Brooklyn and raised in a shuffle of dreary upstate towns.

Hive-spangled, gut roaring with gas and cramp, he survived childhood; at the state university, hand clapped over his chin, he camouflaged torment with smiles and silence. Stumbled through his twenties and into his thirties learning to separate his feelings from his life, counting on nothing. He ate prodigiously, liked a ham knuckle, buttered spuds.

His jobs: distributor of vending machine candy, all-night clerk in a convenience store, a third-rate newspaperman. At thirty-six, bereft, brimming with grief and thwarted love, Quoyle steered away to Newfoundland, the rock that had generated his ancestors, a place he had never been nor thought to go.

A watery place. And Quoyle feared water, could not swim. Again and again the father had broken his clenched grip and thrown him into pools, brooks, lakes and surf. Quoyle knew the flavor of brack and waterweed.

From this youngest son's failure to dog-paddle the father saw other failures multiply like an explosion of virulent cells—failure to speak clearly; failure to sit up straight; failure to get up in the morning; failure in attitude; failure in ambition and ability; indeed, in everything. His own failure.

Quoyle shambled, a head taller than any child around him, was soft. He knew it. "Ah, you lout," said the father. But no pygmy himself. And brother Dick, the father's favorite, pretended to throw up when Quoyle came into a room, hissed "Lardass, Snotface, Ugly Pig, Warthog, Stupid, Stinkbomb, Fart-tub, Greasebag," pummeled and kicked until Quoyle curled, hands over head, sniveling, on the linoleum. All stemmed from Quoyle's chief failure, a failure of normal appearance.

A great damp loaf of a body. At six he weighed eighty pounds. At sixteen he was buried under a casement of flesh. Head shaped like a crenshaw, no neck, reddish hair ruched back. Features as bunched as kissed fingertips. Eyes the color of plastic. The monstrous chin, a freakish shelf jutting from the lower face.

Some anomalous gene had fired up at the moment of his begetting as a single spark sometimes leaps from banked coals, had given him a giant's chin. As a child he invented stratagems to deflect stares; a smile, downcast gaze, the right hand darting up to cover the chin.

His earliest sense of self was as a distant figure: there in the foreground was his family; here, at the limit of the far view, was he. Until he was fourteen he cherished the idea that he had been given to the wrong family, that somewhere his real people, saddled with the changeling of the Quoyles, longed for him. Then, foraging in a box of excursion momentoes, he found photographs of his father beside brothers and sisters at a ship's rail. A girl, somewhat apart from the others, looked toward the sea, eyes squinted, as though she could see the port of destination a thousand miles south. Quoyle recognized himself in their hair, their legs and arms. That sly-looking lump in the shrunken sweater, hand at his crotch, his father. On the back, scribbled in blue pencil, "Leaving Home, 1946."

At the university he took courses he couldn't understand, humped back and forth without speaking to anyone, went home for weekends of excoriation. At last he dropped out of school and looked for a job, kept his hand over his chin.

Nothing was clear to lonesome Quoyle. His thoughts churned like the amorphous thing that ancient sailors, drifting into arctic half-light, called the Sea Lung; a heaving sludge of ice under fog where air blurred into water, where liquid was solid, where solids dissolved, where the sky froze and light and dark muddled.

He fell into newspapering by dawdling over greasy *saucisson* and a piece of bread. The bread was good, made without yeast, risen on its own fermenting flesh and baked in Partridge's outdoor oven. Partridge's yard smelled of burnt cornmeal, grass clippings, bread steam.

The *saucisson*, the bread, the wine, Partridge's talk. For these things he missed a chance at a job that might have put his mouth to bureaucracy's taut breast. His father, self-hauled to the pinnacle of produce manager for a supermarket chain, preached a sermon illustrated with his own history—"I had to wheel barrows of sand for the stonemason when I came here." And so forth. The father admired the mysteries of business—men signing papers shielded by their left arms, meetings behind opaque glass, locked briefcases.

But Partridge, dribbling oil, said, "Ah, fuck it." Sliced purple tomato. Changed the talk to descriptions of places he had been, Strabane, South Amboy, Clark Fork. In Clark Fork had played pool with a man with a deviated septum. Wearing kangaroo gloves. Quoyle in the Adirondack chair, listened, covered his chin with his hand. There was olive oil on his interview suit, a tomato seed on his diamond-patterned tie.

Quoyle and Partridge met at a laundromat in Mockingburg, New York. Quoyle was humped over the newspaper, circling help-wanted ads while his Big Man shirts revolved. Partridge remarked that the job market was tight. Yes, said Quoyle, it was. Partridge floated an opinion on the drought, Quoyle nodded. Partridge moved the conversation to the closing of the sauerkraut factory. Quoyle fumbled his shirts from the dryer; they fell on the floor in a rain of hot coins and ballpoint pens. The shirts were streaked with ink.

"Ruined," said Quoyle.

"Naw," said Partridge. "Rub the ink with hot salt and talcum powder. Then wash them again, put a cup of bleach in."

Quoyle said he would try it. His voice wavered. Partridge was astonished to see the heavy man's colorless eyes enlarged with tears. For Quoyle was a failure at loneliness, yearned to be gregarious, to know his company was a pleasure to others.

The dryers groaned.

"Hey, come by some night," said Partridge, writing his slanting address and phone number on the back of a creased cash register receipt. He didn't have that many friends either.

The next evening Quoyle was there, gripping paper bags. The front of Partridge's house, the empty street drenched in amber light. A gilded hour. In the bags a packet of imported Swedish crackers, bottles of red, pink and white wine, foil-wrapped triangles of foreign cheeses. Some kind of hot, juggling music on the other side of Partridge's door that thrilled Quoyle.

They were friends for a while, Quoyle, Partridge and Mercalia. Their differences: Partridge black, small, a restless traveler across the slope of life, an all-night talker; Mercalia, second wife of Partridge and the color of a brown feather on dark water, a hot intelligence; Quoyle large, white, stumbling along, going nowhere.

Partridge saw beyond the present, got quick shots of coming events as though loose brain wires briefly connected. He had been born with a caul; at three, witnessed ball lightning bouncing down a fire escape; dreamed of cucumbers the night before his brother-in-law was stung by hornets. He was sure of his own good fortune.

He could blow perfect smoke rings. Cedar waxwings always stopped in his yard on their migration flights.

Now, in the backyard, seeing Quoyle like a dog dressed in a man's suit for a comic photo, Partridge thought of something.

"Ed Punch, managing editor down at the paper where I work is looking for a cheap reporter. Summer's over and his college rats go back to their holes. The paper's junk, but maybe give it a few months, look around for something better. What the hell, maybe you'd like it, being a reporter."

Quoyle nodded, hand over chin. If Partridge suggested he leap from a bridge he would at least lean on the rail. The advice of a friend.

"Mercalia! I'm saving the heel for you, lovely girl. It's the best part. Come on out here."

Mercalia put the cap on her pen. Weary of writing of prodigies who bit their hands and gyred around parlor chairs spouting impossible sums, dust rising from the oriental carpets beneath their stamping feet.

Ed Punch talked out of the middle of his mouth. While he talked he examined Quoyle, noticed the cheap tweed jacket the size of a horse blanket, fingernails that looked regularly held to a grindstone. He smelled submission in Quoyle, guessed he was butter of fair spreading consistency.

Quoyle's own eyes roved to a water-stained engraving on the wall. He saw a grainy face, eyes like glass eggs, a fringe of hairs rising from under the collar and cascading over its starched rim. Was it Punch's grandfather in the chipped frame? He wondered about ancestors.

"This is a family paper. We run upbeat stories with a community slant." The *Mockingburg Record* specialized in fawning anecdotes of local business people, profiles of folksy characters; this thin stuff padded with puzzles and contests, syndicated columns, features and cartoons. There was always a self-help quiz—"Are You a Breakfast Alcoholic?"

Punch sighed, feigned a weighty decision. "Put you on the municipal beat to help out Al Catalog. He'll break you in. Get your assignments from him."

The salary was pathetic, but Quoyle didn't know.

Al Catalog, face like a stubbled bun, slick mouth, ticked the back of his fingernail down the assignment list. His glance darted away from the back of Quoyle's chin, hammer on a nail.

"O.k., planning board meeting's a good one for you to start with. Down at the elemennary school. Whyn't you take that tonight? Sit in the little chairs. Write down everything you hear, type it up. Five hunnerd max. Take a recorder, you want. Show me the piece in the A.M. Lemme see it before you give it on to that black son of a bitch on the copy desk." Partridge was the black son of a bitch.

Quoyle at the back of the meeting, writing on his pad. Went home, typed and retyped all night at the kitchen table. In the morning, eyes circled by rings, nerved on coffee, he went to the newsroom. Waited for Al Catalog.

Ed Punch, always the first through the door, slid into his office like an eel into the rock. The A.M. parade started. Feature-page man swinging a bag of coconut doughnuts; tall Chinese woman with varnished hair; elderly circulation man with arms like hawsers; two women from layout; photo editor, yesterday's shirt all underarm stains. Quoyle at his desk pinching his chin, his head down, pretending to correct his article. It was eleven pages long.

At ten o'clock, Partridge. Red suspenders and a linen shirt. He nodded and patted his way across the newsroom, stuck his head in Punch's crevice, winked at Quoyle, settled into the copy desk slot in front of his terminal.

Partridge knew a thousand things, that wet ropes held greater weight, why a hard-boiled egg spun more readily than a raw. Eyes half closed, head tipped back in a light trance, he could cite baseball statistics as the ancients unreeled *The Iliad*. He reshaped banal prose, scraped the mold off Jimmy Breslin imitations. "Where are the reporters of yesteryear?" he muttered, "the nail-biting, acerbic, alcoholic nighthawk bastards who truly knew how to write?"

Quoyle brought over his copy. "Al isn't in yet," he said, squaring up the pages, "so I thought I'd give it to you."

His friend did not smile. Was on the job. Read for a few seconds, lifted his face to the fluorescent light. "Edna was in she'd shred this. Al saw it he'd tell Punch to get rid of you. You got to rewrite this. Here, sit down. Show you what's wrong. They say reporters can be made out of anything. You'll be a test case."

It was what Quoyle had expected.

"Your lead," said Partridge. "Christ!" He read aloud in a high-pitched singsong.

> Last night the Pine Eye Planning Commission voted by a large margin to revise earlier recommendations for amendments to the municipal zoning code that would increase the minimum plot size of residential properties in all but downtown areas to seven acres.

"It's like reading cement. Too long. Way, way, way too long. Confused. No human interest. No quotes. Stale." His pencil roved among Quoyle's sentences, stirring and shifting. "Short words. Short sentences. Break it up. Look at this, look at this. Here's your angle down here. That's news. Move it up."

He wrenched the words around. Quoyle leaned close, stared, fidgeted, understood nothing.

"O.k., try this.

> Pine Eye Planning Commission member Janice Foxley resigned during an angry late-night Tuesday meeting. "I'm not going to sit here and watch the poor people of this town get sold down the river," Foxley said.
>
> A few minutes before Foxley's resignation the commission approved a new zoning law by a vote of 9 to 1. The new law limits minimum residential property sizes to seven acres.

"Not very snappy, no style, and still too long," said Partridge, "but going in the right direction. Get the idea? Get the sense of what's news? What you want in the lead? Here, see what you can do. Put some spin on it."

Partridge's fire never brought him to a boil. After six months of copy desk fixes Quoyle didn't recognize news, had no aptitude for detail. He was afraid of all but twelve or fifteen verbs. Had a fatal flair for the false passive. "Governor Murchie was handed a bouquet by first grader Kimberley Plud," he wrote and Edna, the crusty rewrite woman, stood up and bellowed at Quoyle. "You lobotomized moron. How the hell can you hand a governor?" Quoyle another sample of the semi-illiterates who practiced journalism nowadays. Line them up against the wall!

Quoyle sat through meetings scribbling on pads. It seemed he was part of something. Edna's roars, Partridge's picking did not hurt him. He had come up under the savage brother, the father's relentless criticism. Thrilled at the sight of his byline. Irregular hours encouraged him to imagine that he was master of his own time. Home after midnight from a debate on the wording of a minor municipal bylaw on bottle recycling, he felt he was a pin in the hinge of power. Saw the commonplaces of life as newspaper headlines. Man Walks Across Parking Lot at Moderate Pace. Women Talk of Rain. Phone Rings in Empty Room.

Partridge labored to improve him. "What don't happen is also news, Quoyle."

"I see." Pretending to understand. Hands in pockets.

"This story on the County Mutual Aid Transportation meeting? A month ago they were ready to start van service in four towns if Bugle Hollow came in. You say here that they met last night, then, way down at the end you mention sort of as a minor detail, that Bugle Hollow decided not to join. You know how many old people, no cars, people can't afford a car or a second car, commuters, been waiting for that goddamn van to pull up? Now it's not going to happen. News, Quoyle, news. Better get your mojo working." A minute later added in a different voice that he was doing Greek-style marinated fish and red peppers on skewers Friday night and did Quoyle want to come over?

He did, but wondered what a mojo actually was.

In late spring Ed Punch called Quoyle into his office, said he was fired. He looked out of his ruined face past Quoyle's ear. "It's more of a layoff. If it picks up later on . . ."

Quoyle got a part-time job driving a cab.

Partridge knew why. Talked Quoyle into putting on a huge apron, gave him a spoon and a jar. "His kids home from college. They got your job. Nothing to cry over. That's right, spread that mustard on the meat, let it work in."

In August, snipping dill into a Russian beef stew with pickles, Partridge said, "Punch wants you back. Says you're interested, come in Monday morning."

Punch played reluctant. Made a show of taking Quoyle back as a special favor. Temporary.

The truth was Punch had noticed that Quoyle, who spoke little himself, inspired talkers. His only skill in the game of life. His attentive posture, his flattering nods urged waterfalls of opinion, reminiscence, recollection, theorizing, guesstimating, exposition, synopsis and explication, juiced the life stories out of strangers.

And so it went. Fired, car wash attendant, rehired.

Fired, cabdriver, rehired.

Back and forth he went, down and around the county, listening to the wrangles of sewer boards, road commissions, pounding out stories of bridge repair budgets. The small decisions of local authority seemed to him the deep workings of life. In a profession that tutored its practitioners in the baseness of human nature, that revealed the corroded metal of civilization, Quoyle constructed a personal illusion of orderly progress. In atmospheres of disintegration and smoking jealousy he imagined rational compromise.

Quoyle and Partridge ate poached trout and garlic shrimps. Mercalia not there. Quoyle tossed the fennel salad. Was leaning over to pick up a fallen shrimp when Partridge rang his knife on the wine bottle.

"Announcement. About Mercalia and me."

Quoyle, grinning. Expected to hear they were having a kid. Already picked himself for godfather.

"Moving to California. Be leaving Friday night."

"What?" said Quoyle.

"Why we're going, the raw materials," Partridge said. "Wine, ripe tomatillos, alligator pears." He poured *fumé blanc*, then told Quoyle that really it was for love, not vegetables.

"Everything that counts is for love, Quoyle. It's the engine of life."

Mercalia had thrown down her thesis, he said, had gone blue-collar. Travel, cowboy boots, money, the gasp of air brakes, four speakers in the cab and the Uptown String Quartet on the tape deck. Enrolled in long-distance truck driving school. Graduated summa cum laude. The Overland Express in Sausalito hired her.

"She is the first black woman truck driver in America," said Partridge, winking tears. "We already got an apartment. Third one she looked at." It had, he said, a kitchen with French doors, heavenly bamboo shading the courtyard. Herb garden the size of a prayer rug. In which he would kneel.

"She got the New Orleans run. And I am going out there. Going to make smoked duck sandwiches, cold chicken breast with tarragon, her to take on the road, not go in the diners. I don't want Mercalia in those truck places. Going to grow the tarragon. I can pick up a job. Never enough copy editors to go around. Get a job anywhere."

Quoyle tried to say congratulations, ended up shaking and shaking Partridge's hand, couldn't let go.

"Look, come out and visit us," said Partridge. "Stay in touch." And still they clasped hands, pumping the air as if drawing deep water from a well.

Quoyle, stuck in bedraggled Mockingburg. A place in its third death. Stumbled in two hundred years from forests and woodland tribes, to farms, to a working-class city of machine tool and tire factories. A long recession emptied the downtown, killed the malls.

Factories for sale. Slum streets, youths with guns in their pockets, political word-rattle of some litany, sore mouths and broken ideas. Who knew where the people went? Probably California.

Quoyle bought groceries at the A&B Grocery; got his gas at the D&G Convenience; took the car to the R&R Garage when it needed gas or new belts. He wrote his pieces, lived in his rented trailer watching television. Sometimes he dreamed of love. Why not? A free country. When Ed Punch fired him, he went on binges of cherry ice cream, canned ravioli.

He abstracted his life from the times. He believed he was a newspaper reporter, yet read no paper except *The Mockingburg Record*, and so managed to ignore terrorism, climatological change, collapsing governments, chemical spills, plagues, recession and failing banks, floating debris, the disintegrating ozone layer. Volcanoes, earthquakes and hurricanes, religious frauds, defective vehicles and scientific charlatans, mass murderers and serial killers, tidal waves of cancer, AIDS, deforestation and exploding aircraft were as remote to him as braid catches, canions and rosette-embroidered garters. Scientific journals spewed reports of mutant viruses, of machines pumping life through the near-dead, of the discovery that the galaxies were streaming apocalyptically toward an invisible Great Attractor like flies into a vacuum cleaner nozzle. That was the stuff of others' lives. He was waiting for his to begin.

He got in the habit of walking around the trailer and asking aloud, "Who knows?" He said, "Who knows?" For no one knew. He meant, anything could happen.

A spinning coin, still balanced on its rim, may fall in either direction.

2

Love Knot

In the old days a love-sick sailor might send the object of his affections a length of fishline loosely tied in a true-lover's knot. If the knot was sent back as it came the relationship was static. If the knot returned home snugly drawn up the passion was reciprocated. But if the knot was capsized—tacit advice to ship out.

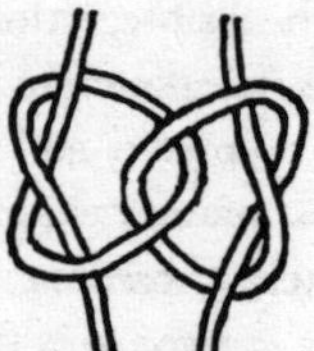

THEN, at a meeting, Petal Bear. Thin, moist, hot. Winked at him. Quoyle had the big man's yearning for small women. He stood next to her at the refreshment table. Grey eyes close together, curly hair the color of oak. The fluorescent light made her as pale as candle wax. Her eyelids gleamed with some dusky unguent. A metallic thread in her rose sweater. These faint sparks cast a shimmer on her like a spill of light. She smiled, the pearl-tinted lips wet with cider. His hand shot up to his chin. She chose a cookie with frosting eyes and an almond for a mouth. Eyed him as her teeth snapped out a new moon. An invisible hand threw loops and crossings in Quoyle's intestines. Growls from his shirt.

"What do you think," she said. Her voice was rapid. She said what she always said. "You want to marry me, don't you? Don't you think you want to marry me?" Waited for the wisecrack. As she spoke she changed in some provocative way, seemed suddenly drenched in eroticism as a diver rising out of a pool gleams like chrome with a sheet of unbroken water for a fractional moment.

"Yes," he said, meaning it. She thought it was wit. She laughed, curled her sharp-nailed fingers into his. Stared intently into his eyes like an optometrist seeking a flaw. A woman grimaced at them.

"Get out of this place," she whispered, "go get a drink. It's seven twenty-five. I think I'm going to fuck you by ten, what do you think of that?"

Later she said, "My God, that's the biggest one yet."

As a hot mouth warms a cold spoon, Petal warmed Quoyle. He stumbled away from his rented trailer, his mess of dirty laundry and empty ravioli cans, to painful love, his heart scarred forever by tattoo needles pricking the name of Petal Bear.

There was a month of fiery happiness. Then six kinked years of suffering.

Petal Bear was crosshatched with longings, but not, after they were married, for Quoyle. Desire reversed to detestation like a rubber glove turned inside out. In another time, another sex, she would have been a Genghis Khan. When she needed burning cities, the stumbling babble of captives, horses exhausted from tracing the reeling borders of her territories, she had only petty triumphs of sexual encounter. Way it goes, she said to herself. In your face, she said.

By day she sold burglar alarms at Northern Security, at night, became a woman who could not be held back from strangers' rooms, who would have sexual conjunction whether in stinking rest rooms or mop cupboards. She went anywhere with unknown men. Flew to nightclubs in distant cities. Made a pornographic video while wearing a mask cut from a potato chip bag. Sharpened her eyeliner pencil with the paring knife, let Quoyle wonder why his sandwich cheese was streaked with green.

It was not Quoyle's chin she hated, but his cringing hesitancy, as though he waited for her anger, expected her to make him suffer. She could not bear his hot back, the bulk of him in the bed. The part of Quoyle that was wonderful was, unfortunately, attached to the rest of him. A walrus panting on the near pillow. While she remained a curious equation that attracted many mathematicians.

"Sorry," he mumbled, his hairy leg grazing her thigh. In the darkness his pleading fingers crept up her arm. She shuddered, shook his hand away.

"Don't *do* that!"

She did not say "Lardass," but he heard it. There was nothing about him she could stand. She wished him in the pit. Could not help it any more than he could help his witless love.

Quoyle stiff-mouthed, feeling cables tighten around him as though drawn up by a ratchet. What had he expected when he married? Not his parents' discount-store life, but something like Partridge's backyard—friends, grill smoke, affection and its unspoken language. But this didn't happen. It was as though he were a tree and she a thorny branch grafted onto his side that flexed in every wind, flailing the wounded bark.

What he had was what he pretended.

Four days after Bunny was born the baby-sitter came to loll in front of the television set—Mrs. Moosup with arms too fat for sleeves—and Petal hauled a dress that wouldn't easily show stains over her slack belly and leaking breasts and went out to see what she could find. Setting a certain tone. And through her pregnancy with Sunshine the next year, fumed until the alien left her body.

Turmoil bubbled Quoyle's dull waters. For it was he who drove the babies around, sometimes brought them to meetings, Sunshine in a pouch that strapped on his back, Bunny sucking her thumb and hanging on his trouser leg. The car littered with newspapers, tiny mittens, torn envelopes, teething rings. On the backseat a crust of toothpaste from a trodden tube. Soft-drink cans rolled and rolled.

Quoyle came into his rented house in the evenings. Some few times Petal was there; most often it was Mrs. Moosup doing overtime in a trance of electronic color and simulated life, smoking cigarettes and not wondering. The floor around her strewn with hairless dolls. Dishes tilted in the sink, for Mrs. Moosup said she was not a housemaid, nor ever would be.

Into the bathroom through a tangle of towels and electric cords, into the children's room where he pulled down shades against the streetlight, pulled up covers against the night. Two cribs jammed close like bird cages. Yawning, Quoyle would swipe through some of the dishes to fall, finally, into the grey sheets and sleep. But did housework secretly, because Petal flared up if she caught him mopping and wiping as if he had accused her of something. Or other.

Once she telephoned Quoyle from Montgomery, Alabama.

"I'm down here in Alabama and nobody, including the bartender, knows how to make an Alabama Slammer." Quoyle heard the babble and laughter of a barroom. "So listen, go in the kitchen and look on top of the fridge where I keep the Mr. *Boston*. They only got an old copy down here. Look up Alabama Slammer for me. I'll wait."

"Why don't you come home?" he pleaded in the wretched voice. "I'll make one for you." She said nothing. The silence stretched out until he got the book and read the recipe, the memory of the brief month of love when she had leaned in his arms, the hot silk of her slip, flying through his mind like a harried bird.

"Thanks," she said and hung up the phone.

There were bloody little episodes. Sometimes she pretended not to recognize the children.

"What's that kid doing in the bathroom? I just went in to take a shower and some kid is sitting on the pot! Who the hell is she, anyway?" The television rattled with laughter.

"That's Bunny," said Quoyle. "That's our daughter Bunny."

He wrenched out a smile to show he knew it was a joke. He could smile at a joke. He could.

"My God, I didn't recognize her." She yelled in the direction of the bathroom. "Bunny, is that really you?"

"Yes." A belligerent voice.

"There's another one, too, isn't there? Well, I'm out of here. Don't look for me until Monday or whatever."

She was sorry he loved her so desperately, but there it was.

"Look, it's no good," she said. "Find yourself a girlfriend—there's plenty of women around."

"I only want you," said Quoyle. Miserably. Pleading. Licking his cuff.

"Only thing that's going to work here is a divorce," said Petal. He was pulling her under. She was pushing him over.

"No," groaned Quoyle. "No divorce."

"It's your funeral," said Petal. Irises silvery in Sunday light. The green cloth of her coat like ivy.

One night he worked a crossword puzzle in bed, heard Petal come in, heard the gutter of voices. Freezer door opened and closed, clink of the vodka bottle, sound of the television and, after a while, squeaking, squeaking, squeaking of the hide-a-bed in the living room and a stranger's shout. The armor of indifference in which he protected his marriage was frail. Even after he heard the door close behind the man and a car drive away he did not get up but lay on his back, the newspaper rustling with each heave of his chest, tears running down into his ears. How could something done in another room by other people pain him so savagely? Man Dies of Broken Heart. His hand went to the can of peanuts on the floor beside the bed.

In the morning she glared at him, but he said nothing, stumbled around the kitchen with the juice pitcher. He sat at the table, the cup shook in his hand. Corners of his mouth white with peanut salt. Her chair scraped. He smelled her damp hair. Again the tears came. Wallowing in misery, she thought. Look at his eyes.

"Oh for God's sake grow up," said Petal. Left her coffee cup on the table. The door slammed.

Quoyle believed in silent suffering, did not see that it goaded.

He struggled to deaden his feelings, to behave well. A test of love. The sharper the pain, the greater the proof. If he could endure now, if he could take it, in the end it would be all right. It would certainly be all right.

But the circumstances enclosed him like the six sides of a metal case.

3

Strangle Knot

"The strangle knot will hold a coil well. . . . It is first tied loosely and then worked snug."

THE ASHLEY BOOK OF KNOTS

A YEAR came when this life was brought up sharply. Voices over the wire, the crump of folding steel, flame.

It began with his parents. First the father, diagnosed with liver cancer, a blush of wild cells diffusing. A month later a tumor fastened in the mother's brain like a burr, crowding her thoughts to one side. The father blamed the power station. Two hundred yards from their house sizzling wires, thick as eels, came down from northern towers.

They wheedled barbiturate prescriptions from winking doctors, stockpiled the capsules. When there were enough, the father dictated, the mother typed a suicide farewell, proclamation of individual choice and self-deliverance—sentences copied from the newsletters of The Dignified Exit Society. Named incineration and strewing as choice of disposal.

It was spring. Sodden ground, smell of earth. The wind beat through twigs, gave off a greenish odor like struck flints. Coltsfoot in the ditches; furious dabs of tulips stuttering in gardens. Slanting rain. Clock hands leapt to pellucid evenings. The sky riffled like cards in a chalk-white hand.

Father turned off the water heater. Mother watered the houseplants. They swallowed their variegated capsules with Silent Nite herbal tea.

With his last drowsy energy the father phoned the paper and left a message on Quoyle's answering machine. "This is your father. Calling you. Dicky don't have a phone at that place. Well. It's time for your mother and I to go. We made the decision to go. Statement, instructions about the undertaker and the cremation, everything else, on the dining room table. You'll have to make your own way. I had to make my own way in a tough world ever since I came to this country. Nobody ever gave me nothing. Other men would of given up and turned into bums, but I didn't. I sweated and worked, wheeled barrows of sand for the stonemason, went without so you and your brother could have advantages, not that you've done much with your chances. Hasn't been much of a life for me. Get ahold of Dicky and my sister Agnis Hamm, and tell them about this. Agnis's address is on the dining room table. I don't know where the rest of them are. They weren't—" A beep sounded. The message space was filled.

But the brother, a spiritual sublieutenant in the Church of Personal Magnetism, did have a phone and Quoyle had his number. Felt his gut contract when the hated voice came through the receiver. Clogged nasals, adenoidal snorts. The brother said he could not come to rites for outsiders.

"I don't believe in those asshole superstitions," he said. "Funerals. At CPM we have a cocktail party. Besides, where did you find a minister to say a word for suicides?"

"Reverend Stain is part of their Dignified Exit meeting group. You ought to come. At least help me clean out the basement.

Father left something like four tons of old magazines down there. Look, I had to see our parents being carried out of the house." Almost sobbed.

"Hey, Lardass, did they leave us anything?"

Quoyle knew what he meant.

"No. Big mortgage on the house. They spent their savings. I think that's a major reason why they did this. I mean, I know they believed in dignified death, but they'd spent everything. The grocery chain went bankrupt and his pension stopped. If they'd kept on living they'd have had to go out and get jobs, clerking in the 7-Eleven or something. I thought Mother might have a pension too, but she didn't."

"Are you kidding? You've got to be dumber than I thought. Hey, Barfbag, if there's anything send my share to me. You got my address." He hung up.

Quoyle put his hand over his chin.

Nor did Agnis Hamm, his father's sister, come to the ceremony. Sent Quoyle a note on blue paper, her name and address in raised letters, pressed with a mail-order device.

> Can't make the service. But I'm coming through next month, around the 12th. Will pick up your father's ashes, as per instructions, meet you and your family. We'll talk then. Your loving aunt, Agnis Hamm.

But by the time the aunt arrived, orphaned Quoyle was again recast by circumstance, this time as an abandoned and cuckolded husband, a widower.

"Pet, I need to talk to you," he'd pled in brimful voice. Knew about her latest, an unemployed real estate agent who pasted his bumpers with mystic signs, believed newspaper horoscopes. She was staying with him, came home for clothes once in a while. Or less. Quoyle mumbled greeting card sentiments. She looked away from him, caught her own reflection in the bedroom mirror.

"Don't call me 'Pet.' Bad enough to have a stupid name like

Petal. They should have named me something like 'Iron' or 'Spike.' "

" 'Iron Bear?' " Showed his teeth in a smile. Or rictus.

"Don't be cute, Quoyle. Don't try to pretend everything's funny and wonderful. Just let me alone." Turned from him, clothes over her arm, hanger hooks like the necks and heads of dried geese. "See, it was a joke. I didn't want to be married to anybody. And I don't feel like being a mama to anybody either. It was all a mistake and I mean it."

One day she was gone, didn't show up for work at Northern Security. The manager called Quoyle. Ricky Something.

"Yeah, well, I'm pretty concerned. Petal wouldn't just 'take off' as you put it without saying something to me." From his tone of voice Quoyle knew Petal had slept with him. Given him stupid hopes.

A few days after this conversation Ed Punch tipped his head toward his office as he walked past Quoyle's desk. It always happened that way.

"Have to let you go," he said, eyes casting yellow, tongue licking.

Quoyle's eyes went to the engraving on the wall. Could just make out the signature under the hairy neck: Horace Greeley.

"Business slump. Don't know how much longer the paper can hold on. Cutting back. Afraid there's not much chance of taking you back this time."

At six-thirty he opened his kitchen door. Mrs. Moosup sat at the table writing on the back of an envelope. Mottled arms like cold thighs.

"Here you are!" she cried. "Hoped you'd come in so's I don't have to write all this stuff down. Tires your hand out. My night to go to the acupuncture clinic. Really helps. First, Ms. Bear says you should pay me my wages. Owes me for seven weeks, comes to three-oh-eight-oh dollars. 'Preciate a check right now. Got bills to pay same as everybody else."

"Did she phone?" said Quoyle. "Did she say when she'd be

back? Her boss wants to know." Could hear the television in the other room. A swell of maracas, tittering bongos.

"Didn't phone. Come rushing in here about two hours ago, packed up all her clothes, told me a bunch of things to tell you, took the kids and went off with that guy in the red Geo. You know who I mean. That one. Said she was going to move to Florida with him, tell you she'll mail you some papers. Quit her job and she is gone. Called up her boss and says 'Ricky, I quit.' I was standing right here when she said it. Said for you to write me out a check right away."

"I can't handle this," said Quoyle. His mouth was full of cold hot dog. "She took the kids? She'd never take the kids." Runaway Mom Abducts Children.

"Well, be that as it may, Mr. Quoyle, she took 'em. May be wrong on this, but it sounded like the last thing she said was they were going to leave the girls with some people in Connecticut. The kids were excited getting a ride in that little car. You know they hardly ever go anywhere. Crave excitement. But she was real clear about the check. My check." The colossal arms disappearing into her coat's dolman sleeves, tweed flecked with purple and gold.

"Mrs. Moosup, there's about twelve dollars in my checking account. An hour ago I was fired. Your pay was supposed to come from Petal. If you are serious about three-oh-eight-oh, I will have to cash in our CDs to pay you. I can't do it until tomorrow. But don't worry, you'll get paid." He kept eating the withered hot dogs. What next.

"That's what *she* always said," said Mrs. Moosup bitterly. "That's why I'm not so cut up about this. It's no fun working if you don't get paid."

Quoyle nodded. Later, after she was gone, he called the state police.

"My wife. I want my children back," Quoyle said into the phone to a rote voice. "My daughters, Bunny and Sunshine Quoyle. Bunny is six and Sunshine is four and a half." They were his. Reddish hair, freckles like chopped grass on a wet dog. Sunshine's wee beauty in her frowst of orange curls. Homely Bunny. But smart. Had Quoyle's no-color eyes and reddish eyebrows, the left one crooked and notched with a scar from the time she fell out of a grocery cart. Her hair, crimpy, cut short. Big-boned children.

"They both look like that furniture that's built out of packing crates," Petal wisecracked. The nursery school director saw untamed troublemakers and expelled first Bunny, then Sunshine. For pinching, pushing, screaming and demanding. Mrs. Moosup knew them for brats who whined they were hungry and wouldn't let her watch her programs.

But from the first moment that Petal raved she was pregnant, threw her purse on the floor like a dagger, kicked her shoes at Quoyle and said she'd get an abortion, Quoyle loved, first Bunny, then Sunshine, loved them with a kind of fear that if they made it into the world they were with him on borrowed time, would one day run a wire into his brain through terrible event. He never guessed it would be Petal. Thought he'd already had the worst from her.

The aunt, in a black and white checked pantsuit, sat on the sofa, listened to Quoyle choke and sob. Made tea in the never-used pot. A stiff-figured woman, gingery hair streaked with white. Presented a profile like a target in a shooting gallery. A buff mole on her neck. Swirled the tea around in the pot, poured, dribbled milk. Her coat, bent over the arm of the sofa, resembled a wine steward showing a label.

"You drink that. Tea is a good drink, it'll keep you going. That's the truth." Her voice had a whistling harmonic as from the cracked-open window of a speeding car. Body in sections, like a dress form.

"I never really knew her," he said, "except that she was driven by terrible forces. She had to live her life her own way. She said that a million times." The slovenly room was full of reflecting surfaces accusing him, the teapot, the photographs, his wedding ring, magazine covers, a spoon, the television screen.

"Drink some tea."

"Some people probably thought she was bad, but I think she was starved for love. I think she just couldn't get enough love.

That's why she was the way she was. Deep down she didn't have a good opinion of herself. Those things she did—they reassured her for a little while. I wasn't enough for her."

Did he believe that pap, the aunt wondered? She guessed that this was Quoyle's invention, this love-starved Petal. Took one look at the arctic eyes, the rigidly seductive pose of Petal's photograph, Quoyle's silly rose in a water glass beside it, and thought to herself, there was a bitch in high heels.

Quoyle had gasped, the phone to his ear, loss flooding in like the sea gushing into a broken hull. They said the Geo had veered off the expressway and rolled down a bank sown with native wildflowers, caught on fire. Smoke poured from the real estate agent's chest, Petal's hair burned. Her neck broken.

Newspaper clippings blew out of the car, along the highway; reports of a monstrous egg in Texas, a fungus in the likeness of Jascha Heifetz, a turnip as large as a pumpkin, a pumpkin as small as a radish.

The police, sorting through singed astrology magazines and clothes, found Petal's purse crammed with more than nine thousand dollars in cash, her calendar book with a notation to meet Bruce Cudd on the morning before the accident. In Bacon Falls, Connecticut. There was a receipt for seven thousand dollars in exchange for "personal services." Looked like she had sold the children to Bruce Cudd, the police said.

Quoyle, in his living room, blubbing through red fingers, said he could forgive Petal anything if the children were safe.

Why do we weep in grief, the aunt wondered. Dogs, deer, birds suffered with dry eyes and in silence. The dumb suffering of animals. Probably a survival technique.

"You're good-hearted," she said. "Some would curse her mangled body for selling the little girls." The milk on the verge of turning. Tan knobs in the sugar bowl from wet coffee spoons.

"I will never believe that, that she sold them. Never," cried Quoyle. His thigh clashed against the table. The sofa creaked.

"Maybe she didn't. Who knows?" The aunt soothed. "Yes,

you're good-hearted. You take after Sian Quoyle. Your poor grandfather. I never knew him. Dead before I was born. But I saw the picture of him many times, the tooth of a dead man hanging on a string around his neck. To keep toothache away. They believed in that. But he was very good-natured they said. Laughed and sang. Anybody could fool him with a joke."

"Sounds simpleminded," sobbed Quoyle into his teacup.

"Well, if he was, it's the first I ever heard of it. They say when he went under the ice he called out, 'See you in heaven.' "

"I heard that story," said Quoyle, salty saliva in his mouth and his nose swelling up. "He was just a kid."

"Twelve years old. Sealing. He'd got as many whitecoats as any man there before he had one of his fits and went off the ice. Nineteen and twenty-seven."

"Father told us about him sometimes. But he couldn't have been twelve. I never heard he was twelve. If he drowned when he was twelve he couldn't have been my grandfather."

"Ah, you don't know Newfoundlanders. For all he was twelve he was your father's father. But not mine. My mother—your grandmother—that was Sian's sister Addy, and after young Sian drowned she took up with Turvey, the other brother. Then when *he* drowned, she married Cokey Hamm, that was my father. Lived in the house on Quoyle's Point for years—where I was born—then we moved over to Catspaw. When we left in 1946 after my father was killed—"

"Drowned," said Quoyle. Listening in spite of himself. Blowing his nose into the paper napkin. Which he folded and put on the edge of his saucer.

"No. Afterwards we went over to stinking Catspaw Harbor where we was treated like mud by that crowd. There was an awful girl with a purple tetter growing out of her eyebrow. Threw rocks. And then we came to the States." She sang " 'Terra Nova grieving, for hearts that are leaving.' That's all I remember of that little ditty."

Quoyle hated the thought of an incestuous, fit-prone, seal-killing child for a grandfather, but there was no choice. The mysteries of unknown family.

When the police burst in, the photographer in stained Jockey shorts was barking into the phone. Quoyle's naked daughters had squirted dish detergent on the kitchen floor, were sliding in it.

"They have not been obviously sexually abused, Mr. Quoyle," said the voice on the telephone. Quoyle could not tell if a man or a woman was speaking. "There was a video camera. There were blank film cartridges all over the place, but the camera jammed or something. When the officers came in he was on the phone to the store where he bought the camera, yelling at the clerk. The children were examined by a child abuse pediatric specialist. She says there was no evidence that he did anything physical to them except undress them and clip their fingernails and toenails. But he clearly had something in mind."

Quoyle could not speak.

"The children are with Mrs. Bailey at the Social Services office," said the mealy voice. "Do you know where that is?"

Sunshine was smeared with chocolate, working a handle that activated a chain of plastic gears. Bunny asleep in a chair, eyeballs rolling beneath violet lids. He lugged them out to the car, squeezing them in his hot arms, murmuring that he loved them.

"The girls look a lot like Feeny and Fanny used to, my younger sisters," said the aunt, jerking her head up and down. "Look just like 'em. Feeny's in New Zealand now, a marine biologist, knows everything about sharks. Broke her hip this spring. Fanny is in Saudi Arabia. She married a falconer. Has to wear a black thing over her face. Come on over here, you little girls and give your aunt a big hug," she said.

But the children rushed at Quoyle, gripped him as a falling man clutches the window ledge, as a stream of electric particles arcs a gap and completes a circuit. They smelled of Sierra Free dish detergent scented with calendula and horsemint. The aunt's expression unfathomable as she watched them. Longing, perhaps.

Quoyle, in the teeth of trouble, saw a stouthearted older woman. His only female relative.

"Stay with us," he said. "I don't know what to do." He waited for the aunt to shake her head, say no, she had to be getting back, could only stay a minute longer.

She nodded. "A few days. Get things straightened up." Rubbed her palms together as if a waiter had just set a delicacy before her. "You can look at it this way," she said. "You've got a chance to start out all over again. A new place, new people, new sights. A clean slate. See, you can be anything you want with a fresh start. In a way, that's what I'm doing myself."

She thought of something. "Would you like to meet Warren?" she asked. "Warren is out in the car, dreaming of old glories."

Quoyle imagined a doddering husband, but Warren was a dog with black eyelashes and a collapsed face. She growled when the aunt opened the rear door.

"Don't be afraid," said the aunt. "Warren will never bite anyone again. They pulled all of her teeth two years ago."

4

Cast Away

"Cast Away, to be forced from a ship by a disaster."

THE MARINER'S DICTIONARY

QUOYLE'S face the color of a bad pearl. He was wedged in a seat on a ferry pitching toward Newfoundland, his windbreaker stuffed under his cheek, the elbow wet where he had gnawed it.

The smell of sea damp and paint, boiled coffee. Nor any escape from static snarled in the public address speakers, gunfire in the movie lounge. Passengers singing "That's one more dollar for me," swaying over whiskey.

Bunny and Sunshine stood on the seats opposite Quoyle, staring through glass at the games room. Crimson Mylar walls, a ceiling that reflected heads and shoulders like disembodied putti on antique valentines. The children yearned toward the water-bubble music.

Next to Quoyle a wad of the aunt's knitting. The needles jabbed his thigh but he did not care. He was brimming with nausea.

Though the ferry heaved toward Newfoundland, his chance to start anew.

The aunt had made a good case. What was left for him in Mockingburg? Unemployed, wife gone, parents deceased. And there was Petal's Accidental Death and Dismemberment Insurance Plan money. Thirty thousand to the spouse and ten thousand to each eligible child. He hadn't thought of insurance, but it crossed the aunt's mind at once. The children slept, Quoyle and the aunt sat at the kitchen table. The aunt in her big purple dress, having a drop of whiskey in a teacup. Quoyle with a cup of Ovaltine. To help him sleep, the aunt said. Blue sleeping pills. He was embarrassed but swallowed them. Fingernails bitten to the quick.

"It makes sense," she said, "for you to start a new life in a fresh place. For the children's sake as well as your own. It would help you all get over what's happened. You know it takes a year, a full turn of the calendar, to get over losing somebody. That's a true saying. And it helps if you're in a different place. And what place would be more natural than where your family came from? Maybe you could ask around, your newspaper friends, tap the grapevine. There might be a job up there. Just the trip would be an experience for the girls. See another part of the world. And to tell the truth," patting his arm with her old freckled hand, "it would be a help to me to have you along. I bet we'd be a good team."

The aunt leaned on her elbow. Chin on the heel of her hand. "As you get older you find out the place where you started out pulls at you stronger and stronger. I never wanted to see Newfoundland again when I was young, but the last few years it's been like an ache, just a longing to go back. Probably some atavistic drive to finish up where you started. So in a way I'm starting again, too. Going to move my little business up there. It wouldn't hurt you to ask about a job."

He thought of calling Partridge, telling him. The inertia of grief rolled through him. He couldn't do it. Not now.

Woke at midnight, swimming up from aubergine nightmare.

Petal getting into a bread truck. The driver is gross, a bald head, mucus suspended from his nostrils, his hands covered with some unspeakable substance. Quoyle has the power to see both sides of the truck at once. Sees the hands reaming up under Petal's dress, the face lowering into her oaken hair, and all the time the truck careening along highways, swaying over bridges without railings. Quoyle is somehow flying along beside them, powered by anxiety. Clusters of headlights flicker closer. He struggles to reach Petal's hand, to pull her out of the bread truck, knowing what must come (wishing it for the driver who has metamorphosed into his father) but cannot reach her, suffers agonizing paralysis though he strains. The headlights close. He shouts to tell her death is imminent, but is voiceless. Woke up pulling at the sheet.

For the rest of the night he sat in the living room with a book in his lap. His eyes went back and forth, he read, but comprehended nothing. The aunt was right. Get out of here.

It took half an hour to get a phone number for Partridge.

"Goddamn! I was just thinking about you the other day." Partridge's voice came fresh in the wires. "Wondering what the hell ever happened to old Quoyle! When you going to come out and visit? You know I quit the papers, don't you? Yeah, I quit 'em." The thought of Mercalia on the road alone, he said, made him go to the truck driver school himself.

"We're a driving team, now. Bought a house two years ago. Planning on buying our own rig pretty soon, doing independent contracting. These trucks are sweet—double bunk, little kitchenette. Air-conditioned. We sit up there over the traffic, look down on the cars. Making three times the money I was. Don't miss newspapers at all. So what's new with you, still working for Punch?"

It only took ten or eleven minutes to tell Partridge everything, from falling in one-way love to riding the nightmares, to leaning over a tableful of maps with the aunt.

"Son of a bitch, Quoyle. You been on the old roller coaster. You had the full-course dinner. Least you got your kids. Well, I'll tell you. I'm out of the newspaper game but still got some contacts.

See what I come up with. Gimme the names of the nearest towns again?"

There was only one, with the curious name of Killick-Claw.

Partridge back on the line two days later. Pleased to be fixing Quoyle's life up again. Quoyle made him think of a huge roll of newsprint from the pulp mill. Blank and speckled with imperfections. But beyond this vagueness he glimpsed something like a reflection of light from a distant hubcap, a scintillation that meant there was, in Quoyle's life, the chance of some brilliance. Happiness? Good luck? Fame and fortune? Who knows, thought Partridge. He liked the rich taste of life so well himself he wished for an entree or two for Quoyle.

"Amazes me how the old strings still pull. Yeah, there's a paper up there. A weekly. They looking for somebody, too. You interested, I'll give you the name I got. Want somebody to cover the shipping news. Guess it's right on the coast. Want somebody with maritime connections if possible. Quoyle, you got maritime connections?"

"My grandfather was a sealer."

"Jesus. You always come at me out of left field. Anyway, it works out, you got to handle work permits and immigration and all that. Deal with those guys. O.k. Managing editor's name is Tertius Card. Got a pencil? Give you the number."

Quoyle wrote it down.

"Well, good luck. Let me know how it goes. And listen, any time you want to come out here, stay with Mercalia and me, you just come on. This is a real good place to make money."

But the idea of the north was taking him. He needed something to brace against.

A month later they drove away in his station wagon. He took a last look in the side mirror at the rented house, saw the empty porch, the forsythia bush, the neighbor's flesh-colored slips undulating on the line.

And so Quoyle and the aunt in the front seat, the children in the back, and old Warren sometimes with the suitcases, sometimes clambering awkwardly up to sit between Bunny and Sunshine. They made her paper hats from napkins, tied the aunt's scarf around her hairy neck, fed her French fries when the aunt wasn't looking.

Fifteen hundred miles, across New York, Vermont, angling up through Maine's mauled woods. Across New Brunswick and Nova Scotia on three-lane highways, trouble in the center lane, making the aunt clench her hands. In North Sydney plates of oily fish for supper, and no one who cared, and in the raw morning, the ferry to Port-Aux-Basques. At last.

Quoyle suffered in the upholstery, the aunt strode the deck, stopped now and then to lean on the rail above the shuddering water. Or stood spraddle-legged, hands knotted behind her back, facing wind. Her hair captured under a babushka, face a stone with little intelligent eyes.

She spoke of the weather with a man in a watch cap. They talked awhile. Someone else reel footing along, said, Rough today, eh? She worried about Warren, down in the station wagon, tossing up and down. Wouldn't know what to make of it. Never been to sea. Probably thought the world was coming to an end and she all alone, in a strange car. The man in the watch cap said, "Don't worry, dog'll sleep the 'ole way across. That's 'ow dogs are."

The aunt looked out, saw the blue land ahead, her first sight of the island in almost fifty years. Could not help tears.

"Comin' 'ome, eh?" said the man in the watch cap. "Yar, that's 'ow it takes you."

This place, she thought, this rock, six thousand miles of coast blind-wrapped in fog. Sunkers under wrinkled water, boats threading tickles between ice-scabbed cliffs. Tundra and barrens, a land of stunted spruce men cut and drew away.

How many had come here, leaning on the rail as she leaned now. Staring at the rock in the sea. Vikings, the Basques, the French, English, Spanish, Portuguese. Drawn by the cod, from the days when massed fish slowed ships on the drift for the passage to the Spice Isles, expecting cities of gold. The lookout dreamed of roasted auk or sweet berries in cups of plaited grass, but saw crumpling waves, lights flickering along the ship rails. The only cities were of ice, bergs with cores of beryl, blue gems within white gems, that some said gave off an odor of almonds. She had caught the bitter scent as a child.

Shore parties returned to ship blood-crusted with insect bites. Wet, wet, the interior of the island, they said, bog and marsh, rivers and chains of ponds alive with metal-throated birds. The ships scraped on around the points. And the lookout saw shapes of caribou folding into fog.

Later, some knew it as a place that bred malefic spirits. Spring starvation showed skully heads, knobbed joints beneath flesh. What desperate work to stay alive, to scrob and claw through hard times. The alchemist sea changed fishermen into wet bones, sent boats to drift among the cod, cast them on the landwash. She remembered the stories in old mouths: the father who shot his oldest children and himself that the rest might live on flour scrapings; sealers crouched on a floe awash from their weight until one leaped into the sea; storm journeys to fetch medicines—always the wrong thing and too late for the convulsing hangashore.

She had not been in these waters since she was a young girl, but it rushed back, the sea's hypnotic boil, the smell of blood, weather and salt, fish heads, spruce smoke and reeking armpits, the rattle of wash-ball rocks in hissing wave, turrs, the crackery taste of brewis, the bedroom under the eaves.

But now they said that hard life was done. The forces of fate weakened by unemployment insurance, a flaring hope in offshore oil money. All was progress and possession, all shove and push, now. They said.

Fifteen she was when they had moved from Quoyle's Point, seventeen when the family left for the States, a drop in the tides of Newfoundlanders away from the outports, islands and hidden coves, rushing like water away from isolation, illiteracy, trousers made of worn upholstery fabric, no teeth, away from contorted thoughts and rough hands, from desperation.

And her dad, Harold Hamm, dead the month before they left,

killed when a knot securing a can hook failed. Off-loading barrels of nails. The corner of the sling drooped, the barrel came down. Its iron-rimmed chine struck the nape of his neck, dislocated vertebrae and crushed the spinal column. Paralyzed and fading on the dock, unable to speak; who knew what thoughts crashed against the washline of his seizing brain as the kids and wife bent over, imploring Father, Father. No one said his name, only the word *father*, as though fatherhood had been the great thing in his life. Weeping. Even Guy, who cared for no one but himself.

So strange, she thought, going back there with a bereaved nephew and Guy's ashes. She had taken the box from sobbing Quoyle, carried it up to the guest room. Lay awake thinking she might pour Guy into a plastic supermarket bag, tie the loop handles, and toss him into the dumpster.

Only a thought.

Wondered which had changed the most, place or self? It was a strong place. She shuddered. It would be better now. Leaned on the rail, looking into the dark Atlantic that snuffled at the slope of the past.

5

A Rolling Hitch

"A Rolling Hitch will suffice to tie a broom that has no groove, provided the surface is not too slick."

THE ASHLEY BOOK OF KNOTS

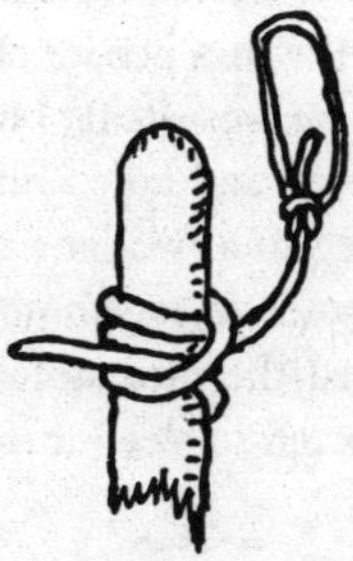

ON THE floor behind the seat Warren groaned. Quoyle steered up the west coast of the Great Northern Peninsula along a highway rutted by transport trucks. The road ran between the loppy waves of the Strait of Belle Isle and mountains like blue melons. Across the strait sullen Labrador. Trucks ground east in caravans, stainless steel cabs beaded with mist. Quoyle almost recognized the louring sky. As though he had dreamed this place once, forgot it later.

The car rolled over fissured land. Tuckamore. Cracked cliffs in volcanic glazes. On a ledge above the sea a murre laid her single egg. Harbors still locked in ice. Tombstone houses jutting from raw granite, the coast black, glinting like lumps of silver ore.

Their house, the aunt said, crossing her fingers, was out on Quoyle's Point. The Point, anyway, still on the map. A house empty for forty-four years. She scoffed, said it could not still stand, but inwardly believed something had held, that time had not cheated her of this return. Her voice clacked. Quoyle, listening, drove with his mouth open as though to taste the subarctic air.

On the horizon icebergs like white prisons. The immense blue fabric of the sea, rumpled and creased.

"Look," said the aunt. "Fishing skiffs." Small in the distance. Waves bursting against the headlands. Exploding water.

"I remember a fellow lived in a wrecked fishing boat," the aunt said. "Old Danny Something-or-other. It was hauled up on the shore far enough out of the storm and he fixed it up. Little chimney sticking up, path with a border of stone. Lived there for years until one day when he was sitting out in front mending net and the rotten hull collapsed and killed him."

The highway shriveled to a two-lane road as they drove east, ran under cliffs, passed spruce forest fronted by signs that said NO CUTTING. Quoyle appraised the rare motels they passed with the eye of someone who expected to sleep in one of them.

The aunt circled Quoyle's Point on the map. On the west side of Omaloor Bay the point thrust into the ocean like a bent thumb. The house, whether now collapsed, vandalized, burned, carried away in pieces, had been there. Once.

The bay showed on the map as a chemist's pale blue flask into which poured ocean. Ships entered the bay through the neck of the flask. On the eastern shore the settlement of Flour Sack Cove, three miles farther down the town of Killick-Claw, and along the bottom, odds and ends of coves. The aunt rummaged in her black flapjack handbag for a brochure. Read aloud the charms of Killick-Claw, statistics of its government wharf, fish plant, freight terminal, restaurants. Population, two thousand. Potential unlimited.

"Your new job's in Flour Sack Cove, eh? That's right across from Quoyle's Point. Looks about two miles by water. And a long trip by road. Used to be a ferry run from Capsize Cove to Killick-Claw every morning and night. But I guess it's closed down now. If you had a boat and a motor you could do it yourself."

"How do we get out to Quoyle's Point?" he asked.

There was a road off the main highway, the aunt said, that showed as a dotted line on the map. Quoyle didn't like the look of the dotted line roads they passed. Gravel, mud, washboard going nowhere.

They missed the turnoff, drove until they saw gas pumps. A sign. IGS STORE. The store in a house. Dark room. Behind the counter they could see a kitchen, teakettle spitting on the stove. Bunny heard television laughter.

Waiting for someone to appear, Quoyle examined bear-paw snowshoes. Walked around, looking at the homemade shelves, open boxes of skinning knives, needles for mending net, cones of line, rubber gloves, potted meats, a pile of adventure videos. Bunny peered through the freezer door at papillose frost crowding the ice cream tubs.

A man, sedge-grass hair sticking out from a cap embroidered with the name of a French bicycle manufacturer, came from the kitchen; chewed something gristly. Trousers a sullen crookedness of wool. The aunt talked. Quoyle modeled a sealskin hat for his children, helped them choose dolls made from clothespins. Inked faces smiled from the heads.

"Can you tell us where the road to Capsize Cove is?"

Unsmiling. Swallowed before answering.

"Be'ind you aways. Like just peasin' out of the main road. On a right as you go back. Not much in there now." He looked away. His Adam's apple a hairy mound in his neck like some strange sexual organ.

Quoyle at a rack of comic books, studied a gangster firing a laser gun at a trussed woman. The gangsters always wore green suits. He paid for the dolls. The man's fingers dropped cold dimes.

Up and down the highway three times before they spied a ruvid strip tilting away into the sky.

"Aunt, I don't think I can drive on this. It doesn't look like it goes anywhere."

"There's tire tracks on it," she said, pointing to cleated tread marks. Quoyle turned onto the sumpy road. Churned mud. The tire marks disappeared. Must have turned around, thought Quoyle, wanting to do the same and try tomorrow. Or had dropped in a bottomless hole.

"When are we gonna get there?" said Bunny, kicking the back of the seat. "I'm tired of going somewhere. I want to be there. I want to put on my bathing suit and play on the beach."

"Me too." Both throwing themselves rhythmically against the seat.

"It's too cold. Only polar bears go swimming now. But you can throw stones in the water. On the map, Aunt, how long is this road?" Hands ached from days of clenching.

She breathed over the map awhile. "From the main road to Capsize Cove is seventeen miles."

"Seventeen miles of this!"

"And then," as if he hadn't spoken, "eleven more to Quoyle's Point. To the house. Whatever's left of it. They show this road on the map, but in the old days it wasn't there. There was a footpath. See, folks didn't drive, nobody had cars then. Go places in the boat. Nobody had a car or truck. That paved main highway we come up on is all new." Yet the signature of rock written against the horizon in a heavy hand; unchanged, unchanging.

"Hope we don't get to Capsize Cove and discover we've got an eleven-mile hike in front of us." The rasp of his nylon sleeve on the wheel.

"We might. Then we'll just turn around." Her expression was remote. The bay seemed to be coming out of her mind, a blue hallucination.

Quoyle and the road in combat. Car Disintegrates on Remote Goatpath. Dusk washed in, the car struggled up a grade. They were on the edge of cliffs. Below, Capsize Cove, the abandoned houses askew. Fading light. Ahead, the main track swallowed in distance.

Quoyle pulled onto the shoulder, wondered if anybody had ever gone over the edge, metal jouncing on rocks. The side track down to the ruined cove steep, strewn with boulders. More gully than road.

"Well, we're not going to make the Point tonight," he said. "This is as far as I think we should drive until we can get a look at the road in daylight."

"You don't want to go back out to the highway, do you?" cried the aunt in her hot voice. So close to the beginning of everything.

"Yeah," said Bunny. "I want to go to a motel with TV and hamburgers and chips that you can eat in bed. And lights that go down, down, down when you turn the knob. And you can turn the television off and on with that thing without getting out of bed."

"I want fried chicken in the bed," said Sunshine.

"No," said Quoyle. "We're going to stick it out right here. We've got a tent in the back and I'm going to set it up beside the car and sleep in it. That's the plan." He looked at the aunt. It had been her idea. But she bent over her purse, rummaging for something private. Her old hair flattened and crushed.

"We've got air mattresses, we've got sleeping bags. We blow up the air mattresses and fold down the backseat and spread them out, put the sleeping bags on them and there you are, two nice comfortable beds. Aunt will have one and you two girls can share the other. I don't need an air mattress. I'll put my sleeping bag on the tent floor." He seemed to be asking questions.

"But I'm so starved," moaned Bunny. "I hate you, Dad! You're dumb!" She leaned forward and hit Quoyle on the back of the head.

"HERE NOW!" The outraged aunt roared at Bunny. "Take your seat, Miss, and don't ever let me hear you speak to your father like that again or I'll blister your bottom for you." The aunt let the blood boil up around her heart.

Bunny's face contorted into a tragic mask. "Petal says Dad is dumb." She hated them all.

"Everybody is dumb about some things," said Quoyle mildly. He reached back between the seats, his red hand offered to Bunny. To console her for the aunt's shouting The dog licked his fingers. There was the familiar feeling that things were going wrong.

"Well, I'm not doing that again," said the aunt, rotating her head, tipping her chin up. "Sleeping in the car. Feel like my neck is welded. And Bunny sleeps as quiet as an eggbeater."

They walked around in the roky damp, in a silence. The car glazed with salt. Quoyle squinted at the road. It curved, angled away from shoreline and into fog. What he could see of it looked good. Better than yesterday.

The aunt slapped mosquitoes, knotted a kerchief under her chin. Quoyle longed for bitter coffee or a clear view. Whatever he hoped for never happened. He rolled the damp tent.

Bunny's eyes opened as he threw in the tent and sleeping bag, but she sank back to sleep when the car started. Seeing blue beads that fell and fell from a string although she held both ends tightly.

The interior of the station wagon smelled of human hair. An arc showed in the fog, beyond it a second arc of faint prismatic colors.

"Fogbow," said the aunt. How loud the station wagon engine sounded.

Suddenly they were on a good gravel road.

"Look at this," said Quoyle. "This is nice." It curled away. They crossed a concrete bridge over a stream the color of beer.

"For pity's sake," said the aunt. "It's a wonderful road. But for what?"

"I don't know," said Quoyle, bringing his speed up.

"Got to be some reason. Maybe people come across from Killick-Claw to Capsize Cove by ferry, and then drive out to Quoyle's Point this way? God knows why. Maybe there's a provincial park. Maybe there's a big hotel," said the aunt. "But how in the world could they make it up from Capsize Cove? That road is all washed out. And Capsize Cove is dead."

They noticed sedgy grass in the centerline, a damp sink where a culvert had dropped, and, in the silted shoulders, hoofprints the size of cooking pots.

"Nobody's driven this fancy road in a long time."

Quoyle stood on the brakes. Warren yelped as she was thrown against the back of the seat. A moose stood broadside, looming; annoyance in its retreat.

A little after eight they swept around a last corner. The road came to an end in an asphalt parking lot beside a concrete building. The wild barrens pressed all around.

Quoyle and the aunt got out. Silence, except for the wind sharpening itself on the corner of the building, the gnawing sea. The aunt pointed at cracks in the walls, a few windows up under the eaves. They tried the doors. Metal, and locked.

"Not a clue," said the aunt, "whatever it is. Or was."

"I don't know what to make of it," said Quoyle, "but it all stops here. And the wind's starting up again."

"Oh, without a doubt this building goes with the road. You know," said the aunt, "if we can scout up something to boil water in, I've got some tea bags in my pocketbook. Let's have a break and think about this. We can use the girls' soda cans to drink out of. I can't believe I forgot to get coffee."

"I've got my camping frying pan with me," said Quoyle. "Never been used. It was in my sleeping bag. I slept on it all night."

"Let's try it," said the aunt, gathering dead spruce branches festooned with moss, blasty boughs she called them, and the moss was old man's whiskers. Remembering the names for things. Heaped the boughs in the lee of the building.

Quoyle got the water jug from the car. In fifteen minutes they were drinking out of the soda cans, scalding tea that tasted of smoke and orangeade. The aunt drew the sleeve of her sweater down to protect her hand from the hot metal. Fog shuddered against their faces. The aunt's trouser cuffs snapped in the wind. Ochre brilliance suffused the tattered fog, disclosed the bay, smothered it.

"Ah!" shouted the aunt pointing into the stirring mist. "*I saw the house*. The old windows. Double chimneys. As it always was. Over there! I'm telling you I saw it!"

Quoyle stared. Saw fog stirring.

"Right over there. The cove and then the house." The aunt strode away.

Bunny got out of the car, still in her sleeping bag, shuffling along over the asphalt. "Is this it?" she said, staring at the concrete wall. "It's awful. There's no windows. Where's my room going to be? Can I have a soda, too? Dad, there's smoke coming out of the can and coming out of your mouth, too. How do you do that, Daddy?"

Half an hour later they struggled together toward the house, the aunt with Sunshine on her shoulders, Quoyle with Bunny, the dog limping behind. The wind got under the fog, drove it up. Glimpses of the ruffled bay. The aunt pointing, arm like that of the shooting gallery figure with the cigar in its metal hand. In the bay they saw a scallop dragger halfway to the narrows, a wake like the hem of a slip showing behind it.

Bunny sat on Quoyle's shoulders, hands clutched under his chin as he stumped through the tuckamore. The house was the green of grass stain, tilted in fog. She endured her father's hands on her knees, the smell of his same old hair, his rumbles that she weighed a ton, that she choked him. The house rocked with his strides through a pitching ocean of dwarf birch. That color of green made her sick.

"Be good now," he said, loosing her fingers. Six years separated her from him, and every day was widening water between her outward-bound boat and the shore that was her father. "Almost there, almost there," Quoyle panted, pitying horses.

He set her on the ground. She ran with Sunshine up and down the curve of rock. The house threw their voices back at them, hollow and unfamiliar.

The gaunt building stood on rock. The distinctive feature was a window flanked by two smaller ones, as an adult might stand with protective arms around children's shoulders. Fan lights over the door. Quoyle noticed half the panes were gone. Paint flaked from wood. Holes in the roof. The bay rolled and rolled.

"Miracle it's standing. That roofline is as straight as a ruler," the aunt said. Trembling.

"Let's see how it is inside," said Quoyle. "For all we know the floors have fallen into the cellar."

The aunt laughed. "Not likely," she shouted joyfully. "There isn't any cellar." The house was lashed with cable to iron rings set in the rock. Streaks of rust, notched footholds in the stone like steps, crevices deep enough to hide a child. The cables bristled with broken wires.

"Top of the rock not quite level," the aunt said, her sentences flying out like ribbons on a pole. "Before my time, but they said it rocked in storms like a big rocking chair, back and forth. Made the women sick, afraid, so they lashed it down and it doesn't move an inch but the wind singing through those cables makes a noise you don't forget. Oh, do I remember it in the winter storms. Like a moaning." For the house was garlanded with wind. "That's one reason I was glad when we moved over to Capsize Cove. There was a store at Capsize and that was a big thing. But then we shifted down the coast to Catspaw, and a year later we were off to the States." Told herself to calm down.

Rusted twenty-penny nails; planks over the ground-floor windows. Quoyle hooked his fingers under the window planks and heaved. Like pulling on the edge of the world.

"There's a hammer in the car," he said. "Under the seat. Maybe a pry bar. I'll go back and get them. And the food. We can make a picnic breakfast."

The aunt was remembering a hundred things. "I was born here," she said. "Born in this house." Other rites had occurred here as well.

"Me too," said Sunshine, blowing at a mosquito on her hand. Bunny slapped at it. Harder than necessary.

"No you weren't. You were born in Mockingburg, New York. There's smoke over there," she said, looking across the bay. "Something's on fire."

"It's chimney smoke from the houses in Killick-Claw. They're cooking their breakfasts over there. Porridge and hotcakes. See the fishing boat out in the middle of the bay? See it going along?"

"I wanna see it," said Sunshine. "I can't see it. I can't SEE it."

"You stop that howling or you'll see your bottom warmed," said the aunt. Face red in the wind.

Quoyle remembered himself crying "I can't see it," to a math teacher who turned away, gave no answers. The fog tore apart, light charged the sea like blue neon.

The wood, hardened by time and corroding weather, clenched the nails fast. They came out crying. He wrenched the latch but could not open the door until he worked the tire iron into the crack and forced it.

Dark except for the blinding rectangle streaming through the open door. Echo of boards dropping on rock. Light shot through glass in slices, landed on the dusty floors like strips of yellow canvas. The children ran in and out the door, afraid to go into the gloom alone, shrieking as Quoyle, levering boards outside, gave ghostly laughs and moans, "Huu huu huu."

Then inside, the aunt climbing the funneled stairs, Quoyle testing floorboards, saying be careful, be careful. Dust charged the air and they were all sneezing. Cold, must; canted doors on loose hinges. The stair treads concave from a thousand shuffling climbs and descents. Wallpaper poured backwards off the walls. In the attic a featherbed leaking bird down, ticking mapped with stains. The children rushed from room to room. Even when fresh the rooms must have been mean and hopeless.

"That's one more dollar for me!" shrieked Bunny, whirling on gritty floor. But through the windows the cool plain of sea.

Quoyle went back out. The wind as sweet in his nose as spring water in a thirsty mouth. The aunt coughing and half-crying inside.

"There's the table, the blessèd table, the old chairs, the stove is here, oh my lord, there's the broom on the wall where it always hung," and she seized the wooden handle. The rotted knot burst, straws shot out of the binding wire and the aunt held a stick. She saw the stovepipe was rusted through, the table on ruined legs, the chairs unfit.

"Needs a good scurrifunging. What mother always said."

Now she roved the rooms, turned over pictures that spit broken glass. Held up a memorial photograph of a dead woman, eyes half open, wrists bound with strips of white cloth. The wasted body lay on the kitchen table, coffin against the wall.

"Aunt Eltie. She died of TB." Held up another of a fat woman grasping a hen.

"Auntie Pinkie. She was so stout she couldn't get down to the chamber pot and had to set it on the bed before she could pee."

Square rooms, lofty ceilings. Light dribbled like water through a hundred sparkling holes in the roof, caught on splinters. This bedroom. Where she knew the pattern of cracks on the ceiling better than any other fact in her life. Couldn't bear to look. Downstairs again she touched a paint-slobbered chair, saw the foot knobs on the front legs worn to rinds. The floorboards slanted under her feet, wood as bare as skin. A rock smoothed by the sea for doorstop. And three lucky stones strung on a wire to keep the house safe.

Outside, an hour later, Quoyle at his fire, the aunt taking things out of the food box; eggs, a crushed bag of bread, butter, jam. Sunshine crowded against the aunt, her hands following, seizing packets. The child unwrapped the butter, the aunt spread it with a piece of broken wood for a knife, stirred the shivering eggs in the pan. The bread heel for the old dog. Bunny at the landwash casting peckled stones. As each struck, foaming lips closed over it.

They sat beside the fire. The smoky stingo like an offering from some stone altar, the aunt thought, watched the smolder melt into the sky. Bunny and Sunshine leaned against Quoyle. Bunny ate a slice of bread rolled up, the jelly poised at the end like the eye of a toaster oven, watched the smoke gyre.

"Dad. Why does smoke twist around?"

Quoyle tore circles of bread, put pinches of egg atop and said "Here comes a little yellow chicken to the ogre's lair," and made the morsels fly through the air and into Sunshine's mouth. And the children were up and off again, around the house, leaping over the rusted cables that held it to the rock.

"Dad," panted Bunny, clacking two stones together. "Isn't Petal going to live with us any more?"

Quoyle was stunned. He'd explained that Petal was gone, that she was asleep and could never wake up, choking back his own grief, reading aloud from a book the undertaker had supplied, *A Child's Introduction to Departure of a Loved One*.

"No, Bunny. She's gone to sleep. She's in heaven. Remember,

I told you?" For he had protected them from the funeral, had never said the word. Dead.

"And she can't get up again?"

"No. She's sleeping forever and she can never get up."

"You cried, Daddy. You put your head on the refrigerator and cried."

"Yes," said Quoyle.

"But I didn't cry. I thought she would come back. She would let me wear her blue beads."

"No. She can't come back." And Quoyle had given away the blue beads, all the heaps of chains and beads, the armfuls of jewel-colored clothes, the silly velvet cap sewed over with rhinestones, the yellow tights, the fake red fox coat, even the half-empty bottles of Trésor, to the Goodwill store.

"If I was asleep I would wake up," said Bunny, walking away from him and around the house.

She was alone back there, the stunted trees pressing at the foot of the rock. A smell of resin and salt. Behind the house a ledge. A freshet plunged into a hole. The color of the house on this side, away from the sun, was again the bad green. She looked up and the walls swelled out as though they were falling. Turned again and the tuckamore moved like legs under a blanket. There was a strange dog, white, somehow misshapen, with matted fur. The eyes gleamed like wet berries. It stood, staring at her. The black mouth gaped, the teeth seemed packed with stiff hair. Then it was gone like smoke.

She shrieked, stood shrieking, and when Quoyle ran to her, she climbed up on him, bellowing to be saved. And though later he beat through the tuckamore with a stick for half an hour they saw no dog, nor sign. The aunt said in the old days when the mailman drove a team and men hauled firewood with dogs, everyone kept the brutes. Perhaps, she said doubtfully, some wild tribe had descended from those dogs. Warren snuffled without enthusiasm, refused to take a scent.

"Don't go wandering off by yourselves, now. Stay with us."

The aunt made a face at Quoyle that meant—what? That the child was nervy.

She looked down the bay, scanned the shoreline, the fiords, thousand-foot cliffs over creamy water. The same birds still flew from them like signal flares, razored the air with their cries. Darkening horizon.

The old place of the Quoyles, half ruined, isolated, the walls and doors of it pumiced by stony lives of dead generations. The aunt felt a hot pang. Nothing would drive them out a second time.

6

Between Ships

Oh make 'er fast and stow yer gear,
Leave 'er, Johnny, leave 'er!
An' tie 'er up to the bloomin' pier,
It's time for we to leave 'er!
OLD SONG

THE FIRE was dying. Dominoed coals gave off the last heat. Bunny lay plastered against Quoyle under the wing of his jacket. Sunshine squatted on the other side of the fire piling pebbles on top of each other. Quoyle heard her murmuring to them, "Get up there, honey, you want the pancakes?" She could not stack more than four before they fell.

The aunt ticked off points on her fingers, drew lines on the rock with a burned stick. But they could not live in the house, said Quoyle, perhaps for a long time. They *could* live in the house, said the aunt, the words lunging at something, but it would be hard. Ah, even if the house was like new, said Quoyle, he couldn't drive back and forth on that road every day. The first part of the road was god-awful.

"Get a boat." The aunt, dreamily, as though she meant a schooner for the trade winds. "With a boat you don't need the road."

"What about stormy weather? Winter?" Quoyle heard his own idiotic voice. He did not want a boat, shied from the thought of water. Ashamed he could not swim, couldn't learn.

"Rare the storm a Newfoundlander couldn't cross the bay in," said the aunt. "In the winter, the snowmobile." Her stick grated on the rock.

"A road still might be better," said Quoyle imagining coffee roaring out of a spigot and into his cup.

"Well, granted we can't live in the house for a while, maybe two or three months," said the aunt, "we can find a place to rent in Killick-Claw where you'll be near your newspaper work until the house is fixed. Let's drive up this afternoon, get a couple of motel rooms and see if we can find a house to rent, line up some carpenters to start on this place. Want a babysitter or a play school for the girls. I've got my own work to do, you know. Locate a work space, get set up. That wind is coming stronger." The coals fountained sparks.

"What is your work anyway, Aunt? I'm embarrassed to say I don't know. I mean, I never thought to ask." Had blundered into the unlikely journey knowing nothing, breathing grief like a sour gas. Hoped for oxygen soon.

"Understandable under the circumstances," said the aunt. "Upholstery." Showed her yellow, callused fingers. "I had the tools and fabric crated up and shipped. Should be here next week. You know, we ought to make a list while we're right here of the work to be done on this place. Needs a new roof, chimney repair. Have you got any paper?" She knew he had a boxful.

"Back in the car. I'll go back and get my notebook. Come on, Bunny, sit here. You can keep my place warm."

"See if you can find those crackers on the front seat. I think Bunny would perk up if she had a cracker." The child scowled. There's a sweet expression, thought the aunt. Felt the wind hard off the bay. A roll of cloud on the edge of the sea and the black and white waves like a grim tweed.

"Let's see," said the aunt. She had thrown new wood on the fire and the flames sprang about under the gusting wind. "Window glass, insulation, tear out the walls, new wallboard, a new door, a storm door, repair the chimneys, stovepipe, new waterline from the spring. Can these children abide an outhouse?" Quoyle hated the thought of their small bottoms clapped onto the roaring seat of a two-holer. Nor did he like the idea for his own hairy rump.

"Upstairs floors need to be replaced, the kitchen floor seems sound enough." In the end Quoyle said it might be cheaper to build a new house somewhere else, the Riviera, maybe. Even with the insurance and what the aunt had, they might not have enough.

"Think we'll manage. But you're right," she said. "We probably should clear a driveway from the mystery parking lot to the house. Maybe the province will do something about the road. We'll probably end up paying. Could be expensive. Lot more expensive than a boat." She stood up, hauled her black coat around and buttoned it to the neck. "It's getting mighty cold," she said. "Look." Held out her arm. Chips of snow landed in the loft of wool. "We better make tracks," she said. "This is not a good place to get caught in a snowstorm. Well do I know."

"In May?" said Quoyle. "Give me a break, Aunt."

"Any month of the year, my boy. Weather here beyond anything you know."

Quoyle looked out. The bay faded, as though he looked through a piece of cheesecloth. Needles of snow in his face.

"I don't believe it," he said. But it was what he wanted. Storm and peril. Difficult tasks. Exhaustion.

On the way out the wind buffeted the car. Darkness seeped from the overcast, snow grains ticking the windshield. On the highway there was already a film of snow on the road surface. He turned in at Ig's Store again.

"Getting some coffee," he said to the aunt. "Want some?"

"There's a big building in there and a parking lot."

"Oh yar. Glove fact'ry it was. Closed up years back." The man slid two paper cups with folded ear handles at him.

Shrieking wind. The bitter coffee trembled.

"Weather," the man said to Quoyle balanced in the doorway with his damp cups.

He bent against air. Cracking sky, a mad burst. The sign above the gas pump, a hand-painted circle of sheet metal, tore away, sliced over the store. The man came out, the door jumped from his hand, wrenched. Wind slung Quoyle against the pumps. The aunt's startled face in the car window. Then the gusts bore out of the east, shooting the blizzard at them.

Quoyle pried the door open. He'd dropped the coffee. "Look at it! Look at this," he cried. "We can't drive to Killick-Claw through twenty miles of this."

"Didn't we see a motel on the way up?"

"Yes we did. And it's back in Bloody Banks." He scraped at the map, his hand spangled with melting snow. "See it? It's thirty-six miles behind us." The car trembled.

"Let's help buddy with his door," said the aunt. "We'll ask him. He'll know some place."

Quoyle got the hammer from under the seat, and they stooped beneath wind. Steadied the door while the man pounded spikes.

He barely looked at them. Things on his mind, Quoyle thought, like whether or not the roof would lift off. But he shouted answers. Tickle Motel. Six miles east. Third time the year the door was off. First time the sign was off. Felt snowly all morning, he bellowed as they pulled onto the highway. Waved them into side-blown snow.

Slick road; visibility nil beyond the hood ornament. All dissolved in spinning particles. The speedometer needle at fifteen and still they skidded and jerked. The aunt leaned this way and that, hand on the dash, fingers widespread, as though by leaning she kept their balance.

"Dad, are we scared?" said Sunshine.

"No, honey. It's an adventure." Didn't want them to grow up timid. The aunt snorted. He glanced in the rearview mirror. Warren's yellow eyes met his. Quoyle winked at the dog. To cheer her up.

The motel's neon sign, TICKLE MOTEL, BAR & RESTAURANT, flickered as he steered into the parking lot, weaving past trucks and cars, long-distance rigs, busted-spring swampers, 4WD pickups, snowplows, snowmobiles. The place was jammed.

"Only thing left is The Deluxe Room and Bridal Suite," said the clerk, swabbing at his inflamed eyes. "Storm's got everybody in here plus it's darts playoffs night. Brian Mulroney, the prime minister, slept in it last year when he come by here. A big one, two beds and two cots. His bodyguards slept on the cots. A hundred and ten dollars the night." He had them over a barrel. Handed Quoyle an ornate key stamped 999. There was a basket of windup penguins near the cash register and Quoyle bought one for each of the children. Bunny broke the wings off hers before they left the lobby. A wet path on the carpet.

Room 999 was ten feet from the highway, fronted by a plate glass window. Every set of headlights veered into the parking lot, the glare sliding over the walls of the room like raw eggs in oil.

The inside doorknob came off in Quoyle's hand, and he worked it back carefully. He would get a screw from the desk clerk and fix it. They looked around the room. One of the beds was a round sofa. The carpet trodden with mud.

"There's no coat closet," said the aunt. "Mr. Mulroney must have slept in his suit." Toilet and shower cramped into a cubby. The sink next to the television set had only one faucet. Where the other had been, a hole. Wires from the television set trailed on the floor. The top of the instrument looked melted, apparently by a campfire.

"Never mind," yawned the aunt, "it's better than sleeping in the car," and looked for a light switch. Got a smoldering purple glow.

Quoyle was the first to take a shower. Discolored water spouted from a broken tile, seeped under the door and into the carpet. The sprinkler system dribbled as long as the cold faucet was open. His clothes slipped off the toilet lid and lay in the flood, for the door hooks were torn away. A Bible on a chain near the toilet, loose pages ready to fall. It was not until the next evening that he discovered he had gone about all day with a page from Leviticus stuck to his back.

The room was hot.

"Take a look at the thermostat," said the aunt. "No wonder." Caved in on the side as though smashed with a war club.

Quoyle picked up the phone, but it was dead.

"At least we can have dinner," said the aunt. "There's a dining room. A decent dinner and a good night's sleep and we'll be ready for anything."

The dining room, crowded with men, was lit by red bulbs that gave them a look of being roasted alive in their chairs. Quoyle thought the coffee filthy, but at other tables they drank it grinning. Waited an hour for their dinner, and Quoyle, sitting with his fractious children, his yawning old aunt and gobs of tartar sauce on both knees, could barely smile. Petal would have kicked the table over and walked out. And she was with him again, Petal, like a persistent song phrase, like a few stubborn lines of verse memorized in childhood. The needle was stuck.

"Thanks," murmured Quoyle to the waitress, swabbing his plate with a bun. Left a two-dollar bill under the saucer.

The rooms on each side of them raged with crashings, howling children. Snowplows shook the pictures of Jesus over the beds. The wind screamed in the ill-fitted window frames. As Quoyle pulled the door closed, the knob came off in his hand again, and he heard a whang on the other side of the door, the other half of the knob dropping.

"Oh boy, this is like a war," said Bunny watching a plywood wall shake. The aunt thought somebody must be kicking with both feet. Turned down the bedcovers, disclosing sheets stitched up from fragments of other, torn, sheets. Warren lapped water out of the toilet.

"It's a little better than sleeping in the car," the aunt said again. "A lot warmer."

"Tell a story, Dad," said Bunny. "You didn't tell us a story for about a hundred years."

Sunshine rushed at Quoyle, grabbed his shirt, hauling herself up into his lap, thumb in her mouth before she even leaned against his chest where she could hear the creaking sounds of his breathing, the thump of his heart, gurglings and squeals from his stomach.

"Not yet, not yet," said Quoyle. "Everybody brush their teeth. Everybody wash their face."

"And say your prayers," said the aunt.

"I don't know any," Sunshine blubbed.

"That's all right," said Quoyle, sitting in the chair beside the bed.

"Let's see. This is a story about hammers and wood."

"No, Dad! Not hammers and wood! Tell a good story."

"About what?" said Quoyle hopelessly, as though his fountain of invention was dry.

"Moose," said Bunny. "A moose and some roads. Long roads."

"And a dog. Like Warren."

"A nice dog, Dad. A grey dog."

And so Quoyle began. "Once there was a moose, a very poor, thin, lonely moose who lived on a rocky hill where only bitter leaves grew and bushes with spiky branches. One day a red motor car drove past. In the backseat was a grey gypsy dog wearing a gold earring."

In the night Bunny woke in nightmare, sobbed while Quoyle rocked her back and forth and said "It's only a bad dream, only a bad dream, it's not real."

"The Old Hag's got her," muttered the aunt. But Quoyle kept on rocking, for the Old Hag knew where to find him, too. Fragments of Petal embedded in every hour of the night.

Warren made bursting noises under the bed. A rancorous stench. Dog Farts Fell Family of Four.

A morning of hurling snow. Stupendous snores beyond the walls. Quoyle dressed and went to the door. Could not find the doorknob. Crept around looking under the bed, in the bathroom, in their luggage, in the jammed drawers of Bibles. One of the kids must have brought it into bed with her, he thought, but when they were up there was no knob. He pounded on the door to attract attention, but got a shout from an adjacent wall to "shut the fuck up or I'll bash yer." The aunt jiggled the phone receiver, hoping for life restored. Dead. The phone book was a 1972 Ontario directory. Many pages ripped out.

"My eyes hurt," said Bunny. Both children had reddened, matter-filled eyes.

For an imprisoned hour they watched the fading storm and the snowplows, banged on the door, called "Hello, hello." Both plastic penguins were broken. Quoyle wanted to break the door down. The aunt wrote a message on a pillowcase and hung it in the window. HELP. LOCKED IN ROOM 999. TELEPHONE DEAD.

The desk clerk opened the door. Looked at them with eyes like taillights.

"All you do is push the alarm button. Somebody come right away." Pointed to a switch near the ceiling. Reached up and flicked it. A clangor filled the motel and set off wall pounding until the motel vibrated. The clerk rubbed his eyes like a television actor seeing a miracle.

The storm persisted another day, winds shrieking, drifting the main highway.

"I like a storm, but this is more than enough," said the aunt, her hair down over one ear from collision with the chandelier, "and if I ever get out of this motel I will lead a good life, go to church regularly, bake bread twice a week and never let the dirty dishes stand. I'll never go out with my legs bare, so help me, just let me get out of here. I forgot what it's like, but it comes back to me now."

In the night it turned to rain, the wind came from the south, warm and with a smell of creamy milk.

7

The Gammy Bird

The common eider is called "gammy bird" in Newfoundland for its habit of gathering in flocks for sociable quacking sessions. The name is related to the days of sail, when two ships falling in with each other at sea would back their yards and shout the news. The ship to windward would back her main yards and the one to leeward her foreyards for close maneuvering. This was gamming.

A WOMAN in a rain slicker, holding the hand of a child, was walking on the verge of the road. As Quoyle's station wagon came abreast she stared at the wet car. The stranger. He lifted his hand a few inches but she had already dropped her gaze. The child's flat face. Red boots. And he was past.

The road to Flour Sack Cove shot uphill from Killick-Claw, over the height of land, then plunged toward houses, a few hauled-up boats. Fish flakes, scaffolds of peeled spruce from the old days of making salt cod. He passed a house painted white and red. The door dead center. A straggle of docks and fishermen's storage sheds. Humped rocks spread with veils of net.

No doubt about the newspaper office. There was a weathered teak panel nailed above the door. THE GAMMY BIRD over a painting of a quacking eider duck. Parked in front of the building were two trucks, a rusted, late-model Dodge and an older but gleaming Toyota.

From inside, shouting. The door snapped inward. A man jumped past, got in the Toyota. The tail pipe vibrated. The engine choked a little and fell silent as though embarrassed. The man looked at Quoyle. Got out of the truck and came at him with his hand. Acne scars corrugated the cheeks.

"As you see," he said, "sometimes you can't get away. I'm Tert Card, the bloody so-called managing editor, copy editor, rewrite man, mechanicals, ad makeup department, mail and distribution chief, snow shoveler. And you are either a big advertiser come to take out a four-page spread to proclaim the values of your warehouse of left-footed Japanese boots, or you are the breathlessly awaited Mr. Quoyle. Which is it?" His voice querulous in complaint. For the devil had long ago taken a shine to Tert Card, filled him like a cream horn with itch and irritation. His middle initial was X. Face like cottage cheese clawed with a fork.

"Quoyle."

"Come in then, Quoyle, and meet the band of brigands, the worst of them damn Nutbeem and his strangling hands. Himself, Mr. Jack Buggit, is up at the house having charms said over his scrawny chest to clear out a wonderful accumulation of phlegm which he's been hawking for a week." Could have been declaiming from a stage.

"This's the so-called newsroom," sneered Card. "And there's Billy Pretty," pointing, as though to a landmark. "He's an old fish dog." Billy Pretty small, late in his seventh decade. Sitting at a table, the wall behind him covered with oilcloth the color of insect wings. His face: wood engraved with fanned lines. Blue eyes in tilted eye cases, heavy lids. His cheek pillows pushed up by a thin, slanting smile, a fine channel like a scar from nose to upper lip. Bushy eyebrows, a roach of hair the color of an antique watch.

His table swayed when he leaned on it, was covered with a church bazaar display. Quoyle saw baskets, wooden butterflies, babies' booties in dime-store nylon.

"Billy Pretty, does the Home News page. He's got hundreds

of correspondents. He gets treasures in the mail, as you see. There's a stream of people after him, sending him things."

"Ar," said Billy Pretty. "Remember the omaloor that brought me some decorated turr's eggs? Hand painted with scenic views. Bust in the night all over the desk. A stink in here for a year afterward." Wiped his fingers on his diamond-pattern gansey, mended in the elbows and spotted with white nobs of glue and paper specks. " 'Omaloor?' As in Omaloor Bay?"

"Oh yes. An omaloor—big, stun, clumsy, witless, simple-minded type of a fellow. There used to be crowds of them on the other side of the bay," he gestured toward Quoyle's Point, "so they named it after them." Winked at Quoyle. Who wondered if he should smile. Did smile.

Near the window a man listened to a radio. His buttery hair swept behind ears. Eyes pinched close, a mustache. A packet of imported dates on his desk. He stood up to shake Quoyle's hand. Gangled. Plaid bow tie and ratty pullover. The British accent strained through his splayed nose.

"Nutbeem," he said. "Nutbeem of the Arctic." Threw Quoyle a half-salute, imitation of a character in some yellowed war movie.

"That's B. Beaufield Nutbeem," said Tert Card, "miserable ugly Brit cast away on the inhospitable Newfoundland shore a year ago and still here. Among other things, imagines he's the foreign news chief. Steals every story off the radio and rewrites it in his plummy style."

"Which bloody misbegotten Card takes the liberty of recasting in his own insane tongue. As the bloody bog-rat's just done."

Nutbeem's news came from a shortwave radio that buzzed as though wracked by migraine. When the airwaves were clear it had a tenor hum, but snarled when auroral static crackled. Nutbeem lay across his desk, his ear close to the receiver, gleaning the waves, the yowling foreign voices, twisting the stories around to suit his mood of the day. The volume button was gone, and he turned it up or down by inserting the tip of a table knife in the metal slot and twisting. His corner smelled of radios—dust, heat, metal, wood, electricity, time.

"Only to save you from accusations of plagiarism, me old son."

Nutbeem laughed bitterly. "I see you've regained your composure, you Newf dung beetle." He leaned at Quoyle. "Yes. Incredible protection from plagiarism. Every sentence so richly freighted with typographical errors that the original authors would not recognize their own stories. Let me give you some examples." He fished in file folders, pulled out a ragged sheet.

"I'll read you one of his gibberish gems, just to open your eyes. The first version is what I wrote, the second is the way it appeared in the paper. Item: 'Burmese sawmill owners and the Rangoon Development Corporation met in Tokyo Tuesday to consider a joint approach to marketing tropical hardwoods, both locally and for export.' Here's what Card did with it. 'Burnoosed sawbill awnings and the Ranger Development Competition met Wednesday near Tokyo to mark up topical hairwood.' " Sat back in his squeaking chair. Let the pages fall into the wastebasket.

Tert Card scratched his head and looked at his fingernails. "After all, it's only a stolen fiction in the first place," he said.

"You think it amusing now, Quoyle, you smile," said Nutbeem, "although you try to smile behind your hand, but wait until he works his damage on you. I read these samples to you so you know what lies ahead. 'Plywood' will become 'playwool,' 'fisherman' will become 'figbun,' 'Hibernia' become 'hernia.' This is the man to whom Jack Buggit entrusts our prose. No doubt you are asking yourself 'Why?' as I have many dark and sleepless nights. Jack says Card's typos give humor to the paper. He says they're better than a crossword puzzle."

The corner at the end of the room fenced with a particleboard partition.

"That's Jack's office," said Card. "And there's *your* little corner, Quoyle." Card waved his arm grandly. A desk, half a filing cabinet, the sawed-off top covered with a square of plywood, a 1983 Ontario telephone book, a swivel chair with one arm. A lamp of the kind found in hotel lobbies in the 1930s stood beside the desk, thick red cord like a rat's tail, plug as large as a baseball.

"What should I do?" said Quoyle. "What does Mr. Buggit want me to do?"

"Ah, nobody but himself can say. He wants you to sit tight

and wait until he's back. He'll tell you what he wants. You just come in every morning and himself'll show up one fine day and divulge all. Look through back issues. Acquaint yourself with *Gammy Bird*. Drive around and learn all four of our roads." Card turned away, labored over the computer.

"I's got to be out and about," said Billy Pretty. "Interview with a feller makes juju-bracelets out of lobster feelers for export to Haiti. Borrer your truck, Card? Mine's got the bad emission valve. Waiting for a part."

"You're always waiting for parts for that scow. Anyway, mine's not starting too good today. She dies just any old place."

Billy turned to Nutbeem.

"I rode the bike today. I suppose you can take the bike."

"Rather walk than snap me legs off on that rind of a bike." He cleared his throat and glanced at Quoyle. But Quoyle looked away out the window. He was too new to get into this.

"Ah, well. I'll hoof it. It's not more than eighteen miles each way."

In a minute they heard him outside, cursing as he mounted the jangling bicycle.

Half an hour later Tert Card left, started his truck, drove smoothly away.

"Off to get soused," said Nutbeem pleasantly. "Off to get his lottery ticket and then get soused. Observe that the truck starts when he wants it to."

Quoyle smiled, his hand went to his chin.

He spent the rest of the day, the rest of the week, leafing through the old phone book and reading back issues of the *Gammy Bird*.

The paper was a forty-four-page tab printed on a thin paper. Six columns, headlines modest, 36-point was a screamer, some stout but unfamiliar sans serif type. A very small news hole and a staggering number of ads.

He had never seen so many ads. They went down both sides of the pages like descending stairs and the news was squeezed into the vase-shaped space between. Crude ads with a few lines of type dead center. Don't Pay Anything Until January! No Down Payment! No Interest! As though these exhortations were freshly coined phrases for vinyl siding, rubber stamps, life insurance, folk music festivals, bank services, rope ladders, cargo nets, marine hardware, ship's laundry services, davits, rock band entertainment at the Snowball Lounge, clocks, firewood, tax return services, floor jacks, cut flowers, truck mufflers, tombstones, boilers, brass tacks, curling irons, jogging pants, snowmobiles, Party Night at Seal Flipper Lounge with Arthur the Accordion Ace, used snowmobiles, fried chicken, a smelting derby, T-shirts, oil rig maintenance, gas barbecue grills, wieners, flights to Goose Bay, Chinese restaurant specials, dry bulk transport services, a glass of wine with the pork chop special at the Norse Sunset Lounge, retraining program for fishermen, VCR repairs, heavy equipment operator training, tires, rifles, love seats, frozen corn, jelly powder, dancing at Uncle Demmy's Bar, kerosene lanterns, hull repairs, hatches, tea bags, beer, lumber planing, magnetic brooms, hearing aids.

He figured the ad space. *Gammy Bird* had to be making money. And somebody was one hell of a salesman.

Quoyle asked Nutbeem. "Mr. Buggit do the ads?"

"No. Tert Card. Part of the managing editor's job. Believe it or not." Tittered behind his mustache. "And they're not as good as they look."

Quoyle turned the pages. Winced at the wrecked car photos on the front page. Sexual abuse stories—three or four in every issue. Polar bears on ice floes. The shipping news looked simple—just a list of vessels in port. Or leaving.

"Hungry Men," a restaurant review by Benny Fudge and Adonis Collard running under two smudged photographs. Fudge's face seemed made of leftover flesh squeezed roughly together. Collard wore a cap that covered his eyes. Quoyle shuddered as he read.

> Trying to decide where to munch up some fast food? You could do worse than try Grudge's Cod Hop. The interior is booths with a big window in front. Watch the trucks on the highway! We did. We ordered the Fish Strip Basket which contained three

> fried fish Strips, coleslaw and a generous helping of fried chips for $5.70. The beverage was separate. The Fish Strip Basket was supposed to include Dinner Roll, but instead we got Slice of Bread. The fish Strips were very crispy and good. There is a choice of packet of lemon juice or Tartar Sauce. We both had the Tartar Sauce. There is counter service too.

Billy Pretty's work, "The Home Page," a conglomeration of poems, photographs of babies, write-away-for hooked rug patterns. Always a boxed feature—how to make birdhouses of tin cans, axe sheaths of cardboard, bacon turners from old kitchen forks. Recipes for Damper Devils, Fried Bawks, Dogberry Wine and Peas and Melts.

But the one everybody must read first, thought Quoyle, was "Scruncheons," a jet of near-libelous gossip. The author knitted police court news, excerpts of letters from relatives away, rude winks about rough lads who might be going away for "an Irish vacation." It beat any gossip column Quoyle had ever read. The byline was Junior Sugg.

> Well, we see the postman has landed in jail for 45 days for throwing the mail in Killick-Claw Harbour. He said he had too much mail to deliver and if people wanted it they could get it themselves. Guess it helps if you can swim. Poor Mrs. Tudge was hit by a tourist driving a luxury sedan last Tuesday. She is in hospital, not getting on too good. We hear the tourist's car isn't too good, either. And the Mounties are looking into the cause of an early morning fire that burned down the Pinhole Seafood fish plant on Shebeen Island; they might ask a certain fellow in a certain cove on the island what he thinks about it. A snowmobile mishap has taken the life of 78-year-old Rick Puff. Mr. Puff was on his way home from what Mrs. Puff called "a screech-in and a carouse" when his machine fell through the ice. Mr. Puff was a well-known accordion player who was filmed by a crew from the university. In the 1970s he served four years for sexual assault on his daughters. Bet they aren't crying either. Good news! We heard Kevin Mercy's dog "Biter" was lost in an

avalanche on Chinese Hill last week. And what's this we read in the overseas papers about kidnappers mailing the left ear of a Sicilian businessman they are holding hostage to his family? The way the foreigners live makes you wonder!

The editorial page played streams of invective across the provincial political scene like a fire hose. Harangues, pitted with epithets. *Gammy Bird* was a hard bite. Looked life right in its shifty, bloodshot eye. A tough little paper. Gave Quoyle an uneasy feeling, the feeling of standing on a playground watching others play games whose rules he didn't know. Nothing like the *Record*. He didn't know how to write this stuff.

On his second Monday morning the door to Jack Buggit's office gaped. Inside, Buggit himself, a cigarette behind his ear, leaning back in a wooden chair and saying "hmm" on the telephone. He waved Quoyle in to him with two hoops of his right hand.

Quoyle in a chair with a splintered front edge that bit into his thighs. Hand to his chin. From beyond the partition he could hear the mutter of Nutbeem's radios, the flicking of computer keys, old Billy Pretty scratching out notes with a nibbed pen he dipped in a bottle.

Jack Buggit was an unlikely looking newspaper editor. A small man with a red forehead, somewhere, Quoyle thought, between forty-five and ninety-five. A stubbled chin, slack neck. Jaggled hair frowsting down. Fingers ochre from chain-smoking. He wore scale-spattered coveralls and his feet on the desk were in rubber boots with red soles.

"Oh yar!" he said in a startlingly loud voice. "Oh yar," and hung up. Lit a cigarette.

"Quoyle!" The hand shot out and Quoyle shook it. It was like clasping a leather pot holder.

"Thick weather and small rain. Here we are, Quoyle, sitting in the headquarters of *Gammy Bird*. Now, you're working at this paper, which does pretty good, and I'll tell you how it is that I come to do this. Set you straight. Because you can see I didn't go to the school of journalism." Shot jets of smoke from the corners of his mouth, looked up at the ceiling as if at mariners' stars.

"Great-great-grandfather had to go to cannibalism to stay alive. We settled Flour Sack Cove, right here, only a few families left now. Buggits fished these waters, sealed, shipped out, done everything to keep going. It used to be a good living, fishing. It was all inshore fishing when I was young. You'd have your skiff, your nets. Finding the fish was a trick. They say true 'the fish has no bells.' Billy Pretty one of the best to find the fish. Knew the water like the hollows in his mattress. He can name you every sunker on this coast, that's the God's truth.

"You worked your cockadoodle guts out, kept it up as long as you could, snatched a little sleep here and there, work in the night by torchlight, sea boils come up all over your hands and wrists, but the work went on. Well, you know, I never got sea boils after I learned a cure. You cut your nails on a Monday, you won't have none. Everybody does it now! You know how fast a clever hand can split fish? No, I see you don't. It won't mean anything to tell you thirty fish a minute. Think of it. Clean thirty fish a minute! My sister could do it in her sleep." He stopped, sat there, breathing. Lit another cigarette, spurted smoke.

Quoyle tried to imagine himself struggling to keep up with fish-splitting athletes, buried in a slippery tide of dulling bodies. Petal swam forward in a long dress of platinum scales, bare arms like silver, white mouth.

"It was a hard life, but it had the satisfaction. But it was hard. Terrible hard in them old days. You'll hear stories would turn your hair blue overnight and I'm the boy could tell 'em. There was some wild, lawless places, a man did what he wanted. Guess *you* know about that, being who you are! But things changed. When the damn place give up on the hard times and swapped 'em in for confederation with Canada what did we get? Slow and sure we got government. Oh yar, Joey Smallwood said 'Boys, pull up your boats, burn your flakes, and forget the fishery; there will be two jobs for every man in Newfoundland.' " He laughed mirthlessly, showing Quoyle four teeth, lit another cigarette.

"Well, I was a sucker, I believed him. I went along with everything the first ten years or so. Sure, I wanted them things, too, the electricity and roads, telephone, radio. Sure I wanted health care, mail service, good education for me kids. Some of it come in. But not the jobs.

"And the fishing's went down, down, down, forty years sliding away into nothing, the goddamn Canada government giving fishing rights to every country on the face of the earth, but regulating us out of business. The damn foreign trawlers. That's where all the fish is went. Then the bloody Greenpeace trying to shut down the sealing. O.k., I says, back when I see I couldn't make it on fish no more, o.k. I says, I'll get smart, I'll get with it, get on the government plan. So, I goes to the Canada Manpower office at Killick-Claw and says, 'Here I am. Need a job. What you got for me to do?'

"And they says, 'What can you do?'

" 'Well,' I says, 'I can fish. Worked in the woods in the winter.'

" 'No, no, no. We don't want fishermen. We'll train you in a marketable skill.' See, they're bringing in industry. Jobs for everybody. First thing they got me into a damn tannery down to Go Slow Harbor. There was only ten or fifteen men working there because it wasn't in full production. The skill they learned me was throwing these stinking hides, come from where, Argentina or somewhere, into vats. I done that all day long for four days, then they ran out of hides and no more come in, so we just stood around or swept the floors. Couple more months the tannery went belly-up. So I goes back home and fishes long as I could. Then to Canada Manpower again.

" 'Fix me up,' I says. 'I needs another job.' "

" 'What can you do?' they says.

" 'I can fish, I can cut wood, I can throw hides in a vat all day long, sweep floors.'

" 'No, no, no. We'll train you. Industrialization of Newfoundland.' They send me down to St. John's where there's a big new plant that's going to make industrial machinery, all kinds of machines, feed mills, crushing machinery for rocks and peanuts, diamond drills, grinders. That was one hell of place. Big. I never seen nothing like it. Five-million-dollar plant. But nobody in it. So I go down there, I get a room I shared with some stinking old bug, I wait. I was down there, half starving, finding what I could for a quarter a day waiting for that damn plant to open up. Son of a bitch never did. Never turned out a single thing. So I goes back home and fishes the season.

"Come fall, I hit Manpower again and says, 'It's gettin' rough. I need that job.' At that time I still believed they was going to find something for me, what with the industrialization and all. 'Well,' the Manpower feller says, never misses a beat, 'there's heartbreak in every trade, Jack. But we're looking out for you. We're going to put you in the Third Mill over to Hyphenville. Going to make cardboard liners.' I worked in that nuthouse for three months. It closed down. They told me next, with my experience, I could get a good job either at the new oil refinery at Bird Wing or at the Eden Falls power project. The refinery wasn't operative yet they said, so they helped me fill out this job application about two miles long, told me to go home and wait for the letter from Eden Falls. I'm still waiting. Yar, they started it up, all right, but there's only a very few of jobs. So I stayed home, doing what fishing I could. Lean times. My wife was sick, we're on the pinch end of things. It was the worst time. We'd lost our oldest boy, you know. So back I goes.

" 'Look, boys, things is hard. I needs a job.' They said they had the perfect thing for me. Saving it all these trial years. And it was right across the Omaloor Bay, a glove factory! Right out there, Quoyle, right out there by your place on the point. They was going to make gloves there, leather gloves. Made it sound like the government built the thing just for me. They said I was a natural for a job due to my experience in the tannery. I was practically a master craftsman of the leather trade! I could prob'ly get an overseer's job! Wasn't I some glad? They got the ferry going. Big crowd showed up to go to work first day. Well, you believe it, we went over there, went inside, there was a lot of people standing around, a nice cafeteria, big stainless steel vats for dyeing, sewing machines and cutting tables. Only two things they didn't have—somebody who knew how to make gloves, and the leather. See, the leather for the gloves was supposed to come from the tannery I worked at years before, but it had folded and nobody ever told the guys building the glove factory, nobody ever told Canada Manpower. That was that.

"So I'm on my way home across the bay, the ferry's making its second and last run. And I'm thinking. I'm thinking, 'If I'd knew this sucker didn't have no leather I could have saved myself a trip.' Now, how do you know things? You read 'em in the paper! There wasn't no local paper. Just that government mouthpiece down to St. Johns, *The Sea Lion*. So I says, not knowing nothing about it, hardly able to write a sentence—I only got to 'Tom's Dog' in school—but I made up my mind that if they could start a glove factory with no leather or nobody that knew how to make 'em, I could start a newspaper.

"So I goes over to Canada Manpower and I says, 'I want to start a newspaper. You fellows think you can help me out?'

" 'How many people you gonna employ?' they says. I takes a wild flyer. 'Fifty. Once I gets going,' I says. ' 'Course there has to be a training period,' I says. 'Develop skills.' They ate it up. They give me boxes and boxes of forms to fill out. That's when my trouble begun, so I got Billy Pretty to give over his fishing and come on board. He writes a beautiful hand, can read like a government man. We done it.

"They sent me off to Toronto to learn about the newspaper business. They give me money. What the hell, I hung around Toronto what, four or five weeks, listening to them rave at me about editorial balance, integrity, the new journalism, reporter ethics, service to the community. Give me the fits. I couldn't understand the half of what they said. Learned what I had to know finally by doing it right here in my old shop. I been running *Gammy Bird* for seven years now, and the circulation is up to thirteen thousand, gaining every year. All along this coast. Because I know what people want to read about. And no arguments about it.

"First I hired Billy, then Tert Card. Good men. Out there in Toronto half the place was filled up with women yakking and laughing and looking the men over, or them looking the women over. Not working at all. Billy knows all you have to know to write the women's stuff up. He's an old bachelor can cook like hell. My wife, Mrs. Buggit, looks it over just in case. I know what my readers wants and expects and I gives 'em that. And what I say goes. I don't want to hear no journalism ideas from you and we'll get along good."

Stopped talking to light another cigarette. He looked at Quoyle whose legs had gone to sleep. Nodding slowly into his hand.

"O.k., Mr. Buggit, I'll do my best."

"Call me Jack. Now here's the rundown on this paper. First of all, I runs the show. I'm the skipper.

"Billy Pretty covers the Home Page, writes Scruncheons—don't you tell NOBODY he's Junior Sugg—handles local news, councils and education. There is more government in Canada than any other place in the world. Almost half the population works for the government and the other half is worked on. And what we got on the local level is meetings up and down the coast going on every minute of the day. Billy does some of the crime, too. And there's more of it than there used to be. See, what used to be called fun and high jinks they now calls vandalism and assault. Billy Pretty. He's been with me since I started *Gammy Bird*."

"I covered the municipal beat at the *Record*," Quoyle croaked, his voice seized up.

"I just told you Billy does that. Now there's Nutbeem writes the foreign, provincial and national news, gets his stories off the radio and rewrites. Also covers sexual abuse. He can't hardly keep up. We run two or three S.A. stories every week, one big one on the front page, the others inside. He does the sports, too, and fillers, some features, but we're not so big on features. He's only been on this paper for seven or eight months. And I won't say he's perfect. He's temporary, anyway. YOU HEAR THAT NUTBEEM?"

"Indeed," from the outer office.

"Tert Card stands in for me when I'm not here, he's the managing editor and a lot of other things. Hands out the assignments, typeset, pasteup, takes the mechanicals to the printer in

Misky Bay, does the labels and mailing, distribution, fills in on some local stories if he's got time. Been here couple years. I heard a lot of complaints about Tert Card and typos, but typos are part of *Gammy Bird*.

"Takes care of the ads. Any fishing stories, I want to hear about 'em first. I knows the problems, being as I'm still in the fishery.

"Now, what I want you to do. I want you cover local car wrecks, write the story, take pictures. We run a front-page photo of a car wreck every week, whether we have a wreck or not. That's our golden rule. No exceptions. Tert has a big file of wreck pictures. If we don't have a fresh one, we have to dip into his file. But we usually have a couple of good ones. The Horncup crowd keeps us supplied. Tert will show you where the camera is. You give the film to him. He develops it at home.

"And the shipping news. Get the list from the harbormaster. What ships come into Killick-Claw, what ones goes out. There's more every year. I got a hunch about this. We're going to play it by ear. See what you can do."

"Like I said on the phone," said Quoyle, "I haven't had much experience with ships." Car wrecks! Stunned with the probabilities of blood and dying people.

"Well, you can tell your readers that or work like hell to learn something. Boats is in your family blood. You work on it. And fill in where Tert Card tells you."

Quoyle smiled stiffly, got up. His hand was on the doorknob when Jack Buggit spoke again.

"One more thing. I'm not no joke, Quoyle, and I don't never want to hear jokes about Newfoundland or Newfoundlanders. Keep it in mind. I hates a Newfie joke."

Quoyle came out of the office. Car wrecks. Stared at the tattered phone books.

"Quoyle!" whispered Nutbeem. "Ahoy, Quoyle, you're not going to go weepy on us, are you? You're not going to go running back to the States, are you? We're counting on you, Quoyle. We're building a cargo cult around you, Quoyle."

Jack Buggit stuck his head out the glass door.

"Billy! Elvis have his pups yet?"

"Yar, he did. Last week. Three of 'em. Every one of 'em's black with white feet."

"Well, I want one of them pups." The door shut again.

8

A Slippery Hitch

"On shipboard the knot is seldom called for, but in small boats, especially open boats that are easily capsized, the necessity frequently arises for instant casting off, and the SLIPPERY HITCH *is found indispensable."*

THE ASHLEY BOOK OF KNOTS

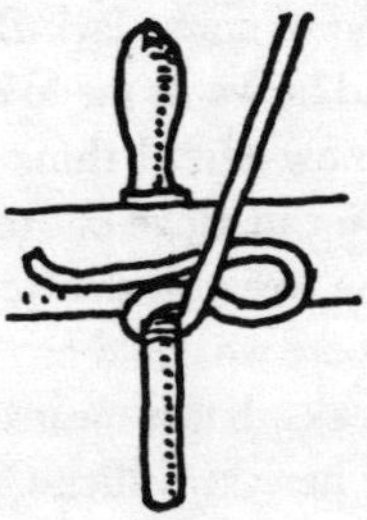

"I DON'T think I can handle this job," said Quoyle. Who had swallowed two beers and eaten a bag of stale popcorn at the Sea Anchor in Killick-Claw wondering if he was strapped into a mistake like a passenger in a plane that briefly rises, then crashes on the runway.

The aunt looked up. She sat on the round bed, knitting a cloud of angora as fast as a machine, Warren slumped at her feet, only the scarlet-rimmed eyes moving. Bunny tear-stained in a chair with a torn cushion. The chair faced a corner of the room. Sunshine ran at Quoyle, bellowing.

"Daddy, she bit me. Bunny bit me on the leg." She showed Quoyle two semicircular dents on her thigh.

"She started it!" shouted Bunny. Scowling like Beethoven.

"You're a rotten bitey shit!" bawled Sunshine.

"For God's sake, pipe down," said the aunt. "Nephew, we've got to do something. These children need a place to go. Out at the house, if we had a lion tamer, we could have them weeding potatoes and sweeping, washing dishes and windows instead of clawing and biting each other. They're cooped up here. And Warren's half dead from lack of exercise."

"Guess what, Dad," said Sunshine. "Warren threw up under your bed."

"She's not herself, that's certain," muttered the aunt. "What did you say about your job?" Brittle voice.

"I said I don't think I can do it. This paper's not like anything I know. The editor's kind of crazy. Jack Buggit. I don't know the area or the people yet and he wants me to cover car wrecks. I can't cover car wrecks. You know why. I think of what happened. Car wrecks. Ships. I doubt we can move out to the house, either. The station wagon won't last a week on that road. How will I get back and forth to work? I suppose we could buy a truck with four-wheel drive and heavy-duty shocks, but it means hours of driving. What about renting something here in Killick-Claw?"

The aunt drove her needles furiously. Wool twitched through her fingers.

"Of course you can do the job. We face up to awful things because we can't go around them, or forget them. The sooner you get it over with, the sooner you say 'Yes, it happened, and there's nothing I can do about it,' the sooner you can get on with your own life. You've got children to bring up. So you've *got* to get over it. What we have to get over, somehow we do. Even the worst things."

Sure, get over it, thought Quoyle. Ten-cent philosophy. She didn't know what he had been through. Was going through.

"Now, I've spent the whole week looking, dragging these kids around Killick-Claw in Tom Rock's taxicab looking for something—a house, apartment, even a couple of rooms. I've got to get my business started up. I've mentioned this every night. But your mind is somewhere else." Wondered how long he would keep wallowing in the dead woman's grave. "We've all got to get a grip here and pull together."

"You're right, Aunt. And I'm sorry you've had to do all the looking." He was here and there was nothing to go back to.

"Well, I haven't found much, either. There is a dark little room with old Mrs. Speck. The government told her to change the sheets and put out a bed-and-breakfast sign. It is worse than this dump, though cheaper. But there's only room for one person. Seems to be a housing shortage in Killick-Claw. Place is having a boom." Her sentences speeding up, tripping out as if to catch time with the clicking needles.

"It's like I said, we need a boat. Cross the bay in half an hour. Foolish to waste money renting a house when we have the old family place right over there that only needs fixing up. I talked today to a carpenter. Dennis Buggit, lives in Killick-Claw. He's not doing much. Says he can work on it right away. His wife is going to take care of the girls tomorrow and I'll go over to the house with Dennis, work up some estimates, see what's involved. Beety, that's the wife. Thinking of starting a day-care in her house. Best news I heard since we got here. These two," jerking her head, "could be the first and best customers."

Bunny kicked the wall. Sniveled.

The only word Quoyle heard was "boat." "Aunt, I don't know anything about boats. They are expensive. They are uncomfortable. They are dangerous. You need a dock or something. I don't want a boat."

"Afraid it's the sensible answer. Unless you want to stay here at a hundred and something a night. That's two days work for the carpenter." Barking. Her eyes hot.

Quoyle pressed the buttons of the television set, forgetting it was dead.

"It doesn't work, Daddy," sobbed Sunshine.

"I hate this place." Bunny, kicking at the wall with her scuffed shoes. "I want to go in a boat. I want to go fix the green house where the aunt was born and have my own room. I will sweep the floor if we can go, Daddy. I'll do everything."

"Let's go have supper," muttered Quoyle. "I can't handle this right now."

"The dining room is closed to the public tonight. It's the curling championship dinner. They fixed us some chowder, but we'll have to go get it ourselves and eat it here in the room."

"I want meat," said Bunny. "I want meat chowder."

"Too bad," said the aunt rather savagely, "it's not on the menu." To herself she added, eat fish or die.

Tert Card in a red shirt and white necktie, on the phone: Billy Pretty on the other line. Billy laughing, choking out dark sentences Quoyle couldn't understand, almost another language. Drumming rain, the bay stippled. The gas heater howled in the corner.

Quoyle looked at Nutbeem. "Is a guy named Dennis Buggit related to Jack? A carpenter? The aunt's talking to him about fixing up the old house. We've got to do something. We can't stay in that damn motel much longer. And the road out to the Point is lousy and there's nothing for rent in Killick-Claw. I don't know what we're going to do. I'll move back to the States before I buy a boat."

Nutbeem dragged his jaw down, raised both hands in mock horror. "Don't like boats? Can be rather amusing, you know. Practical for a place that's all coast and cove and little road. That's how I ended up here, you know, because of my boat. *Borogove*. I call her that because she's mimsy, a bit." Nutbeem's transitory talk. Theatrical speeches like a stump-jumper's spiel, urgent at the time, but forgotten by morning and the speaker on the way to another place.

Quoyle's notebook propped on his tea mug, a half-finished paragraph on a truck accident in the manual typewriter. Everyone else had a computer.

"You'll get one when I give you one," Jack Buggit had said. But not meanly.

"Dennis is Jack's youngest son," said Tert Card, who heard everything, leaning toward them, his foul breath spouting across the room. "He don't get along with the old man. Used to be the apple of the old man's eye, especially after they lost poor Jesson, but not now. You never know, Jack might take it wrong if Dennis works for you. Then again, he might not." The phone trilled like a toy whistle.

"That's him now," said Card, who always knew, and picked it up.

"*Gammy Bird!* Yut, o.k. Got you, Skipper." Hung up, swiveled his chair, looked at the marred sea. Laughed. "Billy! What do you think. He's up at the house with double earache. Says 'You won't see me until tomorrow or next day.' "

"I thought it would be cracked ribs this time," said Nutbeem. "Earache is good. We haven't had that one yet." The phone rang.

"*Gammy Bird!* Yut, o.k., o.k. What's your number? Hold on. Nutbeem, Marcus's Irving station down in Four Hands Cove is on fire. You take it?"

"Why *don't* you get a boat, Quoyle?" Billy Pretty shouted from his corner. He had two laundry baskets on his desk, one of molded plastic, the other of hand-woven stems.

Quoyle pretended he had not heard. But couldn't avoid Nutbeem at the next desk who pushed his radio away, looked excitedly at Quoyle. His face creased, his fingers tapped a beat, remnant of his time in Bahia mesmerized by *afoxés* and *bloco afros*, the music of drums and metal cones, spangled thumb cymbals, the stuttering repique. Nutbeem influenced by the lunar cycle. Had a touch of werewolf. At full moon he burst, talked himself dry, took exercise in the form of dancing and fighting at the Starlight Lounge, then slowly fell back to contemplation.

Before Bahia, Nutbeem said, he had hung around Recife, working for a rum-poached ex-*London Times* man who put out a four-pager in a mixture of languages.

"That's where I got my first idea of owning a boat," said Nutbeem, choosing a date from the packet on his desk. "It was living on the coast, I think, seeing boats and water every day. Seeing the *jangadas*—these extraordinary little fishing boats, just a platform of half a dozen skinny logs—something like balsa—pinned together with wooden dowels and lashed with fiber. Wind driven, steered with an oar. The world was all knots and lashings once—

flex and give, that was the way it went before the brute force of nails and screws. Tells you something, eh? From a distance the fishermen look like they're standing on the water. In fact, they are. The water washes right over the platform. Over their feet." He was up and pacing, raising his chin to the ceiling.

Billy kicked in. "That's how the old komatiks, the sleds, was made. There wasn't a nail in them. All lashed with sinew and rawhide."

Nutbeem ignored the interruption. "I liked the way the boats looked, but I didn't do anything about it. After a blowup with the feculent *Times* bloater—lying there on his waterbed playing the paper comb and drinking black rum—I flew up to Houston, Texas—don't ask me why—and bought a touring bike. A bicycle, not a motorcycle. And I pedaled it to Los Angeles. The most terrible trip in the world. I mean Apsley Cherry-Garrard with Scott at the pole didn't have a clue. I endured sandstorms, terrifying and lethal heat, thirst, freezing winds, trucks that tried to kill me, mechanical breakdowns, a Blue Norther, torrential downpours and floods, wolves, ranchers in single-engine planes dropping flour bombs. And Quoyle, the only thing that kept me going through all this was the thought of a little boat, a silent, sweet sailboat slipping through the cool water. It grew on me. I swore if I ever got off that fucking bicycle seat which was, by that time, welded into the crack of me arse, if ever I got pried off the thing I'd take to the sea and never leave her."

The phone rang again.

"*Gammy Bird!* Yut. Yut, Jack, he's here. No, Nutbeem's just gone to cover a fire. Marcus's Irving station. Four Hands Cove. I dunno. They just give me a number. Yut. O.k. Soon's he comes in. Quoyle, it's Jack again. For you."

"What stories you done this week?" Voice bullets shooting out of the receiver and into his ear.

"Uh. The truck wreck. I just finished that."

"What wreck was that?"

"A semi lost it on the curve coming down into Desolation and rolled. Loaded with new skimobiles. Half of them fell in the water and every boat in the harbor started hauling them out with grapnels. Driver jumped. Nobody hurt."

"Don't forget the shipping news." The phone went dead.

"NUTBEEM! You better get on that fire before it's out and you can't get any nice pictures of leaping flames. And take the camera. It's helpful when you have to take pictures." Scratchy sarcasm.

"Why don't you get a nice little rodney?" said Billy Pretty. "Oh now's the time to pick up a beauty. You could jig for guffies on the weekend, get your picture took by tourists. You'd look good in a boat."

But Nutbeem wasn't ready to leave. "So, Quoyle, there I was back in London, starving again. At least I had my tape collection intact. But I knew I had to have a boat. I was in despair. You may think that the equation is 'boat and water.' It's not. It's 'money and boat.' The water is not really necessary. That's why you see so many boats in backyards. Not having any money I was in despair. I spent an entire year reading books about boats and the sea. I began to hang about boatyards. There was one place where two young chaps were building a rowboat. They seemed to be doing a lot of planing—I've always thought planing rather jolly—and it came to me. Just like that. I would build my own boat. And I would sail it across the Atlantic."

"NUTBEEM!" roared Card.

"Oh go spell 'pterodactyl,' " said Nutbeem, hauling on his jacket and tam-o'-shanter, crashing out the door.

"Christ, he's forgotten the camera. Quoyle, Jack wants me to remind you about the shipping news. Go down to the harbormaster's office and copy off the list of ships. You get the name, the date, vessel's country of origin. They won't give it to you over the phone. You have to go get it."

"I was going to go this afternoon," said Quoyle. "But can do it now. Where's the harbormaster's office?"

"Next to Pubby's Marine Supply on the public wharf. Upstairs."

Quoyle got up, put on his jacket. At least it wasn't a wreck, all glass and dripping fluids, and the ambulance guys fumbling inside smashed mouths.

9

The Mooring Hitch

"The merit of the hitch is that, when snugly applied, it will not slip down the post. Anyone who has found himself at full tide, after a hard day's fishing, with his painter fast to a stake four or five feet below high-water mark, will be inspired to learn this knot."

THE ASHLEY BOOK OF KNOTS

HE DODGED through the rattle of lift trucks and winches on Wharf Road. Boats varnished with rain. Down along he saw the black coastal ferry with its red rails taking on cars, and the Labrador hospital ship. At the government dock orange flank of the Search and Rescue cutter. A dragger coming in to the fish plant.

Wharf Road was paved with worn, blue stone carried as ballast from some distant place. A marine stink of oil, fish and dirty water. Beyond the dives and bars a few provisioners. In one window he noticed an immense pyramid of packaged dates of the kind Nutbeem liked—*Desert Jujubes*—red camels, shooting stars on the label.

The harbormaster's office was at the top of a gritty wooden stair.

THE MOORING HITCH

Diddy Shovel, the harbormaster, watched Quoyle's yellow slicker emerge from the station wagon, watched him drop his notepad on the wet cobbles. Sized him up as strong and clumsy. Shovel had been renowned once for his great physical strength. When he was twenty he started a curious brotherhood called "The Finger Club." The seven members were all men who could suspend themselves from a beam in Eddy Blunt's cellar by a single little finger. Powerful men in those days. As he grew older, he complemented, then replaced, his physical strength with a stentorian voice. Was now the only living member of the Finger Club. His thoughts often stopped at that point.

In a minute Quoyle opened the door, looked through the windows twelve feet high, a glass wall into the drizzled slant of harbor, the public docks and piers in the foreground, and beyond, the sullen bay rubbed with thumbs of fog.

A squeaking sound. Wooden swivel chair spun and the terrible face of the harbormaster aimed at Quoyle.

"You ought to see it in a storm, the great clouds rolling off the shoulders of the mountains. Or the sunset like a flock of birds on fire. 'Tis the most outrageous set of windows in Newfoundland." A voice as deep as a shout in a cave.

"I believe that," said Quoyle. Dripping on the floor. Found the coat hook in the corner.

Diddy Shovel's skin was like asphalt, fissured and cracked, thickened by a lifetime of weather, the scurf of age. Stubble worked through the craquelured surface. His eyelids collapsed in protective folds at the outer corners. Bristled eyebrows; enlarged pores gave the nose a sandy appearance. Jacket split at the shoulder seams.

"I'm Quoyle. New at the *Gammy Bird.* Come to get the shipping news. I'd appreciate suggestions. About the shipping news. Or anything else."

Harbormaster cleared his throat. Man Imitates Alligator, thought Quoyle. Got up and limped behind the counter. The cool high light from the windows fell on a painting the size of a bed sheet. A ship roared down a wave, and in the trough of the wave, broadside, a smaller boat, already lost. Men ran along the decks, their mouths open in shrieks.

The harbormaster pulled up a loose-leaf notebook, riffled the pages with his thumb, then handed the book to Quoyle. ARRIVALS on the cover; a sense of money gain and loss, cargoes, distance traveled, the smell of the tropics.

Followed Quoyle's gaze.

"Fine picture! That's the *Queen Mary* running down her escort, the *Curacoa*. Back in 1942. Twenty miles off the Irish coast in clear sunlight and crystal visibility. The *Queen*, eighty-one thousand ton, converted from passenger liner to troopship, and the cruiser a mere forty-five hundred. Cut her in half like a boiled carrot."

Quoyle wrote until his hand cramped and he discovered he had taken down the names of ships that had called weeks ago.

"How can I tell if ships are still here?"

The harbormaster pulled up another book. Plywood cover, the word DEPARTURES burned in wavering letters.

"Ha-ha," said Quoyle. "I'd think they'd get you a computer. These logbooks look like a lot of work."

The harbormaster pointed to an alcove behind the counter. Computer screen like boiling milk. The harbormaster punched keys, the names of ships leaped in royal blue letters, their tonnages, owners, country of registration, cargoes, arrival and departure dates, last port of call, next port of call, days out from home port, crew number, captain's name, birthdate and social insurance number. The harbormaster tapped again and a printer hummed, the paper rolled out into a plastic bin. He tore off pages, handed them to Quoyle. The shipping news.

Cracking grin that showed false teeth to the roots. "Now you'll remember that we do it two ways," he said. "So when the storm roars and the power's out you'll look in the old books and it'll all be there. Have a cup of tea. Nothing like it on a wet day."

"I will," said Quoyle. Sat on the edge of a chair. Runnels of water coursed down the window glass.

"Get down," said the harbormaster, pushing a cat out of a chair. "It's a good range of vessels we get here now. Bold water in

Omaloor Bay almost to the shoreline. The government put seventeen million dollars into upgrading this harbor two years ago. Reconstructed dock, new container terminal. Sixteen cruise ships pegged to come in this year. They don't stay more than a day or so, but, my boy, when they sets foot on the dock they commence to hurl the money around."

"How long have you been doing this?"

"Depends what you mean by 'this.' I went to sea when I was thirteen years old—deckhand on my uncle Donnal's sixty-ton sailing schooner, working up and down the coast. Where I built up me strength. Oh he fed me royal. And worked me hard. Then I fished for a while on a dory-schooner out on the Belle Isle banks the old way. I worked on a coastal ferry. I was in the Merchant Navy. In World War Two, lieutenant in the Canadian Navy. After the war I joined the Coast Guard. In 1963 I moved into this office as Killick-Claw harbormaster. Thirty years. Next year I'll retire. Seventy years young and they're forcing me out. Intend to learn how to play the banjo. If I can keep from bursting the strings. Sometimes I don't know me own strength. What about you?" Flexed his fingers, making the joints pop like knotwood in a fire. Showed a little finger like a parsnip.

"Me. I'm just working at the paper."

"You look like you come from here but don't sound it."

"My people came from Quoyle's Point but I was brought up in the States. So I'm an outsider. More or less." Quoyle's hand crept up over his chin.

The harbormaster looked at him. Squinted.

"Yes," said Diddy Shovel. "I guess you got a story there, m'boy. How did it all come about that you was raised so far from home? That you come back?" Even now he could perform feats that would make them stare.

Quoyle rattled his teacup on the saucer. "I was—. Ah, it's complicated." And his voice fell away. He jabbed at the pad with his pen. Change the subject.

"That ship there," he said, pointing. "What is it?"

The harbormaster found a pair of binoculars under the chair and looked out into the bay.

"The *Polar Grinder*? Oh yes. She's been tried and tested. Calls here regular to take on fish and sea urchin roe for the Japanese gourmet trade. A refrigerator ship, built in Copenhagen for Northern Delicacies around 1970, 1971. You ever see the way they put the sea urchin roe up at the fish plant?"

"No," Quoyle thinking of the green pincushions in tidal pools.

"Beautiful! Beautiful. Fancy wooden trays. The Japs think they're quite the gourmet delicacy, pay a hundred dollars for a tray of them. They lay them out all in fancy patterns, like a quilt. Umi, Call it umi. Eat them raw. Get them at sushi bars in Montreal. I had them. I tried it all. Buffalo. Chocolate-covered ants. And raw sea urchin roe. Got a cast-iron stomach, I have."

Quoyle sucked at his tea, a little revolted.

"Here. Take the glasses and look. She's got the bulbous forefoot that was coming in when she was built. There's a sister ship, the *Arctic Incisor*. Refrigerator ship, four holds, insulated compartments. Chart and wheelhouse amidships, all the latest electronic navigational aids. Highly automated for her day. Since her misadventures in the storm she's been refitted with new navigational gear, new electronic temperature gauges that you can read on the bridge, all the rest of it.

"When she was built, you know, the fashion was for Scandinavian furniture—that's where all the teak went. That song, 'Norwegian Wood,' remember that?" Sang a few lines in a roaring basso. "That *Polar Grinder* is fitted out with oiled teak furniture. There's a sauna instead of a swimming pool. A lot more useful in these waters, eh? Murals on the walls showing the ski races, reindeer, northern lights and such. You heard about her, I suppose."

"No. She known for something?"

"That's the ship that drove a wedge between father and son, between Jack and his youngest son, Dennis."

"Dennis," said Quoyle. "Dennis is doing some work on our old house. On Quoyle's Point."

"I might have been in that house," said Diddy Shovel in a neutral voice, "when I was a boy. Long, long, long ago. Dennis, now, he is a fine carpenter. Better carpenter than fisherman. And that was a relief to Jack—with all that's happened to the Buggits on the sea. Jack has a morbid fear of it for all he spends as much time as he can on the water. He didn't want his boys to be fishermen. So of course both of them was crazy for it. Jack tells them it's a hard, hard life with nothing to show at the end but broken health and poverty. And a damned good chance of drowning all alone in the freezing boil. Which is what happened to his oldest boy, Jesson. Iced up out on the Baggy Banks with a full load of fish and capsized when the weather went bad. It was forecast a moderate gale but came up storm force all of a sudden. Terrible silver thaw here on shore—the more beautiful they are the more dangerous. More tea." He poured a black cup for Quoyle. Whose tongue was as rough as a cat's.

"So! Dennis apprentices to a well-known carpenter in St. John's, Brian Corkery, his name was, if I remember right, learns the trade from frame to finish. Then what does he do? First job, mind you. He signs on the *Polar Grinder* as ship's carpenter! She was back and forth from the Maritimes to Europe, twice to Japan, down the seaboard to New York. Dennis is just as crazy about boats and the sea as Jack is and Jesson was. He'd rather fish than anything. But Jack won't hear of it.

"The way Jack carried on. Shocking. Thought if Dennis was a carpenter he'd be safe ashore. He was afraid, you see, afraid for him. And what we fear we often rage against. And Jack was right. See, he knows the sea has its mark on all Buggits.

"In due course we had one of our winter storms. As the bad luck would have it the *Polar Grinder* was caught out. About two hundred miles southeast of St. John's. February storm, savage as they come. Cold, forty-foot seas, hurricane-force wind roaring at fifty knots. Have you been at sea in a storm, Mr. Quoyle?"

"No," said Quoyle. "And don't want to be."

"It never leaves you. You *never* hear the wind after that without you remember that banshee moan, remember the watery mountains, crests torn into foam, the poor ship groaning. Bad enough at any time, but this was the deep of winter and the cold was terrible, the ice formed on rail and rigging until vessels was carrying thousands of pounds of ice. The snow drove so hard it was just a roar of white outside these windows. Couldn't see the street below. The sides of the houses to the northwest was plastered a foot thick with snow as hard as steel."

Quoyle's teacup cooled in his hands. Listening. The old man hunched his shoulders, words hissed through his teeth. The past bubbled out of his black mouth.

"Ships tried for safe harbors, distress signals all over the North Atlantic from the Maritimes to Europe. Chemical tanker lost its bridge and the captain went with it. A cargo ship loaded with iron ore went down and all the crew with it. A Bulgarian stern trawler broke in half, all hands lost. Ships in harbor dragged their anchors and slammed into each other. A bad storm. There was no safe place. The *Polar Grinder* had a time of it. The seas not fit to look at. The captain kept just enough speed to maintain steerage way and keep her heading off wind, hoping to ride it out. Oh, you get Dennis to tell you about it sometime. Make your blood seize up, the punishment that ship took. Smashed the wheelhouse windows. Immense seas. All anybody could think of all night long—could she make it until morning? They got through that terrible night. The only difference daylight brought was that they could see the monstrous waves coming down on them, see the fury of the raging sea.

"A little after daybreak there was a sea, a great towering wall that seemed made out of half the Atlantic, then a tremendous detonation. Dennis said he thought the ship had smashed into an iceberg or something exploded on board. Said he was deaf for a while afterward. But it was the sea she took. The *Polar Grinder*'s steel hull cracked amidships under the weight of that wave, a crack almost an inch wide running from starboard to port.

"Well, there they were, rushing back and forth, mixing concrete and trying to plug up the crack with it, shoring timbers, anything to stop the water, it poured in, filling the hold. They were sloshing around in water up to their waists."

Sucked in a mouthful of tea.

"The heavy seas and the tons of water pouring in knocked the ship down. She seemed she was about to go and the captain gave the 'abandon ship.' If you can imagine those small lifeboats in those seas! They lost twenty-seven men. And two peculiar things happened in the end. First, the *Polar Grinder*—as you see—didn't go down. Wallowed along on her side. When he see she was still afloat the captain turned back and reboarded her, and the next day they got a salvage tug out that fastened a tow and finally brought her in."

"And Dennis?"

But the telephone rang and the old man creaked away into his chart room, his voice booming over another wire. Came to the doorway.

"Well, I must cut it short. They've seized a Russian side-trawler inside the two-hundred-mile limit fishing without a license and using a trawl with undersize mesh. Second time they've caught the same ship and captain. The Coast Guard's escorting him in. I've got a bit of paperwork. Come again next week and we'll have a drop of tea."

Quoyle walked along the wharf, craning to get another look at the *Polar Grinder*, but it was lost in the rain. A man in a pea jacket and plastic sandals gazed at the rubber boots in Cuddy's Marine Supply window. Wet, red toes. Said something as Quoyle went past. The liquor store, the marine hardware shop. A longliner drifted toward the fish plant, a figure in yellow oilskins leaning on the rail staring into dimpled water the color of motor oil.

At the end of the wharf, packing crates, a smell of garbage. A small boat was hauled up beside the crates, propped against it a crayoned board: *For Sale*. Quoyle looked at the boat. Rain sluiced over the upturned bottom, pattered on the stones.

"You can have it for a hundred." A man leaning in a doorframe, hands draining into his pockets. "Me boy built it but he's gone, now. Won five hundred dollars on the lottery. Took off for the mainland. Where they lives 'mong the snakes." He sniggered. "Seek his bloody fuckin' fortune."

"Well, I was just looking at it." But a hundred dollars didn't seem like very much for a boat. It looked all right. Looked sturdy enough. Painted white and grey. Practically new. Must be something wrong with it. Quoyle thumped the side with his knuckles.

"Tell yer what," said the man. "Give me fifty, she's yours."

"Does it leak?" said Quoyle.

"Nah! Don't leak. Sound as a sea-ox. Just me boy built it but he's gone now. Good riddance to him, see? I wants to get it out of me sight. I was gonna burn it up," he said shrewdly, taking Quoyle's measure. "So's not to be troubled by the sight of it. Reminding me of me boy."

"No, no, don't burn it," said Quoyle. "Can't go wrong for fifty bucks, can I!" He found a fifty and got a scrawled bill of sale on the back of an envelope. The man's jacket, he saw, was made of some nubby material, ripped, with stains down the side.

"You got a trailer?" The man gestured at the boat, making circles in the air to indicate a rolling motion.

"No. How'll I get it home without one?"

"You'n rent one down at Cuddy's if yer don't mind paying his bloody prices. Or we's'll lash it into the bed of yer truck."

"I don't have a truck," said Quoyle. "I've got a station wagon." He never had the right things.

"Why that's almost as good, long as you doesn't drive too speedy. She'll hang down y'know, in the front and the back some."

"What kind of boat do you call it, anyway?"

"Ah, it's just a speedboat. Get a motor on her and won't you have fun dartin' along the shore!" The man's manner was lively and enthusiastic now. "Soon's this scuddy weather goes off."

In the end Quoyle rented a trailer and he and the man and half a dozen others who splashed up laughing and hitting the man's shoulder in a way Quoyle ignored, shifted the boat onto the trailer. He headed back to the *Gammy Bird*. Hell, fifty dollars barely bought supper for four. The rain ran across the road in waving sheets. The boat wagged.

Saw her. The tall woman in the green slicker. Marching along the edge of the road as usual, her hood pushed back. A calm, almost handsome face, ruddy hair in braids wound around her head in an old-fashioned cornet. Her hair was wet. She was alone. Looked right at him. They waved simultaneously and Quoyle guessed she must have legs like a marathon runner.

Sauntered into the newsroom and sat at his desk. Only Nutbeem and Tert Card there, Nutbeem half asleep with low atmospheric pressure, his ear against the radio, Card on the phone, at the same time whacking the computer keys. Quoyle was going to say something to Nutbeem, but didn't. Instead, worked away on the shipping news. Dull enough, he thought.

SHIPS ARRIVED THIS WEEK
Bella (Canadian) from the Fishing Grounds
Farewell (Canadian) from Montreal
Foxfire (Canadian) from Bay Misery
Minatu Maru 54 (Japanese) from the Fishing Grounds
Pescamesca (Portuguese) from the Fishing Grounds
Porto Santo (Panamanian) from the High Seas
Zhok (Russian) from the Fishing Grounds
Ziggurat Zap (U.S.) from the High Seas

And so forth.

At four Quoyle gave the shipping news to Tert Card, whose moist ear lay against the phone receiver, shoulder hunched while he typed. Suffering from the stiff neck again.

Car doors slammed outside, Billy Pretty's voice seesawed. Nutbeem snapped up alertly.

"There's Mr. Jack Buggit and Billy Pretty back from the car wreck. Moose collision while you were gone, Quoyle. Two dead. And the moose."

Saved again, thought Quoyle.

"I hope they got pictures from every angle, enough to carry us through the thin spots," said Tert Card, typing Quoyle's shipping news.

Minutes passed and the door stayed closed. Billy's voice had stopped. Quoyle knew they were looking at his boat. Well, he'd taken the plunge. Smiled, rehearsing a story of how he'd decided on the spur of the moment to buy a boat and get it over, how he almost felt transformed, ready to take on the sea, to seize his heritage.

The door opened. Billy Pretty scuttled in, went straight to his desk without a look at Quoyle. Jack Buggit, hair studded with raindrops, strode halfway across the room, stopped in front of Quoyle's desk, hissed through a mouthful of smoke, "What the hell you buy that thing for?"

"Why, everybody was after me to buy a boat! It looked as good as any of them. It had a good price. I can get back and forth a lot faster now. It's a speedboat."

"It's a shitboat!" said Jack Buggit. "Best thing you can do is get rid of it some dark night." He slammed into his glass office and they heard him mumbling, striking matches, opening and shutting desk drawers. Nutbeem and Tert Card went to the door and stared out at Quoyle's boat.

"What's wrong with it?" asked Quoyle, throwing out his hands. "What's wrong with it? Everybody tells me to buy a boat and when I buy one they tell me I shouldn't have done it."

"I told you," said Billy Pretty, "I told you buy a nice little rodney, nice little sixteen-foot rodney with a seven-horsepower engine, nice little hull that holds the water, a good flare on it, not too much hollowing, a little boat that bears good under the bows. You bought a wallowing cockeyed bastard no good for nothing but coasting ten feet from shore when it's civil. Hull is as humpy as a lop sea, there's no motor well, the shape is poor, she'll wallow and throw in water, pitch up and down and rear and sink."

Nutbeem said nothing, but he looked at Quoyle as though, in unwrapping a beribboned gift, he had discovered nylon socks. Billy Pretty started up again.

"That boat was built by a dumb stookawn of a kid, Reeder Gouch's kid that run off about a month after he built it. No ability at all. Not only is it no good for nothing, but it makes you cry to look at it. How could anybody build a boat with a stem got a reverse curve in it? I never seen a boat with a stem like that. They don't make them like that here. Reeder was going to burn it, he said. Too bad he didn't. I told you, get a nice little rodney, that's what you want. Or a motor dory. Or a good speedboat. You ought to fill that thing up with stones and launch it to the bottom. Go down to Nunny Bag Cove and talk to those fellers, Uncle Shag Dismal and Alvin Yark and those fellers. Get one of them to build you a nice little craft. They'll give you something that fits the water, something's got a bit of harmony between the two ends of the boat."

Drumroll of rain. Stupid Man Does Wrong Thing Once More.

10

The Voyage of Nutbeem

"Voyage, an outward and homeward passage; although the passage from one port to another is often referred to in insurance policies as a voyage."

THE MARINER'S DICTIONARY

THE AUNT in her woolen coat when Quoyle came into the motel room. Tin profile with a glass eye. A bundle on the floor under the window. Wrapped in a bed sheet, tied with net twine.

"Where are the kids?" said Quoyle. "What's that?"

"They're staying over at Dennis and Beety's house. I thought they'd be better off there, considering. After the experience of this morning. Warren." She pointed at the bundle. "She died during the day under the bed, just her paws sticking out. All alone. I came in and found her." She did not cry, nor did her voice skitter. Quoyle patted the black shoulder, felt the pad stiff under his hand. Dog hairs on the sleeve. The aunt hiding deep in her coat somewhere.

"The girls like it at Beety's. Playing chip-chip and colors with their kids. The Buggits've got kids the same ages. Begged for Sunshine and Bunny to stay over. I didn't think you'd mind. Considering. I told them Warren had to go away. I don't think they knew what I meant. Sunshine is too little, but Bunny wanted to know exactly when Warren was coming back. I hope you can explain it better." Voice even as if reciting the alphabet, halfway between groaning and silence.

"Poor old Warren. I'm sorry, Aunt." And he was sorry. Slouched in the chair, levered the cap from a bottle of beer. Thought of Bunny's murderous dreams that woke them all, the child sweaty, pupils like Billy's ink bottle. Hoped she wouldn't rouse Dennis and Beety in the night.

"What did Dennis say about fixing up the place?" Wearily.

"Well," said the aunt, hanging her coat away, tugging off her boots, "he thinks if he rouses into it with somebody to help him, he could have it so we could get into it—roof over our heads—in two weeks. Believe it or not. With that in mind I tackled the desk clerk and got us the famous bachelor apartment through that door"—pointing at the side wall—"for the rest of the time we're here plus this room for what we're paying for this room alone. Look." She opened the other door, displayed a single bed and a tiny kitchenette. "You can sleep in there. I'll stay on in here with the girls. At least there'll be a little more privacy and a little more room. At least we can fix coffee in the morning, something to eat and not have to test our constitutions downstairs. I'll pick up some food tomorrow." Got out her whiskey bottle, poured a little.

"Now, as to what young Dennis is going to do to the house. Says if you'll help him on the weekends it'll go right along. It'll be rough, but we can manage. It can't be any worse than this place. Fixing up the rest of it will take right on into fall. He thinks we'd want to look into a generator, get a gas stove and couple tanks of propane. He can get hold of a fellow's got a bulldozer to clear a road from the old glove factory to the dooryard. Can do that tomorrow, he says, if we can afford it. I told him we could because we had to. But the first thing is that there's got to be some pilings set, some kind of dock built so Dennis can get back and forth, bring over the building supplies by boat. There's a fellow, he says—I forgot his name—used to build wharves all up and down the coast.

He's retired now, but he could take on a small job like this and finish it up in a few days if he had a crowd to do the heavy bits. Be a lot faster, Dennis says, than driving all the way around."

Quoyle nodded, but his face was dull. The aunt sighed, thought that if she could scrape away her old flesh down to the young bones she would do it herself. *She* could tackle a new job, master a boat, rebuild the house, get over the loss of a cheating mate. She hauled out a wad of sketches and lists, long columns of arithmetic, spread them over the table. Stubby fingers, the nails cut straight across.

"I wish I could find my calculator," she said. "Dennis figures everything up, has to add it three times, loses his place. I can't add at all anymore, seems like. They say if you do sums ten times a day you'll never get senile. But that argues that bankers should be geniuses, so that's not right. Thickest heads in the world." Quoyle hitched his chair around, pretended to take an interest. Man Lukewarm on Ancestral Home Way Out on the Point.

"The biggest problem is putting in the insulation. If we're living in the house, can't very well tear out all that old plaster and lath. Take forever and choke you to death. So he had this other idea. What he'd do is put in new studding right over the existing walls in every room, then lay up the insulation and put your wallboard over it. Be like a double house. Especially since I don't want that vinyl stuff outside. 'Oh,' he says, 'that vinyl siding makes a warm house, never has to be painted, you can buy it on time.' I said I wouldn't have it on my coffin."

She drank her whiskey in two swallows, the single ice cube clanking. Quoyle was surprised to see her pour another. Losing the old dog.

"What do you want to do about Warren?"

"There's no sense trying to bury her," she said. "It's all rock. I'd like to take her out to sea for a sea burial. A short service, you know, a few words. I thought I could drive up the coast and find a likely spot. Consign her to the waves. Poor Warren. She never got to be happy here. Never had a chance to enjoy a real outing, a good walk along the shore. Dogs love that."

"I bought a boat today, aunt. Too bad I didn't get a motor,

too. We could have taken Warren out to sea. If I knew how to handle it."

"You didn't!"

"I did. But Jack Buggit says it's not worth a damn. About all I paid for it. Guy practically gave it to me. Fifty dollars. I mean, Aunt, even if it's not that good it was cheap. I rented a trailer. Now I've got to get a motor. I can learn with this boat."

The aunt peered out into the parking lot. "Can't see it from here," she said. "But you did the right thing. Maybe you could go out with Dennis a few times, see how he manages and all."

"I heard a story about Dennis today. Part of it anyway."

There was a knocking on the door, a knock with a peculiar rhythm. Again the fluttering beat like a drummer striking taut skin. Where had he heard that before? Nutbeem.

"Hello, hello," said Nutbeem, his long legs opening and closing as he came across the room, shook the aunt's hand, handed her a bottle of brown wine, *Vin du France Réserve de Terre Neuve*. Shook Quoyle's hand, looked around smiling as if admiring novel sights. He sat in the chair nearest Warren, his flexed knees halfway up to his shoulders. Glanced at the shroud.

"Thought I'd come by," he said. "Go on telling you about my boat. It's impossible to talk at the paper. Give you the odd pointer on the boat you bought. Old Buggit was rather fierce about it, but you can get some use from it. Just be careful. There's no one else here I can talk to. I haven't talked to anybody since I got here. Eight months, I haven't exchanged a civilized word with anybody. I said to myself 'I'll just drop around after supper, meet Miss, Mrs.—"

"Hamm," said the aunt. "Ms. Agnis Hamm."

"Delighted, Ms. Hamm. You know, one of the tragedies of real life is that there is no background music. I brought some of my tapes. Some Yemenite tin-can stuff, a little Algerian Rai, some of the dub-poets. That sort of stuff. In case you had a tape player. No? This is rather a dump, isn't it? Well, you must come visit *me* and hear them. Although my place is rather small. I live in a trailer. But you'll see. You've got to come for one of my curries. I've even got some tapes from here, you know. There's a weird youth I taped in Fly-By-Night, where I wrecked, he's an expert at what they call chin-music, no instruments, just decides on a tune and then pours out this incredible, nasal stream of nonsense syllables. Like a tobacco auctioneer. "Whangy-uddle-uddle-uddle-uddle-whangy-doodle-ah!' "

The aunt got up. "Gentlemen, I've had a long, hard day and I'm half dead with starving. What do you think about going down to the one-and-only Tickle Motel dining room for a nice plate of cod cheeks? Mr. Nutbeem?" Wondered whether his splayed nose was the original edition or had been flattened.

"Oh, I've had my dinner. Curry, actually. But I'll come down with you. You can eat and I'll talk. Well, maybe I'll have a beer."

Quoyle ordered the fried bologna dinner. It was the only thing on the menu he hadn't tried, but night after night he'd watched diners at neighboring tables wolfing and gnashing, guessed it was a house specialty. The plate came heaped with thick bologna circles, fried potatoes and gravy, canned turnip, and a wad of canned string beans, all heated in a microwave. The overwhelming sensations were of sizzling heat and salt content off the scale. The aunt leaned on her hand, seemed to listen to Nutbeem.

"So there I was, hanging around the boatyards, hanging around the pubs where the builders went, making my pint of bitter last, listening to everything, asking a few questions. Mind you, I knew nothing about boats, had never built anything except a shelf for my uncle's toaster, had never been sailing, never even made a voyage. I always traveled by air. But I listened very assiduously and determined to do it. The idea gripped me.

"Eventually I puzzled out something I could build that would float. A modified Chinese junk built of plywood with a full-batten lug rig. You know, the Chinese have forgotten more about sailing than the rest of the world ever knew. They invented the compass, they invented watertight compartments, they invented stern rudders and the most efficient sail in the world. Junks are ancient boats, more than five thousand years old, and extremely seaworthy, good for long voyages. And I've always been mad for the Chinese poets."

"This is pretty salty," Quoyle said apologetically to the waitress. "I'd better have a pint. If you get a chance."

The aunt's red face bent down, parentheses around her mouth set like clamps. Impossible to know if she was listening to Nutbeem or flying over the Himalayas.

Nutbeem swallowed his lager and signaled for more. As long as the girl was standing there. "I'd been working all this time writing book reviews for a rarefied journal devoted to criticism incomprehensible to anyone but the principals. Bloody dagger stuff. And by sponging off my uncle and living on mutton neck broth I managed to save up enough money to hire a boat designer to draw me up a junk pattern, simple enough that I could build myself out of half-inch marine plywood at home.

"Ah, Ms. Hamm, you should have seen it when I was done. It was ugly. It was a rough and ugly thing, an overall length of twenty-eight feet, a five-foot draft and just that one junk sail, but with a respectable three hundred and fifty square feet. A trim tab rudder hung on the stern. She was heavy and slow. And very ugly. I made her more ugly by painting her rat brown. Piece of foam for a mattress, my sleeping bag. Wooden boxes for chair and table. And that was it. At first I just muffed about near the shore. Surprised how comfortable she was, and she handled well. The sail was a wonder. It's interesting how I got *that*."

The aunt finished her tea, swished the pot about, got another half cup from the spout. There was no stopping Nutbeem, roaring along now with a bone in his teeth.

"You see, I had a friend who worked at Sotheby's, and he mentioned one day that they were going to auction off a lot of marine and nautical curios. So I went—idle curiosity. Just what you might expect, scrimshaw walrus tusks, a nameplate from one of the Titanic's lifeboats, Polynesian palm-rib charts, antique maps. The catalog listed only one item that interested me, and that was a bamboo-batten junk sail from Macau in good condition. I ended up with it for less than the cost of a new one. Bit of a miracle.

"Then I learned just how much of an aerodynamic wonder the batten sail is—it makes a sort of flat curve. It's only reed or canvas sheetlets stiffened horizontally with the battens—the principle of the folding fan, in a way. You fold it and open it up rather like an unhinged fan. One can control the sail very well because of the battened panels—reef or douse in seconds. No stays or shrouds. The small sections let you adjust trim to a fine degree. They say that even with the canvas half full of holes the sail draws. The Chinese call it 'The Ear that Listens for the Wind.' The old junk sailors even used to roll up a reed sail and use it for a life raft if they were shipwrecked. And my auction sail was a good one.

"And so then, that summer, I just set out. Across the Atlantic. There's a point, you know, when you must go forward. I lived off those little packages of Oriental ramen noodles, dried mushrooms, dried shrimp. I had a tiny stove, size of a teacup. You've seen them. Sixty-seven days to Fly-By-Night. It's my plan to keep on around the world."

"You're still here. Saving up money for the next leg?" asked the aunt.

"Ah, that, and I'm finishing some serious repair work. I had planned to go up the St. Lawrence to Montreal, but there was a storm and I got blown off course. I'd never intended coming to Newfoundland at all. If I could help it. It was bad luck I hit one of the worst parts of the coast. Bad rocks. Poor *Borogove*, all that way and her bottom smashed out in Fly-By-Night, a very strange place. That's where I heard the chin-music boy."

"I could go take care of Warren," said Quoyle to the aunt in a low voice. Saw she'd twisted her napkin into a white rope.

"No, no. You stay with Mr. Nutbeem. I'd rather do it myself. Rather be alone." And got up and went out.

"Her dog died," said Quoyle.

Nutbeem waved for more lager.

"My treat," he said, took a fresh breath. But before he started on Fly-By-Night, Quoyle forced an oar in.

"I heard some of Dennis Buggit's adventures on the *Polar Grinder* this afternoon. From Mr. Shovel, the harbormaster. He's quite the storyteller."

"Oh yes. That was something, wasn't it? Makes your flesh creep. My pulse races when Jack comes in. Weird chap. Fellow can read your mind."

"Jack? He didn't say anything about Jack, just that he was mad when Dennis signed on the ship. It was the way he described the storm and abandoning the ship. A sea story. But he had to stop before he got to the end."

"My god, Jack's part is the best part of the story. Well!" Nutbeem leaned back, looked for the waitress with the lager, saw the glass already in front of him.

"As I heard it, Search and Rescue finally gave Dennis and the others up for lost. They picked up two rafts of survivors and all but one of the lifeboats. Six men all tied together with plastic line. Four men still missing. Including Dennis. A week of searching and then they had to call it off. Aircraft, Coast Guard, fishing boats. All this time Jack hardly slept, down by the Coast Guard wharf, pacing back and forth, smoking, waiting for a message. Mrs. Buggit up at the house. Mind you, I wasn't there. Heard it all from Billy and Tert Card—and Dennis himself, of course. They came out and told Jack they had to abandon the search. It was as if he didn't hear them. Stood there, they said, like a stone. Then he turns—you know that sharp way Jack turns—and he says 'He's alive.'

"Went to his brother William in Misky Bay and says 'He's alive and I know where he is. I want to go out for him.' William, you see, had a new long-liner, very seaworthy. But he was worried about going too far offshore. The sea continued rough, even a week after the storm. Never said he wouldn't, mind you, he just hesitated the fraction of an instant. That's all Jack needed. He spun around on his heel and tore back up to Flour Sack Cove. Got a crowd to help him haul his trap skiff out of the water and onto the trailer, and there went Jack, off for the south coast. He drove all night to Owl Bawl, got the skiff in the water, loaded up with his gas cans, and away he went, out to sea alone to find Dennis.

"And he found him. How he knew where to go is beyond logic. Dennis and one other. Both of Dennis's arms were broken and the other fellow was unconscious. How did he get them both in the skiff? Jack never said a word, according to what I heard, until they got to Owl Bawl. Then he said, 'If you ever set foot in a boat again I'll drown you myself.' Of course, soon as the casts were off his arms, Dennis went out squid jigging with his wife. And Jack shook his fist at him and they don't speak."

"How long ago?" asked Quoyle, sending the foam in his glass around in a circle until a vortex formed.

"Oh donkey's years. Long ago. Before I came here."

Miles up the coast the aunt looked at wind-stripped shore. As good a place as any. She parked at the top of the dunes and gazed down the shore. Tide coming in. The sun hung on the rim of the sea. Its flattened rays gilded the wet stones. Combers seethed under a strip of corn-yellow sky.

The waves came on and on, crests streaked tangerine, breaking, receding with the knock of rolling cobbles. She opened the back of Quoyle's station wagon and lifted out the dead dog.

Down past the wrackline, onto hard sand. The fringe of bladder wrack and knot wrack stretched, relaxed, flowed in again on nervous water. The aunt laid Warren on the stones. An incoming wave drenched the sheet.

"You were a good girl, Warren," said the aunt. "A smart girl, no trouble at all. I was sorry they had to pull your teeth but it was that or you know what. Ha-ha. You got a few good bites in, didn't you? Many good years although denied bones. Sorry I can't bury you, but we are in a difficult situation here. Too bad you couldn't wait until we moved out to the house. And too bad Irene never knew you. Would have liked you, I'm pretty sure." Thought, Irene Warren. How I miss you. Always will.

She snorted into her handkerchief, waited in the gathering darkness, moving back a few steps at a time as the tide advanced, until Warren floated free, moved west along the shore, edging out and out, riding some unseen tidal rip. The sea looked as though it would sound if struck. Warren gliding away. Sailed out of sight, into the setting sun.

Just like in the old westerns.

And down the bay Quoyle heard Nutbeem's everlasting story, Tert Card's twilight gathered in his glass of Demerara.

11

A Breastpin of Human Hair

In the nineteenth century jewelers made keepsake ornaments from the hair of the dead, knotting long single hairs into arabesqued roses, initials, singing birds, butterflies.

THE AUNT set out for the house on Friday morning. She was driving her new truck, a navy blue pickup with a silver cap, the extra-passenger cab, a CD player and chrome running boards.

"We need it. Got to have a truck here. Got to get back and forth to my shop. You got a boat, I got a truck. They've got the road fixed and the dock in. Upstairs rooms done. There's an outhouse. For now. Water's connected to the kitchen. Some of that new black plastic waterline. Later on we can put in a bathroom. He's working on the roof this week. If the weather holds. But it's good enough. We might as well get out there. Out of this awful motel. I'll pick up groceries and kerosene lamps. You come out with the girls—and your boat—tomorrow morning."

Her gestures and expressions swift, hands clenching suddenly as though on the reins of a fiery horse. Wild to get there.

The aunt was alone in the house. Her footsteps clapping through the rooms, the ring of bowl and spoon on the table. Her house now. Water boiled magnificently in the teakettle. Upstairs. Yet climbing the stairs, entering that room, was as if she ventured into a rough landscape pocked with sinks and karst holes, abysses invisible until she pitched headlong.

The box holding the brother's ashes was on the floor in the corner.

"All right," she said, and seized it. Carried it down and through and out. A bright day. The sea glazed, ornamented with gulls. Her shadow streamed away from her. She went into the new outhouse and tipped the ashes down the hole. Hoisted her skirts and sat down. The urine splattered. The thought that she, that his own son and grandchildren, would daily void their bodily wastes on his remains a thing that only she would know.

On Saturday morning Quoyle and his daughters came along, suitcases humped in the backseat, the speedboat swaying behind on the rented trailer. He steered over the smoothed road. Starting where the road ended in the parking lot of the glove factory, the bulldozer had scraped a lane through the tuckamore to the house. New gravel crunched under the tires. Clouds, tined and serrated, and ocean the color of juice. The sun broke the clouds like a trout on the line.

"A ladder house," said Sunshine, seeing the scaffolding.

"Dad, I thought it was going to be a new house," said Bunny. "That Dennis was making it new. But it's the same one. It's ugly, Dad. I hate green houses." She glared at him. Had he tricked her?

"Dennis fixed up the inside. We can paint the house another color later on. First we have to fix up the holes and weak spots."

"Red, Dad. Let's paint it red."

"Well, the aunt has the say. It's mostly her house, you know. She might not be crazy about red."

"Let's paint her red, too," said Bunny. Laughed like a hyena.

Quoyle pulled in beside the aunt's truck. He'd wrestle with the trailer and the boat on Sunday. Dennis Buggit on the roof, tossing shingles into the wind. The aunt opened the door and cried "Ta-TA!"

Smooth walls and ceilings, the joint compound still showing trowel marks, the fresh window sills, price stickers on the smudgy window glass. A smell of wood. Mattresses leaned against a wall. The girls' room. Bunny piled wood shavings on her head.

"Hey, Dad, look at my curly hair, Daddy, look at my curly hair. Dad! I got curly hair." Shrill and close to tears. Quoyle picked at melted cheese on her shirt.

In the kitchen the aunt ran water into a sink, turned on the gas stove to show.

"I've made a nice pot of stewed cod," she said. "Dennis brought a loaf of Beety's homemade bread. I got bowls and spoons before I came over, butter and some staples. Perishables in that ice cooler. You'll have to bring ice over. I don't know when we can get a gas refrigerator in here. Nephew, you'll have to manage with the air mattress and sleeping bag in your room for a while. But the girls've got bed frames and box springs."

Quoyle and Bunny put a table together of planks and sawhorses.

"This is heavy," said Bunny, horsing up one end of a plank, panting in mock exhaustion.

"Yes," said Quoyle, "but you are very strong." His stout, homely child with disturbing ways, but a grand helper with boards and stones and boxes. Not interested in the things of the kitchen unless on a platter.

Dennis came down from the roof, grinned at Quoyle. There was nothing in him of Jack Buggit except eyes darting to the horizon, measuring cuts of sky.

"Great bread," said Quoyle, folding a slice into his mouth.

"Yeah, well, Beety makes bread every day, every day but Sunday. So."

"And good fish," said the aunt. "All we need's string beans and salad."

"So," said Dennis. "The caplin run'll be soon. Get a garden in. Caplin's good fertilizer."

In the afternoon Quoyle and Bunny wiped at the lumpy joint compound with wet sponges until the seams were smooth. Bunny intent, the helpful child. But glancing in every corner. On the roof Dennis hammered. The aunt sanded windowsills, laid a primer coat.

In the last quarter-light Quoyle walked with Dennis down to the new dock. On the way they passed the aunt's amusement garden, a boulder topped with silly moss like hair above a face. Scattered through the moss a stone with a bull's-eye, a shell, bits of coral, white stone like the silhouette of an animal's head.

The wood of the new dock was resinous and fragrant. Water slapped beneath. Curdled foam.

"Tie your boat up now, can't you?" said Dennis. "Pick up a couple old tires so she don't rub."

Dennis slipped the mooring lines, jumped into his own boat, and hummed into the dusk on curling wake. The lighthouses on the points began to wink. Quoyle went up the rock to the house, toward windows flooded with orange lamplight. Turned, glanced again across the bay, saw Dennis's wake like a white hair.

In the kitchen the aunt shuffled cards, dealt them around.

"We'd play night after night when I was a girl," she said. "Old games. Nobody knows them now. French Boston, euchre, jambone, scat, All-Fours. I know every one."

Slap, slap, the cards.

"We'll play All-Fours. Now, every jack turned up by the dealer counts a point for him. Here we are, clubs are trumps."

But the children couldn't understand and dropped their cards. Quoyle wanted his book. The aunt's blood boiled up.

"Everlasting whining!" What had she expected? To reconstruct some rare evening from her ancient past? Laughed at herself.

So Quoyle told his daughters stories in the dim bedroom, of explorer cats sighting new lands, of birds who played cards and lost them in the wind, of pirate girls and buried treasure.

Downstairs again, looked at the aunt at the table, home at last. Her glass of whiskey empty.

"It's quiet," said Quoyle, listening.

"There's the sea." Like a door opening and closing. And the cables' vague song.

Quoyle woke in the empty room. Grey light. A sound of hammering. His heart. He lay in his sleeping bag in the middle of the floor. The candle on its side. Could smell the wax, smell the pages of the book that lay open beside him, the dust in the floor cracks. Neutral light illumined the window. The hammering again and a beating shadow in the highest panes. A bird.

He got up and went to it. Would drive it away before it woke the aunt and the girls. It seemed the bird was trying to break from the closed room of sea and rock and sky into the vastness of his bare chamber. The whisper of his feet on the floor. Beyond the glass the sea lay pale as milk, pale the sky, scratched and scribbled with cloud welts. The empty bay, far shore creamed with fog. Quoyle pulled his clothes on and went downstairs.

On the threshold lay three wisps of knotted grass. Some invention of Sunshine's. He went behind the great rock to which the house was moored and into the bushes. His breath in cold cones.

A faint path angled toward the sea, and he thought it might come out onto the shore north of the new dock. Started down. After a hundred feet the trail went steep and wet, and he slid through wild angelica stalks and billows of dogberry. Did not notice knots tied in the tips of the alder branches.

Entered a band of spruce, branches snarled with moss, whiskey jacks fluttering. The path became a streambed full of juicy rocks. A waterfall with the flattened ocean at its foot. He stumbled, grasping at Alexanders, the leaves perfuming his hands.

Fountains of blackflies and mosquitoes around him. Quoyle saw a loop of blue plastic. He picked it up, then a few feet farther along spied a sodden diaper. A flat stick stamped "5 POINTS Popsicle

Pete." When he came on a torn plastic bag he filled it with debris. Tin cans, baby-food jars, a supermarket meat tray, torn paper cajoling the jobless reader.

> . . . perhaps you are not quite confident that you can successfully complete the full program in Fashion Merchandising. Well, I can make you a special offer that will make it easier for you. Why not try just Section One of the course to begin with. This does not involve you in a long-term commitment and it will give you the opportunity to . . .

Plastic line, the unfurled cardboard tube from a roll of toilet paper, pink tampon inserters.

Behind him a profound sigh, the sigh of someone beyond hope or exasperation. Quoyle turned. A hundred feet away a fin, a glistening back. The Minke whale rose, glided under the milky surface. He stared at the water. Again it appeared, sighed, slipped under. Roiling fog arms flew fifty feet above the sea.

A texture caught his eye, knots and whorls down in the rock. The object was pinched in a cleft. He worked it back and forth and then jerked at it. Held it on his palm. Intricate knots in wire, patterned spirals and loops. Wires broken where he had torn the thing loose from the rock. He turned it over, saw a corroded fastening pin. And, turning it this way and that, he caught the design, saw a fanciful insect with double wings and plaited thorax. The wire not wire but human hair—straw, rust, streaky grey. The hair of the dead. Something from the green house, from the dead Quoyles. He threw the brooch, with revulsion, into the pulsing sea.

Climbing again toward the house, he reached the spruce trees, heard a rough motor. A boat veered toward the shore and he thought it was Dennis until he saw the scabbed paint, fray and grime. The dory idled. The man in the stern cut the motor, raised the propeller. Drifted in the fog. The man's head was down, white stubble and gapped mouth. His jacket crudely laced with thrummy twine. Old and strong. Jerked up a line of whelk pots. Nothing. He lowered the propeller, pulled again and again on the greasy rope. The engine settled into a ragged beat. In a minute man and boat were eaten by mist. The motor faded south in the direction of the glove factory, the ruins of Capsize Cove.

Quoyle clawed up. Thought that if he got in there with axe and saw, set some pressure-treated steps in the steepest pitches, built a bridge over the wet spots, gravel and moss—it would be a beauty of a walk down to the sea. Some part of this place as his own.

"We thought the gulls had carried you off." The smell of coffee, little kid hubbub, the aunt in her ironed blue jeans, hair done up in a scarf, buttering toast for Sunshine.

"Dennis was here in his truck. He's got to go cut wood with his father-in-law. Said bad weather was coming, you might want to get the rest of the shingles on. Says it ought to take a day, day and a half. Left you his carpenter's belt. Wasn't sure if you had tools. Said there's five or six more squares under that sheet of plastic. He's not sure when he'll be able to get back. Maybe by Wednesday. Look what he brought the girls."

Two small hammers with hand-whittled handles lay on the table. The throats of the handles painted, one with red stripes, the other with blue.

But Quoyle felt a black wing fold him in its reeking pit. He had never been on a roof, never put down a shingle. He poured a cup of coffee, slopping it in the saucer, refused the toast made from Dennis's wife's bread.

Went to the foot of the ladder, looked up. A tall house. How tall, he didn't know. Steep pitch of roof. In all Newfoundland the roofs were flat, but the Quoyles had to have a wild pitch.

He took a breath and began to climb.

The aluminum ladder bounced and sang as he went up. He climbed slowly, gripped the rungs. At the edge of the roof he looked down to see how bad it was. The rock glinted cruelly with mica. He raised his eyes to the roof. Tar paper stapled down. New shingles halfway. There was a wooden brace nailed above the shingles. Crouch on the brace and nail the shingles? The worst part would be getting up to the brace. Slowly he got back down to the ground.

He heard Sunshine laughing in the kitchen, the tap of the small hammer. Sweet earth beneath his feet!

But buckled on Dennis's carpenter's belt, the pouch heavy with roofing nails, the hammer knocking his leg as he climbed. Halfway up he thought of the shingles, went back down and got three.

Now climbed with only one hand, the other clenching the asphalt pieces. At the top of the ladder he had a bad moment. The ladder rose up several rungs above the roof and he had to step off to the side onto the roof, to crawl up with the deep air beneath him.

He crouched awkwardly on the brace, saw that Dennis put the shingles on in tiers that he could reach comfortably, then set the brace in a new position. The tops of the spruces were like stains in the fog below. He could hear the slow pound of the sea. He did nothing for a few minutes. It wasn't so bad.

Quoyle put his three shingles up behind him on the slant. Took one, slowly butted it to Dennis's last, taking care to maintain the five-inch reveal. He got a few nails out of the apron, gingerly eased the hammer from under his buttock, got it out of the leather loop. He nailed the shingle. As he pounded the third nail home he heard a sliding sound, saw the two loose shingles he had carried up, slipping down. He stopped them with his hammer. Placed a shingle, nailed it. The third. It was not difficult, only awkward and breathless.

Now Quoyle balanced half a square of shingles on his shoulder, climbed back. It was easier, and he got up the roof without crawling, laid the shingles over the ridge and set to work. He glanced at the sea once or twice, saw the profile of a tanker on the horizon like a water snake floating in ease.

He was on the last row. It was fast now because he could straddle the ridge. The nails sank into the wood.

"Hi, Daddy."

He heard Bunny's voice, glanced toward the ground, but the glance stopped high. She stood on one of the rungs above the roof level, straining to put her foot on the roof. She held the hammer with the red-striped neck. Quoyle saw in a tiny vivid window that

Bunny was going to put her foot on the roof, was going to step forward onto the edge of the steep pitch as though on a level path, was going to fall, to pinwheel shrieking to the rock.

"I'm going to help you." Her foot reached for the roof.

"Oh, little child," breathed Quoyle. "Wait there." His voice was low but passionately urgent. "Don't move. Wait there for me. I'm coming to get you. Hold on tight. Don't come on the roof. Let me get you." The mesmerizing voice, the father fixing his child in place with his starting eyes, inching down the evil slope on the wrong side of everything, then grasping the child's arm, her hammer falling away, he saying "Don't move, don't move, don't move," hearing the painted hammer clatter on the rock below. And Quoyle, safe on the rungs, Bunny pinned between his chest and the ladder.

"You're squashing me!"

Quoyle went down with trembling legs, one hand on the rungs, his left arm folded around his daughter's waist. The ladder shook with his shaking. He could not believe she hadn't fallen, for in two or three seconds he had lived her squalling death over and over, reached out time after time to grip empty air.

12

The Stern Wave

"To prevent slipping, a knot depends on friction, and to provide friction there must be pressure of some sort. This pressure and the place within the knot where it occurs is called the nip. *The security of a knot seems to depend solely on its nip."*

THE ASHLEY BOOK OF KNOTS

IT WAS like mirror writing. The slightest change in reverse sent the trailer on the opposite tack, and Quoyle squinted in the side mirror at reflections of opposition. Again and again it folded like a jackknife blade seeking its bed, and twice it gouged the new dock. He was sick of it when finally the thing went straight back and into the water. A trick to it.

Got out and looked at the trailer. Wheels were in the water, the boat poised. His hand was on the tilt latch when he thought of a securing line. That would be fun, launch the boat and watch it float away.

He managed to attach bow and stern lines, yanked the latch. The boat slid down. He got the winch line loose, scrambled onto the dock and made the boat fast. It was something of a two-man operation. Then back to the trailer, close the latch, wind up the cable. The fifty-dollar boat was in the water.

He got in, remembered the damn motor. Still in the station wagon. Carried it onto the dock, put his foot on the gunwale and fell into the boat. Cursed all vessels from floating logs to supertankers.

Quoyle didn't see he'd mounted the motor in a position that would force the bow up like the nose of a bird dog. He poured in gas from the red can.

The motor started on the first pull. There was Quoyle sitting in the stern of a boat. His boat. The motor was running, his hand was on the tiller, wedding ring glinting. He moved the gearshift to reverse, as he had seen Dennis do, and gingerly applied a little power. The boat swung in toward the dock at the stern. Jockeyed back and forth until he was beyond the dock. Shifted into forward. The motor gave a low roar and the boat went—too fast—parallel with the shore. He eased back on the throttle and the boat wallowed. Now forward again, and rocks leaped up ahead of him. Instinctively he pushed the tiller toward the shore and the boat curved out onto Omaloor Bay. The water curled. Traveling on a glass arrow.

He worked the tiller, traced curves. Now faster. Quoyle laughed like a dog in the back of a pickup. Why had he feared boats?

There was an offshore breeze and the waves slapped the boat bottom as he sped at them. A sharp turn and he felt the boat skid. Pushed the throttle back. The stern wave roared up behind him and sloshed over the transom, swirled around his ankles and spread out in the boat. He pulled at the throttle again and the boat leapt forward, but sluggishly, and the water on the floor rushed toward the stern, adding its weight to Quoyle's. He looked for something to bail out the water; nothing. Turned very carefully toward the dock. The boat was vague and unwilling, for the water had altered the trim. Yet he moved forward, not afraid of sinking only two hundred feet from the dock.

As he approached he jerked back on the throttle again, and again the stern wave sloshed over the transom. But close enough to cut the motor and let the boat grind against the dock. He threw his mooring lines over the piles and went up to the house for a coffee can bail.

Back on the water again, he played the throttle delicately, turning with care, wary of the stern wave. There had to be a way to keep the water out when you slowed down.

"Of course there is," said Nutbeem. "Your transom's cut too low. What you need is a motor well, a bulkhead as high as the sides of the boat forward of the motor, with self-bailing drains in each corner. Build one in an hour. I'm flabbergasted they registered it the way it is."

"It's not registered," said Quoyle.

"You'd better hop on down to the Coast Guard and do it," said Nutbeem. "You get caught without a registration, without a motor well, without the proper lights and flotation devices they'll fine your ass off. I suppose you have an anchor?"

"No," said Quoyle.

"Oars? Something to bail with? Distress flares? Do you have a safety chain for your motor?"

"No, no," said Quoyle. "I was just trying it out."

On a Saturday Dennis and Quoyle hauled the boat out of the water. Bunny on the dock, throwing stones.

"She's a rough bugger," said Dennis. "In fact, you might burn her and start over."

"I can't afford to. Can't we put in a motor well? When I tried it out last week it went right along. It was fine until the water came in. I just want to get back and forth across the bay with it."

"I'll put in a bulkhead and give you some advice—only take this thing out on quiet days. If it looks rough better get a ride with your aunt or drive your wagon. It isn't fit, you get in a hard nip."

Quoyle stared at his boat.

"Look at it," said Dennis. "It's just a few planks bunged together. The boy that built it deserves a whack of shot in the backside."

Quoyle's hand went up to his chin.

"Dad," said Bunny, crouched on the pebbles, ramming a stick into the sand. "I want to go in the boat."

Dennis clicked his tongue as though he'd heard her say a dirty word.

"Talk to Alvin Yark. See if he'd make you something. He makes good boats. I'd make something for you, but he'll do it quicker and it'll cost you less. I'll put a bulkhead in, long as nobody sees me doing it, touching this thing, but you better talk with Alvin. You got to have a boat. That's certain."

Bunny ran up to the house, thumb and forefinger pinched together.

"Aunt, the sky is the biggest thing in the world. Guess what's the littlest?"

"I don't know, my dear. What?"

"This." And extended her finger to show a minute grain of sand.

"I want to see." Sunshine charged up and the particle of sand was lost in a hurricane of breath.

"No, no, no," said the aunt, seizing Bunny's balled fist. "There's more without number. There's enough sand for everybody."

13

The Dutch Cringle

"A cringle will make an excellent emergency handle for a suitcase."

THE ASHLEY BOOK OF KNOTS

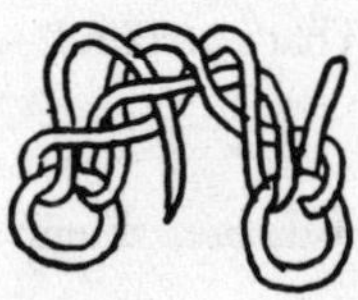

"BOY, there's a sight down here to the wharf. Never the like of it in these waters." The booming voice rattled out of the wire and into Quoyle's ear. "With the smell of evil on it. I wouldn't put to sea in it for all the cod in the world. Better take a look, boy. You'll never see anything like it again."

"What is it, Mr. Shovel? The flagship of the Spanish Armada?"

"No, boy. But you bring your pencil and your camera. I think you can write more than arrival and departure times." He hung up.

Quoyle was not glad. A gusting rain fell at a hard angle, rattling the windowpanes, drumming on the roof. The wind bucked and buffeted. It was comfortable leaning his elbow on the desk and rewriting a Los Angeles wreck story Nutbeem had pulled off the radio. An elderly man stripped naked by barroom toughs, blindfolded and shoved into freeway traffic. The man had just left the hospital after visiting a relative, had gone into a nearby bar for a glass of beer when five men with blue-painted heads seized him. Tert Card said it showed the demented style of life in the States. A favorite story with *Gammy Bird* readers, the lunacy of those from away. Quoyle called back.

"Mr. Shovel, I sort of hate to drop what I'm doing."

"Tell you, it's Hitler's boat. A pleasure boat built for Hitler. A Dutch barge. You never seen anything like it. The owner's on board. They says the paper's welcome to look her over."

"My god. Be there in about half an hour."

Billy Pretty stared at Quoyle. "What's he got, then?" he whispered.

"He says there's a Dutch boat that belonged to Hitler down at the public wharf."

"Naw!" said Billy, "I'd like to see that. Those old days, boy, we had the Germans prowling up and down this coast, torpedoed ships they did right up there in the straits. The Allies got a submarine, captured a German sub. Took it down to St. John's.

"We had spies. Oh, some clever! This one, a woman, I can see her now in a old duckety-mud coat, used to pedal her squeaky old bike up the coast once a week from Rough Shop Harbor to Killick-Claw, then go back down the ferry. I forget what she gave out for a story why she had to do all that bikin', but come to find out she was a German spy, countin' the boats all up and down, and she'd radio the information out to German subs lurking offshore."

"Get your slicker then and come on."

"We always heard they shot her. Just didn't show up one week. They said she was caught down at Rough Shop Harbor and executed. Said she dodged her bike through the paths, screaming like a crazy thing, the men after her, run like engines before they run her down."

Quoyle made a sucking noise with the side of his mouth. He did not believe a word.

There was a hole in the station wagon's floor and through it spurted occasional geysers of dirty rainwater. Quoyle thought enviously of the aunt's pickup. He couldn't afford a new truck. Frightening how fast the insurance money was going. He didn't know where the aunt got it. She'd paid for all the house repairs, put in her share for groceries. He'd paid for the road, the new dock. For the girls' beds, clothes, the motel bill, gas for the station wagon. And the new transmission.

"Wish I'd worn me logans," shouted Billy Pretty. "Didn't know the bottom half of your car was missin'."

Quoyle slowed not to splash the graceful, straight-backed woman in the green slicker. God, did it rain every day? The child was with her. Her eyes straight to Quoyle. His to her.

"Who is that? Seems like I see her walking along the road every time I come out."

"That's Wavey. Wavey Prowse. She's takin' her boy back from the special class at the school. There's a bunch of them goes. She got it started, the special class. He's not right. It was grief caused the boy to be like he is. Wavey was carrying him when Sevenseas Hector went over. Lost her husband. We should of give her a ride, boy."

"She was going the other way."

"Wouldn't take a minute to turn round. Rain coming down like stair rods," said Billy.

Quoyle pulled in at the cemetery entrance, turned, drove back. As the woman and child got in Billy said their names. Wavey Prowse. Herry. The woman apologized for their wetness, sat silent the rest of the way to a small house half a mile beyond the *Gammy Bird*. Didn't look at Quoyle. The yard beyond the small house held a phantasmagoria of painted wooden figures, galloping horses, dogs balanced on wheels, a row of chrome hubcaps on sticks. A zoo of the mind.

"That's some yard," said Quoyle.

"Dad's stuff," said Wavey Prowse and slammed the door.

Back along the flooding road again toward Killick-Claw.

"You ought to see the chair he made out of moose antlers," said Billy. "You set in it, it's comfortable enough, but to the others it looks like you sprouted golden wings."

"She has very good posture," said Quoyle. Tried to cancel the stupid remark. "What I mean is, she has a good stride. I mean, tall. She seems tall." Man Sounds Like Fatuous Fool. In a way he could not explain she seized his attention; because she seemed sprung from wet stones, the stench of fish and tide.

"Maybe she's the tall and quiet woman, boy."

"What does that mean?"

"A thing me old dad used to say."

"There she is." They peered through the streaming windshield. The Botterjacht stood out from every other boat at the wharf, tied up between a sailing yacht whose Australian owners had been there for two weeks, and the cadet training ship. From above, the barge looked like a low tub with strange and gigantic shoehorns on its sides. A crewman in a black slicker bent over something near the cabin door, then walked swiftly aft and disappeared.

"What are those things on the side? Looks like a big beetle with a set of undersize wings."

"Lee boards. Work like a centerboard. You know. You raise and lower a centerboard in a sailing boat so as to add keel. Some calls it a 'drop keel.' You got a shoal draft boat, my boy, she has to work to windward, you'll bless your centerboard. Now, with your lee boards, see, you don't loose any stowage space. The things is hung out on the side instead of down in the gut of the boat. A centerboard trunk takes up space." Billy's worn shape down to the bones, cast Quoyle as a sliding mass.

A light shone in the cabin. Even through the roaring rain they could see the boat was a treasure.

"Oak hull, I guess," said Billy Pretty. "Look at her! Look at the mast on her! Look at that cabin! Teak decks. Flat and low and wide. Never saw a shape like that on a boat in me life—look at them bluff bows. Look how she points up on the stem like a Eskimo knife. See the carving?" Her name was painted on an elaborately carved and gilded ribbon of mahogany—*Tough Baby*, Puerta Malacca. They could hear muffled voices.

"I don't know how you names a boat that," mumbled Billy Pretty, walking up the ramp and jumping on the glistening deck. He bellowed "Ahoy, *Tough Baby*. Visitors! Come aboard?"

A flush-faced man with white hair opened one of the curved-top double doors. He wore madras trousers with a patent leather belt and matching white shoes. Quoyle looked. Everything streaming. Coiled wet rope, dripping ventilator, sheets of water running over the deck. Near the cabin door a wet pigskin suitcase with a worked rope handle.

"Do I know you?" His eyes were bloodshot.

"From the local paper, sir, the *Gammy Bird*, thought our readers would be interested in your boat, we try to do a little story on the more unusual boats that dock in Killick-Claw, never seen anything like this." Quoyle said his piece. The boat felt like the plains under his feet. He smiled ingratiatingly, but *Tough Baby* was not a welcoming boat.

"Ah yes. That incredible harbormaster, what's-his-name, Doodles or whatever it is, mumbled something about a visit from *la presse locale*." The man sighed hugely. Gestured as though throwing away fruit skins. "Well, my darling wife and I are having this sort of totally terrible argument, but I suppose we can do the dog and pony act. I've given lectures on this boat to everybody from Andy Warhol two weeks before that *fatal* operation, to Scotland Yard. She absolutely draws this crowd wherever we go, whether Antibes or Boca Raton. She's absolutely unique." He stepped out into the rain.

"Traditional Dutch barge yacht design, but *marvelously* luxurious with these incredible details. *I* think, the finest Botterjacht ever built. When we first saw her she was a *total* wreck. She was moored in some awful Italian port—belonged to the Princess L'Aranciata—we'd taken a villa in Ansedonia next to theirs for the summer and at one point she mentioned that she had this *wreck* of a Dutch yacht that had belonged to Hitler but bored her to tears. Well! We went up to see it and immediately I could see the possibilities—it was utterly clear, clear, clear that here was an extraordinary, one-of-a-kind *thing*." Rain dripped off the ends of the man's wet hair, his shirt was transparent with it.

"Absolutely flat bottomed so she can go around without *any* damage, you can sail her right up onto shore in storm conditions or for repairs. Incredibly heavy. Almost forty tons of oak. Of *course*, she was designed for the North Sea. Bluff bows. She's absolutely buoyant. You know, my wife *hates* this boat. But I love her."

Billy Pretty's eyes had fallen on a square of Astroturf which he took for a bit of doormat until he saw cigar dog turds. Stared.

"That's for my wife's little spaniel. Great system. Doggie makes doo-doo on the simulated grass, you throw overboard—see the loop on the corner for the line?—and presto, tow until it's squeaky clean again. Great invention. The design dates back to the fifteenth century. The boat, of course, not the doo-doo rug. They're the boats you see in Rembrandt's marvelous paintings. They were royal barges. Henry the Eighth had one, Elizabeth I had one. A royal barge. She was named *Das Knie* when we saw her—means 'The Knee,' and I had to get down on one knee to persuade my darling, darling wife to let me buy it—" he paused for Quoyle's laugh. "Had the same name when the princess bought it—absolutely nobody ever changed it since this sordid German industralist had it after the war. My beloved wife thought it should be named after her, but I called her *Tough Baby*. When I saw what her true character was. This boat will be strong a hundred years from now. Built in Haarlem. Nine years in the building. She's utterly utterly indestructible. Just incredibly massive. The frames are seven and an eighth by six inches on eleven-inch centers."

Billy Pretty whistled and raised his eyebrows. The man's hair plastered against his yellow scalp. Drops hanging from the brims of Billy's and Quoyle's hats like moonstone trim. Quoyle scribbling on his pad, bent over to keep the rain off. Useless.

"The planking—nobody can believe the planking—select grade oak, two and three-sixteenths inches thick with double planking at the bottom. The reason? Because of her shallow home waters, full of sandbars, spits, shifting channels. Unbelievable. The Zuider Zee. Treacherous, treacherous water. You absolutely go aground all the time. The decking isn't flimsy, either. Believe it or not, you are standing on inch and three-quarters teak from pre–World War II Burma! You couldn't buy the wood that's in this boat anywhere in the world today for any amount of money. It's just completely gone today." The pitching voice went on and on. Quoyle saw Billy's hands rammed in his pockets.

"You wretched bastard, who are you talking to?" cried a raw high voice. The drenched man kept talking as though he hadn't heard.

"Let's see, there's a crew of four. She's cutter rigged, two thousand square foot of working sail, takes three incredibly strong men to handle the mains'l and they're always getting these sort of hernias and ruptures. Always quitting and jumping ship. It weighs a thousand pounds. The sail, I mean. And she's slow. Slow because she's heavy. But very, very sturdy." Without a pause he shouted, "I'm talking to the local press about the boat!" Nose wrinkled like a snarling dog.

"Tell them what happened in Hurricane Bob!"

The words poured down with the rain. Quoyle put his sodden notes away, stood with his wet hand over his wet chin. The white-haired man's chest hair showed through the wet silk of his shirt like grey knots. He seemed not to notice the rain. Quoyle saw purple scars on his hands, a ruby the size of a cherry tomato on his ring finger. Could smell the liquor.

"The absolutely marvelous *carving*. The carving is everywhere, these incredible master carvers worked on it for nine years. All the animals known. Zebras, moose, dinosaurs, aurochs, marine iguana, wolverines, we've had internationally known wildlife biologists on board here to identify all the incredible species. And the birds. Utterly, utterly bizarre. It was built for Hitler as I suppose you know, but *he* never set foot on it. There were a thousand delays. Deliberate delays. The extraordinary Dutch Resistance." Words spattering, drops bouncing off the deck.

"Tell them what happened in Hurricane Bob."

"I think my *dear* wife is trying to get our attention," the wet man said. "Just step in the cabin here and take a look at the interior. You'll adore it. As ornate as the carving is outside, they *really* went wild in there." He held a door open, sucked in his stomach to let them pass. Quoyle stumbled in thick carpet. A fire burned in a brick fireplace; there was a satinwood mantle inlaid with orchids worked in mother-of-peal, opal, jasper. Quoyle could not take it in, was conscious of patina, a lamp. Everything looked rare. There was something repellent in the room's beauty, but he didn't know what. Conscious of warping sea-damp, corrosive salt. A woman in a food-splotched bathrobe, hair the color of sewage foam, sat on the sofa. Her hands clashed in bracelets, rings. Feet stretched out, blunt purple ankles. Holding a glass cut with the initial M. Cellos sobbed, imparted a sense of drama. Quoyle saw the CD case on the coffee table, "Breakfast in Satin Sheets." The woman put down the glass. Wet and yellow lips.

"Bayonet, tell them what happened in Hurricane Bob." She ordered the man, did not look at Quoyle or Billy Pretty.

"Her beam is sixteen foot eleven," said the white-haired man taking a glass marked with a J from the mantle. The ice cubes were nearly melted but he drank from it anyway. "There's the Hoogarsjacht, and the Boeierjacht—"

"There's the hockeyjacht and the schnockyjacht and the malarkeyjacht," said the woman. "There's the poppycock and the stockyblock. If you don't tell them what happened in Hurricane Bob, then I will."

The man drank. The hems of his trousers dripped.

Billy Pretty coaxed the woman, lest she draw blood. "Now, m'dear, just tell us what happened in Hurricane Bob. We're anxious to hear it."

The woman's mouth opened but no sound came out. Fixed the man with her stare. He sighed, spoke in a weary singsong.

"Oh. Kay. Keep happiness in the fucking family. We were moored at White Crow Harbor north of Bar Harbor. That's in Maine you know, in the United States. Way up the coast from Portland. Actually there are two Portlands, but the other is on the West Coast. Oregon. Down below British Columbia. Well, *Tough Baby* sort of slipped her moorings at the height of this incredible storm. The sea absolutely went mad. You've seen how *Tough Baby* is built. Utterly massive. Utterly heavy. Utterly built for punishment. Well! She smashed *seventeen* boats to matchsticks. Seventeen."

The woman leaned her head back and cawed.

"Didn't stop there. You've seen she's flat bottomed. Built to go aground. After she absolutely made kindling out of White Crow's finest afloat, the waves kept shoving her on the beach. Like some incredible battering ram. In she'd come. Wham!"

"Wham!" said the woman. The bathrobe gaped. Quoyle saw bruises on the flesh above her knees.

"Out she'd float. She got among the beach houses. These were not your butchers' and bakers' beach houses, no, these were some of the most beautiful houses on the coast designed by internationally known architects."

"That's right. That's right!" Urged him, a dog through a flaming hoop.

"Pounded twelve beach houses, the docks and boathouses, into rubble, absolute rubble. In she'd come. Wham!"

"Wham!"

"Out she'd go. Pulverized them. Brought them down. Wilkie Fritz-Change was trying to sleep in the guest room of one of those houses—he'd been ambassador to some little eastern European hot spot and was recuperating from a breakdown at Jack and Daphne Gershom's beach house—and he barely escaped with his life. He said later he thought they were firing cannon at him. And the most extraordinary thing was that the only damage *she* sustained in this completely mad and uncontrollable rampage was a cracked lee board. Not a dent, not a scratch on her."

The woman, mouth full, shut her eyes, nodded her head. But was bored, now. Tired of these people.

Quoyle imagined the heavy vessel hurling itself onto its neighbors, pounding houses and docks. He cleared his throat.

"What brings you to Killick-Claw? A holiday voyage?"

The white-haired man eager to go on. "Holiday? Up here? On the most utterly desolate and miserable coast in the world? Wild horses couldn't drag me. I'd rather cruise the roaring forties off Tierra del Fuego in a garbage scow. No, we're being reupholstered, aren't we?" A deadly sarcasm whittled his voice to a point. "Silver here, my darling wife, insists on the services of a particular yacht upholsterer. Among thousands. Lived on Long Island, a mere seven miles from our summer place. Now we have to chase up to this godforsaken rock. All the way from the Bahamas to get the dining salon reupholstered. How can anyone live here? My god, we even had to bring the leather with us."

From the way he said the woman's metal name Quoyle thought it was changed from a stodgier "Alice" or "Bernice."

"Yacht upholsterer? I didn't know there were such things."

"Oh absolutely. Think about it. Yachts are full of these incredible, bizarre irregular spaces, utterly *weird* benches and triangular tables. Thousands and thousands of dollars to upholster the dinette alone in a unique yacht like this. Everything custom fitted. And of course every boat is different. Some of the more select yachts have leather walls or ceilings. I've seen leather floors—remember that, Silver? Biscuit Paragon's yacht, wasn't it? Cordovan leather floor tiles. Unbelievable. Of course you fall down a lot."

"What's his name?" asked Quoyle. "A local yacht upholsterer would interest our readers."

"Oh, it's not a him," said the woman. "It's Agnis. Agnis Hamm, 'Hamm's Custom Yacht Interiors and Upholstery.' Tiresome woman, but an absolute angel with the upholsterer's needle." She laughed.

Billy Pretty shifted. "Well, thank-you folks—Bayonet and Silver—"

"Melville. As in Herman Melville." The man pouring another drink, shivering, perhaps because he was wet. They shook the man's hand, Billy Pretty held the woman's cold fingers. Out of the hot cabin into the rain. The wet suitcase was probably ruined.

Inside the cabin heard voices turn loud. Go on, the woman said, get out of here, leave, see how far you get, detestable bastard. Be a tour guide again. Go on. Go. Go on.

14

Wavey

In Wyoming they name girls Skye. In Newfoundland it's Wavey.

A SATURDAY afternoon. Quoyle was spattered with turquoise drops from painting the children's room. Sat at the table with cup and saucer, a plate of jelly doughnuts.

"Well, Aunt," he said, "you are in the yacht upholstery business." Sucking at the tea. "I thought all along it was sofas."

"Did you see my sign?" The aunt sanded a bureau, rubbed the wood with hissing paper, sling of flesh under her upper arm trembling.

Bunny and Sunshine, under the table with cars and a cardboard road that unfolded in racetrack curves. Bunny put a block on the road. "That's the moose," she said. "Here comes Daddy. *Rrrr. Bee-bee-beep.* The moose don't care." She crashed the car into the block of wood.

"I want to do that!" said Sunshine, reaching for the block and the car.

"Get your own. This is mine." There was scrabbling, the knock of skull on table leg and Sunshine's howl.

"Crybaby!" Bunny scrambled out from under the table and threw the block and car at Sunshine.

"Here, now!" said the aunt.

"Calm down, Bunny." Quoyle lifted Sunshine into his lap, inspected the red mark on her forehead, kissed it, swayed back and forth. Across the room Bunny damned all three with killing eyes. Quoyle's smile signaled his disinterest in glares. But it seemed to him the sounds of his children were screaming and scraping. When would they start to be gentle?

"The shop is sixes and sevens at the moment, but at least the sewing machines are set. Getting experienced help is the big problem, but I'm training two women, Mrs. Mavis Bangs and Dawn Budgel. Mavis is an older woman, widow, you know, but Dawn's only twenty-six. Went to university, scholarships and all. Absolutely no work in her field. She's been doing lumpfish processing at the fish plant to fill in—when there's work—and then scraping along on unemployment insurance. That's the lumpfish caviar." Didn't care for it herself.

"No, I didn't see the shop. I interviewed two of your customers, I'm writing about their boat. The Melvilles. It was a surprise. No idea you were a yacht upholsterer."

"Oh yes. I've been waiting for my equipment to come. Opened the shop about ten days ago. I started the yacht upholstery, you see, after my friend died. In 1979. What these days they'd call a 'significant other.' Warren. That's who I named the dog after. In the postal service. Warren was, not the dog." She laughed. Her face flashed elusive expressions. Didn't tell Quoyle that Warren had been Irene Warren. Dearest woman in the world. How could he understand that? He couldn't.

"I swear until today I never knew such a thing existed. I would have been less surprised if you'd been a nuclear physicist." It came to him he knew nearly nothing of the aunt's life. And hadn't missed the knowledge.

"You know, you're very easily surprised for a newsman. It's all simple and logical. I grew up beside the sea, saw more boats than cars, though sure, none of them were yachts. My first job in the States was in a coat factory, sewing coats. The years Warren and I were together we lived on a houseboat, moored it at different marinas on the Long Island shore.

"We got a special rate at Lonelybrook, the marina we were at longest. And if we got tired of seeing the same familiar boats, on Sundays we could drive away to some other harbor, look at their boats, have a dinner. It was like a hobby, like bird-watching. Warren would say 'What do you think about going for a ride, look at some boats?' We dreamed we'd have a nice little ketch someday, cruise around, but it never happened. Always intended to come back here, back to the old house, with Warren, but we put it off, you know. So for me, coming back is a little bit in Warren's memory." More than that.

"I reupholstered an old chair we had on the houseboat, nice lines to it but a sort of mustard brown with the piping all frayed and thready. Got a good upholstery fabric, a dark blue with a red figure in it, took off the old upholstery and used it for a pattern. Just took my time stitching and fitting and pressing. It came out perfect. And I enjoyed doing it. Always liked sewing, working with my hands. Warren thought it was nice. So I did one in leather. That was something, working up leather. This real dark red, burgundy I guess you'd say. The only thing was I didn't get the welting as perfect as I should have. It pooched out a little here and there. And I had a lot of trouble with the tufting. Made me sick to look at how that beautiful leather was spoiled. Because to me it was spoiled. So Warren says—knew I enjoyed it—says 'Why don't you take a workshop in leather upholstery? Some kind of a course?'

"And Warren was the one that noticed the ad in *Upholstery Review*. Got me the subscription for Christmas. A reader. Read anything came into the house, the toothpaste boxes and wine labels. Used to buy a bottle of wine for Friday night supper. Books! My dear, that houseboat was filled with books. So this ad was for a summer course—Advanced Upholstery Techniques—at a school down in North Carolina. Warren wrote off for the brochure. I was just horrified at the cost, and I didn't want to go off alone for a whole summer. It was an eight-week course. But Warren said 'You can't tell, Agnis, you might never get the chance to do this again.' Upshot was, I decided I would."

Sunshine squirmed out of Quoyle's arms and got the blocks. She put one on the road under the table, glanced triumphantly at Bunny. Who swung her legs. Shutting first one eye and then the other, making Sunshine and Quoyle and the aunt hop back and forth. Until it seemed something appeared on the edge of her vision, something out in the tuckamore, a gliding shadow. Something white! That disappeared.

The aunt was rolling, telling Her Story. The romantic version. "It was at college in a little town on Pamlico Sound. There was about fifty people there from all over. A woman from Iowa City who wanted to specialize in museum restoration using antique brocades and rare fabrics. A man who did doll furniture. A furniture designer who kept saying he wanted the experience. I wrote to Warren, glad I came. Told them I didn't have a specialty, just liked working with leather and wanted to improve at it."

She put the sandpaper aside and wiped the tabletop with a waxy rag, long swipes that picked up the dust. Bunny sidled along the wall, came to Quoyle, needing his proximity. Squeezed his arm with both hands.

"About halfway through the course this instructor, he works with the Italian furniture designers, said 'Agnis, I've got a tough one for you.' It was a little twenty-foot fiberglass cruiser that belonged to the school's janitor. He'd just bought a used boat. My job to fit and upholster the odd-shaped cushions that were settees in the daytime and berths at night. There was a triangular bar that he wanted upholstered in tufted black leather, the tufting spelling out the boat's name which was, as I remember, *Torquemada*. I persuaded him that wouldn't look as well as a classic diamond pattern of pleated tufting with a smart padded bumper at the upper rim. I said he could have the boat's name etched on a brass plate to hang behind the bar, or a nice wood sign. He said go for it. It worked.

"I put in some curves, scrolled and rolled edges, gathers and pleats—a very sumptuous style that suited the fellow's dream. Really, there's quite an art to it, and I was upholstering beyond myself. Pure luck." She pried open a tin. Yellow wax. The smell of housekeeping and industry.

"Instructor said I had a touch for boat work, that yacht upholstery paid. Said you got to see some great boats and met a lot of interesting people." Clear enough the aunt let a stranger's praise change her life.

Quoyle was on the floor with his daughters, building a bridge over the road, a town, a city crowded with block cars and roaring engines. Patiently rebuilding bridges that fell as trucks caromed.

"Dad, make a castle. Make a castle in the road." He would do anything they told him.

"On the bus on the way back to Long Island I worked it all out, how I could start up my own little business. I sketched out the sign—Hamm's Yacht Upholstery—with a full-rigged sailing ship under the letters. I intended to rent a storefront down by the wharf at Mussle Harbor. I made a list of the equipment I needed—an industrial-grade sewing machine, button press, pair of padded trestles, taking-down tools—tack lifters and ripping chisels, rebuilding tools—hide strainers, webbing stretchers. I told myself to start small, just get the leather I needed for each job so's I wouldn't tie up a lot of money in leathers."

The castle rose, towers and flying buttresses, one of the aunt's bobby pins with a bit of yarn for a pennant. Now the cars metamorphosed to galloping horses with destructive urges. Bunny and Sunshine clicked their tongues for hoofbeats.

"So home I get, all excited, just pour this out fast as I could talk, Warren sitting there at the kitchen table nodding. I noticed the weight loss, looked sort of grey like how you get with a bad headache or when you're really sick. So I said 'Don't you feel good?' Warren, poor soul! All knotted up. Then just burst out with it. 'Cancer. All through me. Four to six months. Didn't want to worry you while you were taking your course.' "

The aunt got up, scraping her chair, went to the door to get a breath free from the moral stench of wax.

"Turned out, it was over in three months. First thing I did

when I pulled myself together was get that puppy and name her." Didn't explain the need to say part of Irene Warren's name fifty times a day, to invoke the happiness that had been. "She didn't get bad tempered until after she was grown. And then it was only strangers. And after a while I rented the storefront space and started in on yacht upholstery. Warren—my Warren—never saw the shop."

Quoyle lay on his back on the floor, blocks piled on his chest, rising and falling as he breathed.

"That's boats," said Sunshine. "Dad is the water and these are my ferryboats. Dad, you are the water."

"I feel like it," said Quoyle. Bunny back to the window, put two blocks on the sill. Looked into tuckamore.

"Anyway, I've been working at it for the past thirteen years. And when your father and mother went, though I never knew your mother, I thought it was a good time to come back to the old place. Or risk never seeing it again. I suppose I'm getting old now, though I don't feel it. You shouldn't get down on their level, you know." Meaning Quoyle on the floor, covered with blocks. "They'll never respect you."

"Aunt," said Quoyle, his mind floating somewhere between the boats under his chin and the yacht upholstery business. "The woman in your shop. What did you say she studied at university?" He had always played with his children. The first embarrassed pleasure of stacking blocks with Bunny. He took an interest in sand pies.

"Dawn, you mean? Mrs. Bangs never set foot in a grade school, much less university. Pharology. Science of lighthouses and signal lights. Dawn knows elevations and candlepower, stuff about flashes and blinks and buoys. Bore you silly with it. And you know, she talks about it all day long because it's slipping out of her head. Use it or lose it. And she's losing it. Says so herself. But there's no jobs for her, although the shipping traffic is so heavy you can almost lie awake at night and hear it tearing over the ocean. Why, are you interested in Dawn?" The aunt slid her fingers, feeling the waxy surface.

"No," said Quoyle. "I don't even know her. Wondered, that's all."

A fly crawled on the table, stopped to wipe its mouth with its front legs, then limped on, the hind legs more like skids than moving limbs. The aunt snapped her rag.

"Why don't you come by the shop some day next week? Meet Dawn and Mavis. We can have a bite at Skipper Willie's."

"That's a good idea," said Quoyle. Glanced at Bunny staring out into tuckamore.

"What are you looking at, Bunny?" Her scowling gaze.

"When I grow up," said Bunny, "I am going to live in a red log cabin and have some pigs. And I will never kill them for their bacon. Because bacon comes from pigs, Dad. Beety told us. And Dennis killed a pig to get its bacon."

"Is that right?" said Quoyle, feigning amazement.

Tuesday, and Quoyle couldn't get started on the piece. He shoved the page of rain-smeared notes on the Botterjacht under his pile of papers. He was used to reporting resolutions, votes, minutes, bylaws, agendas, statements embroidered with political ornament. Couldn't describe the varnished wood of *Tough Baby*. How put down on paper the Melvilles' savageness? Bunny much on his mind. The door-scratching business in the old kitchen. He shuffled his papers, looked at his watch again and again. Would go into town and take a look at the aunt's shop. Wanted to ask her about Bunny. Was there a problem or wasn't there. And insatiable Quoyle was starving anyway.

Before he started the station wagon the tall woman, Wavey, came to mind. He looked down the road both ways to see if she was walking. Sometimes she went to the school at noon. He thought, maybe, to help in the lunchroom. Didn't see her. But as he came up over the rise and in sight of Jack's house, there she was, striding along and swinging a canvas bag. He pulled up, glad she was alone, that he was, too.

It was books: she worked in the school library twice a week, she said. Her voice somewhat hoarse. She sat straight, feet neatly side by side. They looked at each other's hands, proving the eye's affinity for the ring finger; both saw gold. Knew at least one thing about each other.

Silence, the sea unfolding in pieces. A skiff and bobbing dory, men leaning to reset a cod trap. Quoyle glanced, saw her pale mouth, neck, eyes somewhere between green glass and earth color. Rough hands. Not so young; heading for forty. But that sense of harmony with something, what, the time or place. He didn't know but felt it. She turned her head, caught him looking. Eyes flicked away again. But both were pleased.

"I have a daughter starting first grade this fall. Bunny. Her name is Bunny. My youngest daughter is Sunshine, goes to Beety Buggit's house while I'm at work." He thought he had to say something. Cleared his throat.

"I heard that." Her voice so quiet. As if she was talking to herself.

At the school driveway she got halfway out the door, murmured something Quoyle did not catch, then strode away. Maybe it was thank-you. Maybe it was stop by and have a cup of tea some day. Her hands swung. She stopped for a moment, took a white, crumpled tissue from her coat pocket, blew her nose. Still Quoyle sat there. Watched her run up the school steps and in through the door. What was wrong with him?

Just to see the way she walked, a tall woman who walked miles. And Petal had never walked if she could ride. Or lie down.

15

The Upholstery Shop

The knots of the upholsterer are the half-hitch, the slip-knot, the double half-hitch, and the tuft knot.

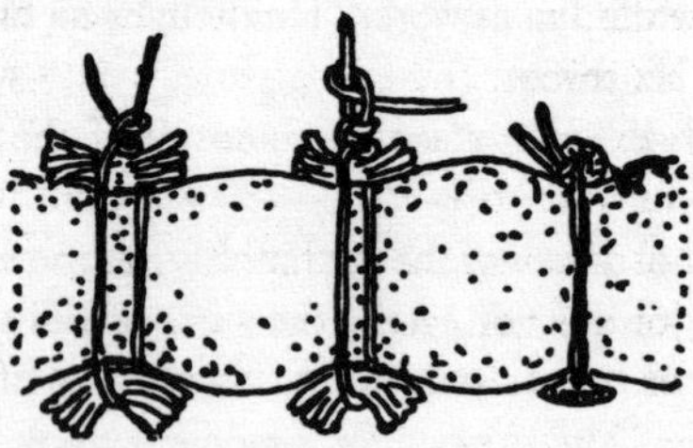

THE AUNT'S shop was in the lane behind Wharf Road. An ochre frame building with wooden flourishes and black shutters. Quoyle liked the row of shops, snug from the wind, yet almost on the wharf. The windows wavery with old glass. A bell jingled as he opened the door. The aunt, working a finger-roll edge on a stuffed pad, looked up. Curved needle halted in midmuslin.

"Here you are," she said. Looked around as though seeing the shop herself for the first time.

A woman with Emily Dickinson hair looped over her ears and symmetrically divided by a wide part sat at a sewing machine. The chattering needle slowed, the muslin slid over the table. The woman smiled at Quoyle, showing perfect teeth between violet lips, then her smile faded, a sadness flowed down her face from brow to mouth. A jabot foamed at her throat.

"Mrs. Mavis Bangs," said the aunt like a master of ceremonies.

At another table, a young woman with a helmet of tight brown curls, scissoring expensively into leather.

"And Dawn Budgel," said the aunt. The woman tense with concentration, did not look up or stop cutting. There was a smell of leather, dye, size and perfume. The perfume came from Mrs. Bangs whose hands were folded now into each other, who stared at Quoyle. His hand went up to his chin.

"Well, this is it," said the aunt. "There's only the two sewing stations and one cutting table set up now, but as I build up business I hope to have six sewing and two cutting. That's what I had back in Long Island. I've got a sailing fishing boat that's like a yacht below decks coming up next week—she was built in the States on the West Coast as a salmon-trolling ketch, but now she belongs to a fellow in St. John's. I've seen a few commercial fishing sailboats in the last year or two. Cheap to run, they say. Working sail might be coming back. Don't I wish."

"Dawn here cutting out the chair backs for the dining salon on the Melvilles' yacht. That color blue matches Mrs. Melville's eyes. She had it specially dyed down in New York. And Mavis is sewing up the liners that go over the foam rubber. Dawn, this is my nephew I told you about. Works for the paper. We're just going to run over across the way to Skipper Will's and get some dinner. Dawn, when you get done cutting you might thread up the other machine with that blue. She had the thread dyed, too."

The aunt clicked out the door on her black heels, and Quoyle, slow in closing it behind her, heard Mrs. Bangs say to Dawn, "Not what you thought, is he?"

A blast of hot oil and scorch came from Skipper Will's exhaust fan. Inside the fug was worse, fishermen still in bloody oilskins and boots hunched over fries and cod, swigged from cups with dangling strings. Cigarette smoke dissolved in the cloud from the fryer. The waitress bawled to the kitchen. Quoyle could see Skipper Will's filthy apron surging back and forth like ice in the landwash.

"Well, Agnis girl, what'll you 'ave today?" The waitress beamed at the aunt.

"I'll have the stewed cod, Pearl. Cuppa tea, of course. This here is my nephew, works for the paper."

"Oh yis, I sees him afore. In 'ere the odder day wit' Billy. 'Ad the squidburger."

"That I did," said Quoyle. "Delicious."

"Skipper Will, y'know, 'e invented the squidburger. Y'll 'ave it today, m'dear?"

"Yes," said Quoyle. "Why not? And tea. With cream." He had learned about the Skipper's coffee, a weak but acrid brew with undertones of cod.

Quoyle folded his napkin into a fan, unfolded it and made triangles of decreasing size. He looked at the aunt.

"Want to ask you something, Aunt. About Bunny." Steeled for this conversation. Petal had said a hundred times that Bunny was a "weird kid." He had denied it. But she was, in fact, different. Something was out of kilter. She was like a kettle of water, simmering and simmering, or in noisy boil before the pot goes dry and cracks, or sometimes cold, with a skim of mineral flowers on the surface.

"Do you think she's normal, Aunt?"

The aunt blew on her tea, looked at Quoyle. Cautious expression. Looked hard at Quoyle as though he were a new kind of leather she might buy.

"Those bad dreams. And her temper. And—" He stopped. Was sayings things badly.

"Well," said the aunt. "Just think of what's happened. She's lost members of her family. Moved to a strange place. The old house. New people. Her grandparents, her mother. I'm not sure she understands what's happened. She says sometimes that they are still in New York. Things are upside down for her. I suppose they are for all of us."

"All of that," said Quoyle drinking his tea savagely, "but there's something"—and his gut rumbled like a train—"something else. I don't know how to say it, but that's what I'm talking about." The words "personality disorder"—the Mockingburg kindergarten teacher's words when Bunny pushed other children and hogged the crayons.

"Give me an example of what you mean."

A dreary cloud settled on Quoyle. "Well, Bunny doesn't like the color of the house. That dark green." That sounded idiotic. It was what had happened in the kitchen. He could overlook the rest. The stewed cod and the squidburger came. Quoyle bit at the squid-burger as though at wrist ropes.

"The nightmares, for one thing. And the way she cries and yells over nothing. At six, six and a half, a kid shouldn't behave like that. You remember how she thought she saw a dog the first day we came to the house? Scared stiff of a white dog with red eyes? How we looked and looked and never saw a track nor trace?" Quoyle's voice roughened. He'd give anything to be away. Yet plowed on.

"Yes, of course I remember." The fork scraping away on the aunt's dish, kitchen heat, the din of knives, swelling laughter. "There was another white dog adventure couple weeks ago. You know that little white stone I had on my garden rock? If you squinted at it it looked like a dog's head? She come pounding on the door, yelling her head off. I thought something terrible'd happened. Couldn't get her to stop yelling and tell me what was the matter. At last she holds out her hand. There's a tiny cut on one finger, tiny, about a quarter of an inch long. One drop of blood. I put a bandage on it and she calmed down. Wouldn't say how she got the cut. But a couple days later she says to me that she threw away 'the dog-face stone' and it bit her. She says it was a dog bite on her finger."

The aunt laughed to show it wasn't anything to have a fit about.

"That's what I *mean*. She imagines these things." Quoyle had swallowed the squidburger. He was stifled. The aunt was making nothing out of something, sliding away from things that needed to be said. The people behind him were listening. He could feel their attention. Whispered. "Look, I'm concerned. I really am. Worried sick, in fact. Saturday morning when you went to pick up your package? We just came in to make lunch. I was going to heat up some soup. Sunshine was struggling with her boots—you know she wants to take her own boots off. Bunny was getting out the box of crackers for the soup, she was opening the box and the waxed paper inside was crackling when all of a sudden she stops. She stares at the door. She starts to cry. Aunt, I swear she was scared to death. She says, 'Daddy, the dog is scratching on the door. Lock the door!' Then she starts to scream. Sunshine sitting there with one boot in her hands, holding her breath. I should have opened the door to show her there was nothing there, but instead I locked it. You know why? Because I was afraid there *might* be something there. The force of her fear was that strong."

"Tch," said the aunt.

"Yes," said Quoyle. "And the minute I locked it she stopped screaming and picked up the cracker box and took out two crackers. Cool as a cucumber. Now tell me that's normal. I'd like to hear it. As it is I'm wondering if she shouldn't go to a child psychologist. Or somebody."

"You know, Nephew, I wouldn't rush to do that. I'd give it some time. There's other possibilities. What I'm getting at is maybe she is sensitive in a way the rest of us aren't. Tuned in to things we don't get. There's people here like that." Looked sidewise at Quoyle to see how he took that. That his daughter might glimpse things beyond static reality.

But Quoyle didn't believe in strange genius. Feared that loss, the wretchedness of childhood, his own failure to love her enough had damaged Bunny.

"Why don't you just wait, Nephew. See how it goes. She starts school in September. Three months is a long time for a child. I agree with you that she's different, you might say she is a bit strange sometimes, but you know, we're all different though we may pretend otherwise. We're all strange inside. We learn how to disguise our differentness as we grow up. Bunny doesn't do that yet."

Quoyle exhaled, slid his hand over his chin. A feeling they weren't talking about Bunny at all. But who, then? The conversation burned off like fog in sunlight.

The aunt ate her fish, a tangle of bones on the side of the plate that the waitress called the devil's nail clippings.

Walked back to the shop. As they came along the sidewalk, through the window he saw the part in Mrs. Bangs's black hair as she bent over a chair seat prying out tacks with a ripping chisel.

"So," the aunt said. "It was good to talk about this. It's a shame, but I've got to stay in late tonight. We've got to tack off the banquettes. We've got to be done with the lot by next Tuesday, finished and installed. If you'll pick up the girls. And don't worry about Bunny. She's still a little girl."

But that had not stopped Guy. She had been Bunny's age the first time.

"Yes," said Quoyle, lightened and rived by a few seconds of happiness. Well, he would wait and see. Anything could happen. "Will you have supper in town or shall we have something for you?"

"Oh I'll just get a bite here. You go ahead. You'll need to get some milk and more ice for the cooler. Don't get all fussed over nothing."

"I won't," said Quoyle, "good-bye," leaning toward the aunt's soft cheek, faintly scented with avocado oil soap. She meant well. But knew nothing about children and the anguish they suffered.

16

Beety's Kitchen

"The housewife's needs are multifarious but most of her requirements are not peculiar and most of what she requires is to be found in the general classifications."

THE ASHLEY BOOK OF KNOTS

A FINE part of Quoyle's day came when he picked up his daughters at Dennis and Beety's house. His part in life seemed richer, he became more of a father, at the same time could expose true feelings which were often of yearning.

The hill tilting toward the water, the straggled pickets and then Dennis's aquamarine house with a picture window toward the street. Quoyle pulled pens from his shirt, put them on the dashboard before he went in. For pens got in the way. The door opened into the kitchen. Quoyle stepped around and over children. In the living room, under a tinted photograph of two stout women lolling in ferns, Dennis slouched on leopard-print sofa cushions, watched the fishery news. On each side of him crocheted pillows in rainbows and squares. Carpenter at Home.

The house was hot, smelled of baking bread. But Quoyle loved this stifling yeast-heat, the chatter and child-yelp above the din of the television. Sometimes tears glazed the scene, he felt as though Dennis and Beety were his secret parents although Dennis was his age and Beety was younger.

Dennis barely looked away from the screen but shouted at the kitchen.

"Make us some tea, mother."

The water faucet gushed into the kettle. A smaller kettle steamed on the white stove. Beety swept at the kitchen table with the side of her hand, set out a loaf of bread. Winnie, the oldest Buggit child, got a stack of plates. As Quoyle sat down Bunny threw herself at him as though he had just arrived from a long, dangerous voyage, hugged, rammed her head against him. Nothing wrong with her. Nothing. Sunshine playing spider with Murchie Buggit, her fingers creeping up his arm, saying tickle, tickle.

Sitting at the kitchen table with children in his lap, eating bread and yellow bakeapple jam, Quoyle nodded, listened. Dennis was deliberate with the day's news, Beety had the crazy stories that branched off into others without ever finishing.

The tablecloth was printed with a design of trumpets and soap bubbles. Dennis said he was disgusted; his buddy Carl had driven into a construction trench across the road up Bone Hill. He was in hospital with a broken neck. Beety put saucers of canned apricots in front of the children. Bunny lifted her spoon, put it down.

"Seems like he's marked. He's the one had a fright, eight, nine years ago. Turned his hair snow-white in a month. He was out fishing, see, with his brother near the Cauldron, and see this limp old thing lying in the water. He thought it was a ghost net, you know, broke loose and come up to the surface. So to it they goes, he gives a poke with his hook, and dear Lord in the morning, this great big tentacle comes up out of the water—" Dennis held his arm above his head, hand curved and menacing, "and seizes him. Seizes him around the arm. He says you never felt such strength. Well, lucky for him he wasn't alone. His brother grabs up the knife he was using to cut cod and commences sawing at that gripping tentacle, all muscle and the suckers clamped tight enough to leave terrible marks. But he cut it through and got the motor started, his heart half out of his mouth expecting to feel the other tentacles coming down on his shoulder. They was out of there. The university paid them money for that cut-off tentacle. And now he busts his neck going into a ditch in the road. What's the point!"

Bunny down and whispering to Beety, getting the bacon from the refrigerator to show Quoyle. The famous bacon from the pig that Dennis had killed. Quoyle widened his eyes and raised his brows to show Bunny he was deeply impressed. But listened to Dennis.

"I never learned nothing about fishing from Dad. He loves fishing—but he loves it for himself. He tried to keep me away from it, tried to keep all of us off the water. It had the effect, see, of Jesson getting in with Uncle Gordon's crowd, and me just wanting to be on the water. Oh, I wanted to be a carpenter, right enough, but I wanted to fish, too," he went on dreamily. "Proper thing. There's something to it you can't describe, something like opening a present every time you haul up the net. You never know what's going to be in it, if it will make you rich or put you under the red line, sculpins or dogfish. So I wanted to fish. Because the Buggits are all water dogs, you know. All of us. Even the girls. Marge is a sailboat instructor in Ontario. Eva's the social director for a cruise ship. Oh, you can't keep us off the boats. But Dad tried his damndest."

"He was afraid for you."

"Yes, that. And it's like he knows something, like he knows something about the Buggits and the sea. Dad's got the gift. He knew when Jesson's boat went down, just like he knew where to go to find me when the *Polar Grinder* was damaged. I'll never forget the time with poor Jesson. You know, Jesson was Mumma's favorite. Always was, from the day he was born."

Quoyle knew how that was.

"Very sudden Dad got up from the table. He'd been sitting there beside the shortwave radio, we's all sitting there, and he said 'Jesson's gone,' and went across the road to his shop—where the *Gammy Bird* office is now—and stayed there by himself all night.

There was the northern lights that night, so beautiful you couldn't believe it, these colored strings shooting out, it was like a web. And in the morning there was these—well, like silver threads was on everything, rigging, houses, telephone wires. Had to come from the northern lights. And mother said it was Jesson's doing as he was in passage from his earthly body."

"After Jesson, he started the paper, right?"

"About right. But you know, Dad don't really run *Gammy Bird*, Tert Card does. The paper is there, you know, and he started it, he decides more or less what goes in it. But he'll phone in, make up some story about being sick, then go out fishing. Everybody knows what he's doing."

"Oh, he runs it," said Quoyle. "Tert Card dances his tune, I think."

"Eat your apricots, Bunny," said Beety, gathering empty saucers.

But Bunny whispered to Quoyle, "Apricots look like little teeny-weeny behinds, Dad. Little fairies' bottoms. I don't want to eat them." And sniveled.

While Dennis talked, a short, wrinkled man came to the doorway, leaned against the frame. He looked like a piece of driftwood, but for his mauve face. Wore a shirt spattered with hibiscus flowers the size of pancakes. Beety gave him a mug of tea, slathered marg on bread which the old man swallowed in one go.

"Alfred!" said Dennis. "Skipper Alfred, come on and sit down. This here is Quoyle, works at the paper. Comes back with Agnis Hamm to the old house on Quoyle's point."

"Yis," said the old man. "I remembers the Quoyles and their trouble. They was a savage pack. In the olden days they say Quoyles nailed a man to a tree by 'is ears, cut off 'is nose for the scent of blood to draw the nippers and flies that devoured 'im alive. Gone now, except for the odd man, Nolan, down along Capsize Cove. I never thought a one of the others would come back, and here there's four of them, though one's a Hamm and the other three never set foot on the island of Newfoundland. But the one I come to see is the carpenter maid."

Dennis pointed at Bunny.

"So, you're the maid was goin' to put on the roof with your little hammer."

"I was going to help Daddy," whispered Bunny.

"Right enough. 'Tis very few that helps their fathers nowadays, lad or maid. So I've brought you a bit of encouragement, like." He handed Bunny a small brass square, the marks worn but still visible.

"You are thinking to yourself 'what is that thing?' Well, 'tis a simple matter. Help you make straight lines and straight cuts. With this and a saw and a hammer and some nails and a bit of timber you can make a hundred little things. I had it when I was your age and I made a box with a lid first thing, six pieces and two bits of leather for the hinges. Wasn't I a proud thing?"

"What do you say, Bunny?" hissed Quoyle.

"I want to make a box with a lid and two bits of hinges."

Everyone laughed except Quoyle, watching Bunny, who flushed red with mortification.

"Then," said Quoyle, "we'll say thank-you Skipper Alfred for the fine square and get off to home if there's going to be time for after-dinner carpentry." Had she heard what he said about the man nailed to a tree?

And in the car, made Bunny put the square flat on the floor in case of a catastrophic ditch in the road.

17

The Shipping News

"Ship's Cousin, a favored person aboard ship . . ."

THE MARINER'S DICTIONARY

PHOTOGRAPHS of the Botterjacht on his desk. Dark, but good enough to print, good enough to show the vessel's menacing strength. Quoyle propped one up in front of him and rolled a sheet of paper into the typewriter. He had it now.

KILLER YACHT AT KILLICK-CLAW

A powerful craft built fifty years ago for Hitler arrived in Killick-Claw harbor this week. Hitler never set foot on the luxury Botterjacht, *Tough Baby*, but something of his evil power seems built into the yacht. The current owners, Silver and Bayonet Melville of Long Island, described the vessel's recent rampage among the pleasure boats and exclusive beach cottages of White Crow Harbor, Maine during Hurricane Bob. "She smashed seventeen boats to matchsticks, pounded twelve beach houses and docks into absolute rubble," said Melville.

The words fell out as fast as he could type. He had a sense of writing well. The Melvilles' pride in the boat's destructiveness shone out of the piece. He dropped the finished story on Tert Card's desk at eleven. Card counting waves, fidgeting through wishes.

"This goes with the shipping news. Profile of a vessel in port."

"Jack didn't say anything to me about a profile. He tell you to do it?" His private parts showed in his polyester trousers.

"It's extra. It's a pretty interesting boat."

"Run it, Tert." Billy Pretty in the corner rapping out the gossip column.

"What about the ATV accident? Where's that?"

"That's the one I didn't do," said Quoyle. "Wasn't much of an accident. Mrs. Diddolote sprained her wrist. Period."

Tert Card stared. "You didn't do the one Jack wanted you to do and you did one he don't know you did. Hell, of course we'll just run it. Proper thing. I haven't seen Jack in a flaming fit for a long time. Not since his fishing boot fell onto the hot plate and roasted. Tell you what, you better leave your motor running when you come in tomorrow morning."

What have I done, thought Quoyle.

"Don't get your water hot about Edith Diddolote. She's in Scruncheons with her sprained wrist and her fiery remarks." Billy's diamond pattern gansey unraveling at the cuffs. The blue eyes still startled.

"Bloody hell, about time you got here. Billy's up at the clinic getting his prostate checked and Jack's on his way down. He wants to see you." Tert Card snapped open a fresh copy of the *Gammy Bird*. Shot black looks from his gledgy eyes. At his desk, Nutbeem lit his pipe. The smoke came up in white balls. Outside the window fog and a racing wind that could not carry it away.

"Why?" said Quoyle apprehensively. "Because of the piece?"

"Yep. He probaby intends to tear your guts out for that Hitler yacht piece," said Tert Card. "He don't like surprises. You should have stuck to what he told you to do."

The roar of the truck engine, the door slam; Quoyle went sweaty and tense. It's only Jack Buggit, he thought. Only terrible Jack Buggit with his bloody knout and hot irons. Reporter Bludgeoned. His sleeve caught on the bin of notes and papers on his desk; paper sprayed over the desk. Nutbeem's pipe twisted in his teeth, tipped out a nugget of burning dottle as he unkinked the telephone cord by letting the receiver hang low and spin. Looked away.

Jack Buggit strode in, ginger eyes jumped around the room, stopped on Quoyle. He hooked his hand swiftly over his head as though catching a fly and disappeared behind the glass partition. Quoyle followed.

"All right, then," said Buggit, "This is what it is. This little piece you've wrote and hung off the end of the shipping news—"

"I thought it'd perk the shipping news up a little, Mr. Buggit," said Quoyle. "An unusual boat in the harbor and—"

" 'Jack,' " said Buggit.

"I don't have to write another one. I just thought—." Reporter Licks Editor's Boot.

"You sound like you're fishing with a holed net, shy most of your shingles standin' there hemming and hawing away." Glared at Quoyle who slouched and put his hand over his chin.

"Got four phone calls last night about that Hitler boat. People enjoyed it. Mrs. Buggit liked it. I went down to take a look at it meself and there was a good crowd on the dock, all lookin' her over. Course you don't know nothin' about boats, but that's entertaining, too. So go ahead with it. That's the kind of stuff I want. From now on I want you to write a column, see? The Shipping News. Column about a boat in the harbor. See? Story about a boat every week. They'll take to it. Not just Killick-Claw. Up and down the coast. A column. Find a boat and write about it. Don't matter if it's a long-liner or cruise ship. That's all. We'll order your computer. Tell Tert Card I want to see him."

But no need to say anything to Tert Card who heard everything over the partition. Quoyle went back to his desk. He felt light and hot. Nutbeem clasped both hands over his head and shook them. His pipe twisted. Quoyle rolled paper into the typewriter but didn't type anything. Thirty-six years old and this was the first time anybody ever said he'd done it right.

Fog against the window like milk.

18
Lobster Pie

"The lobster buoy hitch . . . was particularly good to tie to timber."

THE ASHLEY BOOK OF KNOTS

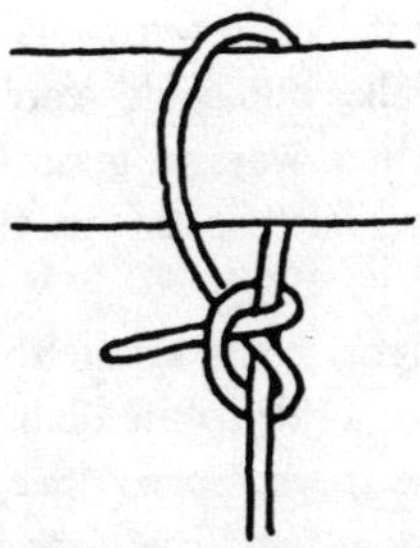

THE BOY in the backseat had plenty to say in wide, skidding vowels that only his mother understood. Quoyle got the sense, though; adventures ran through Herry's talk, a kind of heady exultation in such things as a blue thread on his sweater cuff, the drum of ocherous rain into puddles, a cookie in a twist of tissue. Anything bright. The orange fishermen's gloves. He had a wild sense of color.

"Gove! Gove!"

Or the blue iris in Mrs. Buggit's garden.

"Vars!"

"Nothing wrong with his eyesight," said Quoyle.

Here was a sudden subject for Wavey. Down's syndrome, she said, and she wanted the boy to have a decent life. Not his fault.

Not to be stuffed away in some back room or left to cast and drool about the streets like in the old days. Things could be done. There were other children along the coast. She had asked about other children, found them, visited the parents—her brother Ken took her in his truck. Explained things could be done. "These children can learn, can be taught," she said.

Fervent. A ringing voice. Here was Wavey on fire. Had requested books on the condition through the regional library. Started the parents' group. Specialists from St. John's up to speak. Tell what could be done. Challenged children. Got up a petition, called meetings, ah, she said, they wrote letters asking for the special education class. And got it. A three-year-old girl in No Name Cove had never learned to walk. But could learn, did learn. Rescuing lost children, showing them ways to grasp life. She squeezed her hands together, showing him that anyone alive could clench possibilities.

What else, he thought, could kindle this heat.

She asked Quoyle for a ride to the library. Friday and Tuesday afternoons the only time it was open. "See, Ken takes me when he can, but he's fishing now. And I miss my books. I'm the reader. And I read to Herry, just read and read to him. And get for Dad. What he likes. Mountain climbing, hard travels, going down to the Labrador."

Quoyle got ready Friday morning, put on his good shirt. Cleaned his shoes. Didn't want to be excited. For God's sake, giving someone a ride to the library. But he was.

The library was a renovated old house. Square rooms, the wallpaper painted over in strong pistachio, melon. Homemade shelves around the walls, painted tables.

"There's a children's room," said Wavey. "Your girls might like to have a few books. Sunshine and Bunny." She said their names tentatively. Her hair combed and plaited; a grey dress with a lace collar. Herry already at the bookshelves, pulling at spines, opening covers into flying fancies.

Quoyle felt fourteen feet wide, a clumsy poisoned pig, and

every way he turned his sweater caught on some projecting book. He tumbled humorous essayists, murderers, riders of the purple sage, sermonizing doctors, caught them in midair or not at all. Stupid Quoyle, blushing, in a tiny library on a northern coast. But got into the travel section and found the Erics Newby and Hansen, found Redmond O'Hanlon and Wilfrid Thesiger. Got an armful.

They went back by way of Beety's kitchen to get his girls. Who didn't know Wavey.

A ceremonious introduction. "And that's Herry Prowse. And this is Wavey. Herry's mother." Wavey turned around and shook their hands. And Herry shook everyone's hand, Quoyle's, his mother's, both hands at once. His fingers, palms, as hot as a dog's paws.

"How do you do," said Wavey. "Oh how do you do, my dears?"

Pulled up in front of Wavey's house to the promise of tea and cakes. Sunshine and Bunny fighting in the station wagon to see the yard next door, menagerie of painted dogs and roosters, silver geese and spotted cats, a wooden man in checked trousers grasping the hand of a wooden woman. A wind vane that was a yellow dory.

Then Bunny eyed the plywood dog with its bottle-cap collar. Mouth open, fangs within the lips, the nose sniffing the wind.

"Dad." She gripped Quoyle's collar. "There's a white dog." Whimpered. Quoyle heard her suck in her breath. "A white dog." And caught the subtle tone, the repetition of the awful words, "white dog." Then he guessed something. Bunny was inducing a thrill—working herself up. Girl Fears White Dog, Relatives Marvelously Upset.

"Bunny, it's only a wooden dog. It's wood and paint, not real." But she didn't want to let go of it. Rattled her teeth and whined.

"I guess we'll come for tea another time," said Quoyle to Wavey. And to Bunny he gave a stern look. Nearly angry.

"Daddy," said Sunshine, "where's their father? Herry and Wavey?"

On the weekend Quoyle and the aunt patched and painted. Dennis started the studding in the kitchen. Sawdust on everything, boards, two-by-fours stacked on the floor. The aunt scraping another cupboard to bare wood.

Quoyle chopped at his secret path to the shore. Read his books. Played with his daughters. Saw briefly, once, Petal's vanished face in Sunshine's look. Pain he thought blunted erupted hot. As though the woman herself had suddenly appeared and disappeared. Of course she had, in a genetic way. He called Sunshine to him, wanted to take her up and press his face against her neck to prolong the quick illusion, but did not. Shook her hand instead, said "How do you do, and how do you do, and how do you do again?" Invoking Wavey, that tall woman. Made himself laugh with the child.

One Saturday morning Quoyle went in his boat down to No Name Cove for lobsters. Left Bunny raging on the pier.

"I want to come!"

"I'll give you a ride when I come back."

Put up with the No Name witticisms over his boat. It was an infamous craft that they said would drown him one time. On the way back he skirted a small iceberg drifting down the bay. Curious about the thing, a lean piece of ice riddled with arches and caves. But as big as a bingo hall.

"More than four hundred icebergs have grounded this year so far," he told the aunt. He couldn't get over them. Had never dreamed icebergs would be in his life. "I don't know where they went ashore, but that's what they say. There was a bulletin on it yesterday."

"Did you get the lobsters?"

"Got them from Lud Young. He kept shoving extras in the basket like they were lifesavers. Tried to pay for them but he wouldn't take it."

"Season will be over pretty soon, we might as well eat 'em while we can get 'em. If he wants to give lobster to you, take them. I remember the Youngs from the old days. Hair hanging down in their eyes. You know, the thing that's best," said the aunt, "is the fish here. Wait until the snow crab comes in. Sweetest meat in the world. Now, how do we want to do these lobsters?"

"Boiled."

"Yes, well. We haven't had a nice lobster chowder for a while. And there's advantages to that." She looked toward the other room where Bunny was hammering. "We won't have to hear that screeching about 'red spiders' and fix her a bowl of cereal. Or I could boil them and pull out all the meat and make lobster rolls. Or how about crêpes rolled up with the meat in a cream sauce inside?"

Quoyle's mouth was watering. It was the aunt's old trick, to reel out the names of succulent dishes, then retreat to the simplest dish. Not Partridge's style.

"Lobster salad is nice, too, but maybe a little light for supper. You know, there's a way Warren and I used to have it at The Fair Weather Inn on Long Island. The tail meat soaked in saki then cooked with bamboo shoots and water chestnuts and piled into the shells and baked. There was a hot sauce that was out of this world. I can't get any of those things here. Of course, if we had some shrimp and crabmeat and scallops I could make stuffed lobster tails—same idea, but with white wine and Parmesan cheese. If I could get white wine and Parmesan."

"I bought cheese. Not Parmesan. It's just cheese. Cheddar."

"Well that settles it. Lobster pie. We don't have any cream, but I can use milk. Bunny will eat it without roaring and it'll be a change from boiled. I want to make something a little special. I asked Dawn to come over to supper. I told her six, so there's plenty of time."

"Who?"

"You heard me. I asked Dawn to come over. Dawn Budgel. She's a nice girl. Do you good to talk to her." For the nephew did nothing but work and dote.

There was a prodigious pounding from the living room.

"Bunny," called Quoyle. "What are you making? Another box?"

"I am making a TENT." Fury in the voice.

"A wooden tent?"

"Yeah. But the door is crooked." A crash.

"Did you throw something?"

"The door is CROOKED! And you said you would give me a ride in the boat. And didn't!"

Quoyle got up.

"I forgot. O.k., both of you get your jackets on and let's go."

But just outside the door Bunny invented a new game while Quoyle waited.

"Lie down on your back, see, like this."

Sunshine thumped down on her back, stretched out her arms and legs.

"Now look up near the top of the house. And keep looking. It's scary, it's the scary house falling down."

And their gazes traveled up the clapboards, warped crooked with storms, to the black eaves. Above the peak of the house the thin sky and clouds raced diagonally. The illusion swelled that the clouds were fixed and it was the house that toppled forward inexorably. The looming wall tipped at Sunshine who scrambled up and ran, deliciously frightened. Bunny stood it longer until she, too, had to get up and tear away to safe ground.

Quoyle made them sit side by side in the boat. They gripped the gunwales. The boat buzzed over the water. "Go fast, Dad," yelled Sunshine. But Bunny looked at the foaming bow wave. There, in the snarl of froth, was a dog's white face, glistering eyes and bubbled mouth. The wave surged and the dog rose with it; Bunny gripped the seat and howled. Quoyle threw the motor into neutral.

The boat wallowed in the water, no headway, slap of waves.

"I saw a dog in the water," sobbed Bunny.

"There is *no* dog in the water," said Quoyle. "Just air bubbles and foam and a little girl's imagination. You *know* Bunny, that there cannot be a dog that lives in the water."

"Dennis says there's water dogs," sobbed Bunny.

"He means another kind of dog. A real live dog, like Warren"—no, Warren was dead—"a live dog who can swim, who swims in the water and brings dead ducks to hunters." Christ, was everything dead?

"Well, it looked like a dog. The white dog, Dad. He's mad at me. He wants to bite me. And make my blood drip out." The tears coming now.

"It's not a true dog, Bunny. It's an imaginary dog and even if it looks real it can't hurt you. If you see it again you have to say to yourself, 'Is this a real dog or is this an imaginary dog?' Then you'll know it isn't real, and you'll laugh about it."

"But Dad, suppose it *is* real!"

"In the water, Bunny? In a stone? In a piece of plywood? Give me a break." So Quoyle tried to vanquish the white dog with logic. And headed back to the dock very slowly so there was no bow wave. Getting fed up with the white dog.

In the afternoon Quoyle set the table while the aunt squeezed and folded piecrust.

"Put on the red tablecloth, nephew. It's in the drawer under the stairs. You might want to change your shirt." The aunt stuck two white candles in glass holders although it was still full sunlight outside. The sun would not set until nine.

Bunny and Sunshine were tricked out in white tights, their velvet Thanksgiving dresses with lace collars. Sunshine could wear Bunny's patent leather Mary Janes, but Bunny sulked in grimy sneakers. And her dress was too small, tight under the arms and short. Hot, as well.

"Here she comes," said the aunt, hearing Dawn's Japanese car curving toward the house. "You girls mind your manners, now."

Dawn came up the steps, balancing in white spike heels big enough to fit a man, smiling with brown lips. Her nylon blouse glowed; the hem of the skirt hung low behind. She carried a bottle. Quoyle thought it was wine but it was white grape juice. He could see the Sobey's price tag. The toes of her shoes jutted up at a painful angle.

He thought of Petal in her dress with the fringe, the long legs diving down to slippers embroidered with silver bugles, Petal, darting around in a cloud of Trésor, shooting glances at her reflection in mirror, toaster, glass, flicking her fingers at Quoyle's openmouth desire. He felt a pang for this poor moth.

The conversation dragged, Dawn saying the bare floors and hard windows were "striking." Sunshine heaped grimy bears and metal cars in her lap, it's a bear, it's a car, as though the visitor came from a country where there were no toys.

At last the aunt thumped the fragrant pastry in front of Quoyle. "Go ahead and dish it up, Nephew."

She lit the candles, the flames invisible in the cylinder of sunlight that fell across the table, but the smell of wax reminding them, brought the dish of peas and pearl onions, the salad.

"Let me help," said Dawn, half up, her skirt caught under the chair leg. But there was nothing she could do. Her voice echoed in the hard room.

Quoyle pierced the crust with an aluminum implement. Bunny stuck her fork into the candle flame.

"Don't do that," said the aunt dangerously. A section of lobster pie rose from the steaming dish, slid onto Dawn's plate.

"Oh, is it lobster?" said Dawn.

"Yes, indeed." The aunt. "Lobster pie, sweet as a nut."

Dawn made her voice very warm, addressed the aunt. "I'll just have salad, Agnis. I don't care for lobster. Since I was a girl. We had to take lobster sandwiches to school. We'd throw them in the ditch. Crab, too. Like big spiders!" Tried a laugh.

Bunny looked at the crust and orange meat on her plate. Quoyle braced himself for screeching but it did not come. Bunny chewed ostentatiously, said "I love red spider meat."

Dawn to Quoyle. Confiding. Everything she said overwrought. Pretending an interest.

"It's so awful what those people did to Agnis." Didn't actually care.

"What people?" said Quoyle, his hand at his chin.

"The people in the Hitler boat. The way they just sneaked out."

"What's this?" said Quoyle, looking at the aunt.

"Well, looks like I got stiffed," she said, flames of rage sweeping into her hair roots. "We installed the banquettes on the yacht, all chairs but two done and delivered, all that. And they're gone. The yacht's gone. Pulled out after dark."

"Can't you track them through the yacht registry? That boat's one of a kind."

"I thought I'd wait a little," said the aunt. "Wait to hear. Maybe there was a reason they had to leave in a hurry. Sickness. Or business. They're involved in the oil business. Or she is. She's the one with the money. Or she remembered a hair appointment in New York. That's how they are. Why I didn't say anything to you."

"Didn't you do some work for them back in the States? That would show their address?"

"Yes, a few years ago I upholstered the sofas. But those papers are still back on Long Island. In storage."

"I thought you were having everything sent up here," said Quoyle, noticing again the emptiness of rooms, the lack of the furniture she said was being shipped. Two months now.

Dawn noticed his lips were slippery with butter from the lobster pie.

"It takes time," said the aunt. "Rome wasn't built in a day."

Outside the wind was up and humming in the cables. Bunny at the window.

"Who wants to play cards," said the aunt. Chafing her hands and squinting like a stage villain card shark.

"Know how to play All-Fours?" said Dawn.

"Girl," said the aunt, "you know it."

Glanced at the cupboard where she kept her whiskey bottle. Could bite the top off.

19

Good-bye, Buddy

"The Russian Escape. A prisoner is . . . secured to his guard. . . . In his efforts to escape he rubs his hands together until the heels of his hands pinch a bight of the rope. It is then an easy matter to roll the bight down as far as the roots of the fingers, where it can be grasped with the finger tips of one hand and slipped over the backs of the fingers of the other hand. The prisoner then pulls away and the . . . rope slips over the back of his hand and under the handcuff lashing."

THE ASHLEY BOOK OF KNOTS

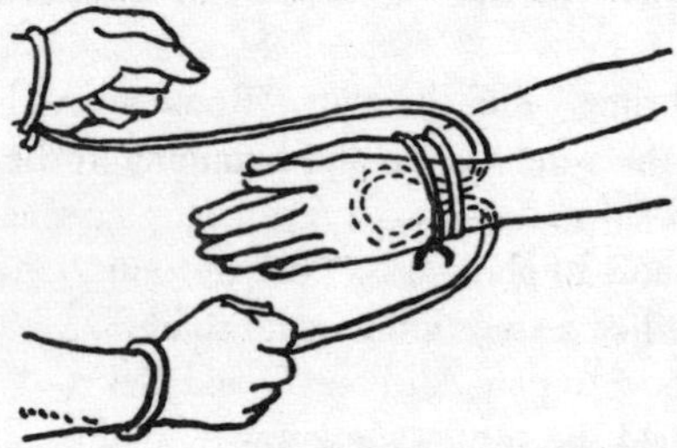

SOMETIMES Tert Card blew everybody out of the place. It was a hot, windless noon hour like a slot between two warring weather systems. They squeezed into Billy's truck, off to the Fisherman's Chance in Killick-Claw for fish and chips, escaped and away from Tert Card who scratched with both hands. Who had the itch in his armpits.

They sat on the public wharf eating out of Styrofoam boxes, stunned by the heat. Quoyle breathed through his mouth, squinted against dazzle. Although Billy Pretty warned, pointed to the north-east horizon at violet clouds pulled from a point as a silk scarf is pulled from a wedding ring. In the southwest they saw rival billows in fantastic patterns, as though a paper marbler had worked through them with his combs making French curls, cascades and winged nonpareil fountains.

"This week I've the most sexual abuse stories I've ever had," said Nutbeem. "Jack ought to be happy. Seven of them. The usual yaffle of disgusting old dads having it on with their kiddies, one more priest feeling up the choirboys, a nice neighborly uncle over in Stribbins Cove who gives the girls rides to Sunday School and buys them sweets if they pull down their knickers for him. One was a bit unusual—gives you a glimpse into the darker side of the Newfoundland character. This lad was a bouncer at a bar down in Misky Bay, tried to throw out some drunk. But the drunk went to his truck, got a tomcod from the ice chest in the back, into the bar again, overpowered the bouncer, ripped his trousers stem to stern and sexually assaulted him with the tomcod." Nutbeem did not laugh.

"What's a tomcod?" asked Quoyle.

Billy leaned against a piling, yawned. "Small one, boy. Small cod. You got your tomcod, your salt cod, your rounders . . . Any way you want to call it, it's fish."

Gazed at the advancing clouds. Tendrils snaking into open blue.

" 'Tis a strange time, strange weather. Remember we had a yellow day on Monday—the sky cast was an ugly yellow like a jar of old piss. Then yesterday, blue mist and blasting fog. Cap it off, my sister's youngest boy called up from St. John's, said there was a fall of frozen ducks on Water Street, eight or ten of them, feathers all on, eyes closed like they was dreaming, froze hard as polar cap ice. When that happens, look out, boys. Like the story I got yesterday over the phone. Same place as Nutbeem's tomcod, Misky Bay. Oh, Misky Bay is going through some kind of band of astral influence. Wouldn't be surprised to hear if they hadn't had a fall of frozen ducks down there, too."

"Give us the story," said Nutbeem, coughing into his pipe.

"Not much of a story, but it shows the feeling that's took hold of Misky Bay. I wouldn't go down there—as I get it from the Mounties a mother of three children went at her grandmother with a metal towel rack, laced her up something shocking, then set fire to the house. They got 'em out, but the poor old lady was bloody as a skinned seal and burned all up and down. And, in the kitchen, the fire volunteers finds a treasure trove. In a bucket under the sink is three hundred dollars worth of religious jewelry shoplifted from Woolworth's over the past year. Each says the other done it."

"I didn't get any car wrecks this week." Quoyle, still thinking of the one in his mind. A breeze ruffled the bay, died.

"Of course," said Nutbeem, "never rains but it floods the cellar. I've got these tremendously nasty sexual assaults, but I've also got my best foreign news story—the Lesbian Vampire Trial's over. Just heard it on the shortwave this morning."

"Good," said Quoyle. "Maybe Jack will give up the car wreck for that. Any pictures?"

"They're rather difficult to get on the older radios," said Nutbeem. "And I think it's unlikely Jack will give up the car wreck spot to an Australian story. That's a standing order: a car wreck and pix on page one. You'll have to use an old one out of Tert's file unless somebody smashes up between now and five o'clock. You got the shipping news and a boat piece, anyway. Right?" Nutbeem, who touched down and flew away.

"Right." Quoyle licked ketchup off the box lid, screwed his napkin into a knot. "The boat that blew up in Perdition Cove Tuesday morning."

Billy stretched and yawned, his withered neck taut again for a few seconds. "I can feel the season changing," he said. "Drawing in. This weather change coming means the end of hot weather. Time I got out to Gaze Island and worked on me poor old father's grave. Put it off last year and the year before." Some sadness straining the words. Billy seemed stored in an envelope; the flap sometimes lifted, his flattened self sliding onto the table.

"What hot weather?" said Quoyle. "This is the first day I can think of over forty degrees Fahrenheit. The rain is always ready to turn into snow. And where's Gaze Island?"

"Don't know where Gaze Island is?" Billy laughed a little. His stabbing blue-eyed look. "Fifteen miles northeast of the narrows. Bunch of whales went aground there once—some calls it Whale

Island, but it is Gaze Island to me. Though it had other names in the beginning. A beauty place. A place of local interest, Quoyle." Teasing.

"Like to see it," said Quoyle who had found his tub of coleslaw. "I've never been on an island."

"Don't be stun, boy. You're on one now, just look at a map. You can come out with me. You ought to know about Gaze Island, you ought. Proper thing. Saturday morning. If the weather's decent I'll go out Saturday."

"If I can," said Quoyle. "If the aunt doesn't have major things planned for me." Kept gazing out at the bay. As if waiting for a certain ship. "There was a newsprint carrier hove to out in the bay yesterday. I was going to write about it." The sunlight fading as the clouds came on.

"Saw her out there. Heard she had some trouble."

"Fire in the engine room. Cause unknown. Diddy Shovel says that five years ago she wouldn't have put in here for mutiny or famine. But now there's the repair dock, the suppliers, the truck terminal. So they're coming in. Plans to enlarge the dockyard. He says they're talking about a shipyard."

"Ar, it wasn't always like this," said Billy Pretty. "Killick-Claw used to be a couple of rickety fish stages and twenty houses. The big harbor, up until after World War II, was at the same damn place we been talking about—Misky Bay. Ar, she was a hot place—them big warships in there, tankers, freighters, troop carriers, everything. After the war, boy, she laid right down flat on the deck. And Killick-Claw come up and give her a kick overboard. Go ahead, ask me what happened."

"What happened?"

"Ammunition. During the war Misky Bay was a ammunition-loading port. They dropped so goddamn many tons of the stuff overboard that nobody dare let down an anchor to this day in Misky Bay. The ammunition and the cables. There is a snarl of telephone and telegraph cables down at the bottom of that harbor would make you think a army of cats with a thousand balls of wool been scrabbling and hoovering around.

"Fact, that's probably when poor old Misky Bay started downhill, when the blast was put on her. You know, that'd be a good head for my towel rack story, 'Misky Bay Curse Still Wrecking Lives.' " The sun obliterated, a chop on the water, stiff breeze.

"Look at that." Billy, pointing at a tug towing a burned hulk. "Don't know what they think they're going to do with that. That must be your story from Perdition Cove. What happened, Quoyle?"

The stink of char came to them.

"Got it here," fishing in his pocket. "Course it's still rough." But he'd spent two days talking to relatives, eyewitnesses, the Coast Guard, electricians, and the propane gas dealer in Misky Bay. Read it aloud.

> GOOD-BYE, BUDDY
>
> Nobody in Perdition Cove will ever forget Tuesday morning. Many were still asleep when the first streak of sunlight painted the stern of the long-liner *Buddy*.
>
> Owner Sam Nolly stepped aboard, a new light bulb in his hand. He intended to replace a burned-out light. Before the streak of sunlight reached the wheelhouse Sam Nolly was dead and the *Buddy* was a raft of smoking toothpicks floating in the harbor.
>
> The powerful blast shattered nearly every window in Perdition Cove and was heard as far away as Misky Bay. The crew of a fishing boat off Final Point reported seeing a ball of fire roll across the water followed by a dense black cloud.
>
> Investigators blamed the explosion on leaking propane gas that accumulated forward overnight and ignited when Sam Nolly screwed in the fresh bulb.
>
> The long-liner was less than two weeks old. It was launched on Sam and Helen (Bodder) Nolly's wedding day.

"A shame," said Billy.

"Not bad," said Nutbeem. "Jack will like it. Blood, Boats and Blowups." Looked at his watch. They got up. A paper blew away, rolled along the wharf and into the water.

Billy squinted. "Saturday morning," he said to Quoyle. Eyes

like a blue crack of sky. Back to Tert Card, the cramped office. Overhead the cloud masses had merged, taken the form of fine-grained scrolls like tide marks on the sand.

After Billy and Nutbeem went in Quoyle lingered, stood in the cracked road a minute. The long horizon, the lunging, clotted sea like a swinging door opening, closing, opening.

20

Gaze Island

"The Pirate and the Jolly Boat.
A pirate, having more prisoners than he has room for, tows one boatload astern.
All knives are taken away, and the boat made fast with the bight of a doubled line. The after end of the line is ring hitched to a stern ringbolt. CLOVE HITCHES *are put around each thwart, and the line is rove through the bow ringbolt and brought to deck. They are told to escape if they can. How do they escape?"*

THE ASHLEY BOOK OF KNOTS

QUOYLE in Billy Pretty's skiff. The old man hopped aboard nimbly, set a plastic bag under the seat and yanked the rope. The engine started—*waaah*—like a trumpet. A blare of wake spilled out behind them. Billy plunged around in a plywood box, dug out a tan plastic contraption, propped it in a corner, sat down and leaned back.

"Ah. 'Tis me Back Buddy—gives the spinal column support and comfort."

There was nothing to say. Haze on the horizon. The sky a sheet of pearl, and through it filtered a diffuse yellow. The wind filled Quoyle's mouth, parted and snapped his hair.

"There's the Ram and the Lamb," said Billy, pointing at two rocks just beyond the narrows. The water swilled over them.

"I like it," said Quoyle, "that the rocks have names. There's one down off Quoyle's Point—"

"Oh, ay, the Comb."

"That's it, a jagged rock with points sticking up."

"Twelve points onto that rock. Or used to be. Was named after the old style of brimstone matches. They used to come in combs, all one piece along the bottom, twelve to a comb. You'd break one off. Sulfur stink. They called them stinkers—a comb of stinkers. Quoyle's Point got quite a few known sunkers and rocks. There's the Tea Buns, a whole plateful of little scrapers half a fathom under the water, off to the north of the Comb. Right out the end of the point there's the Komatik-Dog. You come on it just right it looks for all the world like a big sled dog settin' on the water, his head up, looking around. They used to say he was waiting for a wreck, that'd he'd come to life and swim out and swallow up the poor drowning people."

Bunny, thought Quoyle, never let her see that one.

Billy pulled his cap down against the glare. "You get together with old Nolan yet?"

"No, I think I saw him one morning out alone in an old motor dory."

"That's him. A strange one, he. Does everything the old way. Won't take unemployment. A good fisherman but lives very poor. Keeps to himself. I doubt he can read or write. He's one of your crowd, some kind of fork kin from the old days. You ought to go down to his wee house for a visit."

"I didn't think we had any relatives still living here. The aunt says they're all gone."

"She's wrong on this one. Nolan is still very much among the quick, and I hear he's got it worked up in his head that the house belongs to him."

"What house? Our house? The aunt's house on the point?"

"That's the one."

"This is a fine time to hear about it," muttered Quoyle. "Nobody's said a word to us. He could have come by, you know."

"That's not his way. You want to watch him. He's the old

style of Quoyle, stealthy in the night. They say there's a smell that comes off him like rot and cold clay. They say he slept with his wife when she was dead and you smell the desecration coming off him. No woman would have him again. Not a one."

"Jesus." Quoyle shuddered. "What do you mean, 'old style of Quoyle.' I don't know the stories."

"Better you don't. Omaloor Bay is called after Quoyles. Loonies. They was wild and inbred, half-wits and murderers. Half of them was low-minded. You should have heard Jack on the phone when he got your letter to come to the *Gammy Bird*. Called up all your references. Man with a bird's name. Told Jack you was as good as gold, didn't rave nor murder."

"Partridge," said Quoyle.

"We was on pins and needles waiting to see what come in the door. Thought you was going to be a big, wild booger. Big enough, anyway. But you know, the Quoyles only been on the Point there a hundred years or so. Went there in the 1880s or 1890s, dragging that green house miles and miles across the ice, fifty men, a crowd of Quoyles and their cunny kin pulling on the ropes. Dragged it on big runners, spruce poles made into runners. Like a big sled."

Out through the narrows and Billy set a seaward course. Quoyle had forgotten his cap again and his hair whipped. The skiff cut into the swell. He felt that nameless pleasure that comes only with a fine day on the water.

"Ar," said Billy above the motor and the sound of water rushing off the hull, "speaking of named rocks, we got 'em all along, boy, thousands and thousands of miles with wash balls and sunkers and known rocks every foot of the way. Newfoundland itself is a great rock in the sea, and the islands stribbled around it are rocks. Famous rocks like the Chain Rock and the Pancake up in St. John's, both of them above water and steep-to, and there's old terrors that they've blowed up—the Merlin and the Ruby Rock that was in St. John's narrows. A hundred years ago and more they blew them up. Up along the north shore there's Long Harry. And mad rocks with the seaweed streeling.

"I mind to Cape Bonavista there's Old Harry Rock under two fathoms and he stretches out three mile into the sea and at the far end is a cruel little rise they call Young Harry. In North Broad Cove they've Shag Rock and Hell's Rock. The shag, y'know is the cormorant, the black goose, a stinking black thing that the old people used to say built its nest with dead fish. That's what they called you if you come from Grand Banks. If you come from Fortune you were a gally, a scarecrow. Down on the Burin Peninsula." Billy Pretty tossed his head up and sang in a creaky but lilting tenor:

Fortune gally-baggers and Grand Bank shags
All stuffed into paper bags.
When them bags begin to bust
The Grand Bank shags begin to cuss.

"You heard that one? Now, to rocks again, Salvage Harbor has a big broad one they call the Baker's Loaf and on along you'll find the Cook-room Rock. Funk Islands is snaggy water, reefs and shoals and sunkers. The Cleopatra and Snap Rock. The Fogo Islands, dangerous waters for rocks where many a ship has wrecked. Born and brought up there to find your way through. And sticking out of the water is the Jigger, Old Gappy, Ireland Rock, the Barrack Rock, the Inspector who wants to inspect your bottom.

"Look there, you can see it now, Gaze Island. Been about three years since I come out here. Where I was born and brought up and lived—when I was ashore—until I was forty years old. I shipped out and worked the freighters when I was young for quite a few years. Then I was in two wrecks and thought if there was going to be another, I wanted it to be in home water. There's many of my relatives down under this water, so it's homey, in a way. I come back and fished the shore. Jack Buggit was part of my crowd, even though he come from Flour Cove. His mother was my mother's cousin. You wouldn't know it to look at us, but we're the same age. Both seventy-three. But Jack hardened and I shriveled. The government moved us off Gaze in 'sixty. But you'll see how some of them houses is standing just as straight and firm after thirty-odd years empty. Yes, they *looks* solid enough."

"Like our house down on the Point," said Quoyle. "It was in good shape, endured forty years empty."

"It endured more than that," said Billy.

Gaze Island reared from the water as sheer cliff. Half a mile from the formidable island rocks broke the surface, awash with foam.

"That's the Home Rock. We takes our bearing off it." He changed course toward the southern tip of the island.

Billy worked through an invisible maze of shoals and sunkers. The boat pointed at a red stone wall, waves smashing at its foot. Quoyle's dry mouth. They were almost in the foam. Twenty feet from the face of the cliff he still could not see the entrance. Billy headed the boat at a shadow. The sound of the engine multiplied, beat and shouted at them, echoed off the walls that rose above onyx water.

They were in a narrow tickle. Quoyle could reach out and almost touch the rock. The cliff wall opened gradually, the tickle widened, bent left, and came out into a bay enclosed by a hoop of land. Five or six buildings, a white house, a church with a crooked steeple, a slide of clapboard, old stages and tilts. Quoyle had never imagined such a secret and ruined place. Desolate, and the slyness of the hidden tickle gave the sense of a lair.

"Strange place," said Quoyle.

"Gaze Island. They used to say, over in Killick-Claw, that Gaze Islanders were known for two things—they were all fish dogs, knew how to find fish, and they knew more about volcanoes than anybody in Newfoundland."

Billy brought his boat up to the beach, cut the engine and raised it. Silence except for the drip of water from the propeller, and the skreel of gulls. Billy hawked and spat, pointed down the land curve to a building set away from the shore.

"There's our old place."

Once painted red, greyed it to a dull pink by salt weather. A section of broken fence. Billy seized his bag and jumped out of the boat, bootheels made semicircles in the sand. Secured the line to a pipe hammered into the rock. Quoyle clambered after him. The silence. Only the sound of their boots gritting and the sea murmur.

"There was five families lived here when my dad was a boy, the Prettys, the Pools, the Sops, the Pilleys, the Cusletts. Every family was married with every other family. Boy, they was kind, good people, and the likes of them are gone now. Now it's every man for himself. And woman, too."

He tried to lift a fallen section of fence from the weeds, but it broke in his hands and he only cleared away the tangle from the upright section, braced it with rocks.

They walked up to the high gaze that gave the island its name, a knoll on the edge of the cliff with a knot of spruce in one corner, all hemmed around with a low wall of stones. Quoyle, turning, could look down to the cup of harbor, could turn again, look at the open sea, at distant ships heading for Europe or Montreal. Liquid turquoise below. To the north two starched sheet icebergs. There, the smoke of Killick-Claw. Far to the east, almost invisible, a dark band like rolled gauze.

"They could see a ship far out in any direction from here. They'd put the cows up here in the summer. Never a cow in Newfoundland had a better view."

They walked over the moss and heather to a cemetery. A fence of blunt pickets enclosed crosses and wooden markers, many fallen on the ground, their letters faded by cold light. Billy Pretty knelt in the corner, tugged at wild grass. The top of the wooden marker was cut in three arcs to resemble a stone, the paint still legible:

W. Pretty
born 1897 died 1934
Through the great storms of life he did his best,
God grant him eternal rest.

"That's me poor father," said Billy Pretty. "Fifteen was I when he died." He scraped away, pulling weeds from a coffin-shaped frame that enclosed the grave. It was painted with a design of black and white diamonds, still sharp.

"Painted this up the last time I was over," said Billy, opening his bag and taking out tins of paint, two brushes, "and I'll do it again now."

Quoyle thought of his own father, wondered if the aunt still had his ashes. There had been no ceremony. Should they put up a marker? A faint sense of loss rose in him.

Suddenly he could see his father, see the trail of ground cherry husks leading from the garden around the edge of the lawn where he walked while he ate them. The man had a passion for fruit. Quoyle remembered purple-brown seckle pears the size and shape of figs, his father taking the meat off with pecking bites, the smell of fruit in their house, litter of cores and peels in the ashtrays, the grape cluster skeletons, peach stones like hens' brains on the windowsill, the glove of banana peel on the car dashboard. In the sawdust on the basement workbench galaxies of seeds and pits, cherry stones, long white date pits like spaceships. Strawberries in the refrigerator, and in June the car parked on a country road and the father on his knees picking wild strawberries in the weeds. The hollowed grapefruit skullcaps, cracked globes of tangerine peel.

Other fathers took their sons on fishing and camping trips, but Quoyle and his brother had blueberry expeditions. They whined with rage as the father disappeared into the bushes, leaving them in the sour heat holding plastic containers. One time the brother, face swollen with crying and insect bites, picked only fifteen or twenty berries. The father approached them, arms straining with the weight of two brimming pails. Then the brother began to cry, pointed at Quoyle. Said Quoyle had taken his berries. Liar. Quoyle had picked half a quart, the bottom of his pail decently covered. Got a whipping with a branch torn from a blueberry bush, with the first stroke berries raining. On the way home he stared into the berry pails watching green worms, stink bugs, ants, aphids, limping spiders come creeping up chimneys to the surface of the fruit where they beat the air and wondered. Backs of his thighs on fire.

The man spent hours in the garden. How many times, thought Quoyle, had his father leaned on his hoe and gazed down the rows of string beans, saying "Some sweet land we got here, boy." He'd thought it was the immigrant's patriotic sentiment, but now balanced it against the scoured childhood on a salt-washed rock. His father had been enchanted with deep soil. Should have been a farmer. Guessing at the dead man too late.

Billy Pretty might have heard him thinking.

"By rights," he said, "my dad should have been a farmer. He was a Home boy on his way to Ontario to be hired out to a farmer."

"Home boy?" It meant nothing to Quoyle.

"From a Home. Part orphanage, part a place where they put children if the parents couldn't keep them, or if they were running wild on the streets. England and Scotland just swept them up by the thousand and shipped them over to Canada. My father was the son of a printer in London, but it was a big family and the father died when he was only eleven. It was because he was a printer's son that he could read and write very well. His name was not Pretty then. He was born William Ankle. His mother had all the others, you see, so she put him in a Home. There used to be Homes all over the UK. Maybe there still are. The Barnardo Homes, the Sears Home, the National Children's Homes, the Fegan Home, the Church of England Bureau, the Quarrier Homes and more and more. He was in the Sears Home. They showed him pictures of boys picking big red apples in a sunny orchard, said that was Canada, wouldn't he like to go? He used to tell us how juicy those apples looked. Yes, he said.

"So, a few days later he was on this ship, the *Aramania*, on his way to Canada. This is in 1909. They gave him a little tin trunk with some clothes, a Bible, a brush and comb and a signed photograph of Reverend Sears. He told us about that trip many times. There were three hundred and fourteen children, boys and girls, on that ship, all of them signed on to help farmers. He said many of them were only three or four years old. They had no idea what was happening to them, where they were going. Just little waifs shipped abroad to a life of rural slavery. For you see, he kept in touch with some of the survivors he'd made friends with on the *Aramania*."

"Survivors of what?"

"The shipwreck, my boy, and how he came here. We spoke of the names of rocks on the way out, you'll remember, but there's other things in the sea that's a mortal danger, and they can never have names because they shift and prowl and vanish." He pointed at the icebergs on the horizon. "Remember, in 1909 they didn't have ice patrols and radar and weather faxes. You took your chance in iceberg alley. And my father's ship, like the *Titanic* only three years later, ran onto an iceberg in the bitter June twilight. Right out there, right off Gaze Island. There's no chart for icebergs. Of those three hundred and fourteen children only twenty-four were saved. Official count was twenty-three. And they were saved because young Joe Sop—that was later Skipper Joe, master of one of the last Banks fishing schooners—come up to the Gaze to get the cow and saw the lights and heard the children screeching and crying as they went into the icy water.

"He run down to the houses bawling out there was a shipwreck. Every boat in the place put out, there was two widow women pulled oars and saved three children, and they got what they could, but it was too late for most. You only last a little in that water. Freezes the blood in your veins, you go numb and die in the time it would take us to walk back to the old house.

"Weeks later another shipload of Home children on the way to Canada anchored offshore and sent in a small boat to take the survivors, to send them on to their original destination. But my father didn't want to go. He'd found a home here with the Prettys and they hid him, told the officials there was a mistake in the count of the saved—only twenty-three. Poor William Ankle was lost. And so my father changed his name to William Pretty and here he grew up and led an independent life. And if it was not happy, he didn't know it.

"If he'd gone on with the others he'd likely have gone into a miserable life. You ask me, Canada was built on the slave labor of those poor Home children, worked to the bone, treated like dirt, half starved and crazed with lonesomeness. See, my father kept in touch with three of the boys that lived, and they wrote back and forth. I've still got some of those letters—poor wretched boys whose families had cast them off, who survived a shipwreck and the freezing sea, and went on, friendless and alone, to a harsh life."

Quoyle's eyes moist, imagining his little daughters, orphaned, traveling across the cold continent to a savage farmer.

"Now, mind you, it was never easy at the Prettys', never easy on Gaze Island, but they had the cows and a bit of hay, and the berries, the fish and their potato patches, and they'd get their flour and bacon in the fall from the merchant over at Killick-Claw, and if it was hard times, they shared, they helped their neighbor. No, they didn't have any money, the sea was dangerous and men were lost, but it was a satisfying life in a way people today do not understand. There was a joinery of lives all worked together, smooth in places, or lumpy, but joined. The work and the living you did was the same things, not separated out like today.

"Father'd get those pathetic letters, sometimes six months after they was written, and he'd read them out loud here and the tears would stream down people's faces. Oh, how they wanted to get their hands on those hard Ontario farmers. There was never a one from Gaze Island that voted for confederation with Canada! My father would of wore a black armband on Confederation Day. If he'd lived that long.

"One of those boys, Lewis Thorn, never had a bed of his own, had to sleep in the musty hay, had no shoes or boots and wrapped his feet in rags. They fed him potato peels and crusts, what they'd give to the pig. They beat him every day until he was the color of a dark rainbow, yellow and red and green and blue and black. He worked from lantern light to lantern light while the farmer's children went to school and socials. His hair grew down his back, all matted with clits and tangles. He tried to trim it with a hand-sickle. You can guess how that looked. He was lousy and dirty. The worst was the way they made fun of him, scorned him because he was a Home boy, jeered and made his life hell. In the end they cheated him of his little wage and finally turned him adrift in the Ontario winter when he was thirteen. He went on to another farmer who was worse, if can be. Never, never once in the years he worked on the farms—and he slaved at it because he didn't know anything else until he was killed in an accident when he was barely twenty—never once did anyone say a kind word to him since he got off the ship in Montreal. He wrote to my father that only his letters kept him from taking his life. He had to steal the paper he wrote on. He planned to come out to Newfoundland but he died before he could.

"The other two had a miserable time of it as well. Oh I remember our dad lying on the daybed and stretching out his feet and telling us about those poor lonely boys, slaves to the cruel Canadian farmers. He'd say, 'Count your blessings that you're in a snug harbor.'

"My father taught all his children to read and write. In the winter when the fishing was over and the storms wrapped Gaze Island, my father would hold school right down there in the kitchen of the old house. Yes, every child on this island learned to read very well and write a fine hand. And if he got a bit of money he'd order books for us. I'll never forget one time, I was twelve years old and it was November, 1933. Couple of years before he died of TB. Hard, hard times. You can't imagine. The fall mail boat brought a big wooden box for my father. Nailed shut. Cruel heavy. He would not open it, saved it for Christmas. We could hardly sleep nights for thinking of that box and what it might hold. We named everything in the world except what was there. On Christmas Day we dragged that box over to the church and everybody craned their necks and gawked to see what was in it. Dad pried it open with a screech of nails and there it was, just packed with books. There must have been a hundred books there, picture books for children, a big red book on volcanoes that gripped everybody's mind the whole winter—it was a geological study, you see, and there was plenty of meat in it. The last chapter in the book was about ancient volcanic activity in Newfoundland. That was the first time anybody had ever seen the word Newfoundland in a book. It just about set us on fire—an intellectual revolution. That *this place* was in a book. See, we thought we was all alone in the world. The only dud was a cookbook. There was not one single recipe in that book that could be made with what we had in our cupboards.

"I never knew how he paid for those books or if they were a present, or what. One of the three boys he wrote to on the farms moved to Toronto when he grew up and became an elevator operator. He was the one who picked the books out and sent them. Perhaps he paid for them, too. I'll never know."

The new paint gleamed on the wood, the fresh letters black and sharp.

"Well, I wonder if I'll make it out here again upright or lying down. I'd better have my stone carved deep because there's nobody to paint me up every few years except some nephews and nieces down in St. John's."

Quoyle wondering about William Ankle. "What did it mean, what your father said about the tall, quiet woman. You said it about Wavey Prowse. Something your father used to say. A poem or a saying."

"Ar, that? Let's see. Used to say there was four women in every man's heart. The Maid in the Meadow, the Demon Lover, the Stouthearted Woman, the Tall and Quiet Woman. It was just a thing he said. I don't know what it means. I don't know where he got it."

"You were never married Billy?"

"Between you and me, I had a personal affliction and didn't want anybody to know."

Quoyle's hand to his chin.

"Half that stuff," said Billy, "that sex stuff Nutbeem and Tert Card spews out, I don't know what they mean. What there could be in it." What he knew was that women were shaped like leaves and men fell.

He pointed down the slope, away from the sea.

"Another cemetery there. An old cemetery." A plot lower down enclosed with beach rubble. They walked toward it. Straggling wildness. A few graves marked with lichened cairns, the rest lost in impenetrable tangle. Billy's brilliant eyes fixed Quoyle, waiting for something.

"I wouldn't have known it was a cemetery. It looks very old."

"Oh yes. Very old indeed. 'Tis the cemetery of the Quoyles."

Satisfied with the effect on Quoyle whose mouth hung open, head jerked back like a snake surprised by a mirror.

"They were wrackers they say, come to Gaze Island centuries ago and made it their evil lair. Pirate men and women that lured ships onto the rocks. When I was a kid we'd dig in likely places. Turn over stones, see if there was a black box below."

"Here!" Quoyle's hair bristled. The winding tickle, the hidden harbor.

"See over here, them flat rocks all laid out? That's where your house stood as was dragged away over the ice to Quoyle's Point with a wrangle-gangle mob of islanders behind them. For over the years others came and settled. Drove the Quoyles away. Though the crime that finally tipped the scales was their disinclination to attend Pentecostal services. Religion got a strong grip on Gaze Island in that time, but it didn't touch the Quoyles. So they left, took their house and left, bawling out launchin' songs as they went."

"Dear God," said Quoyle. "Does the aunt know all this?"

"Ar, she must. She never told you?"

"Quiet about the past," said Quoyle, shaking his head, thinking, no wonder.

"Truth be told," said Billy, "there was many, many people here depended on shipwracks to improve their lots. Save what lives they could and then strip the vessel bare. Seize the luxuries, butter, cheese, china plates, silver coffeepots and fine chests of drawers. There's many houses here still has treasures that come off wracked ships. And the pirates always come up from the Caribbean water to Newfoundland for their crews. A place of natural pirates and wrackers."

They walked back to the gaze for another look, Quoyle trying to imagine himself as a godless pirate spying for prey or enemy.

Billy shouted when he saw the gauzy horizon had become a great billowing wall less than a mile away, a curtain of fog rolling over maroon water.

"Get going, boy," shouted Billy, slipping and sliding down the path to the harbor beach, his paint cans knocking together. Quoyle panted after him.

The motor blatted and in a few minutes they were inside the tickle.

21

Poetic Navigation

"Fog . . . The warm water of the Gulf Stream penetrating high latitudes is productive of fog, especially in the vicinity of the Grand Banks where the cold water of the Labrador Current makes the contrast in the temperatures of adjacent waters most striking."

THE MARINER'S DICTIONARY

WHEN they came again into the maze of rocks the fog bank was two thousand yards away.

"Give us ten minutes to get clear of the rocks and the currents and take a course on Killick-Claw and we'll be all right," said Billy, steering the boat through a crooked course Quoyle could only guess at.

"These was the rocks the Quoyles lured ships onto." Shouted. Quoyle thought he felt the haul of the current sweeping along the cliffs, stared into the water as though looking for waterlogged hulks in the depths. They cut around a fissured rock that Billy called the Net-Man.

" 'Cause you'd lose something, floats or pots or a good piece of line and it was uncanny how it'd end up wrapped around the

Net-Man. Some kind of swirly current carried things onto it, I suppose, and they stuck in the clefts."

"There's something on it now," said Quoyle. "Something like a box. Hold on, Billy, it's a suitcase." Billy came around the gurgling rock, handed Quoyle a gaff hook.

"Be quick about it." The suitcase was stranded high on a rock, washed up by the now-retreating tide. It rested on a small shelf, as though someone had just set it down. Quoyle hooked the rope handle and yanked. The weight of the suitcase sent it tumbling into the sea. As it bobbed to the surface he clawed with the hook, drew it near. At last he could reach over and grip the handle. Heavy, but he got it aboard. Billy said nothing, worked the throttled boat through the sunkers.

The suitcase was black with seawater. Expensive looking but with a rope handle. There was something about it. He tried the latches but it was locked. The fog came on them, thick, blotting out everything. Even Billy in the back of the boat was faded and insubstantial. Directionless, no horizon nor sky.

"By God, Quoyle, you're a wracker! You're a real Quoyle with your gaff, there."

"It's locked. We'll have to pick it open when we get back."

"That might take a little while," said Billy. "We'll have to smell our way in. We're not out of the rocks yet. We'll just marl along until we gets clear of them."

Quoyle strained his eyes until they stung and saw nothing. Uneasiness came over him, that crawling dread of things unseen. The ghastly unknown tinctured by thoughts of pirate Quoyles. Ancestors whose filthy blood ran in his veins, who murdered the shipwrecked, drowned their unwanted brats, fought and howled, beards braided in spikes with burning candles jammed into their hair. Pointed sticks, hardened in the fire.

A rock loomed on the starboard bow, a great tower in twisting vapor.

"Ah, just right. 'Tis the Home Rock. Now we're on a straight run. We'll smell Killick-Claw's smoke pretty soon and sniff along in."

"Billy, we saw the Home Rock on the way to the island. It was just a low rock barely a foot out of the water. This thing is enormous. It can't be the same rock."

"Yes, it is. She sticks up a little more now because tide's going out, and she's in the fog. It's fog-loom makes it look big to you. It's an optical illusion, is the old fog-loom. Makes a dory look like an oil tanker."

The boat muttered through the blind white. Quoyle clenched the gunwales and despaired. Billy said he could smell the chimneys of Killick-Claw, fifteen miles across the water, and something else, something rotten and foul.

"I don't like that stink. Like a whale washed up on a beach the third week of hot weather. It seems to get stronger as we go. Maybe there is a dead whale floating along in the fog. You listen for the bell buoy that marks the Ram and the Lamb. We could easy miss the entrance in this fog."

After nearly an hour Billy said he heard the rut of the shore, the waves breaking on stone, and then a pair of needle-shaped rocks rose in the gloom of fog and encroaching night.

"Whoa," said Billy Pretty. "That's the Knitting Pins. We're east of Killick-Claw by a bit. But not far from Desperate Cove. What do y'think, put in there and wait until the fog lifts before heading back up the coast? Oh, there used to be a good little restaurant in Desperate Cove. Let's see now if I can remember how to get in. I never come in here by water since I was a boy."

"For God's sake, Billy, this water is full of rocks." Another foaming mass of black reared from the fog. But Billy knew his way by a rhyme pulled from the old days when poor men sailed by memory, without charts, compass or lights.

When the Knitting Pins you is abreast,
Desperate Cove bears due west.
Behind the Pins you must steer
'Til The Old Man's Shoe does appear.
The tickle lies just past the toe,
It's narrow, you must slowly go.

The old man brought the boat around behind the Knitting Pins and felt his way along current and sucking tide.

"There's a dozen tricks to find your way—listen for the rut of the shore, call out and hear the echo off the cliffs, feel the run of current beneath you—or smell the different flavors of the coves. Me dad could name a hundred miles of coast by the taste of air."

A hump of rock, the sound of licking water, then a slow putter along a breaking ridge of rock. In amazement Quoyle heard a car door slam, heard the engine start and the vehicle drive away. He could see nothing. But in a minute a glow on a stagehead showed and Billy brought the boat up, climbed out and slipped a mooring line over a bollard.

"That stink," he said, "is coming from the suitcase."

"It's probably the leather," said Quoyle. "Starting to rot. How far to the restaurant? I don't want to leave it here."

"The place was right across the road. The tourists come in the summer with their cameras, you know, ar, they'll sit here all day long and watch the water. It's like it's a strange animal, they can't take their eyes off it."

"You'd know why if you came from Sudbury or New Jersey," said Quoyle.

"Here. It's here. I can smell cooking oil stronger than the stink of that suitcase. You leave that suitcase outside."

There were no customers, the waitress and the cook sitting companionably at one of the tables, both tatting lace doilies. A smell of bread, the daily baking for the next day.

"Girl, we're that starved," said Billy.

"Skipper Billy! Give me a start coming in out of the fog that way."

The cook put her tatting aside and stood next to the chalkboard.

"That's all there is now," she said, erasing COD CHEEKS, erasing SHRIMP DINNER. "There's fried squid, m'dear and meatballs. You know that moose Railey got, Skipper Billy? Well, we ground up so much of it like hamburger, you know, and I was wantin' to get the freezer emptied out so I made it up in meatballs this morning in a gravy. It come out good. Mashed potato?" All vertical lines, her face riven, the dark pleats of her skirt.

Billy telephoned Tert Card, leaned against the wall with a toothpick in his teeth.

"Me and Quoyle is down to Desperate Cove, fogbound. I'm going to leave my boat here if you can get us a ride back to Killick-Claw. He's got his car over there and I left my truck down the wharf. Yeah. I'll get it tomorrow. Wracker Quoyle here picked a valise off the Net-Man. We don't know. It's locked. Fog's that thick, so you go easy. There's no hurry. We're eating dinner over here. Yep. No, she made Railey's moose up into meatballs. Ar, I'll tell her."

Quoyle had the squid and a side dish of onion hash. The squid were stuffed with tiny pink shrimp, laid on a bed of sea parsley. Billy worked at his platter of meatballs. The waitress brought them hot rolls with butter and partridgeberry jam.

The cook stuck her long face out of the kitchen.

"I made a old-fashioned figgy duff for Railey, Skipper Billy. There's quite a bit of it on hand. P'raps you'd like to refresh your mouth with some?"

"I would. And Tert Card is comin' down to pick us up. He wants an order of the meatballs to go if you got enough."

So, a dish of figgy duff with a drop of rum sauce, and coffee.

"I'm going to open that suitcase," said Quoyle.

"Wracker Quoyle, that's all you can think of, that bloody suitcase. Go ahead and open it. Pick it open with a fork tine or bash it with a rock. And I hope it's crammed with prizes from the treasure troves of Gaze Island." Billy held his finger up for more tea.

Quoyle dragged the suitcase under the single wharf light. He found a piece of pipe and jabbed the lock. The pipe clinked against the brass. The lock held. Quoyle looked around for something to pry, a screwdriver or chisel, but there was nothing but stone and broken glass. In frustration he raised the pipe over his shoulder and swung as hard as he could at the lock. A metallic crack and, with a frightful wave of stench, the suitcase sprang open.

Under the light he saw the ruined eye, the flattened face and blood-stiff mustache of Bayonet Melville on a bed of seaweed. The gelatinous horror slid out onto the wharf.

22

Dogs and Cats

"The mesh knot is the ordinary way of tying the SHEET BEND *when it is made with a netting needle."*

THE ASHLEY BOOK OF KNOTS

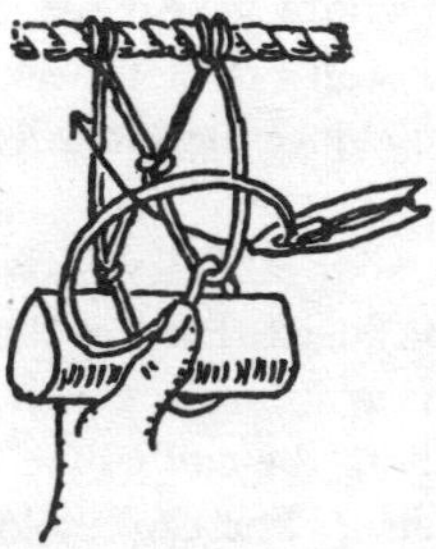

"AGNIS have a manly heart, Agnis do," said Mavis Bangs to Dawn when the aunt went off with her measuring tapes and notebook. "A boldish air, she grasp on things like a man do. That's from living in the States. All the women down there is boldish. See how she was calm? When the nephew was all jelly? Finding that head. She said he couldn't drive for two days he was that shocked. I was shocked myself. What with the Mounties coming in and asking. Questions and questions. Poor Agnis.

"There's the other thing, too. She's a Hamm, but she's a Quoyle. The stories, m'dear. Omond—that was my poor husband—knew them. He come from No Name Cove down the bay from Capsize Cove, that are but one cove from Quoyle's Point. And that little maid they got is a real Quoyle, tilted like a buoy in a raging sea."

Dawn barely heard her. Every time Agnis Hamm's truck pulled away Dawn was at the electronic typewriter. Stayed late some evenings to get at it. Letter after letter.

> Dear Sirs: I am writing to inquire about the position of Auto Sales with your firm. Although my experience is in shipping traffic . . .

> Dear Sirs: I am writing in response to your ad for a Spanish-speaking clerk. Although I do not speak Spanish I have a B.E. in Maritime Traffic Engineering and will relocate. I enclose . . .

Mavis Bangs kept talking. "Tell you a woman that fished alongside her man was Mrs. Buggit. Put the babies with her sister and out they'd go. She was as strong as a man they said. Mrs. Buggit don't go out now, only to the clothesline. She suffers from stress incontinence, they calls it. She can't hold her water. When she stands up or laughs or coughs or whatever. A problem. They was trying to get her to do some exercises, you know, stop and go, stop and go, she said it didn't make a bit of difference except they noticed the dog would stand in front of the bathroom door when she was in there and act real concerned. She was took bad, you know, when they lost the oldest boy. Jesson. Just like Jack, he was. Stubborn! Couldn't tell him a thing. What do you think, Dawn, you think it was Mrs. Melville done it? Whose fancy blue leather we all stitched up? Cut off his head? Agnis's nephew says they was at one another like dogs and cats. Quarreling. And drunk. A woman drunk! And how they went off in the night and didn't pay Agnis for the work we done? Of course, now it looks like it was *she* went off in the night and didn't pay. But to cut a feller's head off and put it in a suitcase! They say she had to have help, a weak old woman like that."

"I don't know," said Dawn. The typewriter had a repeat setting. All she had to do was change the name of the addressee and the position and it spit another letter out.

Dear Sirs: I recently saw your advertisement in *The Globe and Mail* for a research assistant. Although I do not speak Japanese I am willing to learn . . .

Dear Sirs: I recently saw your advertisement in *The Globe and Mail* for a floral designer. Although I do not arrange flowers I am willing to learn . . .

Dear Sirs: I recently saw your advertisement in *The Globe and Mail* for a position in brokerage operations. Although my training is in marine traffic control I am willing to learn . . .

"It's these wicked people coming in. Nothing is like it was. Such ugly things never happened here. We had some good ways in the old times. They may laugh at them now, but they come out true more often than not. One I will never forget, hardly a girl knows it now, because they don't make mats any more, but when there was a new mat made, you know, the girls, the young girls would get a cat, see, and they'd put the cat on the new mat, then fold up the sides and hold it in there. There was always a cat. Newfoundlanders like their cats. Then they'd unfold it, and whoever the cat came to, why she was the next one to be married. Now that was as true as the sun rises."

The goal was twenty-five letters a week, every week. Out of them a reply must come.

Dear Sirs: I recently saw your advertisement for a dog groomer. Although my training is in marine traffic control I am willing to relocate . . .

"My sister worked on a mat all winter, a pattern of roses and codfish on a blue background. Pretty. There I was, fourteen years old. There was five girls there. Liz, that was my sister, and Kate and Jen and the two Marys. They done the cat up in the mat when it was finished. And you know that cat comes straight to me and jumps in my lap. And strange to say, but I was the next one married. Liz was dead of TB before the summer. Kate never married. Mary Genge went to Boston with her folks, and the other Mary I don't know. But I married Thomas Munn. On my fifteenth birthday. As was lost at sea in 1957. A beauty of a man. The black hair. You'd feel like a puff of heat when he'd come in a room. I wasted away with crying. I was down to eighty-seven pounds. They didn't think I would live. But somehow I did. And married Desmond Bangs. Until he went in the air crash. Up in Labrador. I says, 'I'll never marry again, for I can't stand the grief.' Not like some as cuts their husbands' heads off and puts 'em in satchels."

Five more and she would have enough for this week. She'd take anything at first, anything just to get away and out. Not to hear Mavis Bangs. To see something besides fishing boats and rock and water!

I am writing to inquire about the position of visual display person. Although my training is in marine traffic control and upholstery I am willing to learn . . .

"You know, all of us girls was good at the needlework. Liz, of course, making the mats, she was a well-known mat maker. Our mam kept sheep for the wool. I can see her now after supper spinning the wool or knitting. Always knitted after dinner. I can see her now, setting there working a pair of thumbies with her wooden skivers clacking away. Said the wool handled easier at night, was lax because the sheep was lying down, see. Taking their sleep. That old spinning wheel come down to me. Worth a fortune. I used to have it out on the lawn. Des painted it up red and yellow, it was a fine ornament. But we'd have to take it in at night, afraid a tourist would steal it. They do that, you know. They'll take a spinning wheel right out of your yard. I know a woman it happened to. Mrs. Trevor Higgend, goes to my church. What do you think about the nephew, Dawn? You ate supper at their house. Finding a thing like that. You wouldn't want a man who finds what he found, would you? Nothing good ever happened with a Quoyle."

"Never." The keys rattled. The last one for this week. There could be replies in her mailbox right now.

I wish to inquire about the position of architectural draughtsperson. Although my training is in marine traffic control I am willing to relocate and retrain for a career in architectural draughting . . .

Quoyle and Wavey side by side, feeling sympathy for each other, Herry breathing down their necks. The car moaned up the hill through the rain, away from the school. They came over the crest. On Quoyle's side the ocean, bruise grey under the strained wet light.

Gushing through yellow rain. A row of mailboxes, some fashioned as houses with painted windows. Four ducks swayed along the muddy ruts. Quoyle slowed to a crawl behind them until they dodged into the ditch. Past the *Gammy Bird* office, past Buggits' house and on. The square houses painted in marvelous stripes, brave against the rock.

Wavey's little house was mint green on the ground floor, then a red sash. The boy's scarlet pajamas on the clothesline, bright as chile peppers. A pile of tapered logs, sawbuck in a litter of chips and bark, split junks of wood ready to be stacked.

Two fishermen beside the road, lean and hard as rifles, mending net in the rain, the wet beading their sweaters. Sharp Irish noses, long Irish necks and hair crimped under billed caps. One looked up, his glance sprang from Wavey to Quoyle, searching his face, knowing him. Netting needle in his hand.

"Uncle Kenny there," said Wavey to the boy in her low, plangent voice.

"Dawk," cried the child.

There was a new dog in Archie Sparks's yard, a blue poodle among the plywood swans.

"Dawk."

"Yes, a new dog," said Wavey. A wooden dog with a rope tail and a tin-can necklace. Mounted on a stick. Eye like a boil.

In the rearview mirror he saw Wavey's brother coming along the road toward them. The other man watched from a distance, held the net, his hands stilled.

Wavey pulled Herry out of the car. He put his face up to the mist, closed his eyes, feeling the droplets touch him like the ends of cold fine hairs. She pulled him toward the door.

Quoyle held out his hand to the advancing man as he might to an unknown dog stalking toward him.

"Quoyle," he said, and the name sounded like an evasion. The fisherman clamped his hand briefly.

Face like Wavey's lean face, but rougher. A young man smelling of fish and rain. The scrawn of muscle built to last into the ninth decade.

"Giving Wavey a ride home, then?"

"Yes." His soft hand embarrassed him. A curtain moved in the window of the house behind the rioting wooden zoo.

"There's Dad, then, peeping," said Ken. "You'll come in and have a cup of tea."

"No. No," said Quoyle. "Got to get back to work. Gave Wavey a ride."

"Walking keeps you smart. You're the one found the suitcase with the head in it. Would of turned me stomach. You're on the point across," jerked his chin. "Dad sees you over there through his glass on fine days. Got a new roof on the old house?"

Quoyle nodded, got back in his car. But his colorless eyes were warm.

"Going back? I'll take a ride as far as me net," said Ken, striding around the nose of the car and thumping into Wavey's seat.

Quoyle backed and turned. Wavey was gone, disappeared into her house.

"You come along any time and see her," said Ken. "It's too bad about the boy, but he's a good little bugger, poor little hangashore."

"Dear Sirs," wrote Dawn. "I would like to apply . . ."

23
Maleficium

"The mysterious power that is supposed to reside in knots . . . can be injurious as well as beneficial."

QUIPUS AND WITCHES' KNOTS

QUOYLE painted. But no matter what they did to the house, he thought, it kept its gaunt look, never altered from that first looming vision behind the scrim of fog. How had it looked, new and raw on Gaze Island, or sliding over the cracking ice? The idea fixed in him that the journey had twisted the house out of true, wrenched the timbers into a rare geometry. And he was still shuddering over the white-haired man's stiff eye which had sent its dull glare at him.

The aunt's interest in fixing up slowed, veered to something private in her own room where she lay on the bed staring at the ceiling for as long as an hour. Or got up with a yawn, a short laugh, said, Well, let's see now. Coming back from wherever she'd been.

Weekends came to this: the aunt in her room or stirring something or out for a walk. Quoyle hacking his path to the sea, the children squatting in the moss to watch insects toil up stems. Or he split wood against future cold. Thought of Partridge, fired up to cook new dishes and let the children dabble their fingers in mixes and slops, and sometimes let Bunny use the paring knife. While he hovered.

In late August a bowl of cleaned squid stood on the kitchen shelf. Quoyle's intention: calamari linguine when he was done with the painting. Because he owed Partridge a letter. The aunt declared a salad despite fainting lettuce and pale hothouse tomatoes.

"We could have put in a little garden," she said. "Raised our own salads at least. The stuff at the markets is not fit to eat. Celery brown with rot, lettuce looks like it's been boiled."

"Wavey," said Quoyle, "Wavey says Alexanders is better than spinach. You can pick it all along the shore here."

"Never heard of it," said the aunt. "I'm not one for wild plants."

"It's like wild sea parsley," said Quoyle. "I might put some in the calamari sauce."

"Yes," said the aunt. "You try it. Whatever it is." But went to scout a suitable garden patch among the rocks. Not too late to sow lettuce seed. Thinking a glass house would be a good thing.

The day was warm, wind skittering over the bay, wrinkling the water in cat's-paws. The aunt getting the melancholy odor of turned soil. Quoyle smelled paint to the point of headache.

"Someone coming," the aunt said, leaning on the spade. "Walking on the road."

Quoyle looked, but there was no one.

"Where?"

"Just past the spruce with the broken branch. Broken by the bulldozer, I might add."

They stared down the driveway in the direction of the glove factory, the road.

"I did see somebody," said the aunt. "I could see his cap and his shoulders. Some fellow."

Quoyle went back to his paint pot but the aunt looked and finally drove the shovel into the soil to stand by itself, walked toward the spruce. There was no one. But saw footprints of fishing boots angling away into the tuck—moose path she thought that descended to a wild marsh of tea-colored water and leathery shrubs.

She sucked in her breath, looked for dog tracks along the edge of the road. And was not sure.

"It's the old man," said Quoyle. "Got to be."

"What old man?"

"Billy Pretty says he's 'fork kin' of the Quoyles. Says he's a rough old boy. Wouldn't leave Capsize Cove in the resettlement. Stayed on alone. Billy thinks he might have his back up a little because we're in the house. I told you this."

"No, you didn't, Nephew. And who in the world might he be?"

"I remember telling you about it."

The aunt wondered cautiously what the name was.

"I don't know. One of the old Quoyles. I can't remember his name. Something Irish."

"I don't believe it. There's none of 'em left. You know, there was Quoyles didn't have a very good name," said the aunt. Head turned away.

"Heard that," said Quoyle. "Heard Omaloor Bay is called after the Quoyles—like Half-Wit Pond or Six Fingers Harbor or Apricot Ear Brook named for certain other unfortunates. Billy told me how they came here from Gaze Island. Supposed to have dragged the house over the ice."

"So they say. Half those stories are a pack of lies. I imagine the Quoyles was as decent as anybody. And I'm sure I don't know who that fellow you're talking about could be."

Quoyle cleaned his hands of paint, called "Who wants to walk along the shore with me and pick Alexanders?"

Sunshine found two wild strawberries. Bunny threw bigger and bigger stones in the waves; the gouts of water ever closer until a splash doused her.

"All right, all right, let's go back to the house. Bunny can change her britches and Sunshine can wash the Alexanders and I will sauté the garlic and onions."

But when the sauce was nearly done, discovered there was no

linguine, only a package of egg noodles shaped like bows, soft stuff that mounded under the sauce and sent the squid rings sliding to the rims of the plates.

"You've got to plan ahead, Nephew."

Just before dawn again. Something woke him. The bare room rose above him, grey and cool. He listened to hear if Bunny was calling or crying but heard only silence.

A circle sped across the ceiling, disappeared. Flashlight beam.

He got up, went to the seaward window, the husks of flies cracking under his bare feet. Knelt to one side and peered into the diming night. For a long time he saw nothing. His pupils enlarged in the dark, he saw the sky rinsing with the nacre sheen of approaching light. The sea emerged as a silver negative. Far down in the wiry tuck he saw a spark restlessly twitching, and soon it was gone from his sight.

"We ought to go down there," Quoyle said. "Look the old man up."

"I'm sure I don't want to go ferret out some old fourth cousin with a grudge. We've got along this far very well, and it would be better to leave things alone."

Quoyle wanted to go. "We'd take the girls, they'd soften an ogre's heart."

Or more likely, harden it, thought the aunt.

"Come on, Aunt." He urged.

But she was cool. "I've thought about it, wondering who it could be. There was a crowd of my mother's cousins in Capsize Cove, but they were her age if not older, grown adults with children, grandchildren of their own when I was a teenager. So if it's one of them, must be in the late eighties or nineties, probably senile as well. I'd guess the one on the road was somebody from town, maybe walking or hunting, didn't know we were here."

Quoyle said nothing of the flashlight. But coaxed her a little.

"Come on, we'll take a ride down to where the road branches, and walk in. I'd like to see Capsize Cove. The deserted village. Out with Billy that day on Gaze Island—it was sad. Those empty houses, and standing there and hearing about the old Quoyles."

"I never went out to Gaze Island and can't say I feel like I've missed much. Depressing, those old places. I can't think why the government left the houses standing. They should have burned them all."

Quoyle thought of a thousand settlements afire in the wind, flaming shingles flying over the rocks to scale, hissing, into the sea.

In the end they did not go.

24

Berry Picking

"The difference between the CLOVE HITCH *and* TWO HALF HITCHES *is exceedingly vague in the minds of many, the reason being that the two have the same knot form; but one is tied around another object, the other around its own standing part."*

THE ASHLEY BOOK OF KNOTS

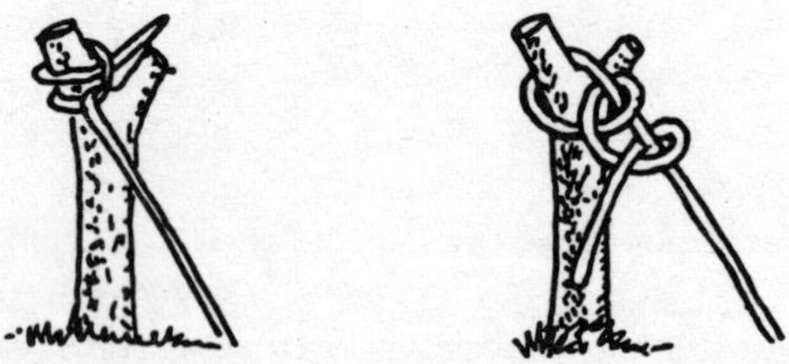

SEPTEMBER, month of shortening days and chilling waters. Quoyle took Bunny to the first day of school. New shoes, a plaid skirt and white blouse. Her hands clammy. Afraid, but refused his company and went through the pushing rowdies by herself. Quoyle watched her stand alone, her head barely moving as she looked for her friend, Marty Buggit.

At three o'clock he was waiting outside.

"How did it go?" Expected to hear what he had felt thirty years before—shunned, miserable.

"It was fun. Look." She showed a piece of paper with large imperfect letters:

BUИ
Y

"You wrote your name," said Quoyle, relieved. Baffled that she was so different than he.

"Yes." As though she'd always done so. "And the teacher says bring a box of tissues tomorrow because the school can't afford any."

Blunt fogbows in the morning trip around the bay. Humps of color followed squalls, Billy Pretty babbled of lunar halos. Storms blew in and out. Sudden sleet changed to glowing violet rods, collapsed in rain. Two, three days of heat as though blown from a desert. Fibres of light crawling down the bay like luminous eels.

On the headlands and in the bogs berries ripened in billions, wild currants, gooseberries, ground hurts, cranberries, marshberries, partridgeberries, squashberries, late wild strawberries, crowberries, cloudy bakeapples stiff above maroon leaves.

"Let's go berrying this weekend," said the aunt. "Just over a ways was well-known berrying grounds when I was young. We'll make jam, after. Berrying is pleasure to all. Maybe you'll want to bring Wavey Prowse?"

"That's an idea," said Quoyle.

She said she would be glad—as if he'd invited her to a party.

"Ken will bring me across—wants to see your new roof."

Ken looked less at the roof than at Quoyle and his daughters; joked with the aunt. Gave Herry a good-bye touch on the shoulder. "Well, I'm off. Business in Misky Bay, so might's well go around the point. Shall I come along later, then?" Eyes like a thornbush, stabbing everything at once. In a hurry to get it all.

"All right," said Wavey. "Thank you, boy." Her berry pails had rope handles finished in useful knots.

The aunt, the little girls, Quoyle, Wavey and Herry walked overland to the berry grounds beyond the glove factory, their pails and buckets rattling, clatter of stones on the path, Sunshine saying, Carry me. The sun laid topaz wash over barrens. Ultramarine sky. The sea flickered.

Wavey in toast-colored stockings, a skirt with mended seams. Quoyle wore his plaid shirt, rather tight.

"People used to come here for miles with their berry boxes and buckets," said the aunt over her shoulder. "They'd sell the berries, you see, in those days."

"Still do," Wavey said. "Agnis girl, last fall they paid ninety dollars a gallon for bakeapples. My father made a thousand dollars on his berries last year. City people want them. And there's some still makes berry ocky if they can get the partridge berries."

"Berry ocky! There was an awful drink," said the aunt. "We'll see what we get," and looked sidewise at Wavey, taking in the rough hands and cracked shoes, Herry's face like a saucer of skim milk. But a pretty boy, they said, with his father's beauty only a little distorted. As though malleable features had been pressed with a firm hand.

The sea glowed, transparent with light. Wavey and Quoyle picked near each other. Her hard fingers worked through the tufted plants, the finger and thumb gathering two, seven, rolling them back into the cupped palm, then dropping them into the pail, a small sound as the berries fell. Walked on her knees. A bitter, crushed fragrance. Quoyle blew chaff away. A hundred feet away Herry and Sunshine and Bunny, rolling like dogs on the cushiony ground. The aunt roved, her white kerchief shrank to a dot. As the pickers spread out they disappeared briefly in hollows or behind rises. The sea hissed.

The aunt called to Quoyle. "Yoo-hoo. Forgot the lunch basket. Back by the glove factory. You get it, I'll watch the children."

"Come with me," said Quoyle to Wavey. Urgent. She looked away at Herry.

"They're playing. Come on. We'll go along the shore. It will be faster walking on the stones than going through the tuckamore. We'll be back in twenty minutes."

"All right."

And she was away on her strong legs, Quoyle stumbling after, running to catch up. The ocean twitched like a vast cloth spread over snakes.

Quoyle swung the basket, walked along the shore past broken bladder wrack, knot wrack, horn wrack and dead-man's-fingers, green sausageweed and coralweed, mats of dulse and in their thousands, crushed clumps of bristly bryozoan, long brown rips of kelp, a blackening coastal string looped by the last week's storm.

Wavey climbed and sprang along the rocks, kicked through the heaped wrack. Quoyle picking his way more slowly, beer bottles clinking in the basket.

"Look," he said. At the mouth of the bay a double-towered iceberg.

"It's tilting."

Wavey stood on a rock, curled her fingers and raised her fists to her eyes as though they were binoculars. The ice mass leaned as though to admire its reflection in the waves, leaned until the southern tower was at the angle of a pencil in a writing hand, the northern tower reared over it like a lover. Soundlessly the distant towers came together, plunged under the water. A fountain of displaced water.

Quoyle below the rock. Suddenly he clasped his hands around her ankles. She felt the heat of his hands through her brown stockings, did not move. Prisoner on the rock. Looked down. Quoyle's face was pressed against her legs. She could see white scalp through snarled reddish hair, fingers curved firm around her ankles hiding her shoes except the pointed toes, the leather perforated in an ornate curl like a Victorian mustache, his heavy wrists and beyond them the sweater cuffs, a bit of broken shell caught in the wool, dog's hair on the sleeves. She did not move. There was a sense of a curtain, of a hand on the rope that could pull it open. Quoyle inhaled the scent of cotton stockings, a salt and seaweed female smell that made him reckless. His fingers unfurled, the hands drew back. She felt the absence. Quoyle staring hard at her. "Come down. Come down." He held out his arms. No mistaking what he meant. Transfixed, she hardly breathed. One flicker of movement and he'd be all over her, pulling her clothes up, wrenching the brown stockings and pressing her down on the stones with the shore flies crawling on bare skin, Quoyle, entering her, ramming his great chin into the side of her neck. And afterwards some silent agreement, some sore complicity, betrayal. She burst out.

"Do you know how he died? My husband? Herold Prowse? I'll tell you. He's in the sea. He's down at the bottom. I never come beside the sea without thinking—'Herold's *there*.' Old Billy tell you about it, did he?"

She slid down the rock, safe now, protected by grief. Quoyle stood away, hands dangling, looking at her. The words gushed.

"Herold was a roustabout on the *Sevenseas Hector*. First decent job he ever had. Wonderful money, steady work. Everything coming fine for us. Biggest, safest oil rig in the world. Three weeks off, three weeks on. He was out on it when it went over. The telephone. Early in the morning. January 29, 1981. I was up and dressed, but lay down again because I felt so bad. I was carrying Herry. A lady's voice come on the phone and she says, she says to me, 'Oh Mrs. Prowse. We have to inform you that they are reporting the *Sevenseas Hector* went over in the storm and the men are considered missing.' Went over in the storm, she said. At first they claimed it was because the storm was so bad.

"But there was other oil rigs out there only a dozen miles away and they stayed up. *Sevenseas Ajax* and *Deep Blue 12*. They didn't have any trouble. Storms like that one comes along every winter. It wasn't a century storm, comes along once every hundred years. Ninety-seven men missing, and not a single body did they ever recover. They saw some of them in a sinking lifeboat, the seas breaking over them and then they was gone.

"It come out little by little. Like a nightmare that gets worse and you can't wake up. The government didn't have any safety rules for these things. The design of the rig was bad. Nobody on the rig knew who was in charge. Was it the tool pusher or the master? Most of the men on board didn't know nothing about the sea. Geologists and cementers, derrickmen, mud watchers, drillers, welders and fitters, they was after the oil, no attention to the water or weather. Didn't even understand the weather reports that come to them. Didn't know enough to close the deadlights when the seas worked up. The glass in the ballast room portlight was weak. The control panel shorted out if water got in it. A sea broke the portlight, come in and drenched the control panel. They wasn't properly trained. No operation manuals. So when the panel went out and they tried to adjust the ballast by hand with some little brass rods they got it all wong, did it backwards, they sent it into a tilt. Just like that iceberg. Over it went. And the lifeboats wasn't any good, and most of the men never made it to the boats because the public address system went out when the control panel failed. The lawyer said it was falling dominoes.

"So, not to hurt your feelings, but that's how it is. I was thinking of it watching that iceberg go down. I think of it every single time I'm at the edge of the water, I look along the shore, half afraid, half hoping that I'll see Herold's drowned body in the seaweed. Though it's years, now."

Quoyle listened. Would he have to bring her to the prairies? And what of Petal's essence riding under his skin like an injected vaccine against the plague of love? What was the point of touching Wavey's dry hand?

They came up the path and onto the barrens, looked toward the pale dot that was the aunt's kerchief, the jumping children like fleas.

Quoyle behind her. Without looking Wavey knew exactly where he was.

Warmth, deep sky, the silence except for their children's far voices. Then, sharply, as a headache can suddenly stop, something yielded, long griefs eased. She turned. Quoyle was so close. She started to say something. Her freckled, rough skin flushed. She fell, or he pulled her down. They rolled over the massed cushions of berry plants, clinging, they rolled, hot arms and legs, berries and leaves, mouths and tears and stupid words.

But when the sea heaved below she heard it, thought of Herold's handsome bones tangled in ghost nets. And shoved Quoyle away. Was up and running toward the aunt, the girls and poor fatherless Herry, the picnic basket bumping against her legs. If Quoyle wanted anything at all he must follow.

Wavey ran to get away, then for the sake of running, and at last because there was nothing else to do. It would look undecided to change her pace, as though she did not know what she wanted. It seemed always that she had to keep on performing pointless acts.

Quoyle lay in the heather and stared after her, watching the folds of her blue skirt erased by the gathering distance. The aunt, the children, Wavey. He pressed his groin against the barrens as if he were in union with the earth. His aroused senses imbued the far scene with enormous importance. The small figures against the vast rock with the sea beyond. All the complex wires of life were stripped out and he could see the structure of life. Nothing but rock and sea, the tiny figures of humans and animals against them for a brief time.

The sharpness of his gaze pierced the past. He saw generations like migrating birds, the bay flecked with ghost sails, the deserted settlements vigorous again, and in the abyss nets spangled with scales. Saw the Quoyles rinsed of evil by the passage of time. He imagined the aunt buried and gone, himself old, Wavey stooped with age, his daughters in faraway lives, Herry still delighted by wooden dogs and colored threads, a grizzled Herry who would sleep in a north room at the top of the house or in the little room under the stairs.

A sense of purity renewed, a sense of events in trembling balance flooded him.

Everything, everything seemed encrusted with portent.

25
Oil

"If there is a vibration from the outside that tilts all your pictures askew, hang them from a single wire which passes through both screw eyes and makes fast to two picture hooks."

THE ASHLEY BOOK OF KNOTS

THE BAY crawled with whitecaps like maggots seething in a broad wound. A rough morning. Quoyle jumped down the steps. He would drive. But walked first down to the dock to look at the water. The boat charged against the tire bumpers. The waves pouring onshore had a thick look to them, a kind of moody rage. Looked at his watch. If he stepped on it there was enough time for a cup of tea and a plate of toast at the Bawk's Nest. Clean up the oil piece then down to Misky Bay to the marine archives. Check boats in the harbor. Supposed to be a schooner there from the West Coast.

Sat at the counter dunking toast into the mug. A folded slice at a time into his maw.

"Quoyle! Quoyle, come back here." Billy Pretty and Tert Card were in a booth at the back, plates and cups spread over the Formica table, Tert Card's cigarette ends stubbed out in his saucer.

"Well, look what the cat dragged in," said Card, giving off whiffs of irritation as strong as after-shave lotion. He was suffering from canker sores in his mouth although he wore knot charms against them. They came with winter. They came when he accidentally bit the inside of his mouth while chewing a bit of boiled pork. He had pulled down his lip that morning and peered into the mirror, revolted by the white rims of three sores like infected punctures. Daubed on a clot of baking soda. No pickles, no black coffee for a few days. And now leaned over a cup of milky tea.

Quoyle ordered more toast. Double grape jelly. Wondered if he should get fried potatoes.

"All we need's Nutbeem and we won't have to go to work." Billy minced his egg into fish hash.

"Like I say, the hope of this place," Tert Card, digging at wax in his ear with the nail of his little finger, "is oil. When they discovered the McGonigle field in 1980 I bought stock, indeed I did. A golden flood is ahead when she starts producing. The petrodollars. Oh, my boy, when the ship comes in I'll be away to Florida."

"The McGonigle?" asked Quoyle.

"Can't believe you're ignorant that they discovered the largest oil reserve in Canada right off our shores, out under the Grand Banks, billions and billions of barrels of oil. That's the McGonigle oil field. We're all going to be rich. Jobs all over the place, dividends for stockholders, manufacturing, housing and supplies. The biggest development project in the country. It's to be golden days."

In the booth in front of them a scrawny man with a mustache like a bar code glanced over his shoulder at Card. Quoyle thought he might be one of the supervisors at the fish plant. He was eating oatmeal with a side dish of bologna.

Billy Pretty snorted. "The only ones getting the jobs and the economic benefits is down to St. John's, I thank you. You watch, by the time they're ready to start pumping the oil out, they'll have the nuclear fusion worked out, make all the clean electricity anybody could ever want out of plain water. Newfoundland will be spiked again."

Quoyle passed a triangle of toast spread with plenty of grape jelly to Billy. How frail the old man looked, he thought, in close quarters with rumpy Tert Card.

"No, boy, they'll never get that fusion going. It's oil. Newfoundland is going to be the richest place in the world. It's a new era. We'll be rolling in money."

Billy Pretty turned to Quoyle. "This is the oil hysteria you're hearing." Then back to Tert Card. "What you'll have is the international oil companies skimming the cream off the pot. How much is going to trickle down to the outports? It's outsiders will get the gold. There's drugs and crime here now, and prostitutes waggling their red behinds, and it's only started. Vandalism, stealing and smashing."

"That's right," said the fish plant supervisor, his oatmeal eaten, the bologna swallowed, puffing the first cigarette and ready to expand. "Look how they burned down the old lighthouse right here in Killick-Claw. Look how they smashed up Fisheries office."

"And," said Billy, swiveling to include his ally, "alcoholism, moral degradation of the lowest kind. Divorce and cruelty and abandoned children moping along the roadside. Pollution! The sea bottom strewn with clits of wires and barrels and broken metal that'll tear up any trawl. And to come? Terrible oil spills will kill off the few midget cod that's left, destroy the fishery entirely, scum the landwash with a black stinking ooze, ruin boats and harbors. The shipping lanes will be clogged with the oil tankers and supply boats." Trembled a dribble of tea into his cup.

"He's away and gone," mocked Tert Card, examining the black knob of wax on his nail. "He's seen the Nile."

Billy Pretty cast his eyes at Quoyle and the fish plant man, opened his mouth to say what he had to say.

Beside him Tert Card swayed, pantomimed playing a violin.

"I'll have an order of fried potatoes and bologna," said Quoyle to the waitress. Billy sucked in a breath.

"I seen the cod and caplin go from millions of tons taken to two or three bucketsful. Seen fishing go from seasonal, inshore, small boats to the deep water year-round factory ships and draggers. Now the fish is all gone and the forests is cut down. Ruined and wrecked! No wonder there's ghosts here. It's the dead pried out of their ground by bulldozers!"

The fish plant man got a word in. "They used to say 'A man's set up in life if he's got a pig, a punt and a potato patch.' What do they say now? Every man for himself."

"That's right," said Billy. "It's chasing the money and buying plastic speedboats and snowmobiles and funny dogs from the mainland. It's hanging around the bars, it's murders and stealing. It's tearing off your clothes and pretending you're loony. It used to be a happy life here. See, it was joyful. It was a joyful life. You wouldn't know what I'm speaking of, Tert Card, you with your terrible need to go to Florida. Why waste my breath." Held the teapot over his cup but nothing came out.

Tert Card's mouth had been waiting a chance. He spoke to all, included the sweating waitress, the cook whose head showed in the order window. "If it was them days now, Mr. Pretty, you'd be dead. You forget the Chinese flu you got a few winters back, in the hospital with it. I seen you in that bed grey as a dead cod, I thought, well, *he's* had it. But they give you antibiotics and oxygen and all and you live to bite the hand that saved you. Nobody, nobody in their right mind would go back to them hard, hard times. People was only kind because life was so dirty you couldn't afford to have any enemies. It was all swim or all sink. A situation that makes people very sweet." Sucking air over his teeth.

The cook called from the kitchen, "I say let the fishery go. Let the oilmen have the free hand. Can't do no worse and might do better." Laughed to show it was a joke. If necessary.

"You better not let some of your customers hear you say that or you will be wallpaper paste." The fish plant man got up, went for a toothpick.

"*I'll* say it to anybody!" Tert Card bellowed. "Oil is strong and fish is weak. There's no contest. The whole world needs oil. There is big money in oil. There's too many men fishing and not enough fish. That's what it comes down to. Now let's get down to the newsroom and put the bloody paper together. Quoyle, you got your boat story?" Shouting still. A full head of steam up.

"Go ahead," said Billy Pretty who had read it, who had listened to Quoyle on the phone talking oil for a week, seen him come back from the Cape Despond spill covered with oil, his notes a greasy wad because he'd plunged in beside the rescuers of ruined seabirds. "You give him that story and we'll watch Tert Card the Oil King expire of a paroxysm. You'd think he had a million dollars worth of oil stock. Ha, he's got two shares of Mobil. Two!" Snakey thrust of his head.

"It's on my desk," said Quoyle.

"I won't forget this, Billy Pretty," said Card, spots the size of coasters burning on his cheeks.

The short parade to Flour Sack Cove, take-out coffee slopping down dashboards, steering wheels gritty with doughnut sugar. Ten minutes later Quoyle handed Card his column, said nothing, watched his eyes zag back and forth. Staff Awaits Paroxysm.

NOBODY HANGS A PICTURE OF AN OIL TANKER

There is a 1904 photograph on the wall of the Killick-Claw Public Library. It shows eight schooners in Omaloor Bay heading out to the fishing grounds, their sails spread like white wings. They are beautiful beyond compare. It took great skill and sea knowledge to sail them.

Today the most common sight on the marine horizon is the low black profile of an oil tanker. Oil, in crude and refined forms, is—bar none—the number one commodity in international trade.

Another common sight is black oil scum along miles of landwash, like the shoreline along Cape Despond this week. Hundreds of people watched Monday morning as 14,000 metric tons of crude washed onshore from a ruptured tank of the *Golden Goose*. Thousands of seabirds and fish struggled in the oil, fishing boats and nets were fouled. "This is the end of this place," said Jack Eye, 87, of Little Despond, who, as a young man, was a dory fisherman with the schooner fleet.

Our world runs on oil. More than 3,000 tankers prowl the world's seas. Among them are the largest moving objects ever made by man, the Very Large Crude Carriers, or VLCCs, up to 400 meters in length and over 200,000 deadweight tons. Many of these ships are single hull vessels. Some are old and corroded, structurally weak. One thing is sure. There will be more oil spills, and some will be horrendous.

Nobody hangs a picture of an oil tanker on their wall.

Tert Card read it, laid it on the corner of his desk and looked at Quoyle.

"You too," he said. "You bloody fucking too."

When the newsroom was empty that evening he stood by the window, addressed an absent Quoyle.

"Keep your bloody American pinko Greenpeace liberalism out of it. Who the hell are you to say this? Oh yes, Mr. Quoyle's bloody precious column! It's against our whole effort of development and economic progress."

And he rewrote the piece, pasted it up with bold fingers, went out and got drunk. To quell the pain of the irksome canker sores. How could they know he swallowed glassful after glassful to comprehend a harsh and private beauty?

A day or two later Tert Card brought in a framed picture from a shipping company's wall calendar. He hung it behind his desk. The gargantuan *Quiet Eye* nosed through a sunset into Placentia Bay. LARGEST OIL TANKER IN THE WORLD. The first time the door slammed it went askew.

Quoyle thought it was funny until noon when Card came back from the printer with the ink-smelling bundles of *Gammy Bird*. Took a copy, turned to see how his Shipping News story came out.

His column had been condensed to a caption accompanying the same calendar page photo that hung on Tert Card's wall.

PICTURE OF AN OIL TANKER

More than 3,000 tankers proudly ride the world's seas. These giant tankers, even the biggest, take advantage of Newfoundland's deep-water ports and refineries. Oil and Newfoundland go together like ham and eggs, and like ham and eggs they'll nourish us all in the coming years.

Let's all hang a picture of an oil tanker on our wall.

Quoyle felt the blood drain out of his head; he went dizzy.

"What have you done!" he shouted at Tert Card, voice an axe.

"Straightened it out, that's all. We don't want to hear that Greenpeace shit." Tert Card whinnied. Feeling good. His cheap face thrust out.

"You cut the guts out of this piece! You made it into rotten cheap propaganda for the oil industry. You made me look like a mouthpiece for tanker interests." He pressed Card into his corner.

"I told you," said Nutbeem. "I told you, Quoyle, to watch out, he'll cobble your work."

Quoyle was incensed, some well of anger like a dome of oil beneath innocuous sand, tapped and gushing.

"This is a *column*," bellowed Quoyle. "You can't change somebody's column, for Christ's sake, because you don't like it! Jack asked me to write a column about boats and shipping. That means my opinion and description as I see it. This"—he shook the paper against the slab cheeks—"isn't what I wrote, isn't my opinion, isn't what I see."

"As long as I'm the managing editor," said Tert Card, rattling like pebbles in a can, "I've the right to change anything I don't think fit to run in the *Gammy Bird*. And if you don't think so, I advise you to check it out with Jack Buggit." Ducked under Quoyle's raised arms.

And ran for the door.

"Don't think I don't know you're all against me." The thick candle that was Tert Card gone somewhere else with his sputtering light.

"You're a surprise, Quoyle," said Billy Pretty. "I didn't believe you had that much steam in your boiler. You blew him out of the water."

"You know how it is, now," said Nutbeem. "I tried to tell you on the first day."

"You watch, though. By tomorrow he'll be back afloat on an even keel. Tert Card snaps right back for all he's a vitrid bugger."

"I'm surprised myself," said Quoyle. "I'm going to call Jack," he said, "and get this straightened out. Either I'm writing a column or I'm not."

"Word of advice, Quoyle. Don't call Jack. He is out fishing, as I assume you know. He don't like *Gammy Bird* business to come into his home, neither. You just leave it alone and let me drop around to the stage tonight or tomorrow night. The crab approach is best with Jack."

"*Gammy Bird*. Tert Card speaking. Oh, yar, Jack." Tert Card held the phone receiver against his sweatered chest, looked at Quoyle. The morning light unkind.

"Wants to talk to you." His tone indicated bad taste or madness on Jack's part.

"Hello." Braced for abuse.

"Quoyle. Jack Buggit here. You write your column. If you put your foot in a dog's mess we'll say it's because you was brought up in the States. Tert will keep his hands off it. Put him back on."

Quoyle held the phone up and motioned to Card. They could hear Jack squawk. Slowly Tert Card turned his back to the room, faced the window, the sea. As the minutes went by he shifted from foot to foot, sat on the edge of his desk, foraged in ears and nostrils. He rocked, switched the phone from one side of his head to the other. At last the phone went quiet and he hung up.

"All right," he said blandly, though the red cheeks flamed, "Jack thinks he wants to try running Quoyle's columns as they come. For now, anyway. So we'll just go along with that. We'll go along with that. But he's got an idea on the car wreck feature. You know there are weeks when we don't have any good wrecks and have to go into the files. Well, Jack wants to include boat wrecks. He says at the fisherman's meeting they said there was more than three hundred dangerous boat accidents and vessel losses last year. Quoyle, he wants you to write up boat wrecks and get some photos, same as you do the car wrecks. There's enough so we'll always have a fresh disaster."

"There's no doubt about that," said Quoyle, looking at Tert Card.

26

Deadman

"Deadman—An 'Irish pennant,' a loose end hanging about the sails or rigging."

THE MARINER'S DICTIONARY

THE END of September, tide going out, moon in its last quarter. The first time Quoyle had been alone at the green house. The aunt was in St. John's for the weekend buying buttons and muslin. Bunny and Sunshine had howled to stay with Dennis and Beety for Marty's birthday.

"She's my best friend, Dad. I wish she was my sister," Bunny said passionately. "Please please please let us stay." And in the Flying Squid Gift & Lunchstop she chose a ring made from pearly shell for Marty's present, a sheet of spotted tissue for wrapping.

Quoyle came across the bay in his scorned boat on Friday afternoon with a bag of groceries, two six-packs of beer. All of his notes and the typewriter. A stack of books on nineteenth-century shipping regulations and abuses. In the kitchen, stooped to put the beer in the ice cooler under the sink, then thought of ice. He'd meant to get some, but the empty cooler was still empty, still in the boat. It didn't matter. In the evening he drank the beer as it was, scribbled by the light of the gas lamp.

On Saturday Quoyle stumped around the underfurnished rooms; dusty air seemed to wrinkle as he moved through it. He split wood until lunch; beer, two cans of sardines and a can of lima beans. In the afternoon he worked at the kitchen table, started on the first draft, banging the keys, swearing when his fingers jammed between them, writing about Samuel Plimsoll and his line.

"FOR GOD'S SAKE, HELP ME"

Everybody has seen the Plimsoll lines or loading marks on vessels. They mark the safe load each ship can carry.

These loading marks came about because of a single concerned individual, Samuel Plimsoll, elected MP from Derby in 1868. Plimsoll fought for the safety of seamen in a time when unscrupulous shipowners deliberately sent overloaded old ships to sea. Plimsoll's little book, *Our Seamen*, described bad vessels so heavily laden with coal or iron their decks were awash. The owners knew the ships would sink. They knew the crews would drown. They did it for the insurance.

Overloading was the major cause of thousands of wrecks each year. Plimsoll begged for a painted load line on all ships, begged that no ship be allowed, under any circumstances, to leave port unless the line was distinctly visible.

He wrote directly to his readers. "Do you doubt these statements? Then, for God's sake—oh, for God's sake, help me to get a Royal Commission to inquire into their truth!" Powerful shipping interests fought him every inch of the way.

When he stopped the evening was closing in again. Cooked two pounds of shrimp in olive oil and garlic, sucked the meat from the shells. Went down to the dock in the twilight with the last beer, endured the mosquitoes, watching the lights of Killick-Claw come on. The lighthouses on the points stuttering.

The Old Hag came in the night, saddled and bridled Quoyle. He dreamed again he was on the nightmare highway. A tiny figure under a trestle stretched imploring arms. Petal, torn and bloody. Yet so great was his speed he was carried past. The brakes did not work when he tramped them. He woke for a few minutes, straining his right foot on the dream brake, his neck wet with anxious sweat. The wind moaned through the house cables, a sound that invoked a sense of hopeless abandonment. But he pulled the sleeping bag corner over his upper ear and slept again. Getting used to nightmares.

By Sunday noon the Plimsoll piece was in shape and he needed a walk. Had never been out to the end of the point. As he pulled the door to behind him a length of knotted twine fell from the latch. He picked it up and put it in his pocket. Then down along the shore and toward the extremity of land.

Climbed over rocks as big as houses, dropping down their sides into damp rooms with seaweed floors. The stones clenched lost nets, beaten into hairy frazzles of mussel shells and seaweed. Gulls flew up from tidal pools. The rock was littered with empty crab shells still wet with rust-colored body fluids. The shoreline narrowed to cliff. He could go no further that way.

So, backtracked, climbed up to the heather that covered the slope like shriveled wigs. Deep-gullied stone. Followed caribou paths up onto the tongue of granite that thrust into the sea. To his right the blue circle of Omaloor Bay, on the left the rough shore that reeled miles away to Misky Bay. Ahead of him the open Atlantic.

His boots rang on the naked stone. Stumbled on juniper roots embedded in fissures, saw veins of quartz like congealed lightning. The slope was riddled with gullies and rises, ledges and plateaus. Far ahead he saw a stone cairn; wondered who had made it.

It took half an hour to reach this tower, and he walked around it. Thrice the height of a man, the stones encrusted with lichens. Built a long time ago. Perhaps by the ancient Beothuks, extinct now, slain for sport by bored whalers and cod killers. Perhaps a marker for Basque fishermen or wrecker Quoyles luring vessels onto the rocks with false lights. The booming thunge of sea drew him on.

At last the end of the world, a wild place that seemed poised on the lip of the abyss. No human sign, nothing, no ship, no plane, no animal, no bird, no bobbing trap marker nor buoy. As though he stood alone on the planet. The immensity of sky roared at him and instinctively he raised his hands to keep it off. Translucent thirty-foot combers the color of bottles crashed onto stone, coursed bubbles into a churning lake of milk shot with cream. Even hundreds of feet above the sea the salt mist stung his eyes and beaded his face and jacket with fine droplets. Waves struck with the hollowed basso peculiar to ovens and mouseholes.

He began to work down the slant of rock. Wet and slippery. He went cautiously, excited by the violence, wondering what it would be like in a storm. The tide still on the ebb in that complex swell and fall of water against land, as though a great heart in the center of the earth beat but twice a day.

These waters, thought Quoyle, haunted by lost ships, fishermen, explorers gurgled down into sea holes as black as a dog's throat. Bawling into salt broth. Vikings down the cracking winds, steering through fog by the polarized light of sun-stones. The Inuit in skin boats, breathing, breathing, rhythmic suck of frigid air, iced paddles dipping, spray freezing, sleek back rising, jostle, the boat torn, spiraling down. Millennial bergs from the glaciers, morbid, silent except for waves breaking on their flanks, the deceiving sound of shoreline where there was no shore. Foghorns, smothered gun reports along the coast. Ice welding land to sea. Frost smoke. Clouds mottled by reflections of water holes in the plains of ice. The glare of ice erasing dimension, distance, subjecting senses to mirage and illusion. A rare place.

As Quoyle descended, he slipped on the treacherous weed, clung to the rock. Reached a shelf where he could stand and crane, glimpse the maelstrom below. Could go no further.

He saw three things: a honeycomb of caves awash; a rock in the shape of a great dog; a human body in a yellow suit, head under the surface as though delighted in patterns of the sea bottom. Arms and legs spread out like a starfish, the body slid in and out of a small cave, a toy on a string tugged by the sea. Newspaper Reporter Seems Magnet for Dead Men.

There was no way down to the body unless he leaped into the foam. If he had brought a rope and grapnel . . . He began to climb back up the cliff. It struck him the man might have fallen from where he now climbed. Yet more likely from a boat. Tell someone.

Up on the headland again he ran. His side aching. Tell someone about the dead man. When he reached the house it would take still another hour to drive around the bay to the RCMP station. Faster in the boat. The wind at his back swept his hair forward so that the ends snapped at his eyes. At first he felt the cold on his neck, but as he trotted over the rock he flushed with heat and had to unzip his jacket. A long time to get to the dock.

Caught in the urgency of it, that yellow corpse shuttling in and out, he cast free and set straight across the bay for Killick-Claw. As though there were still a chance to save the man. In ten minutes, as he moved out of the shelter of the lee shore and into the wind, he knew he'd made a mistake.

Had never had his boat in such rough water. The swells came at him broadside from the mouth of the bay, crests like cruel smiles. The boat rolled, rose up, dropped with sickening speed into the troughs. Instinctively he changed course, taking the waves at an angle on his bow. But now he was headed for a point northeast of Killick-Claw. Somewhere he would have to turn and make an east-southeast run for the harbor. In his inexperience Quoyle did not understand how to tack a zigzag across the bay, a long run with the wind and waves on his bow and then a short leg with the wind on his quarter. Halfway across he made a sudden turn toward Killick-Claw, presented his low, wide stern to the swell.

The boat wallowed about and a short length of line slid out from under the seat. It was knotted at one end, kinked and crimped at the other as if old knots had finally been untied. For the first time Quoyle got it—there was meaning in the knotted strings.

The boat pitched and plunged headlong, the bow digging into the loud water while the propeller raced. Quoyle was frightened. Each time, he lost the rudder and the boat yawed. In a few minutes his voyage ended. The bow struck like an axe, throwing the stern high. At once a wave seized, threw the boat broadside to the oncoming sea. It broached. Capsized. And Quoyle was flying under water.

In fifteen terrifying seconds he learned to swim well enough to reach the capsized boat and grasp the stilled propeller shaft. His weight pulled one side of the upturned stern down and lifted the bow a little, enough to catch an oncoming wave that twisted the boat, turned it over and filled it. Quoyle, tumbling through the transparent sea again, saw the pale boat below him, sinking, drifting casually down, the familiar details of its construction and paint becoming indistinct as it passed into the depths.

He came to the surface gasping, half blinded by some hot stuff in his eyes, and saw bloody water drip.

"Stupid," he thought, "stupid to drown with the children so small." No life jackets, no floating oars, no sense. Up he rose on a swell, buoyed by body fat and a lungful of air. He was floating. A mile and a half from either shore Quoyle was floating in the cold waves. The piece of knotted twine drifted in front of him and about twenty feet away a red box bobbed—the plastic cooler for the ice he'd forgotten. He thrashed to the cooler through a flotilla of wooden matches that must have fallen into the boat from the grocery bag. He remembered buying them. Guessed they would wash up on shore someday, tiny sticks with the heads washed away. Where would he be?

He gripped the handles of the cooler, rested his upper breast on the cover. Blood from his forehead or hairline but he didn't dare let go of the box to reach up and touch the wound. He could not remember being struck. The boat must have caught him as it went over.

The waves seemed mountainous but he rose and fell with them like a chip, watched for the green curlers that shoved him under, the lifting sly crests that drove saltwater into his nose.

The tide had been almost out when he saw the dead man, perhaps two hours ago. It must be on the turn now. His watch was gone. But wasn't there an hour or so of slack between low water and the turn of the tide? He knew little about the currents in the bay. The moon in its last quarter meant the smaller neap tide.

There were, Billy said, complex waters along the west side, shoals and reefs and grazing sunkers. He feared the wind would force him five miles up to the narrows and then out to sea, heading for Ireland on a beer cooler. If only he were nearer to the west shore, the lee shore, where the water was smoother and he might kick his way toward the rock.

A long time passed, hours, he thought. He could not feel his legs. When he rose high on the waves he tried to gauge where he was. The west shore seemed nearer now, but despite the wind and incoming tide, he was moving toward the end of the point.

Later he was surprised to glimpse the cairn he had walked around that morning. Must be in some rip current that was carrying him along the shore toward land's end, toward the caves, toward the dead man. Ironic if he ended up sliding in and out of a booming water cave, companion to the man in yellow.

"Not while I have this hot box," he said aloud, for he had begun to think the red cooler was filled with glowing charcoal. He deduced it because when he raised his chin from the cover his jaw chattered uncontrollably, and when he rested it back against the box the chattering ceased. Only a wonderful heat could have that effect.

He was surprised to see it was almost dusk. In a way he was glad, because it meant he could go to bed soon and get some sleep. He was tremendously tired. The rising and falling billows would be deliciously soft to sink into. This was something he'd worked out. He didn't know why he hadn't thought of it before, but the yellow man was not dead. Sleeping. Resting. And in a minute Quoyle thought he would roll over too and get some sleep. As soon as they shut the lights out. But the hard light was shining directly into his swollen eyes and Jack Buggit was wrenching him away from the hot box and onto a pile of cold fish.

"Jesus Cockadoodle Christ! I *knowed* somebody was out here. Felt it." He threw a tarpaulin over Quoyle.

"I told you that damn thing would drown you. How long you been in the water? Couldn't be too long, boy, can't live in this too long."

But Quoyle couldn't answer. He was shaking so hard his heels drummed on the fish. He tried to tell Jack to get the hot box so he could get warm again, but his jaw wouldn't work.

Jack half-dragged him, half-shoved him into Mrs. Buggit's perfect kitchen. "Here's Quoyle I fished out of the bloody drink," he said.

"If you knew how many Jack has saved," she said. "How many." All but one. She got Quoyle's clothes off, laid hot-water bottles on his thighs and wrapped a blanket around him. She made a mug of steaming tea and forced spoonsful of it between his teeth with the swift competence of practice. Jack mumbled a cup of rum would do more good.

In twenty minutes his jaw was loose enough and his mind firm enough to choke out the sinking of the boat, the illusion of the hot box, to take in the details of the Buggit domicile. To have a second cup of tea loaded with sugar and evaporated milk.

"That's a nice oolong," said Mrs. Buggit. Rum couldn't come near it for saving grace.

Everything in the house tatted and doilied in the great art of the place, designs of lace waves and floe ice, whelk shells and sea wrack, the curve of lobster feelers, the round knot of cod-eye, the bristled commas of shrimp and fissured sea caves, white snow on black rock, pinwheeled gulls, the slant of silver rain. Hard, tortured knots encased picture frames of ancestors and anchors, the Bible was fitted with sheets of ebbing foam, the clock's face peered out like a bride's from a wreath of worked wildflowers. The knobs of the kitchen dresser sported tassels like a stripper in a bawd house, the kettle handle knitted over in snake-ribs, the easy chairs wore archipelagoes of thread and twine flung over the reefs of arms and backs. On a shelf a 1961 Ontario phone book.

Mrs. Buggit stood against the Nile green wall, moved forward to the stove to refill the kettle, her hands like welded scoops. Great knobby kunckles and scarred fingers. The boiling water gushing into the teapot. Mrs. Buggit was bare armed in a cotton dress. The house breathed tropical heat and the torpor of comfort.

She had a voice built up from calling into the wind and stating strong opinions. In this house Jack shrank to the size of a doll, his wife grew enormous in the waxy glitter and cascade of flowers. She searched Quoyle's face as though she had known him once. His teeth clattered less against the mug. The shudders that had racked him from neck to arch eased.

"You'll warm," she said, though she herself could not, coming at him with a hot brick for his feet. A mottled, half-grown dog stirred on the mat, cocked her ears briefly.

Jack, like many men who spend their days in hard physical labor, went slack when he sat in an easy chair, sprawled and spread as if luxury jellied his muscles.

"It was your build there, all that fat, y'know, that's what insulated you all them hours, kept you floating. A thin man would of died."

Then Quoyle remembered the yellow man and told his story again, beginning with the walk on the point and ending with the light in his eyes.

"At the ovens?" Jack went to the telephone in a wedge of space under the stairs to call the Coast Guard. Quoyle sat, his ears ringing. Mrs. Buggit was talking to him.

"People with glasses don't get on with dogs," she said. "A dog has to see your eyes clear to know your heart. A dog will wait for you to smile, he'll wait a month if need be."

"The Newfoundland dog," said shuddering Quoyle, still weak with the lassitude of drowning.

"The Newfoundland dog! The Newfoundland dog isn't in it. That's not the real dog of this place. The real dog, the best dog in the world that ever was, is the water dog. This one here, Batch, is part water dog, but the pure ones all died out. They were all killed generations ago. Ask Jack, he'll tell you about it. Though Jack's a cat man. It's me as likes the dogs. Batch is from Billy Pretty's Elvis. Jack's got his cat, you know, Old Tommy, goes out in the boat with him. Just as good a fisherman."

And at last, Billy Pretty and Tert Card told, the Coast Guard informed of the yellow man, Quoyle's tea mug emptied. Jack went down to the stage to clean and ice his fish. Had saved, now let the wife restore.

Quoyle followed Mrs. Buggit up to the guest room. She handed him the replenished hot-water bottles.

"You want to go to Alvin Yark for the next one," she said.

Before he fell asleep he noticed a curious pleated cylinder near the door. It was the last thing he saw.

In the morning, ravenous with hunger, euphoric with life, he saw the cylinder was a doorstop made from a mail-order catalog, a thousand pages folded down and glued, and imagined Mrs. Buggit working at it day after winter day while the wind shaved along the eaves and the snow fell, while the fast ice of the frozen bay groaned and far to the north the frost smoke writhed. And still she patiently folded and pasted, folded and pasted, the kettle steaming on the stove, obscuring the windows. As for Quoyle, the most telling momento of his six-hour swim were his dark blue toenails, dyed by his cheap socks.

And when her house was empty again, Quoyle gone and the teapot scalded and put away on the shelf, the floor mopped, she went outside to hang Quoyle's damp blanket, to take in yesterday's forgotten, drenty wash. Although it was still soft September, the bitter storm that took Jesson boiled up around her. Eyes blinked from the glare; stiff fingers pulled at the legs of Jack's pants, scraped the fur of frost growing out of the blue blouse. Then inside again to fold and iron, but always in earshot the screech of raftering ice beyond the point, the great bergs toppling with the pressure, the pans rearing hundreds of feet high under the white moon and cracking, cracking asunder.

27

Newsroom

"Galley news, unfounded rumours circulated about a vessel."

THE MARINER'S DICTIONARY

TWO DAYS after Quoyle's spill, Billy Pretty grinning into the newsroom in the afternoon, an old leather flying helmet on his head, the straps swinging, wearing his wool jacket in grey and black squares, face the color of fog.

"They got your drowned man, Quoyle, Search and Rescue got him out of the cave. But he was a bit of a disappointment." Taking a scrap of paper from his pocket, unfolding it. "And it's a page-one story which I've worked out in my head on the way over here. Should have been your story, proper thing, but I've wrote it up already. That was a survival suit he was floating in. Carried up to the ovens by the currents. There was a fellow from No Name Cove washed up in there years ago."

"What do you mean, he was a disappointment?"

"They couldn't tell who he was. At first. Bit of a problem."

"Well don't plague us, Billy Pretty. What?" Tert Card roaring away.

"No head."

"The suitcase?" said Quoyle stupidly. "The head in the suitcase? Mr. Melville?"

"Yes indeed, Mr. Melville of the suitcase. They think. The Mounties and the Coast Guard is howling like wolves at the moon right this minute. Burning up the telephone wires to the States, bulletins and alarms. But probably come to nothing. They said it looks like the body was put in the suit after the head was cut off.

"How do they know?" Tert Card.

"Because the body was inserted in five pieces. Divided up like a pie, he was."

Billy Pretty at his computer pounding out the sentences.

MISSING BODY OF MAN FOUND
GRUESOME DISCOVERY IN OVENS

"I don't know why I never get any good stories," said Nutbeem. "Just the sordid. Just the nastiest stuff for Nutbeem, vile stuff that can't be described except in winking innuendo and allusion. I really won't miss this stuff. The nicest bit I've got is a list of offenses charged against the mayor of Galliambic. He won a hundred thousand in the Atlantic Lottery two weeks ago and celebrated by molesting fourteen students in one week. He's charged with indecent assault, gross indecency and buggery. Here's a depraved lad of twenty-nine went around to the Goldenvale Rest Home and persuaded a seventy-one-year-old lady to come along in his truck for a visit to the shopping mall in Misky Bay. Drove straightaway to the shrubbery and raped her so badly she needed surgery. They took him to the lockup and on court appearance day we all know what he did."

"Tore off all his clothes," droned Quoyle, Billy Pretty and Tert Card in chorus.

"More priests connected with the orphanage. It's up to nineteen awaiting trial now. Here's a doctor at the No Name Medical Clinic charged with sexual assault against fourteen female patients—'provocative fondling of breasts and genitals' is how they put it. The choirmaster in Misky Bay pled guilty on Monday to sexual assault and molestation of more than a hundred boys over the past twelve years. Also in Misky Bay an American tourist arrested for fondling young boys at the municipal swimming pool. 'He kept feeling my bum and my front,' said a ten-year-old victim. And here in Killick-Claw a loving dad is charged with sexually assaulting two of his sons and his teenage daughter in innumerable incidents between 1962 and the present. Buggery, indecent assault and sexual intercourse. Here's another family lover, big strapping thirty-five-year-old fisherman spends his hours ashore teaching his little four-year-old daughter to perform oral sex and masturbate him."

"For Christ's sake," said Quoyle, appalled. "This can't be all in one week."

"One week?" said Nutbeem. "I've got another bloody page of them."

"That's what sells this paper," said Tert Card. "Not columns and home hints. Nutbeem's sex stories with names and dates whenever possible. That was Jack's genius, to know people wanted this stuff. Of course every Newf paper does it now, but *Gammy Bird* was first to give names and grisly details."

"I don't wonder it depresses you, Nutbeem. Is it worse here than other places? It seems worse."

Billy in his corner scribbled, chair turned away. That stuff.

"I don't know if it's worse, or just more openly publicized. Perhaps the priest thing is worse. A lot of abusive priests in these little outports where they were trusted by naive parents. But I've heard it said—cynically—that sexual abuse of children is an old Newf tradition."

"There's an ugly thing to say," said Tert Card. "I'd say a Brit tradition." Scratching his head until showers of dandruff fell into the computer keys.

"What happens to sex offenders here, then? Some rehab program? Or they just simmer in prison?"

"Don't know," said Nutbeem.

"Might make a good story," said Quoyle.

"Yes," said Nutbeem in a droning voice as though his mainspring were winding down. "It might. If I could get at it before I go. But I can't. The *Borogove*'s almost ready and I've got to get out before the ice." A great cracking yawn. "Burned out on this, anyway."

"You better say something to Jack," Tert Card swelling up.

"Oh, he knows."

"What have you got, Quoyle, car wreck or boat wreck? You got to have something. Seems you're out interviewing for the damn shipping news every time there's a car wr ck. Or maybe driving around with Mrs. Prowse? Quoyle, you doing that? You're out of the office more than Jack."

"I've got Harold Nightingale," said Quoyle. "Photo of Harold at the empty dock. It's on your computer. Slugged 'Good-bye to All That.' "

GOOD-BYE TO ALL THAT

There are some days it just doesn't pay to get up. Harold Nightingale of Port Anguish knows this better than anyone. It's been a disastrous fishing season for Port Anguish fishermen. Harold Nightingale has caught exactly nine cod all season long. "Two years ago," he said, "we took 170,000 pounds of cod off Bumpy Banks. This year—less than zero. I dunno what I'm going to do. Take in washing, maybe."

To get the nine cod Mr. Nightingale spent $423 on gas, $2,150 on licenses, $4,670 on boat repair and refit, $1,200 on new nets. To make matters worse, he has suffered the worst case of sea-pups in his 31 years of fishing. "Wrists swelled up to my elbows," he said.

Last Friday Harold Nightingale had enough. He told his wife he was going out to haul his traps for the last time. He wrote out an advertisement for his boat and gear and asked her to place it in the *Gammy Bird*.

He and his four-man crew spent the morning hauling traps (all were empty) and were on their way back in when the wind increased slightly. A moderate sea built up and several waves broke over the aft deck. Just outside the entrance of Port Anguish harbor the boat heeled over to starboard and did not recover. Skipper Nightingale and the crew managed to scramble into the dories and abandon the sinking boat. The vessel disappeared beneath the waves and they headed for shore. The boat was not insured.

"The worst of it is that she sank under the weight of empty traps. I would have taken a little comfort if it had been a load of fish." On his arrival at home Mr. Nightingale canceled his classified ad.

"Ha-ha," said Tert Card. "I remember him calling up about that ad."

Quoyle slumped at his desk, thinking of old men standing in the rain, telling him how it had been. Of Harold Nightingale whose lifework ended like a stupid joke.

He took Partridge's letter from his pocket and read it again. Yo-yo days up and down the coast, furniture for their new house. Mercalia gave Partridge a camcorder for his birthday. They had a pool and something called the Ultima Chef's Gas Grill—cost 2K. He was seriously into wine tasting, had a wine cellar. Had met Spike Lee at a party. Mercalia learning to fly. He'd bought her a leather pilot's jacket and a white silk scarf. For a joke. Found someone to build another clay oven in the backyard. Meat smoker, Columbia River salmon. A three-temperature water bar in the kitchen. They'd installed a great sound system with digital signal processing that could play video laser discs and CDs at the same time in different rooms at different volumes. When was Quoyle going to fly out and visit? Come any time. Any time at all.

Quoyle refolded the letter, put it in his pocket. The bay was an aluminum tray dotted with paper boats. How short the days were getting. He looked at his watch, astonished how the months had fallen out of it.

"Nutbeem. Want to go to Skipper Will's for a squidburger?"

"Absolutely. Let me finish this para and I'm with you."

"Bring me back a takeout of fish and chips." Tert Card pulling wadded bills from his rayon pants.

But Billy opened his lunch box with cartoons of Garfield the cat on the cover, gazed in at a jar of stewed cod, slab of bread and marg. Fixed it himself and thought he was the better for it.

Quoyle and Nutbeem hunched over a table in the back. The restaurant redolent of hot oil and stewed tea. Nutbeem poured a stream of teak-colored pekoe into his cup.

"Have you noticed Jack's uncanny sense about assignments? He gives you a beat that plays on your private inner fears. Look at you. Your wife was killed in an auto accident. What does Jack ask you to cover? Car wrecks, to get pictures while the upholstery is still on fire and the blood still hot. He gives Billy, who has never married for reasons unknown, the home news, the women's interest page, the details of home and hearth—must be exquisitely painful to the old man. And me. I get to cover the wretched sexual assaults. And with each one I relive my own childhood. I was assaulted at school for three years, first by a miserable geometry teacher, then by older boys who were his cronies. To this day I cannot sleep without wrapping up like a mummy in five or six blankets. And what I don't know is if Jack understands what he's doing, if the pain is supposed to ease and dull through repetitive confrontation, or if it just persists, as fresh as on the day of the first personal event. I'd say it persists."

Quoyle called for more rolls, worried the tea bag in the saucer. Would the rolls be enough?

"Doesn't he do the same thing to himself? Going out on the sea that claimed his father and grandfather, two brothers, the oldest son and nearly got the younger? It dulls it, the pain, I mean. It dulls it because you see your condition is not unique, that other people suffer as you suffer. There must be some kind of truth in the old saying, misery loves company. That it's easier to die if others around you are dying."

"Cheery thoughts, Quoyle. Have some more tea and stop

crushing that repulsive bag. You see what Tert Card had stuck on the back of his trousers this morning?"

But Quoyle was deciding on two pieces of partridgeberry pie with vanilla ice cream.

At four o'clock he went to get Wavey.

The cold weather advanced from the north, rain changed to sleet, sleet to snow, fogs became clouds of needlepoint crystals and Quoyle was in an elaborate routine. In the mornings he dropped Sunshine at Beety's, brought Bunny to school, gave Wavey a ride. At four he reversed. Man Doubles as Chauffeur. Tea in Wavey's crazy kitchen if he was done for the day. If he had to work late, sometimes they stayed with her. She cut Quoyle's hair. He stacked her wood on Saturday morning. Sensible to eat dinner at the same table now and then. Closer and closer. Like two ducks swimming at first on opposite sides of the water but who end in the middle, together. It was taking a long time.

"There's no need for it," Mrs. Mavis Bangs whispered to Dawn. "Driving back and forth and giving rides. Those children could ride on the school bus. The school bus would drop the girl at the paper. She could tidy up papers while Agnis's nephew finished up his work. Whatever he does. Writes things down. Don't seem too heavy a work for a man, Mrs. Herold Prowse doesn't need to walk all that way in the weather. She's got her hooks out for him."

"I was thinking, he's got his out for her. He's that desperate for somebody to take care of those brats and do the cooking. And the other, if you know what I mean. Big as he is, he's like he's starving."

In Wavey's kitchen there was a worktable by the window where she applied yellow paint to the miniature dories her father made. Their little stickers on each one, *Woodworks of Flour Sack Cove.* She sanded and painted Labrador retriever napkin holders, wooden butterflies for tourists to nail on the sides of their houses, sea gulls standing on a single dowel leg. Ken took them to the gift shops up along the coast. On consignment, but they sold well enough.

"I know it's just tourist things," she said, "but they're not so bad. Decent work that gives a fair living."

Quoyle ran his finger over the meticulous joinery and glassy finish. And said he thought they were fine.

The little house was full of colors, as though inside Wavey's dry skin an appreciation for riot seethed. Purple chairs, knotted rugs of scarlet and blue, illustrated cupboards and stripes margining the doors. So that, standing in the color she was like an erasing of the human, female form.

Sunshine liked a cabinet with glass doors. Behind the glass a white tureen, a row of plates with swimming fish around the rims, four green wineglasses. On each of the lower doors Wavey had painted a scene; her own house with its painted fence; her father's yard of wooden figures. Sunshine opened the father's door. It made a wheezing squeak. She had to laugh.

28

The Skater's Chain Grip

To rescue someone who has fallen through the ice, the fingers of the rescuer's hand and the victim's hand are bent together in an opposing grip.

"Fingernails should first be close-pared."

THE ASHLEY BOOK OF KNOTS

THE AUNT out for a look around. She'd wanted a breath of air, to get away from Quoyle and his children in the house. To get away from Sunshine's humming and clattering shoes and piercing questions. The tape from Nutbeem that Bunny played endlessly, running down the batteries. The last days of October, a rattle of guns along the coast as the flights of turr came down ahead of the growing ice. Turbot massed off the shelf to the east. Spent salmon lay deep in river pools under the crusting ice or drifted to the sea.

She came upon a small pond. Remembered it, this water oval surrounded by hurts and laurel, women and children moving across the autumn marsh, bakeapples glowing like honeydrops in the slanting light. Leaky boots, birds fluttering up when the berry pickers drew near. Her mother always loved the marshes despite the nippers.

Find a bit of high ground, sleep for a little while under the flying clouds. "Oh," she said, "I could sleep away the rest of my life." How much she had slept through, unknowing! And died in a Brooklyn hospital bed of pneumonia believing she was on the barrens in the northern sun.

The aunt let herself remember an October, the pond frozen, ice as colorless as a sadiron's plate, the clouds in thin rolls like grey pencils in a box. Crowberries encased in ice skins. The wind collapsed. Deepest silence, the vapor of her breath floated from her mouth. Distant soughing of waves. No dead grass trembled, no gull or turr flew. A pearl grey landscape. She was eleven or twelve. Blue knit stockings, her mother's made-over dress. A boiled wool coat, English, tight under the arms, some castoff funneled through the Pentecostal charity. She had a huge pair of man's hockey skates, drew them on over her shoes, laced them tightly. A lace broke. She made a granny knot, poked the metal tip through the eyelet, tied bowknots.

The slanted white marks of the first strokes, then curls and loops like unspooling thread. In the windless twilight she hurtled through the cold. Sound of breathing, skate-risp. Alone on the perfect ice in the red afternoon, the clouds like branches, like a thicket of wavering bleeding branches. Alone. And a pork bun in her pocket. Looked up and saw he was there.

He came onto the ice, unbuttoning his pants, sliding gingerly on the soles of his fishing boots. And although there was no place to go but around and around, although she knew he would get her later if not now, she skated away, evaded his lunging for a long time. Maybe ten minutes. A long time.

She stood now and looked at the pond. Small, uninteresting. No reason to go down to it. The sky was not red but almost black in the southwest. Storms on the way. Soon enough there would be frost on the glass, frost-fur on the sills, the edging of frost that gathered on the quilt where the breath condensed, the timbers of the house contracting in the arctic nights with explosive creakings and snappings. As it was, once. Then, the slide of feet, hot breath on her face. And outside the ravenous wind in the cables, slamming down the chimney and sending rims of smoke up around the stove lids. The raw misery of February. And March, April. Snow until late May. Shuddered.

Well, that life had hardened her, she had made her own way along the rough coasts, had patched and mended her sails, replaced chafed gear with strong, fit stuff. She had worked her way off the rocks and shoals. Had managed. Still managed.

The air tingled. Distant ice was moving down. Snow crystals like shreds of clear plastic formed in cloudless sky, came out of nowhere. She trudged back to the house, the cold in her nostrils like a burned smell. Must listen to the weather forecast. That long drive around. They couldn't put things off much longer.

Inside she hung up her coat, draped her hat over the shoulder, the lined black gloves in the right pocket. Neatly, the fingers inside, the cuffs hanging limp.

The nephew was reading to them. Might as well start some supper. Something simple. Pancakes. And, pouring flour into the bowl, thought about the coming snow. They had to talk about it. The first storm could close the road. He wouldn't know.

The wind came skirling down over the tuckamore, moaned through the house cables.

"Supper!" called the aunt. How loud her voice was in the half-furnished room.

"What I wouldn't give right now," she said suddenly to Quoyle, forking a pancake onto his cold plate, "to be eating a nice dinner at a good restaurant and going to see a good movie. What I wouldn't give to go out and get on a heated bus tomorrow morning instead of driving that truck all around the bay. I tell you frankly, the winter begins to scare me."

As if it had been waiting for the season to be pronounced the snow started, flicking a few grains against the windows.

"You see?" said the aunt as if supported by an ally in an argument.

Quoyle chewed his mouthful of pancake, swallowed tea. He'd thought about it.

"I talked to the bulldozer guy, Dennis's friend. He'll plow the road for a price. If the snow is more than three inches. Your truck can manage that much."

"Twenty-eight miles of plowing! What price might that be?"

"A hundred a pop. Barely pay for the gas. Figured on what the storm frequency is, he estimates he'd have to come out a minimum of twice a week. In five months that's forty plowings. That's four thousand dollars. Another possibility is Dennis. He said he could ferry us back and forth with his boat until it iced up too much. If we could pay for the gas and his time at, say, ten dollars an hour."

"Well, that's a better bargain," said the aunt.

"I don't think so. Figure he has to spend two hours a day—it's twenty minutes across in smooth water. That's the same as the bulldozer, a hundred a week. And by January the bay will be iced in. I don't want to risk the girls on a snowmobile going back and forth across the bay. Dennis says there are weak spots. It's dangerous. Every winter somebody goes through and drowns. You have to know the route. Come to that, I don't like this long drive for them every day, either."

"You have been thinking of all the angles," said the aunt. Dryly. She was used to being the one who figured things out.

He did not say that the day before the capsize he had walked through the bare rooms of the house and guessed her furniture was not coming this year.

"Then," he said, cutting Sunshine's pancake with the edge of his fork to quell her screaking knife, "we could shift across the bay for the winter. Consider this place a summer camp. Nutbeem is leaving in a week or two. His trailer. There's not room for all four of us, but the girls and I could manage. If you could find a room. Or something. Wouldn't Mrs. Bangs know of something?"

But the aunt was astonished. She had gone for a walk and looked at a pond. Now everything had rushed on like an unlighted train in the dark.

"Let's sleep on it," said the aunt.

In the morning five inches of snow and blinding sunlight, a warm wind. Everything dripped and ran. The white blanket on the roof wrinkled, cracked, broke away in ragged cakes that hissed as they slid down and crashed to the ground. By noon only islands of snow on the damp road and in the hollows on the barrens.

"All right," said the aunt. "I want to think about this a little more." Now that it was here, it had come too fast.

"Well, I wondered what happened to you," said Mavis Bangs, the part in her black hair glowing like a wire in the rhomboid of sunlight. "I thought you might be sick. Or have trouble with the truck. M'dear, I was that worried. Or Dawn said maybe it was the snow, but it melted almost as fast as it come, so we didn't think it was. Anyway, noon I went up to the post office and got your mail." She pointed at the aunt's table with her eyes. Importantly. She had jumped into the habit of doing small kindnesses for Agnis Hamm. And would get the mail or pour a cup of tea unbidden. Proffer things with invisible trumpets.

"It was the snow," said the aunt. "You know how snow sticks to a dirt road." She shoveled at the letters. "Fact of the matter we decided it would be better to look for something closer in for the winter. The house be more of a camp, you know. He doesn't want the children to have to travel all that way on school days. So." She sighed.

Mrs. Bangs saw it in a flash. "Was you looking for a house for the all of yous? I knows the Burkes been talking about selling their place for good and moving to Florida. They go down every winter. Got friends there now. A bungalow. They live in a Florida bungalow with a verandah. Mrs. Burke, Pansy, says they have got two orange trees and a palm right in the front yard. Picks the oranges right off. Can you believe it? Now that is a place I'd like to see before I die. Florida."

"I been there," said Dawn. "You can have it. Give me Montreal. Ooh-la-la. Beauty clothes. All those markets, you never saw food like that in your life, movies, boutiques. You can have Miami. Buncha rich Staties."

"What's the Burke place, then," said the aunt offhandedly.

"Well, it's up on the ridge. The road that goes out to Flour Sack Cove, but at this end. Like if you was to go outside and face the hill and start climbing—if you could climb right over the houses, you know—you'd about come on it. Grey house with blue trim. Very nice kept up. Mrs. Burke is a housekeeper. An old-fashioned kitchen with the daybed and all, but they got conveniences, too. Oil heat. Dishwasher. Washing machine and dryer in the basement. Basement finished off. Nice fresh wallpaper in all the rooms."

"Umm," said the aunt. "You think they'd rent?"

"I doubt it. I don't believe they wants to rent. They been asked. I believe they wants to sell."

"Well, you know, actually my nephew is going to take that English fellow's trailer. Works at the paper. Mr. Nutbeem. He's leaving pretty soon."

"So you'd want a separate place, then."

"Ye—es," said the aunt.

"I believe the Burke place would be too much for one person," said Mrs. Bangs. "Even if you was prepared to buy it. It's got nine rooms. Or ten."

"I've put quite a bit of money into the old house. It's a shame. Just to use it for a camp. But getting back and forth is a problem. Like they say, what can't be cured must be endured. I've took a room at the Sea Gull for the rest of the week while we work something out. Nephew and the girls are staying with Beety and Dennis. Kind of cramped, but they're making do. Don't want to get caught by the snow. But let's not worry about it right now. What have we got on the schedule for today? The black cushions for the *Arrowhead*."

"Dawn and me's finished them black cushions Friday afternoon. Shipped 'em this morning."

The aunt looked at her mail. "You're way ahead of me," she said. She turned over a postcard and read it. "That's nice," she said, voice needled with sarcasm. "I thought we'd be seeing the Pakeys on the *Bubble* this week. Now here's their postcard and they say they can't risk coming up here at this time of year. Fair weather sailors, they. No, it's worse. They're having the job done by Yachtcrafter! Those bums." The aunt threw down the postcard, picked up a small package.

"Who do I know in Macau? It's from Macau." Tore it open.

"What is this?" she said. A packet of American currency fell on the table. Tied with a pale blue cord. Nothing more.

"That blue . . ." Mavis Bangs hesitated, put out her hand.

The aunt looked at the blue cord. Untied it and passed it to her. With a significant look. It was not a cord, but a thin strip of pale blue leather.

29
Alvin Yark

"The bight of a rope . . . has two meanings in knotting. First, it may be any central part of a rope, as distinct from the ends and standing part. Second, it is a curve or arc in a rope no narrower than a semicircle. This corresponds to the topographical meaning of the word, a bight being an indentation in a coast so wide that it may be sailed out of, on one tack, in any wind."

THE ASHLEY BOOK OF KNOTS

THE SINGLE advantage of the green house was clear at once. Quoyle, yawning and unshaven in a corner of Beety's kitchen, was combing the snarls out of Sunshine's hair and surrounded by affairs of toast, cocoa, searches for misplaced clothing and homework when Tert Card walked in, poured himself a cup of coffee. Dennis away and gone an hour before. Card looked at Beety, let her see him licking his mouth and winking like a turkey with pinkeye.

He stood then in front of Sunshine and Quoyle, clawing at his groin as though scorched by red-hot underwear. "Quoyle. Just wanted to let you know you should call Diddy Shovel. Something about a ship fire. You'll probably want to go straight along. I put the camera in your car. See if there's a chance for some pix. I'll tell you, Jack Buggit is some smart. People would rather read about a clogged head on a ship than all the car wrecks in Newfoundland." Took his time drinking his coffee. Chucked Sunshine under the chin and scratched again before he ambled out.

"I don't like that yukky man," said Sunshine. Feeling Quoyle's anger through the comb.

"In love with himself," said Beety. "Always has been. And no competition."

"Like this," said Murchie Buggit, hands blurred in demented scratching.

"That's enough," said Beety. "You look like a dog with bad fleas."

"So did he.'" And Sunshine and Murchie screamed with laughter until Murchie choked on toast crumbs and Quoyle had to slap his back.

But before he called the harbormaster the phone rang.

"For you," said Beety.

"Hello?" He expected Diddy Shovel's voice.

"Quoyle," said Billy Pretty, "you stopped by Alvin Yark's to talk about a boat?"

"No, Billy. I haven't even been thinking about it to tell you the truth. Kind of busy the last few weeks. And I guess I'm leery of boats after what happened."

"That's why you must go right back to 'em. Now you been christened. Winter is the finest time to build a boat. Alvin build you something and come ice-out I'll show you the tricks. Since you've been brought up away from the boats and are a danger to yourself."

Quoyle knew he should feel grateful. But felt stupid. "That's kind of you, Billy. I know I ought to do it."

"You just go out there to Alvin's place. You know where his shop is? Get Wavey to show you. Alvin's her uncle. Her poor dead mother's oldest brother."

"Alvin Yark is Wavey's uncle?" He seemed to be treading a spiral, circling in tighter and tighter.

"Oh yes."

While his hand was on the phone Quoyle dialed Diddy Shovel. What was the fire, was there a story in it? Bunny slouched into the kitchen with her sweater on backwards. Quoyle tried to pantomime a command to reverse the sweater, aroused the Beethoven scowl.

"Young man," the great voice boomed, "while you're fiddling around the *Rome* burns. Cargo ship, *Rome*, six-hundred-foot vessel, Panamanian registered, carrying a load of zinc and lead powder is, let's see, about twenty miles out and on fire at thirteen hundred hours. Two casualties. The captain and an unidentified. Rest of the crew taken off by helicopter. Twenty-one chaps from Myanmar. Do you know where Myanmar is?"

"No."

"Right where Burma used to be. Helicopter took most of the crew to Misky Bay Hospital to be treated for smoke inhalation. Ship is in tow, destination Killick-Claw. More than that I do not know."

"Do you know how I can get out to her?"

"Why bother? Wait until they bring her in. Shouldn't be too long."

Yet by three-thirty the ship still had not entered the narrows. Quoyle called Diddy Shovel again.

"Should be here by five. Understand they've had some trouble. Towing cable parted and they had to rig another."

Wavey came down the steps pulling at the sleeves of her homemade coat, the color of slushy snow. She got in, glanced at him. A slight smile. Looked away.

Their silence comfortable. Something unfolding. But what? Not love, which wrenched and wounded. Not love, which came only once.

"I've got to go down to the harbor. So we can pick up the kids and I'll bring you and young Herold straight back. I can drop Bunny off at Beety's for an hour or take her with me. They're towing in a ship that had a fire. Two men dead, including the captain. The others in the hospital. Diddy Shovel says."

"I tremble to hear it." And did, in fact, shudder.

The school came in sight. Bunny stood at the bottom of the steps holding a sheet of paper. Quoyle dreaded the things she brought from school, that she showed him with her lip stuck out: bits of pasta glued on construction paper to form a face, pipe cleaners twisted into flowers, crayoned houses with quadrate windows, brown trees with broccoli heads never seen in Newfoundland. School iconography, he thought.

"That's how Miss Grandy says to do it."

"But Bunny, did you ever see a brown tree?"

"Marty makes her trees brown. And I'm gonna."

Quoyle to Wavey. "Billy says I must get a boat built over the winter. He says I should go to Alvin Yark."

A nod at hearing her uncle's name.

"He's a good boat builder," she said in her low voice. "He'd make you a good one."

"I thought I would go over on Saturday," said Quoyle. "And ask. Take the girls. Will you and Herry come with us? Is that a good day?"

"The best," she said. "And I've got things I've been wanting to bring to Aunt Evvie. We'll have supper with them. Aunt Evvie's some cook."

Then Quoyle and Bunny were off to the harbor, but the *Rome* had been towed to St. John's by company orders.

"Usually they tell me," said Diddy Shovel. "A few years back I'd have twisted 'em like a watch spring, but why bother now?"

On Saturday the fog was as dense as cotton waste, carried a coldness that ate into the bones. The children like a row of hens in the backseat. Wavey a little dressed up, black shoes glittering on the floor mat. Quoyle's eyes burned trying to penetrate the mist. Corduroy trousers painfully tight. He made a thousandth vow to lose weight. Houses at the side of the road were lost, the sea invisible. An hour to go ten miles to the Nunny Bag Cove turnoff. Cars creeping the other way, fog lights as dull as dirty saucers.

Nunny Bag Cove was a loop of road crammed with new ranch houses. They could scarcely see them in the mist.

"They had a fire about six years ago," said Wavey. "The town burned down. Everybody built a new house with the insurance. There was some families didn't have insurance, five or six I guess, the others shared along with them so it all came out to a new house for everybody. Uncle Al and Auntie Evvie didn't need such a big house as the old one, so they chipped in."

"Wait," said Quoyle. "They built a smaller house than their insurance claim paid for?"

"Umm," said Wavey. "He had separate insurance on his boat house. Had it insured for the amount as if there was a new long-liner just finished in it."

"That's enterprising," said Quoyle.

"Well, you know, there might have been! Better to guess yes than no. How many have that happened to, and the insurance was only for the building?"

Mrs. Yark, thin arms and legs like iron bars, got them all around the kitchen table, poured the children milk-tea in tiny cups painted with animals, gilt rims. Sunshine had a Gloucester Old Spot pig, Herry a Silver Spangle rooster and hen. A curly horned Dorset sheep for Bunny. The table still damp with recent wiping.

"Chuck, chuck, chuck," said Herry, finger on the rooster.

"They was old when I was little," said Wavey.

"Be surprised, m'dear, 'ow old they is. My grandmother 'ad them. That's a long time ago. They come over from England. Once was twelve of them, but all that's left is the four. The 'orses and cows are broke, though there's a number of the saucers. Used to 'ave some little glassen plates, but they's broke, too." Mrs. Yark's ginger cookies were flying doves with raisin eyes.

Bunny found all the interesting things in the kitchen, a folding bootjack, a tin jelly mold like a castle with pointed towers, a flowered mustache cup with a ceramic bridge at the rim to protect a gentleman's mustache from sopping.

"You're lucky you saved these things from the fire," said Quoyle. Eating more cookies.

"Ah, well," Mrs. Yark breathed, and Quoyle saw he'd made a mistake.

Quoyle left the women's territory, followed Alvin Yark out to the shop. Yark was a small man with a paper face, ears the size of half-dollars, eyes like willow leaves. He spoke from lips no more than a crack between the nose and chin.

"So you wants a boat. A motorboat?"

"Just a small boat, yes. I want something to get around the bay—not too big. Something I can handle by myself. I'm not very good at it."

A cap slewed sideways on his knotty head. He wore a pair of coveralls bisected by a zipper with double tabs, one dangling at his crotch, the other at his breastbone. Under the coveralls he wore a plaid shirt, and over everything a cardigan with more zippers.

"Outboard rodney, I suppose 'ud do you. Fifteen, sixteen foot. Put a little seven-'orsepower motor on 'er. Something like that," he said pointing at a sturdy boat with good lines resting on a pair of sawhorses.

"Yes," said Quoyle. Knew enough to recognize he was looking at something good.

"Learn yer young ones to row innit when they gits a little stouter."

They went into the dull gloom of the shop.

"Ah," said Yark. "I 'as a one or two to finish up, y'know," pointing to wooden skeletons and half-planked sides. "Says I might 'elp Nige Fearn wid 'is long-liner this winter. But if I gets out in the woods, you know, and finds the timber, it'll go along. Something by spring, see, by the time the ice goes. If I goes in the woods and finds the right sticks you know, spruce, var. See, you must find good uns, your stem, you wants to bring it down with a bit of a 'ollow to it, sternpost and your knee, and deadwoods a course, and breast'ook. You has to get the right ones. Your timbers, you know.

There's some around 'ere steams 'em. I wouldn't set down in a steam timber boat. Weak."

"I thought you'd have the materials on hand," said Quoyle.

"No, boy, I doesn't build with dry wood. The boat takes up the water if 'er's made out of dry wood, you know, and don't give it up again. But you builds with green wood and water will never go in the wood. I never builds with dry wood."

30

The Sun Clouded Over

QUOYLE and his daughters walked from Beety and Dennis's house to the Sea Gull Inn where the aunt roosted, damp and ruffled. Sunshine, grasping Quoyle's hand, slipped again and again. Until he saw it was a game, said, stop that.

The road shone under a moon like a motorcycle headlight. Freezing December fog that coated the world with black ice, the raw cold of the northern coast. Impossible to drive, though earlier he had driven, had made it to Little Despond and back, following up on the oil spill. Closed up. Old Mr. Eye in the hospital with pneumonia. A rim of oil around the cove.

Through the lobby with its smell of chemical potpourri, to the dining room where the aunt waited. Past empty tables. Bunny walked sedately; Sunshine charged at the aunt, tripped, crash-landed and bawled. So the dinner began with tears. Chill air pouring off the window glass.

"Poor thing," said the aunt, inspecting Sunshine's red knees. The waitress came across the worn carpet, one of her shoes sighing as she walked.

Quoyle drank a glass of tomato juice that tasted of tin. The aunt swallowed whiskey; glasses of ginger ale. Then turkey soup. In Quoyle's soup a stringy neck vein floated.

"I have to say, after the first day of peace and quiet, I've missed every one of you. Badly." The aunt's face redder than usual, blue eyes teary.

Quoyle laughed. "We miss you." Sleeping in Beety and Dennis's basement. Did miss the aunt's easy company, her headlong rush at problems.

"Dad, remember the little red cups with the pictures at Wavey's auntie's house?"

"Yes, I do, Bunny. They were cunning little cups."

"I'm writing a letter to Santa Claus to bring us some just like it. At school we are writing to Santa Claus. And I drew a picture of the cups so he would make the right kind. And blue beads. And Marty wrote the same thing. Dad, Marty makes her esses backwards."

"I want a boat with a stick and a string," said Sunshine. "You put the boat in the water and push it with the stick. And it floats away! Then you pull the string and it comes back!" She laughed immoderately.

"Sounds like the kind of boat I need," Quoyle eating the cold rolls.

"And if I get those little red cups," said Bunny, "I'll make you a cup of tea, Aunt."

"Well, my dear, I'll drink it with pleasure."

"Now, who's having the scallops," said the waitress holding a white plate heaped with pallid clumps, a mound of rice, a slice of bleached bread.

"That was my idea," said the aunt, frowning at her pale food, whispering to Quoyle. "Should have gone to Skipper Will's for squidburgers."

"When we're at Beety's house she makes jowls and britches sometimes," said Bunny, "which I LOVE."

"And I hate them," said Sunshine, making a sucking noise in the bottom of her ginger ale glass.

"You do not. You ate them all."

The cod cheeks and chips came.

"Ahem," said the aunt, "This is something of an announcement dinner. I've got an announcement. Good news and bad news. The good news is that I've got a big job that will take most of the winter. The bad news is that it's in St. John's. How it came about, I've been doing a lot of thinking about my yacht upholstery affairs. Let's face it, yacht owners are not as numerous here as on Long Island. Newfoundland is not high in the yachtman's ports of call. So I've been worried. Because I haven't had much work the last six weeks. If it hadn't been for the Mystery Money from Macau, no mystery to me, and to think of that strange woman who dismembers her husband but pays her bills, I'd have been pinched. So I put on my thinking cap. Plenty of commercial shipping in Newfoundland. Am I hoisting the wrong flag? Maybe so. Tried out some new names. Hamm's Yacht Upholstery sure not bringing them in droves. How about, I says to Mrs. Mavis Bangs, what do you think of Hamm's Maritime Upholstery? Could be yachts, could be tankers, could be anything that floats. She thought it was good. So then I called up refitters and boat repair yards in St. John's, introduced myself as Agnis Hamm of Hamm's Maritime Upholstery, and sure enough, there's a need. Right off the bat, a big job, a cargo ship, the *Rome*, that had a bad fire. Destroyed the bridge, upholstery in the ward room, crew lounge, everywhere ruined by smoke and water damage. Months of work. So, I'm taking Dawn and Mrs. Mavis Bangs down to St. John's with me and we'll work until it is done. They want a rich-colored burgundy Naugahyde. And a royal blue, very smart. Leather is not for everyone. It can mould, you know. Dawn is thrilled to be getting to St. John's. Bunny, put your napkin in your collar if you're going to drip ketchup. You're so sloppy."

"Dad," said Bunny. "I can make something. Skipper Alfred showed me it. It's 'The Sun Clouded Over.' "

"Um-hm," said Quoyle twirling a cod cheek in a stainless steel cup of tartar sauce. "But Aunt, where will you stay? A hotel in St. John's for a couple of months will cost a fortune."

"Watch," said Bunny, folding a bit of string.

"That's the good part," the aunt said, chewing scallops. "Atlantic Refitters keeps two apartments just for this kind of thing. Mr. Malt—he's the lad I'm dealing with—says they quite often have to put up experts in certain fields, metal stresses, propeller design, inspectors and such. So we can have one of the company's apartments at no cost—got a couple of bedrooms. It's part of the deal. And there's a work space. Set up the upholstery work. So, Dawn's brother will help us load everything into the back of my truck. They got the Naugahyde coming in from somewhere, New Jersey I believe. And we'll be off by the end of next week. All in the change of a name."

"It sounds quite adventuresome, Aunt."

"Well, I'll be back in the spring. We can move out to the green house again as soon as the road is open. It'll be the sweeter for waiting. I mean, if you still like it here. Or maybe you're thinking of going back to New York?"

"*I'm* not going back to New York," said Bunny. "Marty Buggit is my friend-girl forever. But when I'm big I'll go there."

Quoyle was not going back to New York, either. If life was an arc of light that began in darkness, ended in darkness, the first part of his life had happened in ordinary glare. Here it was as though he had found a polarized lens that deepened and intensified all seen through it. Thought of his stupid self in Mockingburg, taking whatever came at him. No wonder love had shot him through the heart and lungs, caused internal bleeding.

"Dad," said Bunny near tears. "I did it twice and you didn't watch. And Aunt didn't either."

"*I* watched," said Sunshine. "But I didn't see anything."

"I wonder if you need glasses," said the aunt.

"I'm sorry, Bunny girl. Show me one more time. I'm watching like a hawk."

"So am I," said the aunt.

The child pulled a loop of string taut, coiled and arranged it around her fingers in overlapping circles, thumbs and forefingers in the four corner loops.

"Now watch the sun," she said. "The sun is the hole in the middle and the rest is the clouds. Watch what happens." Slowly she drew the loops taut, slowly the center circle grew smaller and at last disappeared.

"It's a cat's cradle," said Bunny. "I know another one, too. Skipper Alfred knows hundreds and hundreds."

"That's extraordinary," said Quoyle. "Did Skipper Alfred give you that string?" He took the smooth line, counted seven tiny hard knots and, joining the ends, one clumsy overhand. "Did you tie these knots?" His voice light.

"I tied *that* one." The overhand. "I found it this morning in the car, Dad, on the back of your seat."

31

Sometimes You Just Lose It

"A sailor has little opportunity at sea to replace an article that is lost overboard, so knotted lanyards are attached to everything movable that is carried aloft: marlingspikes and fids, paint cans and slush buckets, pencils, eyeglasses, hats, snuffboxes, jackknives, tobacco and monkey pouches, amulets, bosuns' whistles, watches, binoculars, pipes and keys are all made fast around the neck, shoulder, or wrist, or else are attached to a buttonhole, belt, or suspender."

THE ASHLEY BOOK OF KNOTS

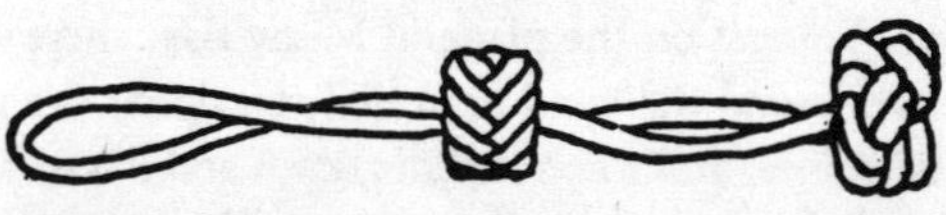

"ON NOVEMBER 21 the *Galactic Blizzard*, a Ro-Ro railcar-ferry with twin rudders and twin controllable pitch propellers left St. John's en route to Montreal," wrote Quoyle, still cold from his dawn excursion to the damaged ship.

> Though ice was forming along the shore it was a fine day. The sky was blue, the sea was calm and visibility was unlimited. An hour after leaving St. John's harbor, the ship struck the south cliff of Strain Bag Island head-on. The collision awakened the officer of the watch who had dozed off. "Sometimes you just lose it," he told Coast Guard investigators.

Tert Card slammed through the door. "I'm shinnicked with cold," he shouted, blowing on his chapped hands, backing his great rear up to the gas heater, "this degree of cold so early in the season takes the heart out of you for the place. Trying to drive along the cliffs this morning with the snow off the ice and the wipers froze up and the car slipping sideways I thought 'It's only November. How can this be?' Started thinking about the traffic statistics. Last January there was hundreds of motor vehicle accidents in Newfoundland. Death, personal injury, property damage. In just one month. That's how the need begins, on a cold day like this coming along the cliff. First it's just a little question to yourself. Then you say something out loud. Then you clip out the coupons in the travel magazines. The brochures come. You put them on the dashboard so you can look at a palm tree while you go over the edge. In February only one thing keeps you going—the air flight ticket to Florida on your dresser. If you make it to March, boy, you'll make it to heaven. You get on the plane in Misky Bay, there's so much ice on the wings and the wind from hell you doubt the plane can make it, but it does, and when it glides down and lands, when they throws open the door, my son, I want to tell you the smell of hot summer and suntan oil and exhaust fumes make you cry with pleasure. A sweet place they got down there with the oranges." He sucked in a breath, exhaled a snotty gust thinking of sleek yellow water like a liqueur. Addressed Quoyle. "Now, buddy, you got some kind of a car or boat wreck this week or not?"

"I wouldn't go down there. I wouldn't set foot on one of they planes." Billy Pretty scratching notes, looking up from his weltering desk, red-rimmed eyes, face like a pricked pastry. "I hope you got all kinds of wrecks Quoyle, because I got not much—couple more unknown bodies and two naked men in court. Here's a boyyo nabbed creeping out of a window loaded down with a sewing machine, the microwave, a shortwave radio, a color television, and the old missus and skipper sleeping away up in their bedroom, all sweet dreams, never woke up. The police patrol saw him hung up on a nail in the windowsill. So down to the Killick-Claw lockup he goes. In the middle of the night he commences to bawl and hoot, tears off all his clothes. They said he was mental. Sent him over to Waterford for observation. It's bloody spreading! Here's another. A young lad, father's a fisherman down to Port aux Priseurs, hit it rich in shrimps so he buys the boy a horse. Builds a barn and buys the boy a horse. Boy wanted a horse. 'All the advantages I never had, blahblah.' Didn't know anything about horses. Put it out in the barn. After a week or so lad gets tired of it and forgets about it. Finally the horse starves to death. They give the kid some kind of dressing-down and fines the dad a thousand dollars. He's got it, y'know, but what d'you think he does? Stands there in the court in front of the judge. Tears off all *his* clothes. So they sent him over to Waterford too.

"Now, over here we got missing persons and unidentified bodies, and none of them match up. Man from Chaw Cove went out hunting. All they found was his mittens. Down here in Puddickton missus finds a cold wet corpus floating under the skipper's dock. Total stranger, and not the feller from Chaw Cove. Not a stitch on him. Makes you wonder if he hadn't been in court recently. The worst one is this dog case. Another shrimp fisherman in Port aux Priseurs. This feller bought some fancy mainland dogs, a couple of pit bulls, couple of rottweilers, couple of Doberman pinschers, kept 'em all out in this big run. Now they can't find the man. Seems he went out to the dog pen and didn't come back. Family's all sitting around watching television. After a couple of hours somebody says 'Where's old dad, then?' They shine a light out at the dog pen, holler yoo-hoo. There's blood all over the snow and some of dad's clothes in a poor condition. So, even though he is missing, they think they know where he is."

Tert Card mooning against the window, staring south. "They ought to give up on the animals in Port aux Priseurs. They don't have the touch. Stick to cars and drugs. Quoyle, you got some kind of a wreck to brighten the front page?"

Nutbeem raised his head, unfolded his arms. "Seeing it's my last week, of course the foreign news is plummy. First, the Canadian Minister of Health has his knickers in a twist over hair removal."

"There are some of us, Nutbeem, who do not think of Canada as a foreign power," said Card.

"Leave him be," said Billy Pretty. "Go on with it, boy."

"All right. Hundreds of doctors are billing Health Insurance Plan for removing unwanted facial hair from women patients. A Ministry of Health official is quoted as saying 'This thing is hot.' Probably means the electrolysis machine. Millions and millions of dollars for millions and millions of electrolysis treatments."

Card sniggered. He was all grease spots and hunger. Fingernails like sugar scoops.

"Thought you'd have a giggle over that," said Nutbeem.

Quoyle was astonished to hear Billy Pretty bellow. "You may laugh, Card, but it's a rotten, bitter thing for a woman to see the shadow of a mustache creeping across her face. You'd be sympathetic now, wouldn't you, if it was men having breast fat removed?" He stared at Card's pointed breasts. A silence hanging for a few seconds, then Tert Card's wet laugh, Billy's snigger. It was only a joke. Quoyle still couldn't recognize a joke when he heard one.

"Ah," said Card, snorting into a tissue, spreading it open in the light of the window. "My sister had the problem, only it was hair on her arms. The old woman had other ways to go at it. We had Skipper Small, was a charmer. He'd write down on a little piece of paper, throw it in the fire, watch it burn until just a pelm laid over the coals, all white and wizzled. He'd take a stick, poke it in and break up the pelm, the bits would fly off to the chimney. 'There,' he'd say, 'there goes your affliction.'"

"Did it fix your sister's arms?"

"Oh yes, boy. Her arms come smooth as silk, they did, it was a pleasure to be squeezed by 'em. So they all said. I hope that's not the extent of your foreign news, Nutbeem, hair removal in Ontario."

"Well, there's the cholera epidemic in Peru. Argentina and Paraguay now refuse to play soccer in Peru. Fourteen thousand cases have been reported in the last six weeks."

"Good. We'll run that story next to the one on unknown insects biting employees in the Social Service office in Misky Bay after a recent influx of Peruvian immigrants." He looked at Quoyle. "Have you got a wreck, buddy?"

"Um," said Quoyle. Giving nothing to Tert Card.

"Well, then, what is it, where is it and did you get pictures?"

"The ship collision on Strain Bag. Then I shot a couple of frames of a vehicle fire—unexplained causes. Truck was parked in front of the funeral home and just burst into flames while the family was inside. Looked like a roasting pan on fire."

"That's a very good tip, Quoyle. If we ever get hard up for pictues we can get a roasting pan, fill it up with oil and set it on fire. Jiggle the camera a little when we take snaps. Who'll ever know?"

"Something in Misky Bay. Apparently a grudge between twin brothers, Boyle and Doyle Cats."

"I know them," said Billy Pretty. "One of them drives a taxi."

"Right. Boyle drives the taxi. There'd been some trouble the night before. Something to do with a drug deal, they think. On Wednesday afternoon Boyle picks up a passenger at the fish plant, makes a U-turn, and is ambushed by a masked man on a late-model blue Yamaha snowmobile with the word PSYCHOPATH painted on the cowling. His brother Doyle is alleged to own such a snowmobile. The snowmobile rider fires a shotgun at the taxi and speeds away, the taxi's windshield is blown out, the vehicle swerves and ends up on the loading ramp of the fish plant. Minor cuts and lacerations. The snowmobile got away."

"Is there snow down there?"

"No."

"I'm going to remember this place for many things," said Nutbeem. "But most of all for the inventive violence and this tearing-off-of-clothes-in-court business. Seems to be a Newfoundland specialty. Here's a fairly simple arson—some chap set his boat on fire—maybe you've got this one too, Quoyle—possibly for the insurance, and he's been sitting in the pokey for a few days. This morning they go to bring him into court and he did the regular."

"Tore off his clothes," droned through the room.

"I can do something with that," said Billy, tapping on the keys.

"Tert," said Nutbeem. "That sister of yours. Is she the one you told us that swallowed the sea wolf?"

"Sea wolf? You stun mope, she swallowed a water wolf. A sea wolf is a submarine. Come down in the dark and took up a dipper of water and swallowed it. When she was a kid. Said she felt something go down. Soon after that she commenced to eat like a horse. Eat and eat. Oh, the old woman knew right away. 'You've swallowed a water wolf,' she said. Nutbeem, I got your S.A. stories running down my computer screen. You writing it by the yard, now? Seven, eight, nine—you got eleven sexual abuse stories here. We put all this in there won't be room for the other news."

"You ought to see my notebook. It's an epidemic." Nutbeem turned to the file cabinets behind him. The khaki metal rang as he wrenched a drawer open. "All this since I've been here. What are you going to do when I'm off, then?"

"Jack's problem. Among others," said Tert Card with a mouthful of satisfaction. "You still leaving Tuesday?"

"Yes, I'll be heading out of the lashing snow sailing on my way to the Caribbean, down through the islands looking for adventure and love."

"It's late to be leaving. Storm and ice could fasten you in here overnight. The ice is formed up in some places. A dangerous time of year for a sailboat. You probably won't make it. It'll be your corpse they find in the ovens next." Tert Card, picking his teeth with the corner of an envelope. The paper jammed and tore, wedged between the yellow incisors.

"That's how it goes here. There's a general emptying out in the late fall. Away they all go to the south," said Billy Pretty. "There's few of us has stuck it out all the years, never been away in winter except when at sea. And Quoyle is the only one I ever see come here to settle. I'm just wondering about him. I suppose he'll be next."

"Obviously staying," said Quoyle. "Alvin Yark's building a boat for me. Bunny's in school, she's doing well. And Sunshine loves it at Beety's. The kids have friends. The aunt will be back from St. John's in the spring. All we need is a place to live."

"I can't see you in Nutbeem's trailer. You looked that place over yet?" Tert Card smiling at some secret.

"He's seeing it Friday. Quoyle's going to help me set up for the party. Getting everything to drink you can think of from screech to ginger beer to champagne."

"Champagne! That's what I enjoy," said Tert Card. "With a ripe peach floating in it."

"Go on. That's something you read. There's never been a ripe peach in Newfoundland."

"I have it when I go down to Florida. I have Mai-tais, Jamaica glows, beachcombers, banana daiquiris, piña coladas—my god, sitting around in your bathing suit on the balcony drinking those things. Baking hot."

"I doubt a man can bring up two little girls on his own," said Billy Pretty. "I doubt it can be done without some savage talk and nervous breakdowns all around."

Quoyle showed he didn't hear him.

32

The Hairy Devil

"To untangle a snarl, loosen all jams or knots and open a hole through the mass at the point where the longest end leaves the snarl. Then proceed to roll or wind the end out through the center exactly as a stocking is rolled. Keep the snarl open and loose at all times and do not pull on the end; *permit it to unfold itself."*

THE ASHLEY BOOK OF KNOTS

DURING the night a warm fluke, a tongue of balmy air, licked out from the mainland and tempered the crawling ice margins. The November snow decayed. On Friday afternoon Tert Card, wild with false spring, cut up at the office, played practical jokes, answered the phone in a falsetto and went to the washroom again and again. They smelled the rum on his breath. Nutbeem's own excitement showed in high voice notes. His departure combined with a waxing moon.

"Going to get Bunny now and take her to Beety's" said Quoyle. "Then I'll be back."

In Beety's kitchen he drank a cup of tea quickly.

"Beety, it's Nutbeem's party tonight. I'm going out early to help him set things up and look over the trailer. God, you make the best bread." Wolfing it down.

"Well, maybe I won't be making it no more if Allie Marvel gets her bakery shop going this spring. Bread keeps you tied down to the house and there's things I'd like to do." She whispered, "If Dennis can stand it."

"Dad," said Bunny, "I want to go to the party."

"Not this one, you don't. This is a men's party. It would not be fun for you."

"Hey, Quoyle," said Dennis from in front of the television set in the living room, "suppose you won't be back *here* tonight."

"Well, I will," said Quoyle, who was sleeping on a cot in the basement workshop until they could move into Nutbeem's trailer. "Because I've got a long day tomorrow. Since the roads are clear. Got to get some things that are still out at the house on the point in the morning, then help Alvin with the boat."

"If the girls have got spare mittens out there," said Beety, "bring them back. Show your dad, Sunshine, what happened to your mitts." The little girl brought a stiff, charred thing.

"She brought in a few junks of wood and her old mitten stuck to a splinter. She didn't notice and Dennis here, he heaves the wood in the firebox and we smell it. There's nothing like the stink of burning wool to get your attention. Got it out, but it's beyond hope. I'm knitting her another one tonight, but you can't have too many kids' mittens."

Sunshine ran to Quoyle, put her mouth to his ear and sent a loud, tickling message in.

"Dad, Beety is showing me how to knit. I am knitting a Christmas present for you. It's very hard."

"Good lord," said Quoyle, astonished. "And you're only four years old."

"It's kind of a trick, Dad, because it's just a long, long, fat string and it turns into a scarf. But I can't show it to you."

"Are you telling a certain secret?" asked Beety.

"Yes," said Sunshine, beaming.

"See you later," said Quoyle.

"See you!" called Dennis eagerly.

It took Quoyle and Nutbeem an hour and a half to get to the trailer. They made long stops at the liquor authority loading boxes of beer and rum into the station wagon until the rear end sagged, stacking the backseat with plastic-wrapped party platters of sliced ham, turkey, cold cuts and red-eyed olives from the town's only supermarket, then on to the fish processing plant for a tub of ice which Nutbeem somehow lashed on top. Early darkness. A few more weeks until the winter solstice.

"Isn't this is too much?" said Quoyle. "Too much everything."

"You're forgetting the contributors and advertisers, and those two discriminating food critics, Benny Fudge and Adonis Collard, who write the food column. Did you read their latest? Sort of a 'Newfoundland Guide to Fried Bologna.' Then there's your pal, the old chap down at the harbor, and the court laddie who gives me the S.A. news. There'll be the odd midnight arrival. And maybe fifty layabouts. You'll see. Killick-Claw is a party town. Why I got six gallons of screech."

"Actually, fried bologna isn't bad," said Quoyle.

"You have gone native."

They drove to the south end, over a one-lane bridge to a trailer behind a cluster of houses. Faded pastel pink with a stenciled frieze of girls with umbrellas, a low picket fence. Nutbeem's scabby bicycle leaned near the steps.

"The Goodlads live in the proper houses," said Nutbeem. "Fishermen. Lambie and John and his mother in the green house, the two younger sons, Ray in the white and red house and Sammy in the blue. The oldest son is a fisheries biologist in St. John's. This is his trailer. He came up once last summer, but left after two days. On his way to New Zealand to study some kind of exotic Southern Hemisphere crab." Nutbeem himself was drawn to crabs in a culinary sense, although a surfeit gave him hives on his forearms.

"Come in," he said and opened the door.

Just another trailer, thought Quoyle, with its synthetic carpet, cubbyhole bedrooms, living room like a sixties photograph except for four enormous brown speakers ranged in the corners like bodyguards, kitchen the size of a cupboard with miniature refrigerator and stove, a sink barely big enough for both of Quoyle's hands. The bathroom had one oddity. Quoyle looked in, saw a yellow spray hose coiled on the mat like a hunting horn, and in the shower cubicle, half a plastic barrel.

"What's this, then?" he asked Nutbeem.

"I longed for a bath—I still do, you know. This is my compromise. They ship molasses in these barrels. So I cut it in half with a saw, you see, and stuck it in here. I can crouch down in it. It's not awfully satisfactory, but better than the cold plastic curtain twining about one's torso."

Back in the living room Nutbeem said "Wait until you hear this," and switched on a tower of sound components. Red and green running lights, flashing digital displays, pulsing contour bands, orange readouts sprang to life. From the speakers a sound as of a giant's lung. Nutbeem slipped a silver disc into a tray and the trailer vibrated with thunder. The music was so loud that Quoyle could not discern any identifiable instrument, nothing but a pulsating sound that rearranged his atoms and quashed thought.

Quoyle rammed the beer bottles into the tub of ice, helped Nutbeem push the table against the wall. The taut plastic over the party platters vibrated visibly.

"When the first guests pull up," shouted Nutbeem, "we'll rip the plastic off."

They looked vainly through the cupboards for a bowl large enough to hold thirty bags of potato chips.

"What about your barrel in the shower?" screamed Quoyle. "Just for tonight. It's big enough."

"Right! And have a beer! Nutbeem's good-bye party has officially begun!" And as Quoyle poured potato chips into the soap-scummed barrel, Nutbeem sent a ululating call into the night.

Through the picture window framed in salmon-pink curtains, they saw a line of headlights approaching the narrow bridge. The beer in Quoyle's bottle trembled in the batter of sound. Nutbeem was saying something, impossible to know what.

Tert Card was the first one through the door, and his stumble carried him against the table with the party platters. He was clenching a rum bottle, wore a linen touring cap that transformed the shape of his head to that of a giant albino ant. He plucked at the plastic wrap, seized a handful of ham and pushed it into his mouth. A crowd of men came in, shouting and swaying, and as though at a ham and cheese eating contest, snatched up the food from the party platters. Crammed potato chips as though stuffing birds for the oven.

The trailer shook on its cinder-block foundation. All at once the room was so packed that bottles had to be passed from hand to hand overhead.

Tert Card was beside him. "There's something I want to tell you," he shouted, raised a squat tumbler with a nicked rim to Quoyle. But before he spoke, disappeared.

Quoyle began to enjoy himself in a savage, lost way, the knots of fatherhood loosened for the night, thoughts of Petal and Wavey quenched. He had only been to two or three parties in his adult life, and never to one where all the guests were men. Ordinary parties, he thought, were subtle games of sexual and social badminton; this was something very different. There was a mood of rough excitement that had more in common, he thought, with a parking-lot fight behind a waterfront bar than a jolly good-bye to Nutbeem. A rank smell of tobacco, rum and dirty hair. Tert Card's touring cap rose and fell in front of him again as though he were doing knee bends. He mopped at his eyebrows with his forearm.

"Everybody asks me about the hairy devil," screamed Tert Card. "But I'll tell you."

Quoyle could barely catch the words of the interminable monologue. "When my father was young up in Labrador . . . Used to call him Skit Card because he was left-handed. Said there was a feeling like he was near a HOLE under the snow. Walk careful or . . . slip straight down SPINNING . . . He walked careful . . . spooky. One day he gets his buddy Alphonse . . . They get to the camp . . . Alphonse says . . . 'NO GOOD, I'm going back.' Father persuades him . . . 'STAY until daybreak' . . . laid down. In the morning Alphonse was GONE. His tracks . . . straight ahead. Then nothing . . . tracks disappeared, snow untouched."

A man with a meaty face the size and shape of a sixteen-pound ham squeezed in front of Quoyle. Although he shouted his voice was distant.

"Hello, Quoyle. Adonis Collard. Write the food column. Wanted to say hello. Don't get up to Killick-Claw much. Down in Misky Bay, you know. For the restaurants." The crowd surged and Quoyle was carried near the beer tub. Nutbeem's sound system was sending out tremendously low snoring and sawing sounds. Then, Tert Card again, a ham slice protruding from his mouth.

"Father got a POLE. Poked around where tracks ended. All of a sudden a sound like a CORK being pulled . . . a deep blue well going down . . . polished steel CYLINDER. He throws in the stick. Whistled like a sled runner."

Someone pushed between them and Quoyle tried to work toward the front door, working his elbows like oars. But Card was in front of him again.

"All of a sudden something BEHIND him. A HAIRY DEVIL jumped down the hole like a HOCKEY puck . . . RED EYES. Says to me father . . . 'BE BACK for you . . . after I washes me POTS AND PANS.' Father . . . ran forty miles."

"My wife," bawled Quoyle, "is dead."

"I know that," said Tert Card. "That's not news."

By ten, Quoyle was drunk. The crowd was enormous, crushed together so densely that Nutbeem could not force his way down the hall or to the door and urinated on the remaining potato chips in the blue barrel, setting a popular example. The deafening music urged madness. In the yard two fights, and the empurpled Diddy Shovel threw Nutbeem's bicycle into the bay. The strong man looked around, called for a beam on which to hoist himself by his little finger. Dennis appeared, scorched and reeling with a rum bottle in his hand. A grim-faced man Quoyle had never seen before pulled his pants off and danced in the mud. A terrible lurch as twenty chanting men lifted the end of the trailer and kicked away the cinder blocks. There was Jack, his arm around Dennis, sharing his bottle. A truck randomly bashed others, shot sparkles of glass over the ground. Billy Pretty lay on the steps singing soundless songs, forcing everyone to walk over him. A swaying, wild madness built up, shouting and bellowing that churned with the drumming music, a violent snorting and capering rage. Accents thickened and fell into the old outport patois. Quoyle couldn't understand a word.

An emaciated black-haired man, a foot taller than the local men who ran to large jaws, no necks, sandy hair and barrel chests, got up on the steps. He raised an axe he'd picked up near Nutbeem's woodpile.

"Ar!" he shouted. "Wants to take 'is leave, do 'e? Us'll 'ave 'im 'ere. Come along, b'ys, axe 'is bo't. Got yer chain saw Neddie?"

Nutbeem screamed "No! No! Don't fucking touch her! Fucking leave her alone!"

With a roar a dozen rushed to follow the black-haired man. Quoyle didn't understand what was happening, saw that he had been left behind. The party had gone somewhere else without him. Just like always. Quoyle left out. Not a damn thing had changed. In a huff of rejection he reeled away down the road toward—what? Something.

"Quoyle, you fucking bitch get back here and help me save her!" But Nutbeem's howl was lost in the cacophony.

The party charged to the dock where the *Borogove* was tied up. Some had gotten chain saws from the back of their pickups, others carried sticks and rocks. The black-haired man was in the lead bellowing "We loves old fuckin' Nutbeem!"

The homely little boat lay at the dock, repaired and ready, provisioned, freshwater tanks filled, new line, the few bits of brightwork polished. Nutbeem staggered along the road crying and laughing as the wild men swarmed over his boat. The black-haired man lifted his axe and brought it down on the deck with all his strength. A chain saw bit into the mast. Tremendous pummeling and wrenching noises, splashes as pieces of the *Borogove* went into the water. The black-haired man got below deck with his axe and in a few minutes chopped through the bottom.

"Every man for hisself," he shouted, rushed forward and jumped onto the pier. In ten minutes Nutbeem's boat was underwater, nothing showing but the roof of the cabin, like a waterlogged raft.

Quoyle did not remember leaving the maelstrom. One moment he was there, the next, on his hands and knees in the ditch on the far side of the bridge. The air was like water in his flaming mouth. Or had he fallen in the water, and was now steaming rudderless in the night? He got up, staggered, looked back at the trailer. The windows glowed in a line of tilted light like a sinking passenger ship. Ships could hear Nutbeem's speakers five miles out at sea, he thought. The howling of the mob.

He started to walk, to lurch along the road into a greater silence. The hell with Nutbeem. He had his own affairs. Past the houses and up the steep streets of Killick-Claw. His head cleared a little as he walked. He did not know where he was going, but climbed up and on. The hill over the town. The same route he took to work every day. He could see the harbor lights below, a large ship coming slowly down the bay. The lighthouse on the point swept its beam over the sea. Quoyle walked on. He felt he could walk to Australia. Down the long hill now, past the dark *Gammy Bird* office. Cold television light in the Buggits' house; Mrs. alone with her snowdrifts of doilies. Looked across the bay where Quoyle's Point was lost in caliginous night. The moon cleared the landmass, cast a sparkling bar on the water.

He was outside her kitchen window. A wry, reedy music within. He knelt at the window. The hard illumination of the neon circle from the ceiling. A clattering. He looked in at Wavey on a kitchen chair, her legs wide, the skirt a hammock for the red accordion on her lap. Her foot rising and falling, slapping the time in a rhythm that was sad in its measured steadiness. And on the empty linoleum stage in front of the stove Herry, dancing and hopping a jig, the pie-face split with a grin of intense concentration.

Quoyle crawled out to the road. The moon's reflection bored into the flat water like a hole into the sea, like the ice well where

Tert Card's father's hairy devil washed his pots and pans. The painted wooden dogs in Wavey's father's yard watched, their bottle-cap collars catching the light as though in convulsive swallowing. He started back toward Killick-Claw, toward the inn where he would rent a room. He had forgotten Beety and Dennis's house, his cot in the basement.

33

The Cousin

"Magic nets, snares, and knots have been, and in some instances probably still are, used as lethal weapons."

QUIPUS AND WITCHES' KNOTS

AT TEN in the morning the chambermaid knocked on Quoyle's door, then stuck her head in and called "Comin' to do the room, m'dear."

"Wait," said Quoyle. "Half hour." Dead boiled voice.

"Guess you was at the party where they sunk the boat! Harriet says the kitchen wants to put away the breakfasts so they can get started on lunch. Shall I tell her to save you a bit of eggs and tea then?"

But Quoyle was on his knees in front of the toilet, retching, suffering, full of self-hatred. Heard her voice like a wasp in a jar. At last he could turn on the shower, stand beneath the hot needles, face thrust near the spray head, feeling the headache move back a little. His legs pained.

The bedroom was icy after the steam. He pulled on clothes, the fabric rucking like metal. Bending to tie his shoes brought the headache into his eyes again and his stomach clenched.

Out the window the sky was dirty, sand swirled in the street. A few trucks passed, exhaust twisting out of tail pipes. Cold. His jacket sleeve was torn from shoulder to wrist.

Downstairs Harriet smirked.

"Hear it was some party," she said. Quoyle nodded.

"You ought to have a cup of tea. Nice hot cup of tea."

"I'll make one out at the house," he said. "Got to get out there this morning and pick up some things." Sunshine's boots, kids' extra mittens, the rest of his shirts, a library book now weeks overdue. Some tools. Supposed to be at Alvin Yark's in the afternoon. He had a recollection of Nutbeem's trailer being pulled apart. Suppose they couldn't live in it? Tried to telephone Nutbeem, fumbled the coins into the slot. No answer.

"They're calling for snow tonight," said Harriet and crackled her papers. "What do you hear from Agnis? She like it in St. John's? I know Dawn likes it. She's my cousin Arky's youngest. Guess she's having the time of her life. Says she'll never come back here."

"O.k., I guess," said Quoyle. Shaking.

In the street he couldn't find his car. Forced his mind back to Nutbeem's party, remembered walking miles and miles out to Wavey's house. Peering in the window. The car must still be at Nutbeem's. Or had he wrecked it, driven it off the road or into the sea? He didn't know. But walked to Harbor Cab and took a taxi to the trailer. There was no place he wanted less to see.

"So this where they 'ad the big pardy," said the driver. "Never know it. I seen pardies go on three, four days. Not no more, my son. Them good days is gone." And drove away.

His station wagon was there, but with an indentation in the door. Seven or eight beer cans in the backseat. Shriveled circles of ham on the fender. The trailer sagged at one end. The yard was glassy with a strew of bottles. No sign of Nutbeem, his bicycle or, at the dock, his boat. Had he sailed away drunk in the night without saying good-bye? Must be pitching on the Atlantic with his head in a vise.

Quoyle thought of the barrel full of piss, the tiny aluminum rooms. He did not want to live in the trailer.

Beety gave him a cool look and a mug of hot tea.

"I stayed at the inn last night," he said, "apparently."

"Look like you slept in the puppy's parlor. I never thought you was the type, Quoyle."

"I didn't think so, either." The tea, scalding hot with two sugars and plenty of milk repairing him. "Is Dennis up?"

"Yes. In a way you could say he's up all night. Come in at daylight with that poor Nutbeem to get some tools, and now he's out rousting the rest of them that sank the boat. Poor Mr. Nutbeem."

"Sank the boat? I didn't see that. I just came from there. I didn't see anything. There was nobody there. Nothing."

"They've gone to get a crane. Dennis says they got in a wild mood last night. Seemed like a good joke to keep poor Nutbeem here by wrecking his boat. So now they've got to fix it."

"My God," said Quoyle. "And I thought Nutbeem had left in the night."

"He didn't look in shape to cross the road."

"Dad. Guess what, Dad, I'm sick. And Bunny's sick, too. And Marty."

Sunshine stood in the door in droopy pajamas, her nose running. Gripping a sheet of paper.

"Poor baby," said Quoyle, lifting her up and dipping a bit of toast in his tea for her.

"They've all got colds," said Beety.

"I was going to take them out to the house with me this morning. You've had them all week, Beety. You must need a break."

"They're like me own," she said. "But perhaps you'll be in tomorrow afternoon? Stay with them all for a bit? Winnie will be here, but I'd like for an adult to be on hand, y'know. Dennis and I was going up to see his mother and father. They says 'come up for evening service, a bite of supper.' We'd take the kids, but they's all sneezing and hawking."

"Glad to stay with them, Beety. You've been all the help in the world. I saw Jack and Dennis together last night. They both looked in a good mood. So I gather the coolness is over."

"That was a lot of gossip. They was *never* cool. Hot under the collar for a while is more like it, but it passed right off. The old gossips made something out of it."

Sunshine felt hot under Quoyle's hand. He looked at her drawing. At the top a shape with cactus ears and spiral tail. The legs shot down to the bottom of the page.

"It's a monkey with his legs stretched out," said Sunshine. Quoyle kissed the hot temple, aware of the crouching forces that would press her to draw broccoli trees with brown bark.

"Nutbeem's trailer looked pretty sad this morning. They lifted one end off the foundation last night. I think I'd rather take the kids into a house than that trailer. If I can find anything. If you hear of anyone who'd rent for a while."

"Did you talk to the Burkes? They're down in Florida. A nice house. They want to sell it but they might rent now. Said they wouldn't at first, but there's been no buyers. It's up on the road to Flour Sack Cove. You go past it twice a day. Grey house with a FOR SALE sign on the front. On the corner, there."

"Black and white picket fence all around?"

"That's it."

He knew the house. Neat house with blue trim, high up, a sailor's wife's view of the harbor.

"I'll see what I can find out on Monday. It might be just the place for us. But I can't buy it. I've put a lot of money into that old house out on the point. I don't have much left. The girls' money's put aside for them. All right, here's the plan," he said, half to Sunshine, half to Beety. "I'm going out to the green house now to pick up the rest of the things. Then I'm going up to Alvin Yark's and help with the boat. Then I'll look in at Nutbeem's and see what's happened with *his* boat. If they fixed it. If Dennis is ready to quit for the day, maybe we'll pick up some pizzas and a movie to watch. How's that, Beety? *Stalk of the Lust Beast*, that's the kind of movie you like isn't it?"

"No! Get out of it. Why don't you bring back a comedy? That Australian one you got before was decent enough."

He wondered if they'd made the Australian lesbian vampire murders into a movie yet.

The gravel road to Quoyle's Point, scalloped ice in the potholes, had never seemed so miserable. The wind dead and the thick sky pressed on the sea. Calm. Flat calm. Not a flobber, Billy would say. The car engine seemed unnaturally loud. Beer cans rolled on the floor. Past the turnoff to Capsize Cove and a thread of smoke, past the glove factory, then he was at the grim house like a hat on a rock.

The abandoned silence. The stale smell. As it was the first time. As though they had never lived in it. The aunt's voice and energy erased.

The house was heavy around him, the pressure of the past filling the rooms like odorless gas. The sea breathed in the distance. The house meant something to the aunt. Did that bind him? The coast around the house seemed beautiful to him. But the house was wrong. Had always been wrong, he thought. Dragged by human labor across miles of ice, the outcasts straining against the ropes and shouting curses at the godly mob. Winched onto the rock. Groaning. A bound prisoner straining to get free. The humming of the taut cables. That vibration passed into the house, made it seem alive. That was it, in the house he felt he was inside a tethered animal, dumb but feeling. Swallowed by the shouting past.

Up the stairs. Someone had laid lengths of knotted twine on the threshold of each room. The dirty clenches at the threshold of the room where his children had slept! Quoyle raged, slammed doors.

He thought of the smoke coming up from Capsize Cove, of what Billy Pretty had said of the old cousin living somewhere down there. Tying his bloody knots! Quoyle seized his shirts from the hangers on the back of the door, found Bunny's boots. No extra mittens that he could see. And slammed out of the house, the lengths of knotted twine in his pocket.

He pulled up at the top of the Capsize Cove road. Would put a stop to this business. The road was beyond repair. In the frozen mud he saw dog tracks. Picked up a stick, was ready to strike a snarler away. Or to shake at a knot-tier. The deserted village came in sight, buildings stacked on one another in steep terraces. Skeletal frames, clapboards and walls gone. A blue façade, a cube of beams and uprights. Pilings supporting nothing, the rotten planks fallen into the sea.

Smoke came from a hut at the edge of the water, more boat shed than house. Quoyle looked around, watching for the dog, noticed a skiff hauled up onshore, covered with stone-weighted canvas. Nets and floats. A bucket. The path from the building to an outhouse behind. The old fish flakes for drying cod, racks for squid. Three sheep in a handkerchief field, a pile of firewood, red star of plastic bag on the landwash.

As he approached the sheep ran from him with tinkling bells. No dog. He knocked. Silence. But knew the old cousin was inside.

He called, Mr. Quoyle, Mr. Quoyle, felt he was calling himself. And no answer.

Lifted the latch and went in. A jumble of firewood and rubbish, a stink. The dog growled. He saw it in the corner by the stove, a white dog with matted eyes. A pile of rags in the other corner stirred and the old man sat up.

Even in the dim light, even in the ruin of cadaverous age, Quoyle saw resemblances. The aunt's unruly hair; his father's lipless mouth; their common family eyes sunk under brows as coarse as horsehair; his brother's stance. And for Quoyle, a view of his own monstrous chin, here a somewhat smaller bony shelf choked with white bristle.

In the man before him, in the hut, crammed with the poverty of another century, Quoyle saw what he had sprung from. For the old man was mad, the gears of his mind stripped long ago to clashing discs edged with the stubs of broken cogs. Mad with loneliness or lovelessness, or from some genetic chemical jumble, or the flooding betrayal that all hermits suffer. Loops of fishing line underfoot, the snarl trodden into compacted detritus, a churn of splinters, sand, rain, sea wet, mud, weed, bits of wool, gnawed sheep ribs, spruce needles, fish scales and bones, burst air bladders, seal offal, squid cartilage, broken glass, torn cloth, dog hair, nail parings, bark and blood.

Quoyle pulled the knotted strings from his pocket, dropped them on the floor. The man darted forward. With stubbed fingers he snatched up the strings, threw them into the stove.

"Them knots'll never undo now! They's fixed by fire!"

Quoyle could not shout at him, even for witch-knots in his daughters' footsteps, even for the white dog that had terrified Bunny. Said, "You don't need to do this." Which meant nothing. And he left.

Back up the gullied road thinking of old Quoyle, his squalid magic of animal parts and twine. No doubt lived by moon phases, marked signs on leaves, saw bloody rain and black snow sweep in on him from the bay, believed geese spent their winters congealed in the swamps of Manitoba. Whose last pathetic defense against imagined enemies was to tie a knot in a bit of string.

Quoyle ducked into the shop. Alvin Yark in the gloom, smoothing at a curved piece of wood with a spokeshave.

"Good stem, looks like," droned Yark. "Going along in the woods and I see that spruce tree and says to meself, there's a nice little stem for Quoyle. Can see it's got a nice flare to it, make a lean boat, not too lean, you know. Made a boat for Noah Day about ten years ago, stem looked pretty in the tree but too upright, you know, didn't 'ave enough flare. So it builds out bluff in the bows. Noah says to me, 'If I 'ad another boat I'd sell this one.' "

Quoyle nodded, put his hand to his chin. Man with Hangover Listens to Boat Builder Project Variables.

"That's what makes your different boats, you know. Each tree grows a little different so every boat you make, you know, the rake of the stem and the rake of the stern is a little different too, and that makes it so you 'as different 'ulls. Each one is different, like men and women, some good, some not so good." Had heard that in a sermon and taken it for his own. He began to sing in a hoarse, low voice, "Oh the *Gandy Goose*, it ain't no use."

Quoyle there among the ribby timbers, up to his ankles in shavings. Cold. Alvin Yark wore mittens, the zipper of his jacket flashed.

Leaning against the walls were the main timbers.

"Them's the ones I cut the week before. Don't cut 'em all now, you know," he explained to Quoyle. "I does the three main ones first, the fore'ook, the midship bend, and the after'ook. Got my molds, you know, my father give 'em to me. 'E used to measure and cut all his timbers with 'em, but quite a few of the sir marks is rubbed out, and some was never keyed, so you don't know what they's meant to be. So I does the three main ones, you know, and the counter. Then I know where I stands."

Quoyle's job was hoisting and lifting. His headache had strengthened. He could feel its shape and color, a gigantic Y that curved from his brain stem over his skull to each eye, in color a reddish-black like grilled meat.

Alvin Yark cut scarf joints, trimmed and smoothed until they fit together like a handclasp. The pieces lay ready. Now they fitted the stem to the keel joint. When Quoyle leaned forward the twin spears of the headache threatened to dislodge his eyes.

"Up the sternpost." Then the deadwood blocks on top of the inboard seams of the joints.

"Put 'er together now," Yark said, driving the four-inch spikes, fastening the bolts. He sang. "Oh it ain't no use, the *Gandy Goose*."

"There's your backbone. There's the backbone of your boat. She's scarfed now. You glance at that, somebody who knows boats, you can see the whole thing right there. But there's nobody can tell 'ow she'll fit the water, handle in the swells and lops until you try 'er out. Except poor old Uncle Les, Les Budgel. Dead now. Would be about a hundred and thirty year old. He was a boat builder along this shore before I saw my first 'ammer and nail. Built beautiful skiffs and dories, butter on a 'ot stove. Last boat he built was the best one. Liked 'is drop, Uncle Les did, yes, pour the screech down 'is gullet by the quart. 'E got old. Strange 'ow we all do."

At the mention of drink Quoyle's head throbbed.

"Wife was gone, children off to Australia. Funerals and pearly gates and coffins got to working on 'is mind. Finally 'e set out to make 'is own coffin. Went down to 'is shop with a teakettle 'alf full of screech and commenced 'ammering. 'Ammering and sawing 'alf through the night. Then 'e crawled back to the 'ouse to sleep it off on the kitchen floor. Me old dad went over to the shop, just as curious as 'e could be to see the wonderful coffin. There she was, coffin with a stem and a keel, planked up and caulked nice, a little six-foot coffin painted up smart. Best thing about 'er was the counter, set nice and low, all ready for 'er little outboard motor."

Quoyle laughed feebly.

Yark bolted a curved spruce piece he called the apron to the inboard of the stem. "Strengthens the stem, y'see. Support for the planks—if we ever gets to them, if I lives that long." He crouched, measured, tapped a nail into one end of the keel, hooked the loop of a chalk line over the nail and drew the blue string to a mark on the far end, snapped. A faint mist of blue powder and the timberline was marked.

"Suppose we might 'ave a cup of tea," murmured Yark, first wiping his nose on the back of his hand, then leaning over the shavings to snort out sawdust and snot. Sang his bit of song. "Oh it ain't no use, 'cause every nut and bolt is loose."

But Quoyle had to go along to Nutbeem's trailer.

At the trailer Nutbeem, Dennis, Billy Pretty and the black-haired man sat on the steps; despite the cold, were drinking beer. Quoyle gagged at the thought. There was no crane, no boat.

"You're lookin' dishy, Quoyle."

"Feel it, too. What's the situation?" He could see that at least the trailer was back on its cinder blocks, the glass raked into a crooked windrow.

"She's gone." Dennis. "Couldn't get the crane, see, but Carl come with his bulldozer. That was a mess. Tore the cabin right off her. Got that diver lives down No Name there, Orvar, come over and put a cable under her. We drags her at an angle to get a line to shore and she breaks in half. Tide was coming in fast and now it seems like she drifted. She's out there somewhere in two pieces. So, on top of everything else, she's a menace to navigation."

"I'm some disgusted," Billy Pretty, mud to his knees, side of his face scraped and raw, the enamel blue eyes bloodshot under the brim of his cap. Sipping as though he drank some aperitif.

Nutbeem swallowed a gassy mouthful and looked at the bay. The sky heavy and low. Although it was only three o'clock, darkness seeped.

"I wouldn't have made it anyway," he said. "Storm coming. Gale warnings, sleet, snow, followed by deep cold, the whole string of knots. By Tuesday there'll be fast ice. I wouldn't have made it."

"Maybe not," said Billy Pretty, "but you could have hauled your boat up until spring."

"No use crying in my beer," said Nutbeem.

A few small flakes of snow drifted down to Billy's knees. He glared at them, breathed to make them melt. A few more fell, widely spaced. "Here's the devil's feathers."

But Nutbeem had the stage. "I've changed my plans as the day has gone along."

"Will you stay on a bit, then? Stay for the Christmas pageant and the times, anyway."

"I don't expect I shall ever want to go to another party," said Nutbeem. "It's like the lad who loved to steal spoonsful of sugar until his grannie sat him down in front of a basin of the stuff, gave him a whacking great stuffing spoon and told him he'd stay right there until the basin was empty. He never had a taste for sugar after that." He laughed in a wretched puff of cheeks.

"At least you can smile at it." Dennis, half-smiling himself.

"If I didn't I'd go round the twist, wouldn't I? No, I've decided to smile, forget and fly to Brazil. Warm. No fog. The water is a lovely swimming-pool green, quite a David Hockney color. Balmy breezes. Perhaps it's still possible to live pleasantly for a few months.

And the fish! Ah, god. Yellowtail steaks. There's this very simple local sauce—you can put it on fish or in other sauces or salads—just squeeze a cup of lime juice, put in a good pinch of salt and let it stand for a few weeks, then you strain it and put it in a corked bottle and use it. It smells rather strange but has a quite wonderful taste. You sprinkle it on a bit of fish smoking fresh off the grill. And Cuban Green Sauce—lime and garlic and watercress and Tabasco and sour cream and lobster coral. And I make a curry, a conch curry, simmered in coconut milk and served with slivers of smoked sailfish that is, if I do say so, heaven on a plate."

"Stop," said Quoyle. Veils of snow swept the bay, dusted their shoulders and hair.

"Dear boy, I haven't even got to the bloody stone crabs. Stone crabs, the glorious imperial yellow, scarlet and ebony exaltations of all the crabs of all the seven seas, the epicure's hour of glory, the Moment of Truth at the table. I like them with drawn butter to which I add a dash of the sour lime sauce and a few drops of walnut pickle liquor, maybe a fleck of garlic."

"You're a poet with the food, Nutbeem," said Billy Pretty. "The time you gave me a plateful of your seal flipper curry. It was a poem."

"I think I'm safe in saying, Billy, that we are the only two people who have ever eaten of that rare dish. And the shrimp. Brazilian style. A big black iron skillet. You heat some olive oil, throw in a few cloves of garlic, then add the shrimp just as they come from the sea—but dry them off a bit, first. When they're cooked to a lovely orange-red you drain them on brown paper bags, toss some sea salt and a grind or two of green pepper or a shake of the Tabasco bottle over them and serve them on the bags. Just bite off the heads, drag the meat out with your teeth and spit out the tails." The snow swept over them. Nutbeem's hair and eyebrows were thick with it as he faced into the wind. The others had gyred around to give their backs to the weather.

"That's how my old friend Partridge used to fix shrimp," said Quoyle.

The silent black-haired man frowned. There were fluffy white epaulets on his shoulders.

"I dunno. It's some good the way they do them at Nell's in No Name Cove. It's them little shrimp, size of your fingernail. She shucks 'em, dips 'em in batter and rolls 'em in crushed graham crackers, then deep-fries 'em and serves with packet of tartar sauce. Proper thing! Good too in the flour sauce on baked beans."

"Yes, those are the sweetest shrimp I've ever tasted," said Nutbeem. "They're very good, those tiny shrimp. Anyway, later I might just drift up the coast, then go over to Pacific Mexico to some of the shark-fishing villages. Very rough places and a very rough sport. I'm not actually planning anything. A certain period of drifting is in order."

"Ar," said Billy, using the edge of his hand as a strigil, scraping the snow off the back of his neck below the tweed cap. "Wish I was young again. I'd go with you. I was to Saõ Paulo and down along the coast. I even had that lime sauce you talk about. Back in the 'thirties. And stone crabs. Been to Cuber, too. And Chiner. Before the war. Ar, Newfoundlanders are your great travelers. I got a nephew was on a troop carrier here lately, carrying the Americans to their Gulf War. Anywhere in the world you go you'll find us. But now I'm past the age of interest. I don't care whether its limes or potatoes, fish or fried."

"When you going, Nutbeem?"

"Tuesday. Same date. Gives me the last chance to whip up a nice helping of bizarre stories for Jack and Tert. 'Elderly Widower Elopes with Lobster!' 'Prime Minister Bathes in Imported Beer.' 'Filthy Old Dad Rapes Childrens' Horse.' Perhaps I shall miss *Gammy Bird*, after all. Oh, Quoyle, a bit of bad news for you. The Goodlads say now they won't rent their trailer out to a newspaperman again. After last night. I pleaded with them, told them you had two sweet little daughters, were a very modest fellow, persnickety housekeeper, never had parties, et cetera, et cetera, but they'll have none of it. I'm awfully sorry."

"I'll find something else," said Quoyle. With every breath a charge of snowflakes in the nostrils. The headache was a dull background throb.

"It's too bad," said Billy Pretty, silvered with snow, changing color with the season. "It's too bad." That seemed to cover everything.

Quoyle squinted at the sky where nothing could be seen but the billions of tossing flakes stirred by a rigorous wind.

"It's a stepmother's breath," said Billy.

34

Dressing Up

Sailors once wore their hair in queues worked two ways; laid up into rattails, or platted in four-strand square sinnets. The final touch called for a pickled eelskin chosen from the brine cask. The sailor carefully rolled the eelskin back (as a condom is rolled), then worked it up over his queue and seized it. For dress occasions he finished it off with a red ribbon tied in a bow.

"QUOYLE, finish that up and I'll take you round the corner to the Heavy Weather and buy you a hot grog." Tert Card, morose and white, staring with hatred at the ice-bound bay. For it had gone very still and cold. Pancakes of submerged ice joined with others into great sheets, the rubbery green ice thickened, an ice foot fastened onto the shore, binding the sea with the land. Liquid became solid, solid was buried under crystals. A level plain stretched nearly to the mouth of the bay. He watched the ice breaker gnawing through, cutting a jagged path of black water.

"I suppose I can." Reluctant. Didn't want to drink with Tert Card but thought no one else would. A quick one. "Let me call Beety and say I'll be a little late." But wanted to collect his daughters and go home to the Burkes' house, a squeaky, comfortable house with many cupboards in unlikely corners. The strangest thing in the place was a lampshade that crackled modestly as the bulb warmed. There was a bathroom with a handmade copper tub wide enough for Quoyle. The first tub he'd ever fit in. Spare rooms for visitors. If any came.

"Then we'll have a glutch or two, or two," grinned Tert Card, the devil plucking at the strings of his throat as if it were a guitar. "Follow me." The vehicles groaned through the cold.

The Heavy Weather was a long room with a filthy linoleum floor and the smell of a backed-up toilet, vomit, stale smoke and liquor. This was where Tert Card drank, the place he scrawled home from, barely able to get up the steps and into his house. Quoyle thought he probably shouted at home. Or worse. The few times he'd seen the wife she looked a bent thing and the children shrank when he said hello to them. For he noticed small children.

Fluorescent halos. A solid row of backs at the bar. Silhouettes of men in caps with earflaps that came down when wanted. Showing each other photographs of boats. The talk was of insurance and unemployment and going away to find work. Quoyle and Tert Card sat at a side table littered with wadded napkins. A smoldering ashtray. Behind them two old slindgers in overcoats and pulled-down Donegal caps, all mufflers and canes and awkward knees. They sat close together on a long bench. Each, a hand on the glass. It might have been a village pub across the water, thought Quoyle.

"What'll you have?" Tert Card, leaning on the table until it rocked. "What'll you have, don't tell me, don't tell me, it's going to be screech and Pepsi." And off he went with his hand worrying his pocket for money.

And back again in the gloom.

They drank. Tert Card's throat worked thirstily and he swallowed again, lifting the cracking arm and beckoning, thrusting two fingers.

"I seen worse than this." He meant the weather. "Two years ago how thick the ice was around the shore. The icebreakers was running full clock. And the storms broke your heart. Just a few years ago, first week in December we had screeching bitter winds, fifty-foot waves thrashing around, it was like the bottom of the ocean was going to come up. You should have seen the way Billy sat in his corner shaking alive, scrammed with cold. Then a week or two later the heaviest rain anybody ever see. Floods and destruction. The Lost Man dam broke. I don't know how many millions of dollars damage it did. December storms are the most treacherous, changeable and cruel. You can go from the warm breeze to the polar blizzard in ten minutes."

On the wall a fisherman's calendar showed the last page. The bare tables reflected. Tert Card's angry yawn. Dark outside, the longest dark of the night. The weather report seeped from a radio behind the bar. A warming trend. Above-normal temperatures forecast.

"That's the weather we get now. Storm, then cold, then warm. A yo-yo, up and down, coldest, warmest, strongest wind, highest tide. Like some Yank advertising company in charge of it all."

An old man, in his eighties, guessed Quoyle, and still working, why not, brought them new drinks. His hair cropped to silver stubble, eyes silvery, too, curved as lunettes, the grey shine of a drop under his nose catching the light. A mustache like spruce needles. Mouth agape, an opening into the skull, showing white tongue and gums, staring stupidly at the money Tert Card thrust.

"Be telling you something," said Tert Card. "Jack and Billy Pretty already knows. I'm leaving, see. I had enough of Killick-Claw. New Year's Day. They wants me down to St. John's, put out the newsletter for the oil rig suppliers. I got the phone call yesterday. Applied a year ago. Oh, there's a waiting list. They only skim the cream. You bet I'm glad to go. If I play me cards right, maybe I'll get to the States, to Texas and the head office. Though it's Florida I loves. I'll think of you, Quoyle, wonder if you're still up here. See, I'm leaving New Year's Day. I bet you'll be the next one to go. You'll go back to the States. Jack and Billy will have to put out the *Gammy Bird* themselves. If they can."

"How will your wife like the city?"

"Wife! She's not going down there. She's staying right here, right at home. Stay home where she belongs. All her family's here. She'll stay right here. A woman stays at home. She'll stay here."

Outraged at the idea it could be any different. But when he signaled for new drinks Quoyle got up, said he was off to his children. A parting shot from Tert Card.

"You know Jack's having Billy take up my job. They'll probably put you on the women's stuff, Quoyle, and hire a new feller to do the shipping news and the wrecks. I believe your days is numbered." And his hand went into his shirt and clawed.

Quoyle was surprised by a fever that swept in with the December storms, as though the demonic energy released by wind and wave passed into the people along the coast. Everywhere he went, saws and rasps, click of knitting pins, great round puddings soaking in brandy, faces painted on clothespin dolls, stuffed cats made from the tops of old stockings.

Bunny talked about the pageant at school. She was doing something with Marty. Quoyle braced for an hour of memorized Yule poems. Did not like Christmas. Thought of the time his brother tore the wrappings off a complete set of Matchbox cars, the tiny intricate vehicles in wonderful colors. He must have gotten some toy, too, but remembered only the flat soft packages that were pajamas or the brown and blue knit shirts his mother bought. "You grow so fast," she accused. Her eyes went back to the moderate-sized brother sending the Alfa Romeo into the red double-decker bus.

He still wasn't over it now and resented the hectoring radio voices counting down shopping days, exhorting listeners to plunge into debt. But liked the smell of fir trees. And had to go to the school pageant. Which wasn't a pageant.

The auditorium was jammed. A sweep of best clothes, old men in camphor-stinking black jackets that gnawed their underarms, women in silk and fine wools in the colors of camel, cinnabar, cayenne, bronze, persimmon, periwinkle, Aztec red. Imported Italian pumps. Hair crimped and curled, lacquered into stiff clouds.

Lipstick. Red circles of rouge. The men with shaved jowls. Neckties like wrapping paper, children in sugar pink and cream. The puff of scented bodies, a murmur like bees over a red field.

Quoyle, carrying Sunshine, could not see Wavey. They sat beside Dennis who was alone in the third row. Beety probably, thought Quoyle, helping in the kitchen. Recognized the old bartender from the Heavy Weather in front of him, a couple of slindgers from the wharves, now with their tan hair wetted and combed, faces swelled with drink and the excitement of being in a crowd. A row of bachelor fishermen waiting to hear of jobs away. The slippery boys. Whole truckloads of clans and remote kin squeezing into folding chairs. Sunshine stood on her chair and made a game of waving to people she didn't know. He could not spot Wavey and Herry. A smell of face powder. She'd said they would be there. He kept looking.

The principal, dressed in her brown suit, came on the stage, a spotlight wavered across her feet and the junior choir began. Shrill, pure voices flooded over the audience.

It was not what he thought. Yes, children lisped comic or religious poems to thunderous applause. But it was not just schoolchildren. People from the town and the outlying coves came onstage as well. Benny Fudge, the black-haired rager who led the attack on poor Nutbeem's boat—for he was "poor Nutbeem" now—sang "The Moon Shines Bright" in a fruity tenor and finished with two measures of finger snapping and clogging.

"When I was a kid they came around at night and sang outside the door," whispered Dennis. "Old Sparky Fudge, Benny's granddad, you see, had a renowned voice. Lost off the Mummy Banks."

Then Bunny and Marty stood alone on the edge of the stage.

"Hi Bunny!" screamed Sunshine. "Hi Marty!" A ripple of laughter.

"Quiet, now," whispered Quoyle. The child like coiled wire.

Bunny and Marty wore matching red jumpers. Beety had let them sit at the sewing machine and stitch the long side seams. Quoyle could see Bunny's knees trembling. Her hands clenched. They began to sing something Quoyle had heard seeping from behind a door, a haunting little tune in a foreign language which he guessed was an African tongue. How had they learned it? He and Dennis mopped at their eyes and snorted with embarrassment.

"Pretty good," croaked Quoyle.

"Oh, aye," said Dennis in a robber chief's voice.

Quoyle remembered Nutbeem's tape. Had the children memorized some pagan song of unknown meaning from that tape? He hoped so.

A woman, perhaps seventy, glowing hair in a net like a roll of silver above her forehead came smiling onto the stage. Bunched cheeks over her smile like two hills above the valley. Eyes swimming behind lenses. A child ran out and placed a soccer ball on the floor behind her.

"Oh, this is good," said Dennis, nudging Quoyle. "Auntie Sofier's chicken act."

She stood still a few seconds, long old arms in her jersey, the tweed skirt to the knees. Yellow stockings, and on her feet red slippers. Suddenly one of the legs scratched at the stage, the arms became wings, and, with a crooning and cackling, Auntie Sofier metamorphosed into a peevish hen protecting an egg.

Quoyle laughed until his throat ached. Though he had never found hens amusing.

Then Wavey and Herry. The boy wore a sailor suit, clacked across the stage in tap shoes. Wavey, in her grey, homemade dress sat on a chair, the accordion across her breast like a radiator grill. The few false notes. Wavey said something that only the boy heard. A strained silence. Then, "One, two, three," said Wavey and commenced. The hornpipe rolled into the audience and at once hundreds of right heels bounced against the floor, the boy rattled his way up and down the blank boards. Quoyle clapped, they all clapped and shouted until Herry ran forward and bowed from the waist as his mother had taught him, smiling and smiling through the hinges of his face.

The showstopper was Beety.

The black cane appeared first from behind the curtain and a roar went up in the audience. She came out jauntily. Strutted. Wore dance tights and tunic covered with sequins and glass bugles, rondels, seed beads, satinas and discs, crow beads, crystal diamonds, cat's-eyes, feather drops and barrels, sputniks and pearls, fluted twists, bumpy-edges and mother-of-pearl teardrops. She had only to breathe to send shimmering prisms at them. A topper that took the light like a boomerang. Leaned on the cane. Twirled the hat on one finger, flipped it in a double somersault and caught it square on her head.

"We all know Billy Pretty's ways," she said, voice charged with tricks and amusements, a tone Quoyle'd never heard. He glanced at Dennis who leaned forward, mouth half open, as eager as anyone for her next word.

"Proper thing to save a dollar, eh Billy?"

The audience, laughing, twisted around in their seats to stare at Billy who sat near the back, strangling. The cane twirled.

"Yes, we knows 'is ways. But 'ow many knows the time last winter, February it was, time we 'ad that silver thaw when Billy wanted to 'ave the old grandfather clock in 'is kitchen repaired? It was like this, m'dears." The cane walked around. "Billy called up Leander Mesher."

The audience creaked and twisted in their seats again to look at the grocer whose hobby was repairing antique watches.

"Leander's been known to fix a few watches at 'is kitchen table. The old kind. There may be a few 'ere remember them. You used to wind them up. Every day. S'elp me, it's true! Every day. Life was terrible 'ard in the old days. So! Calls Leander up on the telephone. It was a local call. No charge." She became an uncanny Billy Pretty, hooped over the phone.

" 'Leander,' he says. 'Leander, what would you ask to repair me old grandfather clock that's 'ere in me kitchen the 'undred years past. I winds it up with a key. It is not battery operated.'

" 'Ah,' says Leander. 'Could be about a hundred and ten dollars. The cost comes in getting it 'ere. Pickup and delivery. Got to charge fifty each way. Got to 'ire two strong lads, gas and oil for the truck. Insurance. Air in the tires.'

" 'There's no cost to air in the tires,' says Billy.

" 'Where 'ave you been, Billy? 'Tis called 'inflation.'

"Well, m'dears, Billy thought about it a bit. We knows 'e lives up on the 'ill and Leander's 'ouse is down at the bottom and in between a dozen streets. Billy 'as it all figured out. 'E'll carry the clock down to Leander 'imself. Save fifty dollars. Leander can bring it back. Uphill. After all, it's not that it's all that 'eavy, being mostly an empty space for the pendulum, but it's awkward. Very awkward." She measured off the dimensions of the grandfather clock, reaching high with the cane to touch the wooden dove that everyone knew topped Billy's clock, widening her arms, stooping and dusting a bit of lint from the carved fruitwood foot. Quoyle twisted around, saw Billy roaring with pleasure at the resurrection of his clock on the stage. Someone in the audience went TICK TOCK.

" 'E gets a good length of rope, you see, knotted and looped around nicely where 'is arms'll go. And 'oists 'er up on 'is back and out the door! 'Eading for Leander's." Now she was Billy teetering down the steep, icy hill.

" 'Awful slick,' says our Billy." Taking careful little steps.

"Now, down near the bottom of the hill is where Auntie Fizzard lives, ninety years old, isn't that right m'dear?"

And everyone stretched forward to see the elderly lady in the front row who raised thick canes in tremulous salute and drew cheers and clapping.

"Ninety years old, and there she goes, got 'er galoshes on with the little bit of fur around the tops, 'as frosters pounded in the 'eels so's she won't slip, wearing 'er black winter coat and a woolly knitted hat, got a cane in each 'and, and each cane got a red rubber tip on the end. She couldn't fall down if she was pushed. She thinks." Now Beety was Auntie Fizzard, inching along, casting fierce glances to the left and the right, watching for those who push ninety-year-old women.

"Up at the top of the 'ill . . ." The audience roared.

"Up at top of the 'ill you might say there was a bit of trouble. First our Billy runs a few little steps to the right and slides, then 'e catches and trips to the left and 'e slips, and 'e goes straight on and 'e skids, and then the 'ill is steeper and the ice glares like water, and 'e's on his way, then over 'e goes, clock-side down and picking up speed like 'e's on a big komatik 'e can't steer.

"Poor Auntie Fizzard 'ears the 'issing noise and she glances up, but 'tis too late, the clock clips 'er and belts 'er into the snowbank. There's an awful silence. Then Billy gets up and starts to haul 'is precious clock out of the snow, get it on 'is back again. 'E's still got a few steps to take to Leander's 'ouse, you see. Glances over and sees Auntie Fizzard's boots sticking out of the snow. Sees them frisk around a bit, then 'ere comes Auntie Fizzard out of the snow, 'er 'at crooked, one cane buried until spring, black coat with so much snow on it's white.

" 'You! You Billy Pretty!' She blasted 'im." The cane twirled.

"Says,"—a long, long pause—"says, 'Why don't you wear a wristwatch like everybody else?' "

A tremendous roar from the audience. Young men tossed their watches into the air.

"Ah, she's something, she's something, isn't she?" Dennis pounding Quoyle's back, leaning forward to touch old Mrs. Fizzard's shoulder.

"Not a word of truth in it," she screamed, purple with laughing. "But how she makes you think there was! Oh, she's terrible good!"

And a few days later Quoyle gave Wavey a clear glass teapot, a silk scarf printed with a design of blueberries. He'd ordered them both through the mail from a museum shop in the States. She gave him a sweater the color of oxblood shoe polish. Had knitted it in the evenings. It was not too small. Their faces close enough for breath to mingle. Yet Quoyle was thinking of the only gift that Petal ever gave him. She had opened dozens of presents from him. A turquoise bracelet, a tropical-fish tank, a vest beaded with Elvis Presley's visage, canary eyes and sequin lips. She opened the last box, glanced at him. Sitting with his hands dangling, watching her.

"Wait a minute," she said and ran into the kitchen. He heard the refrigerator open. She came back with her hands behind her back.

"I didn't have a chance to buy you anything," she said, then held both closed hands toward him. Uncurled her fingers. In each cupped palm a brown egg. He took them. They were cold. He thought it a tender, wonderful thing to do. She had given him something, the eggs, after all, only a symbol, but they had come from her hands as a gift. To him. It didn't matter that he'd bought them himself at the supermarket the day before. He imagined she understood him, that she had to love him to know that it was the outstretched hands, the giving, that mattered.

On Christmas day a hunch of cloud moved in. But the aunt was up from St. Johns, and they had Christmas dinner with Dennis and Beety in Mrs. Buggit's kitchen, people in and out, the fire bursting hot and stories of old-time teak days and mummers and jannies. Jack skulked around the edges pouring hot rum punch. Some distance away they heard sporadic and celebratory shotgun fire.

Dennis's mustache white with frost. He and Quoyle on the Saturday morning after Christmas cutting next winter's firewood back in the spruce at the bottom of the bay. Quoyle with the chain saw, for which he had an affinity, Dennis limbing and trimming. The blue scarf knitted by Sunshine barely wrapped around Quoyle's neck. At noon they stood over the small fire sucking hot tea.

"Beety says we ought to take a look in at old Nolan there in Capsize Cove. Seeing as we're not that far away. Finish up a little early and run in there. Dad or somebody usually goes over early part of the winter to see if he's got enough wood and food. A little late this year. Beety makes him a cake and some bread. I see his smoke there in the morning, but you can't tell."

"I didn't even think about him," said Quoyle. Guilty.

They went up the bay in a great curve, Dennis shouting stories of drunken snowmobilers who sank forever beneath the ice because they didn't know the routes.

"Bloody cold," he shouted, squinting at the notch in the shoreline. The empty houses of Capsize Cove were in sight like a charcoal drawing on rough paper. A long banking turn onto shore.

Smoke coming out of the metal pipe of the old cousin's shack. The snowmobile's whine throttled back to stuttered idling.

"Leave it running," said Dennis.

Worse than Quoyle remembered. The stink was gagging. The old man too weak or befuddled to get to the outhouse. A skeleton trembled before them. The dog near the stove didn't move. But was alive. Quoyle could not help it. He retched and staggered to the doorway. In the fenced pasture three humps under the snow. Frozen sheep.

"Uncle Nolan," he heard Dennis say. "It's Dennis Buggit, Jack Buggit's boy, from across the bay. My wife's sent you some bread." He drew the bread out of the carrier bag. The sweet, homely perfume of bread. The skeleton was upon it, crushing the loaf into his mouth, a muffled howling coming out of the twitching crust.

Dennis came outside, spat. Cleared his throat and spat again.

"Some stinking mess. Poor old bugger's starving. Christ in the early morning, what a mess. He'd better go into a home, don't you think? He's off his rocker. Burning the walls of his house, there. You see where he's ripping the boards off? He's your kin, so it's up to you. What to do with him. They take him away, I'll come back over, drown the old dog. Half dead anyway."

"I don't have any idea what to do about him."

"Beety will know who to call up about this. She gives time to that Saving Grace place that helps the women. And the Teenage Mothers. Knows all them groups. Her and Wavey."

"Beety and Wavey?" Quoyle's face flaming with guilt. He should have looked out for the wretched old cousin the first time he saw him. Didn't think.

"That Saving Grace, Beety and Wavey started it. Couple years ago. Councilman lived over near us beat his wife up one winter, pushed her out naked-ass in the snow. She come to Beety. Blue with cold, deaf and blood in her ears. Next day Beety calls up Wavey. Wavey knows how to set up them groups, get something started, after she got the special ed group up. Get the Province's ear, see? Make them pay attention."

"Some women," said Quoyle. But thought, oh you should have

seen Petal, you should have seen my lovely girl. A preposterous thought, Petal in Killick-Claw, and not funny. She would have screamed, jumped on the next plane out. Never, never to be seen again.

"My son," said Dennis, "you don't know the half of it," and gunned the snowmobile out onto the wind-scoured bay.

35

The Day's Work

"Day's Work, consists, at least, of the dead reckoning from noon to noon, morning and afternoon time sights for longitude, and a meridian altitude for latitude."

THE MARINER'S DICTIONARY

"WANT to talk to you, Quoyle." Jack, shouting down the wire. "Pick you up tomorrer morning. So they know who you are down to Misky Bay." Bristling cough. Hung up before Quoyle could say anything. If he'd had anything to say.

By January it had always been winter. The sky blended imperceptibly into the neutral-colored ice that covered the ocean, solid near shore, jigsaw floes fifty miles out and heaving on the swells. Snow fell every day, sometimes slow flakes, as if idling between storms. Deepened, deepened; five, eight, eleven feet deep. The roads were channels between muffling banks, metal, wood silenced. And every ten days or so, by Quoyle's reckoning, another storm.

Jack's truck heater blasted, yet their breaths iced the side windows. Quoyle scraped with his fingernails to look for the harp seals that began to dot the far ice now like commas and semicolons. Half listening to Jack. Thinking of seals. Wavey's older brother, Oscar, had a pet seal. Devoted to the local scallops. Jack had things on his mind and talked like a rivet gun. The new groundfish fishing season had opened, a maze of allocations and quotas that threw him into reverse.

"Einstein couldn't understand it. They've made a fucking cockadoodle mess out of it, those twits in Ottawa who don't know a lumpfish from their own arse." Jack at his medium range of temper.

"It's like this." Combing his hair with his hand so it bristled up. "Goddamn, you just get something working good and it quits. Seems like I'm always lashing things up with wire."

Quoyle slouched in his enormous maroon anorak. Had remembered the name of Oscar's seal. Pussels. What they called the local scallops.

"O.k. Quoyle, Billy wants to stay with the Home Page so you're the new managing editor. You'll do Tert Card's job, put it together, handle the phone, assignments, bills, advertisers, printer. You got to watch the son of a bitch printer. Why I'm taking you down there. If a mistake can be made, he'll make it. Let's see. Want you to keep writing the Shipping News."

Quoyle startled, hand halfway to his chin.

"Like to try Benny Fudge on the court reports and auto wrecks, the sexual abuse stories. Drop the restaurant stuff and the foreign news. Everybody knows all the restaurants and nobody cares about what happens somewhere else. Get that off the telly."

The truck climbed the twist of road over the headlands and they came into a zone of perpetual light snow.

"What do you think, get a new slant on the home page? Can call it 'Lifestyles.' See, Billy and me been knocking this 'round for a couple of years. There's two ways of living here now. There's the old way, look out for your family, die where you was born, fish, cut your wood, keep a garden, make do with what you got. Then there's the new way. Work out, have a job, somebody tell you what to do, commute, your brother's in South Africa, your mother's in Regina, buy every goddamn cockadoodle piece of Japanese crap you can. Leave home. Go off to look for work. And some has a hard time of it. Quoyle, we all know that *Gammy Bird* is famous for its birdhouse plans and good recipes, but that's not enough. Now we got to deal with Crock-Pots and consumer ratings, asphalt driveways, lotteries, fried chicken franchises, Mint Royale coffee at gourmet shops, all that stuff. Advice on getting along in distant cities. Billy thinks there's enough to make the home section a two-page spread. He'll tell you what he's got in mind. You work it out with him."

"We could get some who've gone away to write a guest column in the form of a letter once in a while. Letter from Australia, Letter from Sudbury, how it is," said Quoyle.

"Guess I'd read that if I was twenty-one and had to get moving. It'll be a different paper. In more ways than one."

"Nutbeem handled touchy stories very well. I don't know how Benny will be with the sex crime stuff."

"Well, let's just wait and see how the feller does before we sink our graples in him, eh? You live with this, Quoyle?" Coming into the Misky Bay traffic, a circle of unnamed streets and steep one-way hills complicated by mounds of snow.

He nodded. Swore to himself by St. Pussel there would never be a typo.

"Come up the stage tonight and I'll tell you the rest of it. O.k., now here's where you makes your turn, see, then you cuts along behind the firehouse. It's the shortcut."

"Well," said Quoyle, sitting where Tert Card had sat, although he had cleared off the desk and torn up the picture of the oil tanker, "what have we got for news this week. Benny, how'd you do with the S.A. and the police court stories?" Pitching his voice low.

Benny Fudge sat with his hands folded tightly on his clean desk as though at an arithmetic lesson. His puffed hair made Quoyle think of Eraserhead.

"I'll tell you. I read about fifty of Nutbeem's stories to see how he handled the abuse cases but I can't string it together the way he did. I tried, because I felt like I owed it to Nutbeem. After the boat. But I couldn't get it rolling. Best I can do."

> A charge of incest against a 67-year-old Misky Bay man was dismissed Tuesday when his 14-year-old daughter refused to testify.
>
> Dr. Singlo Booty, 71, of Distant Waters has been arrested and charged with nine counts of sexual assault involving seven patients from May 1978 to July 1991. He will appear in provincial court January 31.

Waited, biting his thumbnail.

Quoyle looked at Billy who moved his eyebrows very slightly. Nutbeem would have squeezed out two heart-wrenching stories.

"The other stuff was excellent. The other court stuff? I've got lovely stuff."

"What might the lovely stuff be?" asked Quoyle.

"Two fellers here charged with everything in the book. Had a run-in with wildlife officers. Charged with carrying firearms in closed season, obstruction of wildlife officers doing their duty, assaulting wildlife officers with sharp branches and lobster pots, breaking wildlife officers' Polaroid sunglasses, uttering threats against wildlife officers. Another story about buddy here, charged with possession of copper wire. About four thousand dollars worth. He's also charged with trafficking in hashish. And I got a Youth on a Crime Spree. Stole a bicycle in Lost All Hope, rode it eleven miles to Bad Fortune, there he stole a motorcycle and made it to Never Once. But the boy was ambitious. Abandoned the motorcycle and stole a car. Drove the car into the sea and swam ashore at Joy in the Morning. Where two Mounties by chance were parked in their patrol car, eating doughnuts. And five Unemployment Insurance fraud charges. And four dragger captains fined two thousand apiece for fishing redfish in closed waters. A guy down in No Name got thirty days for jigging fish in inland waters. All kinds of car wrecks. And a lot of photos. I like taking photos. See, I can have a dual career. Reporter and photographer."

"Write them up with a little more detail than you put into the S.A. stories." Quoyle acted gruff, hard-boiled.

"Yeah, I could write crime stuff all day. But not the sex stuff." A prim mouth. "I see the crime stories and the camera work as my big chance."

Chance for what, Quoyle wondered. But there he was at Tert Card's window frame with the phone against his ear, running the stories through the computer, pasting up the pages, driving the mechanicals down to Misky Bay to the print shop. When the paper came out that week he tore out the editorial page where the masthead ran and mailed it to Partridge. *Managing Editor: R. G. Quoyle.*

And so it went, stories of cargo ships beset by ice, the Search and Rescue airlift of a sailor crushed in power-operated watertight doors, a stern trawler adrift after an explosion in the engine room, a factory freezer trawler repossessed by the bank, a sailor lost overboard from a scientific survey vessel in rough seas, plane crashes and oil spills, whales tangled in nets, illegal dumping of fish offal in the harbor, plaques awarded to firemen and beauty queens, assaulting husbands, drowned boys, explorers lost and found, ships that sank in raging seas, a fishing boat hit by an icebreaker, a lottery winner, seizure of illegal moose meat.

And he sent a copy of a police bulletin to the aunt. Mrs. Melville captured in Hawaii with the steward from *Tough Baby*. A handsome man thirty years younger than she, wearing Giorgio Armani clothes and driving a Lexus LS400 with the cellular telephone. "I did it for love," she confessed. The steward said nothing.

All in the day's work.

36

Straitjacket

Straitjacket: A coat of strong material, as canvas, binding the body closely for restraining the violently insane or delirious, violent criminals, etc. Some confine the arms to the body, others have long sleeves, without openings, which may be knotted together.

THE NORTH tilted toward the sun. As the light unfolded, a milky patina of phytoplankton bloomed over the offshore banks along the collision line of the salt Gulf Stream and the brack Labrador Current. The waters crosshatched in complex layers of arctic and tropic, waves foamed with bacteria, yeasts, diatoms, fungi, algae, bubbles and droplets, the stuff of life, urging growth, change, coupling.

A Friday afternoon. Quoyle at home, changing into old clothes. He watched through the kitchen window for Jack's skiff. Rain-colored distance though none fell where Quoyle was. A stern trawler left the fish plant, probably heading offshore for the Funk Island Banks. Ten days with a fourteen-man crew, towing the net, the slow haul back, the brief moment of excitement when the cod end of the net came up, the cod pouring into the hold. Or nothing much. And down to gut and bleed. And tow again and haul back. And mend net. And again. And again.

There was Jack's skiff, working down toward Flour Sack Cove. The rain curtain sagged east, left smears of blue behind it. Quoyle picked up the phone.

"Hey, Billy? I'm going along to Jack's now. See him heading in."

"You just had a call from the States. I gave him your number there so you might wait a minute. And heard a rumor Sea Song might be closing down three fish plants next month. Anonymous source. No Name Cove supposed to be on the list. You tell Jack. If it's true, I don't know what people are going to live on down there.

"You talk to somebody at Sea Song yet?"

"Ar, the manager's got the face of a robber's horse and he'll give me the brazen old runaround. But we'll try."

Quoyle gave it five minutes, had his hand on the doorknob when the phone rang. Partridge's voice, almost five thousand miles away, lagging and sad.

"Quoyle? Quoyle? This is a lousy connection. Listen, you following the riots?"

"Some," said Quoyle. "They give it about ten seconds on the news here. It looks bad."

"Bad, all right. Not only LA. It's like the whole country got infected with some rage virus, going for their guns like it used to be you'd look at your watch. Remember Edna the rewrite woman on the *Record*?"

"Yeah. She never smiled at me. Not once."

"You had to earn Edna's smiles. Listen. She just called me up. They had a disaster, a tragedy at the *Record*. Some nut came in yesterday afternoon with a fucking machine gun and killed Punch, Al Catalog, three or four others. Wounded eight more."

"Jesus! Why?"

"Oh, it's part of the scene here and something to do with the Letters to the Editor. If you can believe it. This guy sent an anonymous letter saying riots were necessary to purge the system and redistribute wealth and they didn't print it. So he came down with a machine gun. Edna says the only reason he didn't get her was because she was under the copy desk looking for paper clips when the shooting started. Remember how there was never enough paper clips? Quoyle, they shot at Mercalia on the freeway last week. Show you how crazy the scene is, I made a joke about living in California, about LA style. Fucking bullet holes through her windshield. Missed her by inches. She's scared to death and I'm making jokes. It hit me after Edna called what a fucking miserable crazy place we're in. There's no place you can go no more without getting shot or burned or beat. And I was laughing." And Quoyle thought he heard his friend crying on the other side of the continent. Or maybe he was laughing again.

A deep smell to the air, some elusive taste that made him pull in conscious breaths. Sky the straw-colored ichor that seeps from a wound. Rust blossoms along the station wagon's door panels. He could have been dead in Mockingburg, New York.

Jack stood in the skiff, pronging cod onto the stage. Quoyle pulled on a slicker, his gloves. He seized his knife, picked up a cod. In the beginning it had seemed a strange way to conduct an editorial meeting.

"Hands might as well be doing something while we talk," said Jack, scrambling up. "Always hated the sight of five, six grown men sitting around a table, doing nothing but work their jaw. You see them doodle away, rip pieces of paper, wagging their foot, fooling with paper clips."

Quoyle didn't want to think about paper clips. Told Jack about the machine gunner, the random shot on the freeway, the riots.

"Well known how violent it is in the States. Worst you'll get *here*," said Jack, "is a good punch-up and maybe your car pushed over the cliff." They worked silently.

Jack said the cod were small, five or six pounds on average, you rarely got one that went more than fifty nowadays, though in early times men had caught great cod of two hundred pounds. Or more. Overfished mercilessly for twenty years until the stocks neared collapse. Did collapse, said Jack, up at the table, his knife working.

"Why I don't stop fishing, see," he said, deftly ripping up, jerking out the entrails, cigarette in the corner of his mouth, "even if I wanted to, is because I'd never get my licenses for lobster or salmon fishing again. Don't know why, I loves lobster fishing best. You let your cockadoodle license lapse just one season and it's gone forever."

"Billy said to tell you there's a rumor Sea Song might be closing three plants next month. Says he hears No Name might be one."

"Jesus! You think it can't get worse, it gets worse! This business about allocating fish quotas as if they was rows of potatoes you could dig. If there's no fish you can't allocate them and you can't catch them; if you don't catch them, you can't process them or ship them, you don't have a living for nobody. Nobody understands their crazy rules no more. Stumble along. They say 'too many local fishermen for not enough fish.' Well, where has the fish gone? To the Russians, the French, the Japs, West Germany, East Germany, Poland, Portugal, the UK, Spain, Romania, Bulgaria—or whatever they call them countries nowadays.

"And even after the limit was set, the inshore was no good. How can the fish come inshore if the trawlers and draggers gets 'em all fifty, a hundred mile out? And the long-liners gets the rest twenty mile out? What's left for the inshore fishermen?" He spat in the water. Watching Quoyle's clumsy work with the knife. "You got the idea. That's all there is to it. Just keep at it steady."

"Those ads, Jack. I'd like to drop the fake ads. We need the news space. Last week we had the sawmill story, story on the new National Historic Park in Misky Bay, demonstration over foreign fishing off the Virgin Rocks, another demonstration against the high electric rates, the shrimp processors' strike—good, solid local stories—and we had to cramp 'em in very hard. No pix. I mean, it would be different if it was real ads."

"Ar, that was Tert Card's idea, make up fake ads for big outfits down to St. John's. Make it look like we're big, y'know. Punch up the local advertisers a little. Go ahead, pull them ads out if you need the space. See, we didn't have that much news when we started. And the ads looked good."

One by one the cleaned fish went into the grey plastic fish box. Jack hurled the guts and livers into the water.

"Fishery problem? Fuckin' terrible problem. They've made the inshore fishermen just like migrant farm workers. All we do is harvest the product. Moves from one crop to another, picks what they tells us. Takes what they pays us. We got no control over any of the fishery now. We don't make the decisions, just does what we're told where and when we're told. We lives by rules made somewhere else by sons a bitches don't know nothin' about this place." A hard exhalation rather than a sigh.

But, Quoyle thought, that's how it was everywhere. Jack was lucky he'd escaped so long.

Late in February papers came from St. John's for him to sign as next of kin, papers to put the old cousin away forever. Delusions, senile dementia, schizophrenic personality; prognosis poor. He sat looking at the dotted lines. Could not sign away the rest of the life of an unknown man to whom he'd spoken a single sentence, who had only tied knots against him. He thought he would go down to the city and see the old cousin before he signed anything. Suppose he was wild-eyed, drooling and mad? He expected it. Suppose he was lucid and accusatory? Expected that, too.

At the last hour he asked Wavey to come along. He said it would be a change of scene. They could go to dinner. A movie. Two movies. But knew he was saying something else.

"It will be fun." The word sounded stupid in his mouth. When had he ever had "fun"? Or Wavey, chapped face already set in the lines of middle age, an encroaching dryness about her beyond stove heat and wind? What was it, anyway? Both of them the kind who stood with forced smiles watching other people dance, spin on barstools, throw bowling balls. Having fun. But Quoyle did like movies, the darkness, the outlines of strangers' hair against the screen, the smell of peanuts and shampoo, popcorn squeaking in teeth. He could fly away from his chin and hulking shape into the white clothes and slender bodies on the screen.

Wavey said yes. Herry could stay with her father. Yes, yes indeed.

A few torn pieces of early morning cloud the shape and color of salmon fillets. The tender greenish sky hardening as they drove between high snowbanks. A rim of light flooded up, drenched the car. Quoyle's yellow hands with bronze hairs, holding the wheel, Wavey's maroon serge suit like cloth of gold. Then it was ordinary daylight, the black and white landscape of ice, snow, rock and sky.

Quoyle's romping thoughts left him with nothing to say, nothing to crack the silence swelling between them. Mumbled a stupid question about Alvin Yark's endless song. But didn't care. It was just to get started.

"Sung that long as I can remember. The *Gander Goose* sank at sea and the *Bruce* was the one they shipped the moose on. Moose from New Brunswick. I don't know when, back around the First World War. Newfoundland didn't have moose until they brought them in." Nor was it anything to her, but the exchange of voices in the humming car encouraged. She thought of a boy in school who had wept over his lunch of mildewed crackers. She had given him her meat sandwich, cut from a cold moose roast.

"There's enough of them now," said Quoyle, laughing, wanting to seize the chapped hand. It seemed an omen when they saw one of the animals in a frozen wallow beside the highway.

By noon there were open harbors, and the sight of blue water made them both happy. Blue, after months of ice.

Wavey in the shops on Water Street, exhilarated and startled by the smells of new leather, perfumed magazines, traffic exhaust. She bought a toy cow for Herry, a pair of long underwear for her father. Box of greeting cards for all occasions, on sale. A paring knife with a red handle to replace the stub in the kitchen drawer. A floral-print brassiere in jewel colors. There was lovely Shetland wool that would make a Fair Isle sweater. But it was too expensive. She noticed a monger's window where, on a bed of ice, a wonderful scene was worked in fish. A skiff made of flounder fillets rode waves of shrimp and blue-black mussels. A whole salmon was a lighthouse, shot out rays of glittering mackerel. All framed by a border of crab claws.

She had Quoyle's list, his envelope of money for clothes for Bunny and Sunshine. Tights, corduroy pants, a pullover for Sunshine, socks and panties. What enormous pleasure in shopping for little girls. She added barrettes, socks edged with scallops of lace, two lovely woolly tams, teal and mauve. Careful to guard against the pickpockets that abounded in cities. Ate a roast beef sandwich for lunch and spent the afternoon twacking through rich stores, looking over everything and never spending another cent.

Quoyle shopped, too, circled the shelves of the asylum gift shop wanting to bring something to the old cousin. Who knew what his memories were? Who knew what his life had been? He'd fished. Pulled up whelk pots. Had owned a dog. Walked at night. Tied knots.

He looked among the wrestling magazines and machine-embroidered sachets, found a sentimental photograph of a poodle in a stamped metal frame. It would have to do. There was no point in wrapping it, he told the woman at the register and put it in his jacket pocket.

The old cousin sat in a plastic chair with wooden arms. Sat alone near a window. He was very clean and dressed in a white nightgown, a white robe. Paper slippers on his veiny feet. He stared at a television set in a bracket near the top of the wall, the picture blurred enough to show two mouths, four eyes, an extra rim of cheeks on every face. A bald man talked about diabetes. An explosive blue commercial for antifreeze showing fragments of a hockey game, a spray of ice.

Quoyle got on a chair and adjusted the controls, lowered the volume. Stood down, sat down. The old cousin looked at him.

"You come 'ere, too?"

"Yes," said Quoyle. "I came to see you."

"Damn long ride, ent it?"

"Yes," said Quoyle, "it is. But Wavey Prowse came along for company." Why tell that to the old cousin?

"Oh, aye. Lost 'er 'usband."

"Yes," said Quoyle. There seemed nothing wrong with the old man's mind to Quoyle. He looked around for knotted strings, saw none. "Well, what do you think?" he asked cautiously. Could mean anything.

"Oh! Wunnerful! Wunnerful food! They's 'ot rainbaths out of the ceiling, my son, oh, like white silk, the soap she foams up in your 'and. You feels like a boy to go 'mongst the 'ot waters. They gives you new clothes every day. White as the driven snow. The television. They's cards and games."

"It sounds pleasant," said Quoyle, thinking, he can't go back to that reeking sty.

"No, no. It's not entirely pleasant. Bloody place is full of loonies. I knows where I is. Still, the creature comforts is so wunnerful I play up to 'em. They asks me, 'Who are you?'—I says 'Joey Smallwood.' Or, 'Biggest Crab in the Pot.' 'Oh, 'e's loony,' they think. 'Keep 'im 'ere.' "

"Um," said Quoyle. "There's a Golden Age home in Killick-Claw. There might be a chance—." But wasn't sure if they would take him. Reached in his pocket for the photograph of the poodle, handed it to the old cousin.

"Brought you a present."

The old man held it in his trembling claw, looked. Turned away from Quoyle toward the window, toward the sea, his left hand came up, fingers spread over the eyes.

"I tied knots 'gainst you. Raised winds. The sheep is dead. Whiteface can't get in."

Painful. Quoyle wished he'd gotten a box of chocolates. But persevered.

"Cousin Nolan." How strange the words sounded. But by uttering them bound himself in some way to this shriveled husk. "Cousin Nolan Quoyle. It's all in the past. Don't blame yourself. Can you hold on while I look into the Golden Age home? There's quite a few from Killick-Claw and No Name Cove there. You know you can't go back to Capsize Cove."

"Never wanted to be there! Wanted to be a pilot. Fly. I was twenty-seven when Lindbergh crossed the Atlantic. You should have seed me then! I was that strong! 'E was 'ere in Newfoundland. 'E took off from 'ere. They was all 'ere, St. Brendan, Leif Erikson, John Cabot, Marconi, Lucky Lindy. Great things 'as 'appened 'ere. I always knowed of it. Knowed I was destined to do fine things. But 'ow to begin? 'Ow to get away and begin? I went to fishing but they called me Squally Quoyle. See, I was a jinker, carried bad winds with me. I 'ad no luck. None of the Quoyles 'ad no luck. 'Ad to go on me own. In the end I went down in me 'opes."

Quoyle said he would find out things about the Golden Age home in Killick-Claw. Thought, in the meantime he would sign nothing.

The old cousin looked beyond Quoyle to the doorway.

"Where's Agnis? She ent come see me a once."

"To tell the truth, I can't say why," said Quoyle.

"Ah, I knows why she don't want to come by. Shamed! She's shamed, knowing what I knows. 'Er was glad enough to be in my 'ouse though when she were a girl. Come to the old woman with 'er trouble, begged for 'elp. Snivel and bawl. Women's dirty business! I seen 'er digging up the root. Squinty little Face-and-Eye berry, the devil's evil eyes watching out from the bushes. Boiled them roots up into a black devil's tea, give it to 'er in the kitchen. She was at it all night, screeched a bomb, the bawling so's I couldn't get no rest. See 'er there in the morning, she wouldn't look up, turned 'er dishy face to the wall. There was something bloody in the basin.

" 'Well,' I says, 'is it over then?'

" 'It is,' says the old woman. And I goes out to me boat. It was 'er brother done it, y'see, that clumsy big Guy Quoyle. Was at 'er from when she was a little maid."

Quoyle grimaced, felt his chapped lower lip split. So the aunt had been to the Nightmare Isles as well. His own father! Christ.

"I'll come by in the morning," he mumbled. "If there's anything you need." The old man was looking at the photograph of the poodle. But Quoyle, turning from him, thought he saw the mad glint now, remembered Billy's vile story about the man's dead wife. The old woman. Assaulting the corpse. Ah, the Quoyles.

In the hotel dining room Quoyle ordered wine. Some obscure Bordeaux, corky and sour. Wavey's graceful lifting of her glass. But it went straight to their heads and they both talked wildly of what—nothing. He heard her dark voice even when she was silent. Quoyle forgot the old cousin and all he had said; felt wonderful, wonderful. Wavey described the things in the stores, Sunshine's new cobalt blue sweater that would set off her fiery curls. She was conscious of the new brassiere under her dress and slip. Samples from the perfume counter cast exquisite scents from her wrists every time she raised her fork. They looked at each other over the table. Briefly at first, then with the prolonged and piercing gazes that precede sexual congress. Wineglasses clinked. Butter melted on their knives. Quoyle dropped a shrimp and Wavey laughed. He always dropped shrimp, he said. They both had veal scaloppine. Another bottle of wine.

After such a dinner the movie was almost too much. But they went. Something about a French recluse who peeped through Venetian blinds and played with a bread knife.

And at last to bed.

"Oh," said Wavey, lying dazed and somewhat bruised in Quoyle's large arms, "this is the hotel where Herold and I came on our honeymoon."

In the morning the attendant said the old man could not be seen. Had broken the glass from the poodle picture and stabbed at all who came near. And was tranquilized. No question of a Golden Age home for him.

37

Slingstones

"The slingstone hitch . . . is used in anchoring lobster pots. It may be tied either in the bight or in the end. Pull the ends strongly, and the turns in the standing part are spilled into the loops."

THE ASHLEY BOOK OF KNOTS

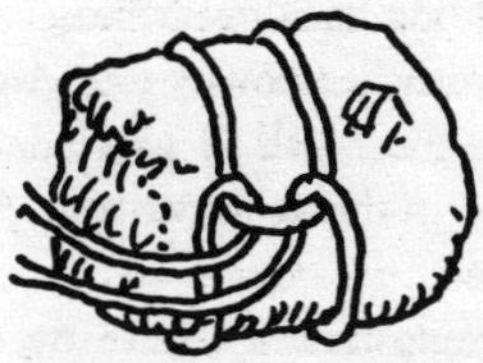

WEEKS of savage cold. Quoyle was comfortable enough in his sweater and anorak. The old station wagon sputtered and slugged, at last quit in sight of the *Gammy Bird* office. He got out, put his shoulder to it, steering with one hand. Got it rolling, jumped in and turned the key, popped the gearshift. The engine caught for a few seconds, then died again as he rolled up behind Billy's decayed Dodge. Ice in the gas line, he thought. Maybe Billy had some dry gas.

Billy had phone messages. Two calls from the principal of Bunny's school. Call back right away. He dialed, heart in his mouth. Let Bunny be all right.

"Mr. Quoyle. We've had some trouble with Bunny this morning. At recess. I'm sorry to say she pushed one of the teachers,

Mrs. Lumbull. Pushed her very hard. In fact, Bunny knocked her down. She's a large and strong child for her age. No, it was not an accident. By all accounts it was deliberate. I don't need to tell you Mrs. Lumbull is upset and mystified why the child would push her. Bunny will not say why. She's sitting right across from my desk and refuses to speak. Mr. Quoyle, I think you'd better come down and pick her up. Mrs. Lumbull didn't even know Bunny. She's not in her class."

"Billy, borrow your truck? Got ice in my line."

Bunny had been moved to the outer office where she sat with her hat and coat on, arms folded, face crimson and set. Wouldn't look at Quoyle. Holding back everything.

The principal with her downy face, wearing the brown wool suit. Fingernails like the bowls of souvenir spoons. Held a pencil as though interrupted in the act of writing. An authoritarian voice, perfected by practice.

"Under the circumstances I have no choice but to suspend Bunny from school until she explains her action and apologizes to Mrs. Lumbull. Now, Bunny, this is your last chance. Your father's here now and I want you to make a clean breast of it. Tell me why you pushed poor Mrs. Lumbull."

Nothing. Quoyle saw his child's face so full of rage and misery she could not speak.

"Come on," he said gently, "let's go get in Billy's truck." Nodded to the principal. Who put her pencil on the desk with a hard sound.

In the truck Bunny bawled.

"You push that teacher?"

"Yes!"

"Why?"

"She's the worst one of all!" And would say no more. So Quoyle drove her to Beety's, thinking here we go again.

"Mrs. Lumbull, eh?" Beety's eyebrows up. "Be willing to bet three cookies you had your reasons."

"I did," said Bunny, snorting back tears. Beety pushed Quoyle toward the door. Gave him a little wave.

He heard the story in the afternoon. From Beety by way of Marty.

"Mrs. Lumbull is a float teacher, takes classes when the main teacher is sick or at a conference. Today she took the special ed class. Got 'em all bundled up, outside. Herry Prowse is in that class. Poor Herry hits the cold air and decides he has to go pee. Tries to tell Mrs. Lumbull. Hopping up and down. You know how Herry talks. Not only does she not understand him—or maybe she does—but she makes him stand at attention against the brick wall to cure his fidgeting and every time he tries to tell her his problem she mimics him, pushes him back. Herry's blubbering away and finally wets his pants and is humiliated. And here comes the avenging angel, Miss Bunny Quoyle, full speed ahead, and rams mean Mrs. Lumbull right behind the knees. The rest is history. If she was mine, Quoyle, I'd give her a medal. But it's going to be tough straightening this out with the school. The principal don't want to hear there's trouble with a teacher. Teachers are hard to get. Even teachers like Mrs. Lumbull. So she'll try to bull it out."

That evening Quoyle talked to the aunt on the phone, didn't know he would set her in motion. A screech over the wire like a sea gull. She caught an early plane, would not be turned back, and in the morning the principal saw three generations of Quoyles advancing up the frozen driveway. The aunt's new St. John's hairstyle like a helmet, Quoyle's chin jutting, and Bunny between.

Got an earful from the aunt. But it was Quoyle who smoothed things out, explained in a reasonable voice, coaxed the principal and Bunny into mutual apologies and promises. Easy enough for the principal who knew that Mrs. Lumbull was moving to Grand Falls to open a Christian bookstore. Hard for Bunny who still measured events on a child's scale of fair and unfair.

Certain wheels had turned, certain cogs enmeshed. Quoyle went on Saturday afternoon, as usual, to Alvin Yark's, Wavey and the children with him. Wavey turned to the backseat. Looked at Bunny, not as adults look at children, checking guilt or comprehension, fingernails, zipped jackets and hats, but as one adult may look at another. Saying a few things without words. Took Bunny's hand and squeezed it.

"How do you do, how do you do," said Herry, who always caught connections.

The car achieved some sort of interior balance on the way to Nunny Bag Cove, a rare harmony of feeling that soothed all the passengers.

Wavey and her Auntie Evvie were hooking a floor mat with a design of seabirds copied from a calendar. Wavey worked at the puffin. Bunny went with her storybook to the rocker at the window. Here the Yark cat, when the glass wasn't frosty, watched boats as though they were water rats. Sunshine and Herry shook toys from Herry's red backpack. Though later Sunshine was pulled to the women, the flicking hooks jerking up loops of wool, inventing turrs and caplin. She got the sneeze-provoking smell of burlap backing. Wavey aimed a wink. Sunshine moved in, put her finger on the puffin. Dying to try it.

"This way," said Wavey, hand closing over the child's, guiding the hook to seize the pale wool. Bunny turned the pages and smoothed the cat with her stockinged foot. A storm of purring. She looked up.

"Petal was in a car accident in New York and she can't come here. Because she can never wake up. I could wake her up but it's too far away. So when I'm grown up I might go there."

What brought that on, wondered Wavey.

In the shop Yark fretted. The snow was deep, storms and gales raged still, but the ice was breaking up, seal were moving into the bays, the cod and turbot spawning, herring were on the dodge. He felt change and life, the old seasonal longing to get out. Take a few seal. Or shoot at icebergs. Anyway, get moving. But his eyes were too weak for that, watered in the light from snow blindness twenty years earlier, even though his wife had put tea compresses over his eyes. The reason he had to work now in a darkened shop.

During the past weeks he had set and wedged the keel into floor blocks, leveled, braced, and immovably secured the boat's backbone.

"Now it'll start to look like something. Today we marks out the main timbers."

With his scraped and worn tape he measured back from the top of the stem along an invisible line, muttered to Quoyle. He calculated the midpoint of the hull length and marked the keel a second time a few inches forward of the midpoint mark. Measured from the sternpost to mark the afterhook placement. Quoyle tidied up rows of chisels and saws, peered out the sawdust-coated window at the bay ice. Still the measurements were not over. Yark calculated the position of the bottom of the counter up from the timberline by rules and patterns he carried in his head.

"Leave me take that saw, boy," said the old man. His words seemed to come out of a mouthful of snow. Quoyle handed the saw, the chisel, the saw, the chisel, leaned over the work watching Yark notch the timberline to take the timber pairs. At last he could help set in the timbers, holding them while the old man fastened them to the floor with stout braces he called spur shores.

"Now we notches the sternpost, my son." Bolted on the counter, the metal biting into the wood with its fast grip. Put his hands on his hips and leaned back, groaning. "Might as well quit while we're ahead. Wavey come?"

"Yes. And the kids."

"You needs kids about. Keeps you young." Cleared his throat and spat in the shavings. "When are you two going to do the deed?"

He switched off the light, turned in the gloom of the shop and looked at Quoyle. Quoyle wasn't sure which deed he meant. The crack that was Yark's mouth elongated, not a smile so much as a forcing apart of seams that went with the blunt question. To force Quoyle's seams apart. And other forced seams implicit.

Quoyle's exhalation that of someone doing heavy work.

"I don't know," he said.

"Is it the boy?"

Quoyle shook his head. How to say it? That he loved Petal,

not Wavey, that all the capacity for love in him had burned up in one fast go. The moment had come and the spark ignited, and for some it never went out. For Quoyle, who equated misery with love. All he felt with Wavey was comfort and a modest joy.

But said, "It's Herold. Her husband. He's always in her mind. She's very deeply attached to his memory."

" 'Erold Prowse!" The old man closed the door. "Let me tell you something about 'Erold Prowse. There was a sigh of relief went up in some places when he was lost. You've heard of the tomcat type of feller, eh? That was 'Erold. He sprinkled his bastards up and down the coast from St. John's to Go Aground. It was like a parlor game down in Misky Bay to take a squint at babies and young children, see if they looked like 'Erold. 'Appen they often did."

"Did Wavey know this?"

"Of course she knew. 'E made her life some miserable. Rubbed her nose in it, 'e did. Went off for weeks and months, swarvin' around. No sir, boy, don't you worry about 'Erold. Far as keeping 'Erold's memory green and sacred goes, of course 'e turned into a tragic figure. What else could she do? And then there was the boy. Can't tell a lad born under those circumstances that 'is dad was a rat. I know she makes a song and dance about 'Erold. But 'ow far does that get 'er?" He opened the door again.

"Not far from Herold, I guess." said Quoyle, who answered rhetorical questions.

"Depends how you look at it. Evvie's made bark sail bread. We might as well get the good of it with a cup of tea." Clapped Quoyle on the arm.

The seal hunt began in March, a few foreigners out on the Front, the bloody Front off Labrador where the harp seals whelped and moulted in the shelter of hummocky ice. Men had burned and frozen and drowned there for centuries, come to a stop when televised in red color, clubbing.

Thousands of seals came into the bays as well and excited landsmen put out after them in anything that would work among the ice floes.

In the 4:00 A.M. fluorescent brightness Jack Buggit drank a last cup of tea, went to the hook behind the stove for his jacket and hood. Hands into wife-knitted thumbies, took the rifle, box of cartridges in his pocket. Shut off the light and felt through the dark to the latch. The door silent behind him.

The cold air filled his throat like ice water. The sky a net, its mesh clogged with glowing stars.

Down at the stage he loaded gear into the frost-rimed skiff. Rifle, club—wished he had one of the Norwegian hakapiks, handy tool for getting up onto the ice again if you went in. Well, a fisherman had to take his chance. His sealer's knife, anti-yellow solution, axe, crushed ice, buckets, nylon broom, line, plastic bags. For Jack pelted on the ice. And it had to be right or it was no good at all.

Checked the gas. And was out through the bay ice to the ice beyond.

By full light he was crawling on his belly through jagged knots toward a patch of seals.

Shot the first harps before eight. Jack glanced briefly at a dulled eye, touched the naked pupil, then turned the fat animal on its back and made a straight and centered cut from jaw to tail. Sixty years and more of practice on the seal meadows. Used to be out with a crowd, none of this Lone Ranger stuff. Remembered Harry Clews, a famous skinner who pelted out the fattest with three quick strokes of the knife. Oh what a bad breath the feller had, indoors they couldn't abide him. Women put their hands over their noses. Lived in his boat, you might say. The hard life, sealing. And in the end, Harry Clews, expert of a bitter art, was photographed at his trade, put on the cover of a book and reviled the world over.

He slipped the knife in under the blubber layer and cut the flipper arteries, rolled the seal onto its opened belly on clean slanted ice. Smoked a cigarette while he watched the crimson seep into the snow. Thought, if there is killing there must be blood.

Now, barehanded, cut away the pelt from the carcass, keeping the blubber layer an even thickness, cut out the flippers and put them aside. The holes small and perfectly matched. He rinsed the pelt in the sea, for the iron-rich blood would stain and ruin it, laid it on clean snow, fur down, not a nick or scrape on it, and turned to the carcass.

Grasped and cut the windpipe, worked out the lungs, stomach, gut, keeping the membrane intact, cut up through the pelvic bone, then worked the sharp knife cautiously around the anus, never nicking the thin gut. And gently pulled the whole intact mass away from the carcass. Tossed buckets of seawater to cool and wash the meat. A pool in the body cavity.

He carried the pelt twenty feet away to a clean patch, laid it fur side up, swept the waterdrops off with his broom, then worked anti-yellow into the fur and along the edges. Perfect. That's she, by god, he said to himself.

Wavey came at suppertime one evening to the Burkes' house. Carried a basket, Herry swinging along behind her, scratched the edge of the road with a stick. Sea still light under iridescent cauliflower clouds. She opened the Burkes' kitchen door, went in where Quoyle boiled spaghetti water. Of course she had walked, she said. In the basket she showed a seal flipper pie.

"You said you never ate it yet. It's good. From the shoulder joint, you know. Not really the flippers. From a seal Ken got. His last seal, he says. He's away to Toronto soon." She would not stay. So Quoyle stuffed his children into their jackets, left the pie on the table for a few minutes to drive her home. Pulled up in front of the picket fence. Her hand on the basket handle, his hand on hers. The heat of her hand lasted all the way back to the Burkes' house.

The pie was heavy with rich, dark meat in savory gravy. But Sunshine ate only the crust, itching to get back to her crayons. A pinpoint cross above a page of undulating lines. "It's Bunny," she said. "Flying over the water." And laughed with her mouth wide open, showing small teeth.

In the night Quoyle finished the whole thing and licked the pan with a tongue like a dishclout. Was still standing with the pan in his hand when the kitchen door opened and Wavey came in again.

"Herry's sleeping at Dad's," she said. "And I'm sleeping here." Breathless with running.

Real Newfoundland kisses that night, flavored with seal flipper pie.

Three or four days later he was still thinking about seal flipper pie. Remembered the two raw eggs Petal gave him. That he had invested with pathetic meaning.

"Petal," said Quoyle to Wavey, "hated to cook. Hardly ever did." Thought of the times he had fixed dinner for her, set out his stupid candles, folded the napkins as though they were important, waited and finally ate alone, the radio on for company. And later dined with the children, shoveling in canned spaghetti, scraping baby food off small chins.

"Once she gave me two eggs. Raw eggs for a present." He had made an omelet of them, hand-fed her as though she were a nestling bird. And saved the shells in a paper cup on top of the kitchen cabinet. Where they still must be.

"Sure, she must have made a bit of toast from time to time."

"She wasn't home much. She worked—in the daytime. And at night and weekends—I guess she was out with her boyfriends. I know she was out with them."

"Boyfriends!"

He would say it. "Petal went with men. She liked other men," said Quoyle. "A lot." Unclear whether he meant the degree of liking or the number of men. Wavey knew, hissed through her teeth. Hadn't she guessed there was a nick in the edge of that axe? The way Quoyle talked of his love, but never the woman? Could pull out one from her own skein of secrets.

"You know," she said, "Herold." Thought of Herold stumbling in at dawn smelling of cigarettes, rum and other flesh, coming naked into the clean sheets, pubic hair sticky and matted from his busy night. "It's just cunt juice, woman," he'd said, "now shut up." She exhaled, said "Herold," again.

"Um," said Quoyle.

"Herold," said Wavey, "was a womanizer. He treated me body

like a trough. Come and swill and slobber in me after them. I felt like he was casting vomit in me when he come to his climax. And I never told that but to you."

A long silence. Quoyle cleared his throat. Could he look at her? Almost.

"I know something now I didn't know a year ago," said Quoyle. "Petal wasn't any good. And I think maybe that is why I loved her."

"Yes," said Wavey. "Same with Herold. It's like you feel to yourself that's all you deserve. And the worse it gets the more it seems true, that you got it coming to you or it wouldn't be that way. You know what I mean?"

Quoyle nodded. Kept on nodding and breathing through pursed lips in a whistling way as though considering something. While handsome Herold and ravishing Petal scuttled in and out of ratholes of memory. Something like that.

Quoyle couldn't get used to the sight of Benny Fudge knitting. Wolf down his sandwich and haul out the stocking, ply the needles for half an hour as rapidly as the aunt. No sooner done with the blue stuff than he was tearing into white wool, some kind of a coat, it looked like.

Quoyle tried to make a joke about it. "If you could write like you knit." Benny looked up, hurt.

"More than knitting. Benny was champion net mender. He knows the twine needle better'n he knows his wife, isn't that right, Benny?" Billy winked at Quoyle.

"In a different way," said Benny, black hair falling over his face as he bent to the work.

His writing was not that bad, either, said Quoyle, mollifying. Billy nodded, still on the subject of knitters and busy hands.

"Jack knits a little still, not like he used to of course. He was a good knitter. But he never had the grip on it Benny does. Benny's like that transport driver, you know, drove a container truck between St. John's and Montreal?"

Quoyle thought of Partridge. He'd call him up that night. Tell him. What? That he could gut a cod while he talked about advertising space and printing costs? That he was wondering if love came in other colors than the basic black of none and the red heat of obsession?

"This driver used to barrel right across Nova Scotia and New Brunswick, had his arms sticking through the steering wheel, knitting away like a machine. Had a proper gansey knit by the time he got to Montreal, sell it for good money as a Newf fisherman's authentic handicraft."

"Might as well," said Benny Fudge. "Happen to know what he got for one?"

"No. But I can tell you about the time buddy was ripping along down the Trans-Canada knitting about as fast as the truck was going when this Mountie spies him. Starts to chase after him, doing a hundred and forty km per. Finally gets alongside, signs the transport feller to stop, but he's so deep in his knitting he never notices."

One of Billy's jokes. Quoyle smiled faintly.

"Mountie flashes his light, finally has to shout out the window, 'Pull over! Pull over!' So the great transport knitter looks at the Mountie, shakes his head a bit and says, 'Why no sir, 'tis a cardigan.' "

Benny Fudge didn't crack a smile. But Billy screeched like rusty metal.

At the end of the seal hunt Jack switched to herring. He had his herring trap.

That was what Quoyle loved best, it seemed, sitting on the stony shore out of the wind behind a rock, holding the grill of silvery herring over coals. These cold picnics on the lip of the sea. Wavey made a table from a piece of driftwood and a few stones. Herry trailed rubbery seaweed. The sun warmed a grassy bit of sheep pasture where Bunny and Sunshine raced across the slope.

"Wavey!" Sunshine's shrill voice. "Wavey, did you bring marshmallows?"

"Yes, maid. The little ones."

The Maids in the Meadow thought Quoyle, looking at his

daughters. And as though something dropped in place, he matched Billy's father's verse with his life. The Demon Lover. The Stout-hearted Woman. Maids in the Meadow. The Tall and Quiet Woman.

Then Bunny ran at them with her hands cupped. Always an arrow flying to the target. A stiff, perfect bird, as small as a stone in a child's hand. Folded legs.

"A dead bird," said Wavey. "The poor thing's neck is broken." For the head lolled. She said nothing about sleep nor heaven. Bunny laid it on a rock, went back to look at it twenty times.

The herrings smoked, the children dodged around, saying Dad, Dad, when are they ready. Dad, said Herry. And put his pie-face up, roaring at his own cleverness.

"Cockadoodle Christ, you're worse than the gulls." Jack, watching Quoyle shovel herring into a bucket.

"I could eat the boatload."

"If you wasn't getting out the paper you ought to take up fishing. You're drawn to it. I see that. What's good, you know, you bring a little stove in the boat, frying pan and some salt pork, you can have you the best you ever ate. Why you never see a fisherman take a bag of lunch out. Even if he goes hungry now and then. Nothing made ashore that's as good as what you pull out of the sea. You'll come out with me one time."

Two weeks later the herring were unaccountably gone and the *Gammy Bird* took a temporary dive in size while Billy and Quoyle and Dennis helped Jack overhaul his lobster pots, build a few new ones. And Benny Fudge went to Misky Bay to have all his teeth pulled.

"I don't know if I'll be fishing lobster for meself or all of yous."

"I wish I was going out," said Billy. "Oh there's money in lobster. But you can't get a license. Only way anyone here could have a license for lobster is if you turned yours over to Dennis, here."

"I'm ready," said Dennis.

"Won't be tomorrow," said Jack. Short and hard. Jealous of

his fishing rights. He was. And wanted to keep his last son ashore.

"Come a nice day we'll have a big lobster boil, eh?" said Billy. "Even if we have to buy them off somebody down at No Name Cove. Too bad there isn't some kind of occasion to celebrate." Winked at Dennis, rolled his eyes at Quoyle.

"There is," said Quoyle. "The aunt's coming back this Saturday and we're having a welcome home party at my house. But I doubt there'll be lobster."

Jack had a pile of stones at the corner of his shack. Anchors for the lobster pots, he said. Slingstones.

38

The Sled Dog Driver's Dream

"A leash for a large dog of rawhide belt lacing. Taper and skive four thongs, form a a loop with the small end of the longest strand, and seize all strands together. Lay up a FOUR-STRAND SQUARE SINNET. *Surmount it with a large* BUTTON KNOT. *Cover the seizing with a leather shoestring* TURK'S HEAD.*"*

THE ASHLEY BOOK OF KNOTS

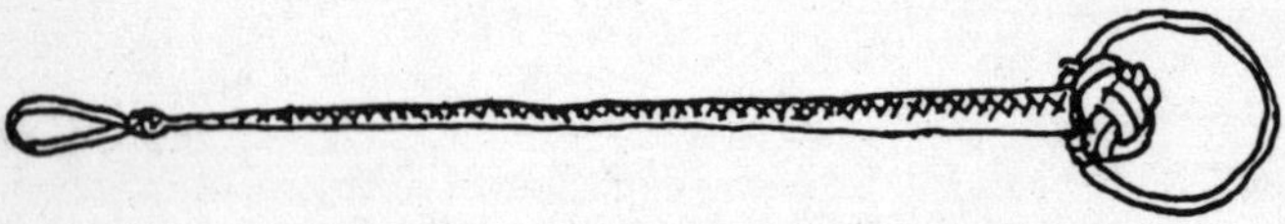

ALVIN YARK'S sweater zipper rattled as he hooked his worn measure out of the pocket. Time to get to the work. Had got cleaned out the day before with a quart of steeped she-var needles, had moved his bowels and was ready now to move the earth. Marked the keel with his pencil stub for the timber pairs, still uncut from curved planks. The window showed empty road. Humming, singing, he turned to the overhead rack that ran the length of the shop and pulled down wood ribbands, tacked them the length of the frame, from forehook to midship bend to the afterhook timbers. And there was the boat.

" 'E missed the best part, did Quoyle. Missed seeing 'er come out of nothing." Checked the window again. Nothing but April water streaked with white like flashing smiles, like lace tablecloths snapping open in slow motion. Clots of froth bobbed against the pilings. Beyond the headland, bergy bits, pans and floes, a disintegrating berg like a blue radiator in the restless water.

At last the mud-throwing hump of Quoyle's station wagon moved into Yark's view. He stopped in the doorway, the oxblood sweater caught on a nail. Picked fussily at the wool loop where another would have yanked, said he had to be back in good time. For the aunt's welcome home supper. He and Wavey had spent the morning, he said, making enough fish chowder to sink a tanker and Alvin and Evvie had better come to help put it away.

"I enjoys a bit of a time," said Yark. "Agnis in or comin' in?"

Quoyle had picked up the aunt in Deer Lake at noon. She looked fit. Full of energy and ideas.

But Quoyle dreamed, thoughts somewhere else. He picked up the wrong tool when Yark pointed.

"Hundred things going on," he mumbled. The Lifestyles page was on his mind. Mail pouring in. They'd never run another birdhouse plan but what was the cure for homesick blues? Everybody that went away suffered a broken heart. "I'm coming back some day," they all wrote. But never did. The old life was too small to fit anymore.

Yark half-sang his interminable ditty, "Oh the *Gandy Goose*, it ain't no use, cause every nut and bolt is loose, she'll go to the bottom just like the *Bruce*, the *Gandy Goose*, and kill a Newfound-LANDER," while he transferred the measurements to the rough boards.

"You'll 'ave your boat next Saddy. She'll be finished." Thank God, thought Quoyle. Man Escapes Endless Song. A pale brown spider raced along the top ribband.

"Weather coming on. I see the spiders is lively all day and my knees is full of crackles. Well, let's cut them timbers. 'Oh it was the *Bruce*, who brought the moose, they lives so good out in the spruce.' "

Quoyle looked at his boat. The timbers were the real stuff of it, he thought, mistaking the fact for the idea. For the boat had existed in Yark's mind for months.

As Yark sawed and shaped, Quoyle leaned the timbers against the wall. Their curves made him think of Wavey, the lyre-shape of hip swelling from waist, taut thighs like Chinese bridges. If he and Wavey married, would Petal be in the bed with them? Or Herold Prowse? He imagined the demon lovers coupling, biting and growling, while he and Wavey crouched against the footboard with their eyes squeezed shut, fingers in their ears.

The twilight drew in, their breaths huffed white as they set and braced the timbers.

"It ain't no use, it ain't no use, I gots to get some tea into my caboose," sang Yark as they stepped from gloom into green after-glow. Sea and sky like tinted glass. The lighthouse on the point slashed its stroke, house windows flowered pale orange.

"Hear that?" said Yark, stopping on the path. Arm out in warning, fingers splayed.

"What?" Only the sucking draw of the sea below. He wanted to get home.

"The sea. Heard a big one. She's building a swell." They stood below the amber sky, listening. The tuckamore all black tangle, the cliff a funeral stele.

"There! See that!" Yark gripped Quoyle's wrist, drew his arm out to follow his own, pointing northeast into the bay. Out on the darkling water a ball of blue fire glimmered. The lighthouse flash cut across the bay, revealed nothing, and in the stunned darkness behind it the strange glow rolled, rolled and faded.

"That's a weather light. Seen them many times. Bad weather coming." Although the trickster sky was clear.

Cars and trucks parked along the road in front of the Burkes' house, and through the window he could see people in the kitchen. He stepped into music. Wavey playing "Joe Lard" on her accordion and Dennis thumping at a guitar. Who was singing? Beety pulled pans out of the oven, shouted a joke. A burst of laughter. Mavis Bangs told Mrs. Buggit about a woman in St. John's who suffered from a caked breast. Ken and his buddy leaned against the wall with their arms folded, watching the others. For they were in a

Toronto of the mind, at a sophisticated party instead of an old kitchen scuff.

"Dad." Bunny, pulling at Quoyle, his jacket half off, whispering urgently. "I been waiting and waiting for you to come home. Dad, you got to come up to my room and see what Wavey got for us. Come on, Dad. Right now. Please." On fire about something. He hoped it wasn't crayons. Dreaded more broccoli trees. The refrigerator was covered with them.

Quoyle let himself be dragged through the company, eyes catching Wavey's eyes, catching Wavey's smile, oh, aimed only at him, and upstairs to Bunny's room. On the stairs an image came to him. Was love then like a bag of assorted sweets passed around from which one might choose more than once? Some might sting the tongue, some invoke night perfume. Some had centers as bitter as gall, some blended honey and poison, some were quickly swallowed. And among the common bull's-eyes and peppermints a few rare ones; one or two with deadly needles at the heart, another that brought calm and gentle pleasure. Were his fingers closing on that one?

Herry and Sunshine were lying on the floor. Marty pushed a bowl of water toward a husky puppy. White fur, the tail curled up like a fern. The puppy galloped at Bunny, seized the loop of her shoelace and pulled.

"It's a white dog." Could hardly say it. Watched her from the corner of his eye.

"She's a sled dog, Dad. Wavey got her for me from her brother who raises sled dogs."

"Ken? Ken raises sled dogs?" He knew it wasn't Ken, but was groping to understand this. Man Very Surprised to See White Dog in Daughter's Chamber.

"No, the other brother. Oscar. That's got the pet seal. Remember we saw the pet seal, Dad? But Ken drove us over. And Oscar's going to show me how to train her when she gets big enough. And I'm going to race her, Dad. If she wants to. And I'm going to ask Skipper Al if he'll help me make a komatik. That's the sled, Dad. We saw one at Oscar's. I'm going to be a dog-team racer when I grow up."

"Me too," said Sunshine.

"That's the most wonderful thing I've ever heard. My dog-team kids. Have you named her yet?"

"Warren," said Bunny. "Warren the Second."

"Warren the Second," said Herry.

Quoyle saw his life might be spent in the company of dynastic dogs named Warren.

"Dad," whispered Bunny, "Herry's getting a dog too, it's Warren the Second's brother. Tomorrow. But don't tell him. Because it's a secret."

Quoyle went downstairs to hug the aunt and then Wavey. Because he was so close then, and in bravado, he kissed her. A great true embrace. Her teeth bruised his lip. The accordion between them huffed a crazy chord. A roar and clapping at this public intimacy. As good as an announcement. Wavey's father sat at the table, one hand on his thigh, the other tapping cigarette ash into a saucer. A lopsided smile at Quoyle. A wink of approval rather than complicity. That must be where Wavey got her little winks. But Jack was in the pantry looking out the window at the dark.

"Jack," called Beety, "what are you fidgeting at in there?" She set out a tall white cake plastered with pink icing. Candy letters spelled "Welcome Agnis." Quoyle ate two slices and tried for a third but it went to Billy Pretty who came in late with snow in his hair. Stood near the stove. Importantly. Every man in the room looked at him. Though he had said nothing.

"Marine forecast don't say much, but I tell you it's shaping up for a good one. Snowing hard. I'd say gusting to thirty knots anyway. Out of the east and backing. I'd say she's going to be a regular screecher. Listen at it." And as the accordion's lesser wind wheezed and died they heard the shriek of air around the corner of the house.

"Must be one of them polar lows they can't see coming until it's gone. I'd better say my greetings and get off home. I don't like the feel of it," said Billy through cake.

Nor did anyone else.

"I'm going to bore up home, buddy," shouted Jack to Quoyle. "Y'know, I felt it coming. Smash me boat to drumsticks if I don't haul her up. Mother'll go with Dennis." And pointed at his wife, at Dennis. Understood.

By nine o'clock the uneasy guests had gone, thinking of drifted roads and damaged boats.

"Looks like you brought it with you, Aunt." They sat in the kitchen, surrounded by plates, the aunt with her noggin of whiskey. A skeleton of forks in the sink.

"Oh, don't ever say that. Don't ever tell somebody they brings a storm. Worst thing you can say." But seemed glad.

A pendulum clock brought from the equator to a northern country will run fast. Arctic rivers cut deepest into their right banks, and hunters lost in the north woods unconsciously veer to the right as the earth turns beneath their feet. And in the north the dangerous storms from the west often begin with an east wind. All of these things are related to the Coriolis, the reeling gyroscopic effect of the earth's spin that creates wind and flow of weather, the countering backwashes and eddies of storms.

"Backing wind, foul weather," Billy Pretty said to himself, steering sideways down a hill. The wind angling to the north now.

He had seen wind hounds a few days before, lozenges of light in a greasy sky. Imagined wind in his inner eye, saw its directions in the asymmetrical shapes of windstars on old maps, roses of wind whose elongated points pictured prevailing airs. The storm star for his coast included a backing point that shifted from the northeast to the southwest.

By midnight the wind was straight out of the west and he heard the moan leap to bellowing, a terrible wind out of the catalog of winds. A wind related to the Blue Norther, the frigid Blaast and the Landlash. A cousin to the Bull's-eye squall that started in a small cloud with a ruddy center, mother-in-law to the Vinds-gnyr of the Norse sagas, the three-day Nor'easters of maritime New England. An uncle wind to the Alaskan Williwaw and Ireland's wild Doinionn. Stepsister to the Koshava that assaults the Yugoslavian plains with Russian snow, the Steppenwind, and the violent

Buran from the great open steppes of central Asia, the Crivetz, the frigid Viugas and Purgas of Siberia, and from the north of Russia the ferocious Myatel. A blood brother of the prairie Blizzard, the Canadian arctic screamer known simply as Northwind, and the Pittarak smoking down off Greenland's ice fields. This nameless wind scraping the Rock with an edge like steel.

Billy mumbled prayers in his pillow for poor souls caught on the waves tonight, riding a sea striped with mile-long ribbons of foam. The stiff tankers, old trawlers with bad hulls would break apart.

At last he had to get up. The electricity was out. He fumbled in the dark, found the flashlight and shone it through the window. Could see nothing inches away but snow hurling at velocities that made the air glow.

Cautiously he opened the door, felt it leap as the wind smote it. And wrestled it closed. A fan of snow across his kitchen floor, his naked footprint in it. Every window in the house rattled, and outside a cacophony of rolling buckets, slapping rope, snapping tarpaulins against the roar. The wires between his house and the utility pole keened discordancies that made his scalp crawl. The cold was straight from the glaciers, racing down the smoking ocean. He thrust junks of wood onto the coals, but the chimney barely drew. The wind, he thought, was blowing so hard it was like a cap over the chimney. If that was possible.

"Blow the hair off a dog," he said. And his own dog, Elvis, twisted her ears, the skin on her back shuddered.

In the Burkes' house the aunt marked the beating of the sea, a pummeling sound that traveled up through the legs of the bed. Up the road Mrs. Buggit recognized the squealing gasps of a drowning son. Herry, rigid in his blankets, experienced immensity, became a solitary ant in a vast hall. And down in St. Johns in his white bed the old cousin trembled with pleasure at what he had conjured with wind-knots.

But Bunny went up the howling chimney, sailed against the wind and across the bay to the rock where the green house strained against the cables. She lay on stone, looked up. A shingle lifted, tore away. A course of bricks flew off the chimney like cards. Each of the taut cables shouted a different bull-roarer note, the mad bass driving into rock, the house beams and timbers vibrating. The walls chattered, shot nails onto the heaving floors. The house strained toward the sea.

A crack, a whistle as a cable snapped. Glass burst. The house slewed on grating sills. The cables shrilled.

Bunny watched, flat on her back, arms outstretched like a staked prisoner and powerless to move. The house lifted at the freed corner, fell, lifted. Glass broke. A second cable parted. Now the entire back of the house rose as if the building curtsied, then dropped. Cracking beams, scribbles of glass, inside the pots and pans and beds and bureaus skidding over the floors, a drawer of spoons and forks down the tilt, the stairs untwisting.

A burst of wind wrenched the house to the east. The last cables snapped, and in a great, looping roll the house toppled.

Shrieking. Awake. Scrambling across the floor to get away. The wind outside proving the nightmare. Quoyle lurched through the door, grasped the kicking child. He was frightened for his daughter. Who was mad with fear.

Yet in ten minutes she was calm, swallowed a cup of warm milk, listened to Quoyle's rational explanation of wind noises that caused nightmare, told him she could go back to sleep if Warren the Second slept on the bed. When he asked cautiously what she had dreamed, she couldn't remember.

At the *Gammy Bird* Quoyle ran a special issue, OUR BATTERED COAST, featuring shots of boats in the street, marooned snowplows. A thousand stories, said Billy Pretty in a worn voice. Ships lost, more than forty men and three women and one child drowned between the Grand Banks and the St. Lawrence Seaway, boats crippled and cargoes lost. Benny Fudge brought in photographs of householders digging out their buried pickups.

The weather service predicted a heat wave.

On Monday it came, a shimmering day of heat, the land

streaming with melting snow and talk of global warming. A riddled iceberg scraped past the point. Quoyle in shirtsleeves, squinting his way through glare. When he could shunt thoughts of Bunny onto a siding, he felt spasms of joy. For no reason that he could think of except the long daylight, or the warmth, or because the air was so clear and sweet he felt he was just learning to breathe.

Late in the morning the newsroom door opened. There was Wavey. Who never came there. She beckoned. Whispered in his ear, her breath delicious against his cheek. The auburn braid a rope of shining hairs which he had experienced undone. Yellow paint on her knuckle, faint scent of turpentine.

"Dad says you must come by this noon. He wants to show you something." But said she didn't know what. Some kind of men's business. For Archie was an expert at dividing the affairs of life into men's business and women's business. An empty cupboard and a full plate were the man's business, a full cupboard and an empty plate the concern of the woman.

He was leaning on his fence when Quoyle drove up. Must have heard the station wagon start up half a mile away, for the exhaust system was shot. Quoyle knew he should have walked the distance, needed the exercise, but it was quicker to drive. He'd start walking tomorrow if the weather was good.

Archie leaned, his wooden zoo behind him, held old-fashioned binoculars. A cigarette in his mouth. Years ago the first thing he'd seen through the binoculars had been the Buggit boys out on the grainy ice, copying, jumping from one pan to another. Could see the snot running from their noses. Never a miss for an hour. Then Jesson fell short, clenched the edge of the ice, the other one tried to haul him up. Archie was out there with his boat in a few minutes, saving the boy, yanking him out of the sishy drift. At the time, thought it was lucky he had those binoculars. But later saw it for an omen. No one could stop the hand of fate. Jesson was born to be drowned.

He raised the binoculars now as Quoyle came toward him, scanned the far shore, examined Quoyle's Point as illustration for what he had to say.

"You know, I believe your 'ouse is gone. Take a look." Held out the binoculars.

Quoyle standing on snow-rived rock. Moved the binoculars slowly back and forth. And again.

Archie reeked of cigarettes. His face fissured with thousands of fine lines, black curved hairs growing out of his ears and nostrils. The fingers orange. Couldn't speak without coughing.

"No, you won't find 'er for she's not there. I looked out for 'er this morning, but she's not where she was. Thought you might want to go along down and see if she was just tipped over or sailed away. Was some shocking 'ard wind we 'ad. How many years was them cables 'olding 'er down?"

Quoyle didn't know. Since before the aunt's time, what sixty-four years and many more. Since the old Quoyles dragged the house across the ice.

"She'll take it hard if it's gone," he said. "After all the work." And even though he knew his secret path was still there, felt as if he'd lost the place where the whiskey jacks flitted through the tunnels among the spruce branches, the place where he jumped down onto the beach. As if he'd lost silence. Now there was only town. The Quoyles on the shift again.

Thanked Archie and shook his hand.

"Good thing I had the binoculars." Archie drew on his cigarette, wondered what shrouded meaning might be in this.

Beety said yes, Dennis was cutting wood for his buddy Carl who still couldn't lift more than a fork, had to wear a collarlike thing around his neck. Yes he had the snowmobile. Though the snow was spotty. Down the highway by the blue marker; Quoyle'd see the truck parked on the side of the road. Not far from where they'd been cutting after Christmas. There was a wood path going in. He'd find it. Sure he would.

Dennis in a fan of raw stumps and Quoyle had to shout above the chain saw's racketing idle. He said his house was missing. And they were up the road for the track through slumping drifts, past the Capsize Cove turnoff. Gravel showing through. Past the glove factory. Whiskey jacks there, anyway. The smell of resin and exhaust. Trickle of melt water.

The great rock stood naked. Bolts fast in the stone, a loop of cable curled like a hawser. And nothing else. For the house of the Quoyles was gone, lifted by the wind, tumbled down the rock and into the sea in a wake of glass and snow crystals.

"All our work and money and it's just away like that? To stand forty years empty, and then go in the flicker of an eyelid! Just when we had it fixed up." The aunt in her shop, sniveling into a tissue. A silence. "What about the outhouse?"

He could hardly believe what he heard. The house gone and she asked about the crapper.

"I didn't notice it, Aunt. But I didn't make a special effort to look, either. The dock is still there. We could build a little camp out there, use it on fine weekends and in the summer, you know. I've been thinking we could buy the Burkes' house. It's a nice house and it's convenient. It's big enough. Nine rooms, Aunt."

"I'll get over this," she said. "I've always been good at it. Getting over things."

"I know," he said. "I know some of the things you've managed to get over."

"Oh, my boy, you couldn't even guess." Shaking her head, the stiff smile.

That sometimes irked. Quoyle blurted, "I know about what my father did. To you. When you were kids. The old cousin told me, old Nolan Quoyle."

He did know. The aunt hauled in her breath. The secret of her whole life.

Didn't know what to say, so she laughed. Or something like it. Then sobbed into her palms while the nephew said there, there, patting her shoulder as if she were Bunny or Sunshine. And it was Quoyle who thought of a cup of tea. Should have kept his mouth shut.

She straightened up, the busy hands revived. Pretending he'd never said a thing. Was already throwing out ideas like Jack pitched fish.

"We'll build a new place. Like you say, a summer place. I'd as soon live in town the rest of the year. Fact, I was thinking of it."

"We'll have to make some money first. Before we can build anything out on the point. And I don't know how much I can put into it. I'm thinking I'd like to buy the Burke house."

"Well," said the aunt, "money to rebuild out on the point isn't a problem. There's the insurance, you know."

"You had insurance on the green house?" Quoyle incredulous. He was not insurance-minded.

"Of course. First thing I did when we moved up last year. Fire, flood, ice, act of God. This was an act of God if I ever saw one. If I was you I'd ask the Burkes about that house. It'll be a good roomy house for you. For children and all. For I suppose that you and Wavey have about come to that point. Though you haven't said."

Quoyle almost nodded. Dipped his chin. Thought while the aunt talked.

"But I've got other plans." Making some of it up as she went along. Couldn't live with the nephew now. Who knew what he knew.

"I've been thinking about that building where my shop is. I've looked into buying it. Get it for a song. I've got to expand the work space. And upstairs is nice and snug with a view of the harbor. It could make a handsome apartment. And I wouldn't be going into it alone. Mavis—Mavis Bangs, you know Mavis—wants to go partners in the business. She's got a little money set aside. Oh, this's all we talked about all winter. And it makes sense if we both live upstairs over the shop. So that's what I'm thinking we'll do. In a way it's a blessing the old place is gone."

As usual, the aunt was way out front and running.

39

Shining Hubcaps

"There are still old knots that are unrecorded, and so long as there are new purposes for rope, there will always be new knots to discover."

THE ASHLEY BOOK OF KNOTS

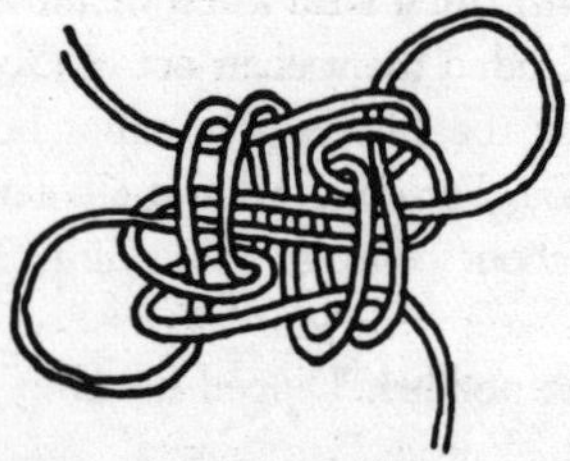

PACK ice like broken restaurant dishes still in the bay but the boat was finished. The last curl looped out of Yark's plane. He stood away, slapped the graceful wood, made a palm-sized cloud of dust. Seemed made of saw scraps himself. Humming.

"Well, that's she," he said. "Get some paint on 'er and there you go." And while Quoyle and Dennis wrestled the boat onto the trailer, the old man watched but took his ease. His part was finished. His mouth cracked open. Quoyle, guessing what was coming, got there first, roared "Oh the *Gandy Goose*, it ain't no use," sang it to the end, swelling the volume until the lugubrious tune took warmth from his hot throat. Old Yark believed it was a salute, embroidered stories for half an hour before he went up to his tea, the tune still warm in his ears as a hat from behind the stove.

A platter of fried herrings with bacon rashers and hashed potatoes. A quart jar of mustard. Beety back and forth, stepping over Warren the Second who wished to live forever beneath the tablecloth or with the boots but could not decide. Quoyle and Wavey were supper guests, full of kind laughter and praise for what they ate. Boiled cabbage. And blueberry tarts to finish, with cream. Double helpings from every dish for Quoyle. Although the cabbage would produce gas.

Sunshine flexed a herring backbone and sang "birch rine, tar twine, cherry wine and turbletine." Bunny and Marty sharing a chair, arms entwined, each with a bag of candy hearts saved from Valentine's Day, allowed themselves one each. LUCKY IN LOVE. OH YOU KID.

At the table, Dennis fidgeted, up and down. Opened a drawer, closed it.

"What's the matter with you?" asked Beety. "You're like a cat with his bum on fire tonight."

An offended look from Dennis while Quoyle bit his lip.

"Don't know, woman! Seems like I'm looking for something. Don't know what. That's one thing."

"You want more tea?"

"No, no, I's full up."

But there were things. No work for weeks, none in sight, he said to Quoyle. Not a good way to live, always anxious about income. Sick of it. Be different if he could do a little fishing. Up again, to pick up the teapot, look in it. Quoyle was lucky to have a job. Wasn't there more tea to be had?

"It's your father's paper," said Quoyle. "Can't you work on the paper? God knows we could use you. Ah, we're shorthanded every way." Bungled his spoonful of sugar, spilling half on the good tablecloth.

"Christ, no! Rather have me arms cut off at the shoulder. I hates messing with little squiddy words, reading and writing and that. Like scuffing through dead flies." He showed his blunt hands. "We're talking"—nodded at Beety, whose eyes were cast down at the moment—"about going to Toronto for a year or two. Don't want to, but we could save up and then come back. There's good work there for carpenters. There's nothing here." Drummed on the table, which set all the children off, small fingers trying to produce the hollow galloping. Dennis glared. Unconvincingly.

Beety and Wavey scraped the dishes, talked of Toronto. Beety's voice as limp as a hot rag. How it might be. Would the kids like it. Maybe better if they didn't. Maybe. Maybe.

Quoyle could hardly say, don't go. Knew they would be lost forever if they went, for even the few who came back were altered in temper as a knife reclaimed from the ashes of a house fire. Poor Bunny, if she had to lose Marty. Poor Quoyle, if he had to lose Dennis and Beety.

When all were yawning, Quoyle carried Herry, more or less asleep on the living room carpet. Sunshine gripped Wavey's hand because there was ice. The dog was first in the car and tried every seat.

"Wavey," said Sunshine, "if you ironed a fish would it be as big as a rug?"

"I think, bigger," said Wavey. "If unfolded."

Dennis walked out with them. Rust pattered on the ground when Quoyle slammed Wavey's door.

"When are you going to get rid of this old clunker?" Morose. Braced his hand against the station wagon until it started to move away. Watched their taillights dwindle, then walked across the road and looked. Nothing to be seen but the lighthouse's electronic stutter. The sea flat as boards.

In the sleeping house Quoyle ran a hot bath. He soaked in the water, pinched his nose and slid down into the heat. With gratitude. Fate could have given him Nutbeem's molasses barrel.

Out of the tub he rubbed with a towel, wiped off the full-length mirror on the back of the bathroom door. He looked at his naked self, steam rising from his flesh in the cool air. Saw he was immense. The bull neck, the great jaw and heavy cheek slabs stubbled with coppery bristles. The yellowish freckles. Full shoulders and powerful arms, the hands as hairy as a werewolf's. Damp fur on the chest, down to the swelling belly. Bulky genitals bright red from the hot bathwater in a nest of reddish hair. Thighs, legs like tree stumps. Yet the effect was more of strength than obesity. He guessed he was at some prime physical point. Middle age not too far ahead, but it didn't frighten him. It was harder to count his errors now, perhaps because they had compounded beyond counting, or had blurred into his general condition.

He pulled on the grey nightshirt which was torn under the arms and clung to his wet back. Again, a bolt of joy passed through him. For no reason.

Came out of sleep to hear the phone ringing. Down to the kitchen, stumbling over a dirty shirt he had dropped. Dennis on the wire.

"Don't like to wake you up but thought you ought to know. Mumma called a few minutes ago. He's not back yet. Been out since four this morning. He should have been back dinnertime. It's ten o'clock now. Something's wrong. I called the Search and Rescue. I'm on my way to Mumma's now. I felt like something was off all day. We's braced for the worst."

"Let me know as soon as you hear anything." Quoyle shivered in the chilly kitchen. The clock said six minutes past ten. He could not hear the sea.

At midnight Dennis called again, voice hoarse and drained. As though some long struggle had ended badly.

"They found the boat. They found him. He's drownded. They said efforts to resuscitate failed." No heartbeat, no breath, lying on the rescue ship's emergency room table. "Looks like he caught his foot in the slingstone line when he threw a lobster trap over. They're bringing him and the boat in now. You call Billy? I'm taking Mumma down. She wants to be there when they bring him in."

In the morning, breakfastless and shaky from seven cups of coffee, heart and stomach aching, Quoyle went to the wharf on his way to Wavey. There was Jack's skiff tied up beyond the orange Search and Rescue vessel, trucks and cars and a knot of people looking at the boat of the drowned man.

Wavey fell against him like a cut sapling, tears wetting his shirt. Quoyle backed against the sink in her little kitchen. He said he would drive Herry and Bunny to school to keep balance in their day. Sunshine would stay with Wavey, who, after the brief luxury of Quoyle's shoulder, was making school lunches. Not to trouble Beety.

A stillness. Mist the depth of a hand on the water, blurred the jumbled shore. Rock ledges like black metal straps held the sea to the land. Quoyle inhaled, cold air rushed up his nose and he was guilty because Jack was dead and here he was, still breathing.

Paper-faced Billy had every detail, had gone to the wharf the night before, had put his hand on Mrs. Buggit's arm, touched Dennis's shoulder and said he was sorry for their trouble. Had seen Jack brought back to the house and carried in. Helped pull Jack's clothes off, cover him with a sheet. Observed the matching mole below his left nipple that, when balanced by the eye against the right nipple, suggested punctuation ready for an inscription to be written around the torso.

Jack. It is himself: he was a fisherman was

Had seen Mrs. Buggit and her sisters with the basins of water and scissors to prepare Jack for his suit, to shave and tonsure, to clip his nails. An embroidered pillow was ready to put under his head, brought from a trunk, the tissue unfolded. *His Voyage Ended.* Worked decades before in the north light of the window.

Quoyle and Benny Fudge leaned on their desks, watching Billy who seemed made of translucent fish bones, whose talk pelted them like handfuls of thrown pebbles.

"They found the skiff out by the Pook Rock. Jack never set a lobster trap there in his life. Can't figure it out, what he was doing there. You know that cat he liked so well, called him Skipper. Skipper Tom. Still on the boat. The Search and Rescue comes up along, shines the searchlight and there's Skipper Tom, prowling back and forth with his tail lashing as if he knowed Jack needed help and couldn't work out how to give it. They could see Jack clear as day under the water. The line going overboard. He was upside down, just under the boat. The slingstone line of the lobster trap wrapped around his ankle and yanked him overboard. He couldn't get loose. It was tangled kind of crazy. His hand was jammed in his pocket. He had to of been feeling for his knife, you know, cut himself free. But there wasn't a knife there. Could be he dropped it or lost it somehow as he went over and didn't realize. I don't know if he carried it loose in his pocket, but when *I* was fishing *my* knife was in my right pocket and there was a lanyard that secured it to me belt loop. Because if you lose it when you're upside down under the water like poor Jack, that's all, you're gone." Hoarse as a raven.

Quoyle imagined Jack's clothes rippling underwater like silk, his moonstone face and throat and hands glimmering under the sea.

"Amen," said Benny Fudge. "There's many a lobsterman goes that way."

"How's Mrs. Buggit taking it?" Thinking of the woman in the perpetual freeze of sorrow, afloat on the rise and fall of tatted billows.

"Surprising calm. She said she's been expecting it since the first week they was married and Jack was thought lost out on the ice. Sealing. She's been through the agony now three times over. There's one relief that's helping her bear up. See, they recovered the body. She can bury Jack. They've took him up home to lay him out. Jack will be the first Buggit in a long time to be buried in the earth. It's a comfort for her to have the body."

Stones crowded in close company in the Killick-Claw cemetery, for someone lost at sea did not need six feet of space.

"They're laying him out now. The wake is tonight and the burial service tomorrow, Quoyle. You do bring Wavey to poor Jack's house at seven tonight. Dennis told me to tell you. And asks if you'll be a pallbearer for poor Jack."

"Yes," said Quoyle. "I will. And we'll run a special edition this week dedicated to Jack. Billy, we'll want a front-page obit. From the heart. Who better than you? Talk to everybody. I wonder if there's any pictures of him. I'll see if Beety knows. Benny, forget whatever you're doing. Go down to Search and Rescue and get the details of them finding Jack. Get some shots of his skiff. Play up the cat. What's his name? Skipper Tom."

"What's going to happen with the *Gammy Bird*?" said Benny Fudge, tossing lank black hair. "Will it be put to rest?" His big chance slipping away. Even now he played with a piece of string as if it was yarn.

"No. A paper has a life of its own, an existence beyond earthly owners. We're going to press tomorrow as usual. Have to work like hell to make it. What time's the wake, Billy?" Quoyle began to rip up the front page.

Billy reached for his notebook. "Seven. I don't know if Dennis can build a coffin or if they'll have to buy one."

Benny Fudge slipped out the door, in his hand the new laptop computer, on his head a mail-order fedora, his face firmed up with new teeth and ambition.

Thickening mist on the water. Vaporous spirals writhed, the air thickened and filled in, that other world disappeared as if down a funnel leaving only wet rock, the smothered sea and watery air. From a distance the hoarse and muffled call of the foghorn like a bull in a spring meadow bellowing with longing.

Quoyle was exhausted, keyed up, getting ready for the wake. He squeezed into his black funeral trousers. He'd have to go back to the paper as soon as he could decently leave and finish pasting up Billy's long piece. They had a fine picture of Jack, ten years younger but looking the same, standing beside his freshly painted skiff. Quoyle had had a big nine-by-twelve print framed for Mrs. Buggit.

Dreaded seeing Jack lying in his parlor in a froth of knotted doilies. Thought of the corpse as wet, as though they could not dry him off, the seawater running from him in streams, dripping loudly on the polished floor and Mrs. Buggit, worried, stooping to mop it up with a white cloth bunched in her hand.

His old tweed jacket was too small as well. In the end he gave up and pulled on the enormous oxblood sweater he wore every day. It could not be helped. But would have to buy a new jacket next day for the funeral. Get it in the morning in Misky Bay when he took the paper in to be printed. Tying his good shoes when Wavey called and said Bunny had something to ask.

Tough little voice. Only the second time he'd talked to her on the phone. She'd never make a living selling insurance.

"Dad, Wavey says I have to ask you. I want to go to the awake for Uncle Jack. Wavey says you have to say if we can. Dad, you are going and Marty and them is going and Herry and Wavey is going and me and Sunshine has to be with the aunt in her shop full of needles and I don't want to, I want to go to the awake.

"Bunny, it's 'the wake,' not 'the awake.' And Marty and Murchie and Winnie are going because Jack was their grandfather. Let me talk to Wavey about this."

But Wavey thought it was right for them to go.

Quoyle said there had been too much death in the past year.

"But everything dies," said Wavey. "There is grief and loss in life. They need to understand that. They seem to think death is just sleep."

Well, said Quoyle, they were children. Children should be protected from knowledge of death. And what about Bunny's nightmares? Might get worse.

"But, m'dear, if they don't know what death is how can they understand the deep part of life? The seasons and nature and creation—"

He didn't want her to get going toward God and religion. As she sometimes did.

"Maybe," said Wavey, "she has those nightmares because she's afraid if she sleeps she won't wake up—like Petal and Warren and her grandparents. Besides, if you look at the departed you'll never be troubled by the memory. It's well-known."

And so Quoyle agreed. And promised not to say that Jack was sleeping. And he would come along and get them all in the station wagon. In about fifteen minutes.

The verge of the road crowded with cars and trucks. They had to park far back and walk to the house, toward a roar of voices that carried a hundred feet. A line of people filed through the parlor where, among lace whirligigs, Jack's coffin rested on black-draped sawhorses. They sidled in, edging through the crowd to the parlor. Quoyle held Bunny's hand, carried Sunshine. Jack like a photograph of himself, waxy in his unfamiliar suit. His eyelids violet. Actually, thought Quoyle, he did look like he was sleeping. Had to jerk Bunny away.

Joined the line sifting into the kitchen where there were cakes and braided breads, the steaming kettle, a row of whiskey bottles and small glasses. The talk rose, it was of Jack. The things he had done or might have done.

Billy Pretty speaking, a glass in his hand. His face gone blood-red with whiskey and the words tumbling out in ecstatic declamation, tossing in the lop of his own talk. "You all know we are only passing by. We only walk over these stones a few times, our boats float a little while and then they have to sink. The water is a dark flower and a fisherman is a bee in the heart of her."

Dennis in a serge suit with flared cuffs and Beety with her hand on Mrs. Buggit's trembling shoulder. A collar of heavy lace imprinting the black silk. Dennis rummaged through boxes and drawers, looking for Jack's lodge pin. Which was missing, had been missing for years. Now it was needed.

Children played outside. Quoyle could see Marty in the yard throwing crusts to hens. But Bunny would not go to her, eeled back into the parlor and took up a station beside the coffin.

"I'll get her," said Wavey. For the child's staring was unnatural. While Dennis showed his mother the pin, found in a cup on the top shelf of the pantry. An enameled wreath and the initial R. She took it, rose and moved slowly toward the parlor. To pin it in Jack's lapel. The final touch. Leaned over her dead husband. The pin point shook as she tried to pierce the fabric. A respectful silence from the watching mourners. Sudden sobbing from Beety. Wavey tugged Bunny's hand gently. A fixed gaze on the corpse. She would not come, yanked her hand away.

A cough like an old engine starting up. Mrs. Buggit dropped the pin into the satin, turned and gripped Dennis's arm. Her throat frozen, eyes like wooden drawer knobs. Wavey seized Bunny away. Dennis it was who shouted.

"Dad's come back to life!"

And lurched to help his father get his shoulders out of the coffin's wedge. A roar and screaming. Some stumbled back, some surged forward. Quoyle pushed from the kitchen, saw a knot of arms reaching to help grey Jack back to the present, water dribbling from his mouth with each wrack of his chest. And across the room heard Bunny shout "He woke up!"

Quoyle drove shaky Dennis to the hospital through the fog, followed the ambulance. They could see Mrs. Buggit's profile in the howling vehicle. Behind them the whiskey was going fast, there was an immense babble of disbelief and cries of holy miracle. To Quoyle Dennis repeated all that had happened, what he thought, what he felt, what he saw, what the ambulance doctor said as though Quoyle had missed it.

"They says they's worried about pneumonia! And brain damage! But I'm not!" Dennis, laughing, pounding the car seat, saying follow that ambulance, his hands full of papers that he'd grabbed up somewhere. He talked like a windmill in high-pitched, whirling sentences. Rustling and sorting papers as they drove. Punching Quoyle's shoulder.

"There he is, struggling to sit up. He's wedged in pretty good. Gets half up and looks at us. He coughs again. The water fairly squirts out of him. Can't talk at all. But seems to know where he is. The doctor comes with the rig there says he'll probably make it, tough as he is. Says it's kids usually that survives immersion. Adults is rare. But they don't know Dad. See, it's the cold of the water shuts down the system and the heart beats very slow. For a while. Doctor says he couldn't have been in the water long. Says he bets he'll make it. And Mother! The first thing she says when she could talk, she says, 'Dennis found your lodge pin, Jack. That's been missing so long.' "

Quoyle saw it on the front page, knocking everything else sky-high. Dennis dropped papers on the floor of the car.

"Slow down, I gots to get these in order."

"What are they?"

"For Dad to sign. His lobster license. Sign it over to me. They's taking some beauties now."

Wavey sat with Bunny on the edge of the bed in the Buggit's spare room, where Quoyle had slept with hot-water bottles.

"Look," said Wavey. "Do you remember that dead bird you found down by the shore a few weeks ago? When Dad cooked the herring?" For they were all calling him "Dad."

"Yes." Bunny's fingers working at the bedspread.

"That bird was dead, not sleeping. Remember, you looked at it and every time it was the same? Dead. When something is dead it can never wake up. It is not sleeping. Goes for dead people, too."

"Uncle Jack was dead and he woke up."

"He wasn't really dead, then. They made a mistake. Thought he was dead. Wouldn't be the first time it happened. Happened to a boy when I was in school. Eddie Bunt. They thought he was drowned. He was like in a coma."

"What is a coma?"

"Well, it's where you're unconscious, but you're not dead and you're not asleep. Something in your body or head is hurt and the body just waits for a while until it gets good enough to wake up. It's like when your dad starts the car in the morning and lets it warm up. It's running, but it's not going anywhere."

"Then Petal is in a coma. She's sleeping, Dad says, and can't wake up."

"Bunny, I'm going to tell you something straight. Petal is dead, she is not in a coma. She is not sleeping. Your dad said that so you and Sunshine wouldn't be too sad. He was trying to be gentle."

"She could be in a coma. Maybe they made a mistake like Uncle Jack."

"Oh Bunny, I'm sorry to say it but she is really and truly dead. Like the little bird was dead because its neck was broken. Some hurts are so bad they can't get better."

"Was Petal's neck broken?"

"Yes. Her neck was broken."

"Dennis's friend Carl got a broken neck and he's not dead. He just has to wear a big collar."

"His neck was only a little bit broken."

Silence. Bunny picked at the crocheted stars of the bedspread. Wavey saw the questions would come for a long time, that the child was gauging the subtleties and degrees of existence. Downstairs the hubbub and laughing increased. Upstairs, difficult questions. Why was one spared and another lost? Why did one rise and not another? Ah, she could be years and years explaining and never clear up the mysteries. But would try.

"Wavey. Can we go see if the bird's still there?" Tense little fingers, pulling the crocheted work.

"Yes," she said. "We'll go look. But remember we had a bad storm and such a small thing as a dead bird could blow away, or the waves come up and take it. Or maybe a gull or cat claim it for a lunch. Chances are we won't find it. Come on. We'll see if Ken will give us a ride. Then we'll go to my house and I'll make cocoa."

The rock was there, but no bird. A small feather in a tuft of grass. It could have come from any bird. Bunny picked it up.

"It flew away."

In the weeks that followed Jack's resurrection, his slow gain on the pneumonia and voicelessness that followed, he whispered out details of his round trip to the far shore and back.

Decent kind of a day. Not many lobsters but some. On the way in the motor had run bad. Then quit. Flashlight battery dead. Fiddled with the motor in the dark for two hours and couldn't get it running. Couple of skiffs went past, he shouted for a tow. Didn't hear him. Later and later. Thought he'd be there all night. Flicked his lighter and looked at his watch. Five to ten. Skipper Tom meowing and hopping around like he had the itch. Then dumped a load of cat crap all over a lobster trap. Jack threw it overboard to rinse it, and that's all she wrote buddy, he was jerked into the water. Pulled at the cord on his belt attached to his knife. Felt the knot slip, the knife strike him on the side of the head as it fell. Breathed water. Convulsed. Peed and shat and twisted. And as consciousness faded, came to believe vividly that he was in an enormous pickle jar. Waiting for someone to draw him out.

Quoyle experienced moments in all colors, uttered brilliancies, paid attention to the rich sound of waves counting stones, he laughed and wept, noticed sunsets, heard music in rain, said I do. A row of shining hubcaps on sticks appeared in the front yard of the Burkes' house. A wedding present from the bride's father.

For if Jack Buggit could escape from the pickle jar, if a bird with a broken neck could fly away, what else might be possible? Water may be older than light, diamonds crack in hot goat's blood, mountaintops give off cold fire, forests appear in mid-ocean, it may happen that a crab is caught with the shadow of a hand on its back, that the wind be imprisoned in a bit of knotted string. And it may be that love sometimes occurs without pain or misery.

ACCORDION CRIMES

E. Annie Proulx

From the author of *The Shipping News*, the intriguing story of a green, two-row button accordion. Its Sicilian maker has a vision of freedom and a future in La Merica. New Orleans brings a violent end to the musician's tale, but the accordion's story is only just beginning.

'This novel confirms Proulx as one of the greatest American writers.' *Independent*

£6.99 1 85702 575 X

HEART SONGS

E. Annie Proulx

The first collection of short stories from the author of *The Shipping News.*

'Matchlessly capturing the rewards and rigours of life in the rural remoteness of America's north-east, the stories in *Heart Songs* focus on characters almost elementally close to the harsh landscapes and hard ways of life. Tough knowledgeableness about their circumstances goes along with a style that is elatingly fresh and crisp with sensuous delicacy.' *Sunday Times*

£6.99 1 85702 404 4